A Texas Kind
of Christmas

BOOKS BY JODI THOMAS

BOOKS BY JODI THOMAS (cont.)

Ransom Canyon

RANSOM CANYON
RUSTLER'S MOON
LONE HEART PASS
SUNRISE CROSSING
WILD HORSE SPRINGS
INDIGO LAKE
MISTLETOE MIRACLES

Whispering Mountain

TEXAS RAIN
TEXAS PRINCESS
TALL, DARK, AND
  TEXAN
THE LONE TEXAN
TEXAS BLUE
WILD TEXAS ROSE
PROMISE ME TEXAS

BOOKS BY CELIA BONADUCE

Tiny House Novels

TINY HOUSE ON THE
  HILL
TINY HOUSE ON THE
  ROAD
TINY HOUSE IN THE
  TREES

Fat Chance, Texas Series

WELCOME TO FAT
CHANCE, TEXAS

SLIM PICKINS' IN FAT
  CHANCE, TEXAS
LIVIN' LARGE IN FAT
  CHANCE, TEXAS

Venice Beach Romances

THE MERCHANT OF
  VENICE BEACH
A COMEDY OF ERINN
MUCH ADO ABOUT
  MOTHER

BOOKS BY RACHAEL MILES

Muses' Salon

RECKLESS IN RED
ENCHANTING
  OPHELIA

CHARMING OPHELIA
TEMPTING THE EARL
CHASING THE HEIRESS
JILTING THE DUKE

A Texas Kind
of Christmas

JODI THOMAS
CELIA BONADUCE
RACHAEL MILES

KENSINGTON BOOKS
www.kensingtonbooks.com

KENSINGTON BOOKS are published by

Kensington Publishing Corp.
119 West 40th Street
New York, NY 10018

Compilation copyright © 2020 by Kensington Publishing Corp.
"One Night at the St. Nicholas" © 2019 by Jodi Thomas
"Birdie's Flight" © 2019 by Celia Bonaduce LLC
"Spirit of Texas" © 2019 by Rachael Miles

All Kensington titles, imprints, and distributed lines are available at special quantity discounts for bulk purchases for sales promotion, premiums, fund-raising, educational, or institutional use.

Special book excerpts or customized printings can also be created to fit specific needs. For details, write or phone the office of the Kensington Sales Manager: Kensington Publishing Corp., 119 West 40th Street, New York, NY 10018. Attn. Sales Department. Phone: 1-800-221-2647.

Kensington and the K logo Reg. U.S. Pat. & TM Off.

ISBN-13: 978-1-4967-2131-0 (ebook)
ISBN-10: 1-4967-2131-4 (ebook)
Kensington Electronic Edition: November 2019

ISBN-13: 978-1-4967-2130-3
ISBN-10: 1-4967-2130-6
First Kensington Trade Paperback Printing: November 2019

10 9 8 7 6 5 4 3 2 1

Printed in the United States of America

Contents

One Night at the St. Nicholas

JODI THOMAS

Thank you, Celia, for calling me New Year's Eve to ask me to join you and Rachael on this fun adventure.

Chapter 1

Texas, 1859
Christmas Eve

Rain hung in the air so thick Cody Lamar couldn't see the sunset as he rode into Dallas. He swore into the wind. This was the dumbest idea he'd ever had in his life.

He was thirty-four, old enough to know better, but here he was going courting at some fancy party, looking for a girl he hadn't seen in years.

Probably half the single men in the state would be at the St. Nicholas Hotel tonight, lined up to propose if they'd heard the same rumors he had. A Texas princess, who came with a dowry of cattle and land, was looking for a husband. Shy, rarely seen, Miss Jacqueline Hartman, daughter of one of the richest ranchers in Texas, would be married by the new year or rumor was her father planned to disown her.

Cody had been twenty when he met his neighbor Harry Hartman, and his daughter Jacqueline had been about seven.

The day hadn't been much better than today; funeral weather, he'd thought then.

He couldn't remember what the little girl had looked like that morning they all huddled around her mother's grave. Harry had stood like stone in the rainstorm, but his daughter looked like she might blow away. She'd clenched her hands behind her back as the preacher shouted above the thunder. Cody wondered if she was stubbornly refusing to touch her father, or simply frozen in place.

Little Jacqueline Hartman wore a coat a few sizes too big with a hood covering her face. Cody remembered brown hair or maybe it had been wet blond. She was skinny, though. He noticed that. Bony as a fence post with that big coat flapping around her like a black flag.

She'd spent most of the funeral standing behind her daddy, who ignored her. When one of the cowhands tossed the first shovel of dirt on her mother's casket, the girl started crying.

No one moved to comfort her. No one said a word. Harry finally noticed her. He swore so loud it raveled the storm. He picked her up and loaded her in the back of the buckboard as if she was simply a newfound burden.

All the other families stood in the rain watching as he climbed on the seat and grabbed the reins.

When the wagon finally disappeared in the dreary fog, Cody could still hear her sobs carried on the icy wind.

He had felt sorry for her that day, but he hadn't known what to say. Afterwards, he'd watched for the kid at barn raisings and when he went to town. A sad little girl with a bull of a father raising her. Once he thought he saw her in the schoolyard sitting all alone. He'd noticed her asleep in the wagon while her father went about his business in town, and again a few years later when she rode wild across open pasture.

Cody had left his land for a while, raising money by serving in the war with Mexico. By the time he'd gotten back, folks said they never saw her in town at all. She'd grown up so shy she never left her father's spread.

He remembered being happy for her when Harry married again. Folks bragged that Margaret Hartman was the most beautiful bride they'd ever seen. The new Mrs. Hartman was one of those rare women who takes up all the air in a room. She acted as if all others were simply around to entertain her. Harry paraded her about like she was a prize heifer and she talked baby talk to him as if she was too dumb to sneeze without directions.

Cody didn't really care. The war had hardened him and all he wanted to do was live in peace on his land. On the rare occasions he saw Mr. and Mrs. Hartman, Harry's daughter was never with them.

Now, over a dozen years since the day he'd seen Jacqueline cry, she was the belle of the ball. She was long into marrying age at twenty-one and her father and stepmother seemed set on the idea that she find a husband tonight.

Cody pushed memories aside as he slowed his mount into the heavy traffic of a dozen wagons. Dallas wasn't much of a town, but bigger than most this far north of the Rio.

He stabled his horse across the street from the St. Nicholas and stomped through the mud suddenly in a hurry to get his chore finished. He planned to propose to Miss Hartman whether she was pretty or homely. Something he never figured he'd do. If she needed a husband he could handle that job.

He was about to walk into some elegant ball wearing worn clothes and ask a girl he'd never spoken to if she'd be interested in marrying him. He didn't want a wife, but he'd treat her right. Talk to her now and then. Finish building the house he'd started years ago. Take her to town once a month whether they needed supplies or not.

With the land she'd be getting when she married Cody, he'd be able to grow his herd. Otherwise, he'd have to pack up and move farther north to expand.

Marriage seemed less trouble than moving beyond the fort line into Indian Territory.

But, he'd never tell her he loved her. He'd given up being that kind of fool years ago. She'd have to agree to that term. Cody had a feeling she was used to no one caring about her.

Chapter 2

Nathaniel Ward lowered his bowler and tried to ignore the three mismatched passengers across from him on the stage heading toward a settlement known as Dallas.

First was a plump little woman who never stopped talking to her barrel-chested husband, a farmer, who didn't bother listening to his wife. He was trying to sleep while their son, about six, refused to settle in one spot.

On every stop of the dusty two-day journey people had gotten on or off, but they all had the same look of disgust when they glanced at Nate.

Maybe it was the hat, Nathaniel decided. Most of these Texans wore wide-brimmed, high-crowned hats or wide sombreros with a Mexican flare. No one but an Easterner would wear a bowler in this wild windy country.

Of course, their frowns might be because Nathaniel hadn't had a bath in a week. Or maybe it was the bloodstains on his coat. He thought of telling them that it wasn't his blood, but somehow he doubted that would offer much comfort.

And then, there was the fact that he was handcuffed to the rawhide, mean lawman.

Marshal Cash Calaber might think of himself as Texas's best, seeing he was a lawyer, a marshal, and mentioned to every passing voter that he'd be running for governor the next election. But all Nate saw was six feet of nasty wrapped in self-righteous lectures and seasoned with bullshit.

Nate had been watching him for days. Studying him carefully. He had expensive boots with his initials sewn into the leather and a valise branded in the same style.

Cash was about Nate's build, but the blowhard carried himself full-sized. Reminding Nate of a toad puffed up to fight.

If no one in the coach acted like they were listening to him, the man would talk louder as if giving a speech to a whole hall of people. He had enough stories to have lived a dozen lifetimes. A few, he claimed were personal experiences, but Nate had read them in dime novels. To stay awake, the marshal sometimes ran down all the rules of law. He'd say, "I know enough law to pass the bar in every state, but I don't want to dumb myself down to a solicitor's level. I'll run this state in five years."

If no other passenger commented, Cash talked about his parents' ranch down near Austin or about the rich girl he was going to meet in Dallas as soon as he turned over this outlaw. "I've never met her, but she's a true Texas princess. Her folks were part of the Old Three Hundred, the first settlers Stephen F. Austin brought out in 1825. All I got to do before I claim her is see this bad guy hang first. Duty before pleasure, I always say."

He'd elbow Nate every time he repeated his goals and Nate would play his part by growling.

"Captured him all by myself even though my duties are usually called for at the capital. But, it was my obligation to keep the great state of Texas safe from outlaws and killers."

Nate thought of adding that the capture wasn't very hard. He'd been sitting on the steps of his burned theater trying to drink himself to death when Cash marched up, pulled his gun, and arrested him.

Nate noticed Cash wasn't the brightest of men. For one, he never allowed anyone else to talk and two, he hadn't figured out that Nate wasn't the outlaw he'd been looking for.

Not that Nate was a saint, but he'd never robbed the banks the marshal claimed he had. He didn't even own a gun.

Calaber might think Nathaniel Ward was a criminal, but in truth, Nate was simply an actor on hard times. He'd spent his last dollar to buy a theater in Austin, only to find the place had burned down six months ago. He'd thought Texas might be his chance, but things weren't going so well. Chained to a marshal trying to make a name for himself and headed toward his own hanging didn't sound like much of a career choice.

"Hey, Mister? You kill somebody?" the squirmy kid asked.

Both of the parents frowned and glared at Nathaniel.

An out-of-work actor is still an actor. Nate twisted a smile on one side of his mouth like he'd seen the marshal do. "Yep. Killed a snot-nosed kid who bothered me with questions back at the last watering hole."

The boy paled and Marshal Cash laughed. "Hell, Ward, you sound just like me. What happened to that Yankee accent of yours?"

Grinning, Nathaniel added, still in the marshal's accent, "Southern with a hint of Irish, you are, partner. I've been cooped up with you for almost three days. It was bound to rub off."

Calaber turned back to the boy. "He ain't no killer, kid. He's a thief, a pretender. Almost had me convinced he was an actor and not a bank robber but I caught him just around the corner from the bank. You ask me, acting isn't no kind of job. Ain't much different than a robber. Breath will go out of either one when the rope tightens."

Now the chubby little woman in a hat bigger than her head gasped. "An actor. I've heard of them but haven't ever seen one."

The marshal grinned. "Most of the time he just acts like he's an actor. I don't think he's any good. I've never heard of him and I've been around."

Nathaniel pushed his hat back down, deciding Calaber just liked to needle him. The man had probably never seen a play. Despite all his talk, Nate could honestly say that the marshal had the manners of a prairie dog, but he'd be insulting the pup.

Cash had bragged that tonight he'd be at some big ball and he planned to court a rich rancher's only daughter. He claimed she'd look good in the governor's mansion.

The stage stopped at a crossroads and the driver yelled, "This is y'all's last stop if you're not heading toward Dallas."

As the family bumped their way out, the man looked back at Marshal Calaber. "Take care. The last leg north runs right through outlaw country. Keep your gun fully loaded and at the ready. Next forty miles is dangerous."

"Thanks for the warning," Nathaniel said in the marshal's voice. "But I've got a schedule to keep and a pretty princess to charm."

Calaber slugged Nate in the chest with his free fist as the farmer closed the stage door. "That will be enough out of you, parrot. We're making Dallas before dark and it won't be soon enough to get rid of you."

When they were around people, Calaber was civil, but the minute they were alone, the lawman was downright bothersome, Nate decided. Men like that were pretenders. In public, all smiles and righteous, but behind doors they were twisted.

Nate acted like he was hurt, which usually satisfied Cash. The marshal had no way of knowing that a few blows were nothing compared to the treatment of orphans running the streets of New York.

That's where Nate had learned to pretend. Immigrants from all over were crammed into the slums and Nate had learned to shift his body, change the way he talked, even cuss in the language of each street. Someone told him a nun had dropped him off at the orphanage and said his name was Nathaniel. When Nate ran away at seven, he'd picked the name over the door where he'd slept. Ward.

Calaber pulled out a bottle and took a long draw, something else he never did in front of people. "By midnight I'll bed that princess." He tossed his wide-brimmed hat across to the empty seat, rolled his leather jacket up as a pillow, and stretched his legs atop his valise. "You'll be in jail and I'll be sleeping at the St. Nicholas. I already got my room booked and a maid name of Katie waiting for me to chase her around the hallways." He laughed. "She's a wild one. She'll fight and fight, but in the end I'll win, and she'll never say a word about what I'll do to her."

Nate had worked at a hotel as a kid. He knew the maids never told no matter what the hotel guests did for fear of getting fired. Their job was all that stood between them and starvation.

While the marshal slept and the miles flew by, Nate thought of how he could get out of this mess. Cash had already told him that his trial wouldn't take more than an hour. The clerk who'd seen him rob the bank remembered a dark-haired man in a bowler hat. He'd described half the men east of the Mississippi, including Cash, but that didn't seem to matter to the marshal.

"You fit the bill, Ward. You'll be swinging from a rope in the midnight breeze." The lawman had said it so many times it was starting to echo.

All Nate needed was one break. A blink when Calaber forgot to watch him, a minute to run. He'd vanish so fast the marshal would never find him.

Rain tapped on the coach and Nate could hear the driver cussing to the man riding shotgun.

Pulling his hat off with his unshackled hand, Nate thought about tossing it out the window. All he needed was a pinch of luck. One moment to run, then he'd lay low. Grow his hair long like the Texans did. Stay in the sun until his skin tanned. He'd find work somewhere and remain silent until he picked up an accent that was so far south everyone would think he was born and raised on the Rio Grande.

Give him a month, maybe two, and the marshal wouldn't know Nate if they bumped into each other on the street.

Lightning flashed and thunder shook the earth. The stagecoach rocked Nate out of his planning as the horses screamed. He pulled the flap on the window open but couldn't see through the downpour. If he hadn't been chained, he'd kick the door open and roll out into the mud. No one could see more than a few feet.

If he wasn't shackled to the near-drunk sheriff, he'd vanish.

"Damn driver better slow down. He'll roll the coach if he hits a hole." Cash stuck his arm out of the window as if the driver might see it. "Slow down, you idiot."

As if his words took action the right front wheel slammed into something and the stage shifted. Nate heard the crack of wood, screams of the horses and driver. A moment later the hooves thundered away, no longer tethered to the coach as it rocked once before slamming on its side.

Cash's body smashed against the window, his free hand caught outside the window beneath the stage.

Nate plummeted into the lawman, his elbow falling against his jawline like a hammer. Cash's body seemed to melt into a pile of rags.

Slowly, Nate's head stopped spinning and he shifted off Calaber, dragging the marshal's arm along as far as his could. The chain held, but the body didn't move.

All was dark as tiny waterfalls dripped through the cracks and windows. Nate had no idea if the marshal was dead, or just out cold. He tried to pull the lawman up, but his arm was wedged beneath the overturned coach.

Nate weighed the facts. The marshal was silent, whether unconscious or dead. And this was Nate's chance to escape.

In total blackness, he patted the lawman's chest until he felt the shackles' key in his vest pocket. In seconds, he unlocked the chains and opened the coach door that now faced skyward.

Waterlogged light blinked into the coach. The drunken marshal looked like a man sleeping it off with scattered clothes and whiskey and weapons around him.

Just before he jumped out, Nate snatched the valise and crammed as many items as he could find into it. A Colt. The marshal's badge. A shaving kit. Any clothes he could reach.

He left the chains, the lock, and the whiskey. On impulse, he crammed the bowler hat on Calaber's head and traded for the sheriff's wide-brimmed hat and leather coat.

As he climbed out the stagecoach, Nate spotted the driver and guard. They were headed down the road the coach had just traveled with no sign of the horses. The axle that had once been tied to the horses lay in pieces in the mud and lightning still blinked against the southern sky.

Time for Nate to vanish.

He followed the trail from a distance so no one traveling the road would see him. He guessed Dallas couldn't be much farther. It would be dark soon.

The rain eased and he began to run. It would take the driver an hour or more to catch the horses, if he caught them, then he'd need time to right the coach. If the wheel was broken, that meant more work, more time. He might just decide to spend the night and leave the repairs until dawn.

If Cash were dead, there would be no hurry to ride in and report an accident. If the marshal were still alive, he'd probably be yelling for them to hurry. Since Nate hadn't felt any blood, he guessed Calaber was alive.

Either way Nate figured he had several hours' head start.

A half hour later he was too tired to run and began to recalculate.

He couldn't turn off the road into the wild. Survival had always been in towns and cities. Never in the country. He had no choice but to stay on the road.

Nate had slowed to a walk and was half asleep when he almost bumped into a cart stuck in mud halfway off the road. The horse had wandered far enough to graze, and the driver had fallen backward into the wagon bed. From the smell of it, Nate guessed he was dead drunk.

"Don't worry, partner," Nate said softly in his best Texas slang. "I'll help you get home."

Within minutes he had the horse trotting at a pace that rocked the drunk back to sleep, and with the dying sun's light he made out the outline of a settlement. Dallas.

By twilight they'd reached town. The sound of carolers singing Christmas songs seemed out of place in the cold, dusty town.

He asked a kid selling papers where the St. Nicholas Hotel was and within minutes Nate climbed out of the wagon with the sheriff's valise in one hand and his wide-brimmed hat in the other.

Without bothering to tie the reins, he let the horse continue on, obviously heading for his barn. The drunk would simply wake up in the morning thinking that his horse had found his own way home.

The clerk looked overwhelmed with duties when Nate walked up to register. He wore the marshal's hat low and set the monogrammed luggage on the counter.

The entire lobby and every parlor were open and looked like Christmas had exploded inside. Since Nate had never celebrated Christmas, he turned away, concentrating on signing the logbook.

"We received the telegram you'd be in tonight, Marshal," the clerk said with his back to Nate as he fetched a key. "We have your room ready. Your dress clothes for the ball have been pressed and put in your room."

Nate nodded once and took the key. "Thanks. Is it too late to get a meal delivered?"

The clerk's voice sounded harsh when he said, "No. I'll see Katie brings it up."

Nate remembered how Cash bragged about teasing the girl and he suddenly felt sick at his stomach for pretending to be such a man. Without another word, Nate rushed upstairs.

Ten minutes later, when a petite maid brought in a tray, Nate stood in the shadows by the window so she couldn't see his face. "Just leave it on the table, Katie."

As she backed away, he added, "There's two bits on the dresser. Take it for your trouble." He would have liked to leave her more but didn't want to draw attention.

She backed all the way to the door with the money in her fist, then ran.

Nate ate his first real meal in days as he tried to make his tired mind think. If there was a big ball at the fancy hotel tonight, that meant there was probably going to be a high-stakes poker game in one of the rooms. The cash in the pocket of the marshal's bag gave him plenty of pocket money. Nate would be gambling with time if he showed up at the ball, but if Cash was hurt, or delayed long enough, Nate might just win enough to travel back to Chicago in style. At the very least he'd fill up on whatever kind of food they have at balls.

He reached in the valise and pulled out a roll of bills. If he lost, no problem. He was playing with the marshal's money. They could only hang him once.

Chapter 3

Jacqueline Hartman stood before a long mirror in her suite on the top floor of the St. Nicholas. All she saw were her flaws. Plain brown hair that refused to hold a curl no matter how hot the iron, skin too tanned to be fashionable. Too tall. Too ordinary.

Her father's new wife had spent years reminding Jacqueline of all her shortcomings. The second Mrs. Hartman, Jacqueline's stepmother, was beautiful even into her forties with golden hair and a peach complexion that made her seem twenty years younger. She made it plain to all the staff that she was the reigning queen of the Double H Ranch and Jacqueline was never to receive any special treatment for being Harry's daughter.

Margaret Hartman even joked, when Jacqueline's father wasn't around, that it was lucky Harry was rich because she'd never find a beau otherwise. Men might outnumber women three to one in Texas, but that wasn't enough odds to help Harry's poor pitiful daughter.

Jacqueline grinned as she set aside the frilly pink gown with ribbons flowing down the length of the skirt. She'd been told to wear the pink, but she picked up a simple midnight blue dress. Her mother's dress had been packed away in the attic, as if waiting for Jacqueline to find it. It was cut low, showing off her shoulders and the top of her well-rounded breasts. Her father wouldn't approve if he even remembered the dress. Her stepmother would be shocked. But if Jacqueline was forced into going fishing, she might as well dress the bait.

She'd show them that she was not a child to be paraded out. She was a woman who had the sense to pick her own mate or better yet, pick no mate at all. This might be her one chance to break free before she disappeared completely.

"If this doesn't work," she said, winking at her reflection, "I'll become an outlaw, or a pirate." All the time she'd been hiding away from people, she'd been reading books filled with adventures. In every story there was always a call to action, a quest. Maybe tonight she'd be strong enough to accept the challenge. She'd step out of her shell and start charting her own destiny.

Deep in her heart she knew she'd never be truly brave, but if wishing it so could work, she might be brave enough to run away tonight. She'd kept in touch with her first teacher, a widow who moved to Austin. Mrs. Eden would welcome her in. Plus, Jacqueline had saved enough money to live until she found employment.

With each cut her stepmother made, each joke, each reminder of what she'd never be, Jacqueline withered until she became exactly what her stepmother wanted, little more than a shadow who haunted the attic rooms of Hartman Headquarters. But, inside, she'd planned for someday and that someday was about to come.

When her father threw one of his big parties on the ranch, his daughter was rarely seen. If she did step from the background,

Margaret was always there hinting at what a fool she was to even try. "You've got all you want in your room, Jacqueline. Your books, your drawings. Don't try to be something you're not."

Only last month Jacqueline turned twenty-one, and being invisible was no longer an option. Harry began teaching his daughter to run the ranch and suddenly Margaret wanted her gone. Two women in the house was one too many. Jacqueline's father was growing old and more manageable for his younger wife. A grown daughter might prove bothersome if not a full-out threat should Harry die, so Margaret whined and begged and bullied until she got her way.

When the St. Nicholas Hotel began to plan for a Christmas ball, Margaret went to work. Her project suddenly had a deadline. Harry's child would be married and gone by the New Year.

Jacqueline watched her stepmother's plan form before her eyes without being able to stop it. They'd all go to a fancy ball in Dallas. Margaret insisted her stepdaughter would find happiness. It was Harry's duty to help the poor child, and half the wealthy men in Texas would be in one place.

Whispers circled faster than invitations. Harry Hartman's only daughter was looking for a husband. The lucky man to win her hand would also get a fourth of one of the biggest land grant ranches in Texas as a wedding present along with a starter herd of two hundred head of cattle.

Jacqueline grinned at her reflection. Margaret hadn't liked the idea of a dowry, but she accepted what Harry allotted his only child. After all, Harry was mellowing as he aged and she'd soon have control over more money than she'd ever be able to spend.

Maybe her stepmother figured three-fourths of the ranch would be enough to handle as a widow.

Though Jacqueline resented the whole auction that was about to take place tonight, she had one ace in the hole her stepmother didn't know about. Her father had agreed to let her decide if more than one man offered for her hand, and he swore he'd give her any fourth of his ranch she wanted.

"You pick what you want, darlin'," Harry said. "I know there's no man good enough, but if you like one fellow, that's your choice. If he don't act right once you're married, I'll come over and horsewhip him into shape every Wednesday."

Jacqueline smiled. Her daddy might ignore her most of the time, but he held to his word and not even Margaret's whining could bend his promise.

As Jacqueline stepped into her blue velvet gown she felt, for the first time, beautiful. She hadn't let the maid try to curl her hair tonight. She wore it straight, like a waterfall down her back.

One of the hotel maids, a woman named Katie, stepped in to lace the dress. "You look different tonight, Miss Jacqueline. You excited to go find you a man?"

"No," Jacqueline answered honestly. "I'm excited to start an adventure." At dawn tomorrow she'd be on a stage to Austin even if some man did propose.

The maid laughed. "Good for you. Picking a husband is like playing poker blind. There ain't no telling what you have when the dealing's done."

Jacqueline turned to Katie. "You want to marry someday?"

"I would, Miss, but no man offers marriage to a maid almost in her thirties, and I want no part of a man who offers anything else."

Jacqueline took one more look in the mirror, and fear made her whole body shake. She wasn't sure she could do this. Walk around for all to stare at. They'd feel sorry for her. She wasn't like her stepmother. Attention terrified her. "I . . ."

Katie seemed to understand. She stood just behind her. "Go down now, Miss. Hardly anyone is here yet. Get yourself a glass of wine and figure out where the hidden corners are in every room. Then if you panic, just melt into a corner. There's places in this hotel that no one will look if you need to vanish. I'll tell you where they are while I brush your hair."

"Sounds like a great plan." Maybe she could watch the men. Pick one she liked. A nice man. Maybe introduce him to her father. Margaret would think her plan to get rid of Jacqueline was working.

Then, at dawn Christmas Day, while everyone slept, she'd make her escape. She'd be in Austin before anyone knew she was gone.

She feared this might be just a wild dream, like so many others, but this one fantasy had kept her going while her stepmother calculated ways to get her out of the house forever.

Someday, she'd be brave enough to stand up to her stepmother's scheming and her father's indifference, and tonight Jacqueline had to take the first step.

As she reached for the doorknob, the maid asked, "What should I do with this dress, Miss? It's so lovely."

"I don't care. It's yours if you like. I'll never wear it." Jacqueline didn't look back as she stepped out of the room with her plan in mind. Walk around. Have a glass of wine. Talk to a few people. Find the hiding places.

And, most important of all, find a man to introduce to her father before the ball was over. Let them believe she was playing along.

Chapter 4

Cody thought finding the shy neighbor's daughter would be easy, but now, staring at the outside of the hotel decorated up like a Christmas cake, he wasn't so sure. If she had any other offer, he'd be coming in second. Men dressed in fine suits walked the newly graveled sidewalk, and soldiers polished and ten years younger than him stood smoking cigars before they stepped inside for the evening.

He hadn't even bothered to shave. Hell. She'd think him more bear than man.

He pulled off his duster, not caring if he got wet as he walked up the steps. His black suit, even wet, was presentable. His best clothes were funeral worn, but they'd have to do. If Miss Jacqueline said yes, he'd let her know he was grateful, he swore. After all, he'd cared about her since she was a kid even if he'd never talked to her.

In his mind, he was already glimpsing the future. Meals when he got home every night. Having her on his arm when he had to go to socials. Talking to her on Sunday afternoons.

In truth, he'd rarely talked to women. A few saloon girls,

who did most of the talking, and a few cowhands' wives. Cody tried to be polite to both. In truth, he figured he frightened most women. He was bigger than most and a hard man who didn't know how to court. By fourteen he'd grown to six feet and was earning a man's wages. By nineteen he had his own ranch but times were hard and he was needed to fight in a war. By the time he made it back to his land he had enough money saved to make a strong start on building his ranch.

Now, he was about to take another step. Marriage. He'd ask her, if she didn't run when she saw him.

The realization that he'd have to talk to the girl before he proposed made him sweat on the coldest night of the year. His only chance tonight was to close his eyes and pretend she was older. He could talk to the old widows at church on the rare times he attended potluck suppers. Of course, they were usually holding cobblers or pies. Maybe he'd just pretend Jacqueline was holding a pie.

He'd even proposed to Mrs. Pratt twice. She made the best peach pie he'd ever tasted. She might be near eighty, but if she'd said yes, he would have considered them engaged.

As he walked through the huge hotel doors he wondered how he'd pick Jacqueline Hartman out in the crowd. She'd probably still be thin. He hoped she hadn't filled out because that was the only detail he had to go on.

Cody had worked herds of cattle all his life but he'd never worked a crowd of people. He'd put his back to the wall and study everyone who walked in. There were bound to be a few signs of who was who and if any young woman would talk to him, he'd do his best to keep the conversation going. After all, it wouldn't hurt to practice.

The place sparkled like a diamond mine. A hundred fancy lamps reflected off china like he'd never seen. And the people all looked like they were dressed up to stand in some expensive tailor's windows. They were all smiling or laughing.

Cody brushed the edges of his mouth and pushed up the corners. He hadn't smiled in so long he may have lost the ability.

Cody figured he must be early because the place wasn't crowded. He took a deep breath, taking in the aroma of baked pies and seasoned meats. He'd fill a plate before he left even if he didn't talk to Jacqueline. If he did that, whether the lady said yes or no wouldn't matter so much.

He'd made it ten feet into the foyer before he spotted Margaret Hartman. She crossed the room, making her whole body float on the music that drifted from the next room. She might be well into her forties now, but she still turned heads.

"Well, if it isn't my neighbor, Cody Lamar. I can't believe you left your land." She offered her hand, then pulled it back as if only waving. "You're a bit early for the dancing so don't bother to ask me to waltz. My mother always told me to beware of a man with brown eyes. But then, I do see adventure when I stare in yours."

She had a way of swaying when she was standing still and her eyes seemed to be sending signals he couldn't read. She was still a beauty but like a candle, bits seemed to be about to drip.

"You sent me an invitation, Mrs. Hartman. It would have been impolite not to come."

Now her over-painted eyebrows were moving. "You're welcome anytime, Cody. A man like you doesn't need an invitation." She leaned closer and whispered, "I can tell by the cut of a man's jaw whether he knows how to treat a woman or not."

Cody fought the urge to run. He'd sooner face down a drunk gunfighter than Mrs. Hartman. "I think I should pay my respects to Harry and Miss Jacqueline."

Her face settled. "Good luck with that. Harry is playing poker with the men who hate to dance. Just follow the cigar smoke. I don't know where Jacqueline is. I bought her a lovely pink dress with ribbons that drift around her. Had it shipped from New Orleans in the hope of making her look presentable." She waved her hands. "Oh, I know it's Christmas and I should have bought a red dress, but she's such an untouched flower, if you know what I mean. I thought she should wear pink. Never had one fellow and now her father wants her married." She grinned and fine wrinkles rippled across her powdered face. "I told her I'd need to explain the facts of life to her and the poor girl looked like she'd faint. I'll be so glad when this mothering chore is done. I've endured enough."

Luckily, a middle-aged couple hurried up to Margaret gushing over her stunning crimson dress and Cody backed away toward the wall. He had a feeling poor little Jacqueline was probably the one who had endured.

Grumbling to himself, he swore he should have stayed home. He was no good at conversation. His hands were too rough to hold a lady's fingers during a dance. Hell, no chance of that. He didn't know how to dance anyway.

Maybe he could melt into the woodwork and watch from the shadows.

To his surprise a woman in blue velvet was standing so still he hadn't noticed her next to the drapes until she giggled.

"Excuse me, Miss." He nodded once. "I almost backed into you. I hope you didn't hear me talking to myself. Habit of mine."

When she didn't speak, he said more to himself than her, "I had to get away from that lady fast."

The woman in blue laughed. Her beautiful eyes matched the color of her dress and Cody thought her a simple kind of pretty.

"Most people are drawn to Margaret Hartman, I understand," she whispered. "I'm told men flock to her like bees to honey."

"Really?" he said without thinking. "Who told you that?"

"Margaret." The lady easily ten years younger than him

laughed again. "I know how you feel. I try to stay out of her way too. She's like a porcupine always on full alert."

He leaned, almost touching the young lady's bare shoulder. "To tell the truth, I don't want to be here. I'm not much for parties. I'm only staying in hopes of finding the food. I could smell it when I stepped inside but can't see it."

They watched Margaret flutter around the room, then move on to the next parlor. The woman in red seemed to think the night was all about her.

"I didn't want to come either. I can't dance or talk to strangers, but my father thinks I need to get out and meet people." She frowned. "I'm afraid the food won't be served for another hour."

"Too bad. I'm not sure I can hang around that long." He looked out at the people. "Trust me, most of this crowd isn't worth knowing. Rustlers, gamblers, and bankers." Cody couldn't believe he was being so honest with a total stranger. "And, young lady, you are talking to a stranger right now."

She blushed. "Maybe it's because I don't know you."

"Then, we'll never introduce ourselves and we can visit here in our own little corner." He smiled at her. "How about we make up stories about all these fancy people? I don't plan on taking the time to know any of them, so you can fill me in."

She nodded and they began to whisper wicked observations about the crowd. Some true, some lies. The preacher's wife who finished every glass of wine left on any table. The three sisters, dressed alike, who traveled in a tight little pack. The banker who checked his watch as if he needed to run over and close the place down.

Cody kept an eye out for a woman in a pink dress. He saw red and all shades of green. He saw one gold and a few white, but no pink. With his luck he'd just ridden half a day from his ranch for nothing. Shy little Jacqueline Hartman probably ran away from home at the thought of marrying a man like her father.

"You dance, Mr. Nobody?" the woman in velvet blue asked.

"Nope."

"Play cards?"

"Not much. I figure the weather in Texas is about all the gambling I can handle."

"Then, tell me, why are you here?"

"I need land. My small ranch is boxed in on all sides, and the only way I can spread out is to marry the neighbor's daughter. So I decided to come ask her."

"She's a friend of yours?"

"Nope. Haven't seen her in years."

"How will you spot her?"

"She's about your age. Skinny, I think, and according to Margaret she's wearing a pink dress with ribbons."

The woman in blue looked confused. "You'd marry someone you don't know, much less love, just to get more land?"

"I told myself all the way into town that I would, but I don't know if that would be right for her or me. I've got the money to buy the land, maybe I'll just make old Harry another offer. I can foresee a problem with my plan. What if I get her home and she don't like me? I can't keep a cook around the place. What chance would I have with a wife?"

"Are you a hard man to live with?"

He nodded. "I am. I've been told I have a stern look about me."

"And a strong chin," she whispered with laughter in her tone.

"You heard Margaret say that?"

"Many times," the lady in blue answered. "At every party."

Cody didn't know whether to laugh or cuss so he just shrugged. It felt good to just talk with someone about nothing important.

He spotted Margaret weaving her way toward him and felt the girl in blue slipping behind him. Fully aware that he was sacrificing himself for a stranger, Cody took a few steps toward the overdressed, over made-up woman.

Margaret almost bumped her nose against his chest. "Who was that woman beside you a minute ago? I didn't see her face but there was something familiar about the way she moved."

Cody fought down a gag as a cloud of perfume made his eyes water. One more thing Margaret overdid. "I don't remember any woman," he lied. "All ladies seem to disappear when you're around, Mrs. Hartman. You must outshine them all."

She patted her overdone hair. "I don't see her now. Probably nobody I need to know. Dallas is getting too full of drifters and farmers lately. It's also becoming quite crowded in here. I can hardly catch my breath. Would you like to step out on the porch with me to take in a bit of the night air?"

"No," he answered. "I take it in every night. Let me get you a drink, Mrs. Hartman. You do seem a little flushed."

"Thank you, Cody, and do call me Margaret."

Cody would have run, but he'd topple too many people. When he made it to the bar, he directed a waiter to deliver a tray of drinks, one of whatever they were serving, to the lady in red.

When the waiter followed his pointed finger, he frowned. Apparently, her beauty didn't charm everyone in the room.

"Tell her I'm in the poker room if she asks."

"She won't join you in there, sir. Her husband is there."

Cody winked. "I know."

The waiter grinned, obviously understanding exactly what Cody wasn't saying. "I'll be happy to pass the message on, sir."

Cody was tall enough to see over most heads in the room. The woman in the dark blue dress had vanished and if he was smart he'd do the same until Mrs. Hartman found some other man to bother.

The evening wasn't working out as he'd hoped. He'd been here an hour and hadn't seen Miss Jacqueline or found the table of food. At this rate he'd be heading home alone and hungry.

Moving through the hallways, he ended up at the kitchen. The round little cook took one glance at him and smiled. "You leaving, Mister?"

Cody nodded. "Not my kind of place, ma'am. I'm too much of a bull to stay around all this china, but I got to tell you this kitchen smells mighty good."

Without another word she wrapped up four rolls stuffed with sliced ham. "A man shouldn't leave before dinner is served. I'll pack you up something for the road."

"Thanks, ma'am. You wouldn't marry me, would you?"

"Sure would if I already didn't have a man and six kids waiting for me at home."

"Just my luck." He stepped out the side door, calling himself a dozen names for even thinking this had been a good idea. He'd been honest with the woman in blue velvet. He couldn't marry just to get land; it wouldn't be right. And, there was no chance of some woman falling for him in one night. He might as well go over to the livery and bed down beside his horse until sunup.

The velvet lady had asked him if he'd be hard to live with and he'd answered correctly. He rarely talked. He worked from dawn to dusk. During roundup he often slept in his clothes to save time. If he took out an ad for a wife in the *Dallas Herald* and was honest, no one would answer.

He stepped out on a small porch that led to what might have been a garden in warmer days. On this moonless night the glow from inside cast an eerie light over the dead plants walled in by brick and iron. The shadows reminded him of black lace hanging over stone. The night was so dark beyond the wall he could almost believe the world ended.

There, in the little walled-in patio, where empty pots lined the top of the fence like sentinels and candlelit lanterns sparkled around a wide walkway, was a woman whirling. Dancing alone to the music drifting out. Waltzing with the breeze.

He couldn't stop staring. Cody had never seen anyone so lost in a dance. He felt like he'd stumbled into a magical place. He'd always been a man who looked reality straight on. But suddenly, a fairy danced before him, seeming more dream than truth. Tall and slender with hair that flew about her in rays of sunshine. A vision more lovely than his mind could have created.

If he moved, if he even breathed, she might disappear. So, Cody leaned against the back door and simply watched.

Then one fact registered.

The woman wore pink, with long ribbons drifting around her.

Chapter 5

Jacqueline quickly tiptoed her way up the back staircase usually reserved for staff at the St. Nicholas.

"Miss Hartman," a bellboy in his early teens said as he passed her on his way down. "You shouldn't be here. Guests use the front stairs." He shuffled a box of small lanterns to one arm as if he needed to point the direction.

"I know." She fought down panic that always seemed to want to choke her. "I only need a minute to be alone." She'd become an expert at hiding, at being invisible, since her father brought Margaret home. Only tonight she was in foreign territory.

The kid must have read the fear in her eyes. He seemed to understand. "Yes, Miss. I'll see you to your room."

"No. I need to be totally alone. Someplace where no one will find me." The boy could have no idea how angry her stepmother would be if she found Jacqueline hiding.

He smiled. "That won't be easy to find, Miss. All three floors are packed with guests and staff and it wouldn't be safe for you to go outside alone. Dallas is a rough town. Mrs. Cockrell is even having the maids who live in town bunk in with the single girls who stay in the attic. She says she doesn't want any of her girls out late tonight trying to dodge drunks on their way home."

"I just need a bit to think before I have to face so many people. There must be a hideout somewhere."

"Afraid of strangers, are you?"

"No. Mostly afraid of my stepmother, to be honest."

His kind face relaxed a bit and nodded slightly, telling her he comprehended. "Don't ever tell Mrs. Cockrell, but I know a place. Sometimes I hide there to rest and everyone else thinks I'm just in another part of the house."

"I swear. I'll never tell anyone." Jacqueline crossed her heart across blue velvet. She knew all the staff, including the owner, Widow Cockrell, had been putting up with Margaret's demands for three days. "I just need to disappear for a while."

The boy reversed his direction and headed up the stairs without even looking back to see if she was following. His words came in rhythm to his steps. "We store the empty trunks up here until the guests need to pack. Folks wouldn't be able to move around in their rooms if we left the trunks with them. No one will be coming up here tonight. Too much going on."

He hurried toward the back of the third-floor hallway, then opened a door hidden beneath what looked like attic stairs. Trunks of all sizes lined the room, and hatboxes were stacked up like funny round Christmas trees. "You'll be alone here, Miss. I'll leave a candle and a flint for you."

"Thank you." She took the little lantern that looked more like a decoration than real. "I don't think I'll need it. I'm used to the shadows."

"Sam, Miss. Sam Barkley. Someday I'm going to own a fine hotel, bigger than this one."

"I have no doubt."

He held the door as she slipped in.

"Thank you, Sam. When you have that fine hotel, I'll remember your kindness." She met his eyes. "Swear you'll never tell where I am. No matter what, you'll keep my secret."

He bowed slightly. "I swear, Miss Hartman. You'll be warm here. The heat from downstairs will rise and there's slits near the ceiling that lets a bit of light in from the hallways."

Silently he closed the door.

Jacqueline moved among the luggage, feeling a bit like a giant crossing over rows of houses. She carefully maneuvered her way to the far corner. She sat on one trunk and placed the candle on another, but she didn't light the tiny lantern. She thought it brilliant that the room had been built with slits near the floor as well as the ceiling to allow just a bit of light and air in. Maids and footmen retrieving luggage wouldn't bother lighting a candle or lantern. It would be easier to simply move in the shadows.

"You can't spend the rest of your life hiding," she whispered to herself. Her only real escape for years had been in books. The one expense her father never denied her.

This morning Margaret threatened to burn her entire library if she didn't follow instructions tonight.

The plan was simple. Pick a man from the hundred attending the ball. Marry one. Get out of her father's house.

She covered her face, letting her long hair curtain her in. "Why can't I simply hide away at home?" Her words sounded hollow in the still, dusty air.

"Why not? Hiding isn't so bad," a low voice drifted on the still air. "I'm an expert at it of late."

Jacqueline jumped up. "Who's there?"

With a bit of laughter the voice came again. "Would you believe the Ghost of Christmas Past?"

"No." She relaxed at bit. Anyone who knew Dickens couldn't be too bad.

"I'm no one," a male voice answered. "Just another soul hiding out from the crowd. Don't be afraid. I won't bother you, lady. I just need to be invisible for a while too."

She could barely make out the outline of a man sitting on the floor five feet away. He didn't look all that threatening and he wasn't moving toward her. A book lay beside him and by the way he held it, she knew his fingers were used to bending the spine.

"You have to leave. This isn't a library."

"I know. I went to the trouble of stealing this book from the parlor shelf only to discover it's too dark in my hideout to enjoy it."

She straightened and frowned at him. "*My* hideout. I came in here to be alone. So, go."

His laugh held no humor. "I was thinking *you* should leave. After all, I was here first."

"But, you should be the gentleman and disappear."

He shook his head. "You are right, dear lady, but I fear my need to vanish is far greater than yours. So, like it or not, I stake my claim on this cave."

Jacqueline twisted on the trunk to face him and was suddenly proud of herself for being so brave. "You tell me your story and I'll tell you mine, and we'll see who has the greatest need."

He leaned forward and set one elbow atop his knee. "All right. Why not? If I leave this room, there is a good chance I'll be arrested. I might as well plead my case to you as some judge.

"Want to tell me your name, lady, before I begin? By the time I confess all my sins, there's a good chance we'll be enemies."

She thought about the tall cowboy who had talked to her in the ballroom. He'd had a hard frown on a rugged face, but his eyes had surprised her. Intelligent brown eyes that missed little. She'd called him Mr. Nobody. He hadn't guessed who she was. The big cowboy had even told her he'd come to propose to Harry's daughter. He'd never thought that he was talking to

Harry's only child. If she could fool the cowboy, maybe she could easily fool this younger man as well.

This stranger couldn't know anything about her. She'd have to drip lies atop the bones of truth. "I'm Jacqueline, but my mom called me Littlebird. She died before I turned seven. She'd read to me every night since I was born, and when she passed no one comforted me, not even my father. I think he was too lost in his own grief. No one read to me again. For a long time I thought my father hated me because he'd had to share her love."

"Nice to meet you, Littlebird. Only tonight in that beautiful gown Bluebird seems a more fitting name. Sorry to hear about your mom. I never knew my folks. My name's Nathaniel Ward and I grew up on the streets of New York.

"I was an actor first in New York, then Boston until a few months ago. I scraped together all the money I could and bought a theater in Austin. When I got there a few weeks ago, I realized the former owner forget to tell me that the place burned. I was busy drinking my sorrows away when a marshal named Cash Calaber decided I was an outlaw. He was hauling me to Dallas to hang when the stage wrecked and I escaped."

"Mr. Ward, you're dressed very well for a broke, unemployed actor about to be tried as an outlaw."

"I stole the clothes, and these fine stovepipe boots as well." He stood and took a bow.

"Sure you did." She didn't buy a word he said.

The only bit that made her question his lie was the fact that she'd met a marshal named Calaber once. He'd had dinner with her father. She hadn't liked him. The man never spoke to her but he patted Margaret on the bottom twice when he thought no one was looking. "If you're telling the truth, what happened to the marshal?"

"Last time I saw him his arm was trapped under the coach. I think I might have knocked him unconscious with my elbow when I tumbled on top of him as the coach rolled. Or, maybe I killed him." The actor examined his elbow as if hoping to find a weapon.

"I'll need more details before I believe you, sir."

Nate didn't seem to mind. He was a natural storyteller. By the time he finished with all that had happened, he'd made her laugh at the passengers they'd encountered and she found herself believing every word.

She liked how he mimicked all the passengers' voices and how he noticed details.

"I'm worthless, lady," Nate finally said. "I stole the clothes I have on. I'll probably be dead tomorrow but, on the bright side, I didn't rob a bank and I've never killed anyone. Course, I can't speak for my elbow. My only chance of getting out of this mess is to hide in here until the marshal gives up looking for me and I'll probably starve before that happens."

"I'll have breakfast delivered. I'll share."

"That's kind of you, Littlebird. Now it's time to tell me why you're here. Your need for a hideout cannot possibly be as great as mine."

Jacqueline remembered the maid Katie and the pink dress. "I work here at the hotel." She looked down at her beautiful low-cut velvet dress. "I stole this dress in hopes of mixing with the rich ranchers and finding me a husband. I'm all alone in this world and scrubbing these rooms every day will age me fast."

"Then why did you come up here, lady? Shouldn't you be downstairs mixing? The pickings will only get worse as the party ages and there are no rich husbands up here hidden in trunks."

She tried to remember the plots of the books she read. A damsel in distress. She needed to be poor. Really poor. Penniless. And being chased by an evil villain with a long mustache and a peg leg. No, that might be too much. She was orphaned very young and left on the streets. No, that was his story. She'd say she was kicked out of her home because her parents couldn't feed all the kids. She'd been forced to work from dawn to dusk. Maybe sold by her drunken father to a madam. She hadn't been old enough to entertain gamblers and thieves, so she did laundry all day.

She began to ramble through her story.

When he raised one dark eyebrow, she added, "Can you imagine how many sheets a day have to be washed in a brothel? And when I finally slept, rats ran over my clothes looking for crumbs from the one slice of bread I got for dinner."

By the time she finished, she'd used every plot she'd ever read.

Nate listened without saying a word. When she finally stopped to breathe, he whispered, "Dear lady, I've never been so attracted to a woman's mind in all my twenty-four. Your imagination enchants me." He moved closer, lifted her hand, and kissed her palm, then smiled and said, "Littlebird, I think I'm in love with you. You blended every story I've ever heard into your life story."

"You don't believe me?" She tried to act insulted.

"Not a word, but I loved hearing it. Pretty lady, you were born to be a great writer."

Jacqueline didn't know whether to be offended or flattered. She held back a cry and decided to be honest about one thing. "If you could see me better, you wouldn't say that I'm pretty. I'm plain. Ask anyone. I couldn't stay at the ball downstairs. I'm too shy. I fall over words. People would pity me. I can't dance. I don't—"

"You don't see the person I see. No one must," he answered.

She laughed. "You can't see me at all. We're huddled in a dark room where shadows cross."

"I see you better here in the twilight than anyone will see you downstairs and believe me, you are beautiful. You're a wonder to behold."

He stood and shoved a few empty trunks aside. "Shall we dance, Littlebird? If I'm to be jailed and you will be forced into a loveless marriage, we might as well have one last dance."

He hadn't believed her story. She'd believed every word of his, but somehow it didn't matter. In the darkness they saw each other. Maybe he was a man trying to be kind? Maybe he was mad? She only knew one thing for sure. He would be the first man she danced with.

"I don't know how," she whispered.

"I'll teach you."

Pulling her near he closed his eyes as he hummed a tune. They moved around the room, bumping into trunks, stepping on each other's toes, laughing, dancing.

When they heard the doorknob rattle, they ducked like children behind a trunk.

A woman stepped in quickly and dropped two hatboxes, then was gone with only the melody of "Sweet Lorena" left in her wake.

He laughed and took her hand. "Shall we continue?"

She giggled.

Light from the floor below blinked through the cracks and tiny slits in the boards as they swayed. He leaned close to her ear. "Littlebird, we're dancing on stars."

She looked down and smiled. "We are indeed."

Chapter 6

Cody stood in the shadows of the back door off the hotel kitchen and watched the woman in pink dance. Her hair flowed around her shoulders as she hummed a tune he'd never heard.

He found himself wishing that she wasn't the rich girl he'd come to propose to. But she wore pink with ribbons. She had to be Jacqueline Hartman.

Now and then he'd let himself believe that he'd somehow find a woman just right for him. It'd be luck though, not some planned plot just to make him richer.

Even if the vision before him said yes to his proposal and he loved her every day for the rest of his life, he'd always wonder if a part of the attraction hadn't been the land. Or maybe she'd be the one to wonder. She'd never trust his love and that would eat at him.

Finally, she waltzed close to the doorway and glanced in his direction. Fear flashed brighter than the candlelight shining in the windows.

He raised his hand as she backed away searching for an escape.

"Wait," he said harsher than he'd meant. "I didn't mean to interrupt you. I was just watching you dance, Miss Hartman. I swear, I mean you no harm."

She shook her head and backed away into the shadows. Green eyes filled with fear.

"You know me. I'm Cody Lamar, your neighbor to the north."

She shook her head again and held her hand up as if she could stop him.

"I should have let you know I was here but I've never seen someone dance like that. So free. So lost. It was a wonder." Cody knew he was making a fool of himself but he had no idea how to talk to her.

He calmed his voice. "How about we start over. I came here hoping to meet you. Then I changed my mind and was leaving out the back door before I embarrassed us both."

"I'm not Miss Hartman," she said as she lowered her hand. "You have me mixed up with another."

She was young, but not twenty-one, he guessed as he tried to see her face more clearly in the shadows.

"All right." He didn't know if she simply didn't want him to know who she was or she thought the lie would turn him away. For all she knew he was some outlaw come to kidnap her. If her dad would offer land to any man who'd marry her, he might offer money for ransom. "I don't care who you are, just don't be afraid of me. I've been a hard man all my life, but I swear I mean you no harm."

She watched him as if she thought he might strike at any moment. "I've heard of you, but I'm no one you know, Mr. Lamar. You shouldn't talk to me."

He decided to play along. "I can't very well call you no one. What's your name?" He frowned. Could have said that a bit nicer. Was it possible he'd hardened to an old man at thirty-four?

"Katie," she answered. "I'm Katie McCord."

"Well, Katie, would you like to go back inside? I think they about have supper ready in this fancy hotel."

"No. I don't belong at the party."

He could see that she was starting to shiver. "All right. I understand that. I don't feel like I belong either." He leaned inside the back door and pulled a red tablecloth from a stack on the counter. "May I offer you a cape, Katie?"

She nodded slightly and stepped closer. "Thank you, Mr. Lamar."

"Call me Cody, Katie, and what is it you've heard about me?"

"I've heard it said that you're a fair man and a war hero." She hesitated.

"And what?"

"That you have no family but you still work hard as if you had someone to leave your land to."

"That's true. I have no one. My parents died when I was fourteen. There was no one to claim as kin after that. I left to make my fortune. Told the neighbor girl I'd come back and marry her. By the time I made it back, she'd had two husbands and six kids." He smiled. "I guess she wasn't one to wait.

"In the early years this part of the country was too wild to even think of bringing a wife out and now I'm too set in my ways to look." The fear was leaving her eyes so he kept talking.

"Strange how I'm rattling on to you. I don't usually do that."

"I'm alone too. It's easy to recognize another." She hugged herself and took one more step toward him.

"It's going to snow soon." He didn't step away, but didn't dare move an inch closer to her. "Wrap up in this, Katie."

She finally moved into the folds of the tablecloth and he was careful not to touch her as he wrapped her in linen.

"It's warmer inside."

"No. I won't go in."

He heard a bit of steel in her tone and respected her for it. Now close he saw that she was nearer his age. Maybe she wasn't the Hartman girl.

"There's a fire in the shed next to the livery." He pointed across the street. "If you don't want to go inside, we could sit over there by the fire. I've got biscuits in my pocket. Not a proper dinner but it's the best I can offer you."

"You'd be a gentleman?" Suddenly she looked very young. She didn't trust easy.

"Of course. You have my word. I'm headed that way anyway to check on my horse. We'll just be two people sharing a fire."

"And biscuits," she added.

He moved to the garden gate and pulled the bolt. "You can see the fire burning from here. When you get ready to come back, I'll see you get home safely. I'd just like to talk to someone besides myself for a change. I rode all the way into town, might as well stay a bit longer."

She didn't look like she believed him, but she obviously didn't want to go back inside the hotel.

"You hungry?" he asked.

"I've been busy. No time to eat today. I am hungry."

"Me too. I made up my mind to ride in after I'd worked until noon. Never been to a fancy party like this before." He wanted to put his arm around her to keep her warm, but Cody doubted that would be a good idea. "You don't like balls?"

A hint of a smile lifted the corner of her mouth. "I've never been to one either."

He laughed. "Then let's take a break from this party we don't seem to be a part of and visit."

When they reached the shed, he saw her hesitate. "We can leave the door open and sit behind the fire. We should be plenty warm enough and can watch the people coming and going without them even noticing us."

She lifted her dress as she tiptoed to the sidewalk. "Will you tell me about your ranch? All I've seen of this country was from the window of the coach when I arrived."

"How long ago was that?"

"More than six months. I've been busy helping get the hotel up and running."

"I will tell you all about my place, if you'll tell me how you learned to dance so beautifully."

She looked up at him. "No one has ever seen me dance."

"I'm honored to have been the first."

She laughed as she stopped at the edge of the walk and looked out over the muddy street.

"If you wouldn't be offended, Miss, I could carry you. I'd hate to see that dress stained."

When she didn't answer he lifted her up slowly. It took several steps, but she finally relaxed a bit and put her arm around his shoulders.

"Where are the livery boys? I've seen them sitting in the shed when people are coming and going after dark." Her breath brushed against his throat and he thought of asking if he could carry her like this forever.

Cody spotted the boys across the street watching the ball from a side window. When he pointed out his find, she smiled. "They're part of the unseen tonight."

"Like us," he added as he carefully lowered her near the fire. "You're the second lady I've met tonight who doesn't want to be seen. I'm beginning to believe we're the lucky ones. All those folks inside dancing are pretending to be happy."

He pulled up two stools and then waited for her to sit down. Then he offered her one of the napkins the cook had bundled for him.

For a while they ate in silence, watching the fire, listening to the music and growing used to each other's presence. A stray dog wandered from the barn and stood next to her as if knowing she'd share. She did.

"Your dog?" he asked.

"No. We're just friends."

"Does the pup have a name?"

She shook her head. "Tell me what it's like to be out all alone at night with only the stars to keep you company?"

He thought he heard a hint of the Irish in her words. Maybe she was just a woman named Katie, or maybe she was trying to fool him. Cody decided he didn't care as long as she was talking to him. "I'm north of the Double H. Doubt you could see my place from there even if you tried. I got good water. Lots of grazing land. But if I try to run more cattle, I'll overgraze the land."

She looked at him. "I used to love running across an open field in spring. I'd imagine I was a deer. The land we lived on in Ireland wasn't ours, but my father worked it. When we were pushed off we came to America on ships they called coffin ships because so many died. I thought, once we landed, I'd be in sunshine again, but I worked at a factory and rarely saw the sun. Even now, I long to get out in the sunshine."

He studied her for a moment before she laughed. "If we're going to have a conversation, Mr. Lamar, you have to talk after I talk. That's the way it works."

"Right," he managed to say, then admitted, "I'm sorry, but I can't stop looking at you. You really are lovely. You've bewitched me, Katie."

"I know," she answered without hesitation. "I blew fairy dust on you while I danced." She reached across the few inches separating them and touched his arm, then pulled away. "When I was little, my mother used to tell me stories of the fairies in Ireland. She said there are trees called fairy trees. That's where they live and no one must ever cut them down for fear of having five generations of bad luck."

"And do the fairies live in the trees?"

"Under them, I think. I don't remember. All I know is that if you see a fairy tree, it's wise to leave a shiny trinket for good luck."

Cody couldn't believe he was even listening to such nonsense, but somehow everything about this night no longer seemed real. The shy lady he'd talked to in the corner of the parlor had made him laugh with her stories of all the people in the room. If he ever saw her again he'd call her friend. But when she'd vanished he had the feeling that the party was all wrong for him too.

He'd been heading out when he found Katie, who seemed to want to talk. She had no idea what a rare gift she was giving him.

One fact he knew. The little dancer in pink had charmed him. As the fire burned low, he told her of his life. Of growing up in Tennessee without a mother. Of leaving his family farm at fourteen with five twenty-dollar gold pieces in his pocket. Of fighting in a war he didn't understand. He even told her of his dreams to come to Texas and become a rancher and how he'd worked so hard those first few years he swore he sometimes slept standing up.

She hung on his every word, those big green eyes never leaving his face. She wasn't just listening; she was traveling through his memories on his words, asking details.

When she shivered he put more wood on the fire and started to take his coat off.

"No," she said as she touched his arm again. "Let's share."

He opened his jacket and she fit under his arm, wrapped in his nearness. Then, she spread the tablecloth over their knees. It had been so many years since anyone had done anything to comfort him, Cody could only watch.

Cody thought of telling her he was already warm, but there was something so caring about the way she spread the cloth over his leg before she cuddled in next to him.

"You're no longer afraid of me, Katie?"

"No. I know you. You've shared your struggles, your fears, and your dreams."

He kissed her hair. "Will you share yours?"

"No," she answered. "I've given up on dreams. You'd look at me different if you saw all. I'm no one, going nowhere."

"But you dance?"

She grinned even though sadness still shone in her eyes. "Yes, I do."

Cody shook his head. "I doubt that you will never dream again. Maybe someday the sorrow in those green eyes will pass. Can you tell me if this thing you'll never tell me about has anything to do with how frightened you looked when you first saw me?"

She nodded.

"If that fear ever threatens you again, all you have to do is squeeze my hand and I'll make it go away."

A tear drifted down her cheek, but she smiled up at him. "Thanks for offering, but I'll have to face my fear myself one day."

He held her for a long while. She didn't pull away. If she felt safe with him near, he'd stay as long as she wanted him to.

Chapter 7

Nate stepped from the trunk closet and moved down the hallway, making sure no one saw him. It was past nine and his littlebird claimed she was starving.

As he hurried toward the sound of voices and the music, he fought the urge to turn around. What if his lady disappeared? He was twenty-four and he'd never met anyone like her. Shy. Funny. Newborn to the world, yet so smart. How could a woman in the middle of nowhere be so well read? Why hadn't she run the minute she realized they were alone? He felt she was so right for him, if he was looking for someone, but he knew he was all wrong for her.

He slowed his steps as anger washed through him. Why had she stayed? The answer was obvious. She was more afraid of what was outside the room than she was of being alone with a stranger. It hurt his heart that someone had been cruel to her and probably still was.

Nate wanted to turn around and run back to her. He needed to hold her and tell her all would be all right. But he couldn't make that promise. He had nothing to offer. No way to protect her.

All he could do for her was make it unnoticed downstairs, slip between all the people, and collect something to eat. Then they'd talk the rest of the night away, and somehow he'd make her forget about her unkind world, if only for a few hours.

He tried to remember the last time he'd spent the evening with a lady. Never, he decided. He'd shared meals after a performance but never one-on-one. Never in their own little private hideaway. Never with a lady.

He'd spent money to enjoy a willing woman's company a few times, but it was only pretend. He wasn't loving; he was simply paying for a lesson and he didn't like the man in the mirror when he looked at himself the next morning.

As he walked slowly down the stairs, he forced reality in his mind. Dreaming needed to be hidden away. There was too much danger outside of the shadows.

He wondered what happened to the marshal. Surely the driver and the guard had fixed the coach by now and were heading into town. Maybe they'd left the coach and ridden bareback. Calaber would be riding with them and he'd be mad as hell.

Nate smiled. Even if the marshal got to the hotel and managed to get another key to his room, he couldn't go to the ball. Nate was wearing his clothes. Calaber would see Nate's dirty, bloody clothes in a pile and probably explode in rage. The marshal would have him hanged immediately, then shake him back alive and shoot him dead again for the trouble Nate had caused him.

As Nate reached the ground floor, he straightened into the part he must play, even tried to act slightly inebriated as he walked around the dancers. No one wants to engage a drunk in conversation.

The music was lively. The crowd loud. The ball was in full swing. No one would notice him. They were too busy having fun.

He'd reached the long buffet table before noticing a group of men huddled in the back hallway. As he filled his plate, he realized these men didn't belong. Two held Sharps rifles resting in the crook of their arms. One had a long knife strapped to his waist. All wore heavy coats and thick boots.

They looked ready to ride through the night. But they were there, circled around someone sitting in one of the high-backed dining chairs.

One of the men standing glanced over his shoulder and Nate caught the flash of a badge on his chest. Something besides dancing was going on, and Nate had a sinking feeling that it might have something to do with him.

Then, he caught a glimpse of the man sitting in the center of the small group. His boots were stretched out between two men. Fancy boots branded with double Cs.

The urge to run raged through Nate's muscles like wildfire. But, if he moved, he'd attract attention and that was the last thing he wanted to do. Growing up he'd become an expert at moving unnoticed through crowds. His skill would come in handy now. He had to collect food and make it back to her. A few more hours in the shadows was all he'd hope for.

Five men plus the marshal were not good odds.

Every man standing was heavily armed.

Nate wouldn't have a chance and if a gun was fired in the crowded room, someone besides him might be killed. He didn't want that guilt even though the next shot would probably end his life.

If he died, what would the lady upstairs think? That he'd left her? She already thought she wasn't pretty. He'd like to get his hands on whoever convinced her of that notion. Everything about her enchanted him. Her skin, her long hair, her mind, the way she laughed.

And somehow he knew that her fate lay in his hands.

Like he did before each curtain rise, Nate barred his emotions inside and hid behind the mask of an actor.

He turned to an old man waiting in line to fill his plate and played his best Calaber voice. "You know what's happening over yonder, partner?"

"Word is the local sheriff's been called in. Hartman thinks his daughter has been kidnapped. They can't find her anywhere." The old man shrugged. "It is hard for anyone to get excited about a woman that no one's seen."

Nate bobbled his head like a drunk agreeing with something he didn't understand.

"If that ain't enough trouble for the night, a loud mouth marshal from Austin just arrived in town claiming his prisoner attacked him while he was bringing the outlaw in. Broke his arm. The lawman claims his escaped prisoner probably did the kidnapping." The old guy snorted. "I think it's part of the entertainment if you ask me. Gives folks something new to talk about."

"I agree." Nate laughed the same way the old man did. "How would a kidnapper get a lady out past all these people?"

The old man agreed and added, "Why would anyone kidnap a homely girl when there are so many pretty ones here tonight?"

"Is Hartman's daughter really as ugly as they say?"

"Heard she was. According to Hartman's wife, they have to offer land and cattle to find someone willing to marry her. Folks say she's so shy she stays in her room when folks come to the ranch to visit."

Slowly Nate walked away from the table with two plates. Conversations drifted around him, but he gave no hint that he was listening. The old man was right. People were all talking about the mystery of Jacqueline Hartman's disappearance. Calaber was probably the only one trying to solicit help by claiming the two were connected. If he could convince the posse that Nate was linked to a kidnapping, the trial would be over before the thirteen twists of a hangman's knot could be completed.

Within minutes he was climbing the stairs two at a time, a plate in each hand and a bottle of wine under his arm. If he only had a short time left, he wanted to spend it with his shadow lady.

For a moment he stood in front of their hideout. If he had any brains, he'd take off for wild country. The barn would be packed with horses. No one would miss one. By midnight he'd be far enough out of town Calaber would never find him. No one would think of him heading north past the fort lines. So, that might be his best chance of survival.

His entire body froze. If he had any heart still in him, he had to stay. If he had a brain, he had to go.

If he stayed tonight, a few more hours would be all the time they had together. Maybe all the time he had left on earth. Eventually the marshal would search the hotel. Nate knew he'd be swinging from a rope an hour after he was caught, and she'd be married off to some fool who only wanted her land. He hadn't believed the sad story she'd told, but he believed she was the missing princess and somehow the real story was so much sadder than the make-believe one.

If he stayed they might have tonight and one night was more then he'd ever dreamed to have with a woman like Jacqueline. One night. Maybe, if he tried, it would be enough to last her a lifetime.

He tapped the toe of his boot on the storage door and waited. Finally, his littlebird opened it slightly, then stepped back so quickly that he only caught a glimpse of her bare shoulder, but he knew she was beautiful. He didn't need the light to tell him that. For this one night with his lady, Nate swore he'd be whatever she needed him to be. He'd be the one memory she carried in her heart.

"I almost left," she whispered. "I'm starving."

"If you'd vanished, pretty lady, I'd have to eat both meals."

"Oh, no," she giggled. "I'll have to stay."

They set up a proper dining table with trunks and boxes. He

told her about seeing the marshal. "What would you say if I told you I was the outlaw he's chasing?"

"I'd say take me with you. I've always wanted to be an outlaw or maybe a pirate. Only we'll only steal from mean people."

"I agree." He leaned across the table and kissed her cheek. "And when we're caught, we'll die in each other's arms."

"No. That's not a grand ending. I'll save you the moment before death, then we'll run off to see Paris, or England, or New York. I've always dreamed of seeing the world. Once I saw a map of Paris in the back of a book and I memorized it just in case I'd need to know someday."

They made up all the tragedies that might happen on their travels and all the adventures she'd write about. He even acted out a few of their plans.

"When we're exhausted, we'll come back here and live out our days on the prairie. But, you'll have to marry me." Her words were light as though she was making up a story.

"I'd gladly do that. Then I could read to you in bed and you could cook me breakfast every morning."

"I can't cook."

"Great, we're back to starving." This time when he leaned across their food, he kissed her lips. "Every plot of our life seems to end in death."

"No. Remember, I'll save you." She leaned back far enough to only be a shadow once more. "Will you kiss me again, later?"

"I will, pretty lady."

When the food was gone he spread out a shawl she'd found in one of the trunks and they sat in the darkest corner of the storage room, holding hands as they talked.

"Tell me your greatest fear," he whispered as he pushed her hair back away from her face.

"Of never having someone to love," she answered simply. "I wouldn't even care if he really loved me. If someone would just let me love him. Of course, he'd have to be worth the loving."

"How could he not be?" Nate whispered. "You'd never pick a man who wasn't."

She laced her fingers in his. "You're worth the loving."

Nate could think of nothing to say. He wished he had been honest from the first. He kissed her cheek and answered, "I wish I were a better man. A man worth that kind of love."

He held her then for a long time. She finally rested her head against his heart and whispered, "Tell me a story."

"Your wish is my command."

He told her the stories he'd seen in plays and the ones he'd read in books. He told her stories that had drifted through his mind when his days were endless boredom. He told her his dreams.

Tomorrow's forecast was probably death by hanging, or shooting, or even some lawman choking him to death, so he might as well get all the what-might-have-beens out.

When he finished talking, she was asleep. He pulled her close against him and rested his head atop hers and whispered, "I wish I was worth your love. Since we only have tonight, know whatever happens I'll love you to my last breath."

Chapter 8

Carolers walked the street passing between the small shed and the grand St. Nicholas Hotel. Even when Cody couldn't see them he could hear their voices carried on the frosty wind. Christmas had never meant much to him. Just another day to work most years but tonight memories drifted in his thoughts.

Once, when he was about five or six, his dad took him to a neighbor's house for a Christmas Eve meal. They'd had a tree decorated with berries and candy for the kids. He'd heard the same songs that night that echoed in the air tonight.

If he'd had a mother would he be different? Maybe the reason he'd never finished the big house he'd started was simply because he had no family to put in it.

He laid his big hand over Katie's, noticing that his touch was rough against her fingers. "Katie, what happened to your parents?"

"They were frail when we left Ireland. They didn't make the crossing."

He was silent for a while, then added, "It's nice being with you like this. I guess we're the last of both our families. Maybe we were the strongest." His fingers closed gently over hers.

She smiled. "It is nice tonight. It's like, for a moment, the world's slowing down so we can just relax and breathe. You're a big man, but a gentle man, Mr. Lamar."

"No one has ever called me that. I was a good soldier and my men say I'm a fair boss."

She pulled her hand from his grip and placed her warmed fingers on his cheek. "They don't see you like I do. We might have just met, but I feel like I've known you all my life. You are someone I've been waiting to meet. You're my chance encounter. My mom used to say that there are people you meet for only a moment who change you."

"I don't believe in chance."

He had no more words, but he felt what she'd meant. In watching her dance and talking with her on this cold night, she'd somehow changed him. Maybe it was just the night, the music in the air, everyone happy. Maybe, for once in his life, he'd simply stumbled on something good that was meant to be. He should just relax and enjoy the moment. He had a feeling it would soon be his favorite memory.

Cody was aware that something was going on at the hotel long before he mentioned it to Katie.

She relaxed against his side and watched the fire. But Cody missed little that happened beyond the shed they'd found. His years in the military and being constantly on guard against rustlers had honed his skills.

Men, not dressed for a ball and well armed, had stormed their way in the side door. One man with his arm in a sling marched with them shouting orders as if he was boss, but Cody watched the men turn to another, a small man who gave directions with the movement of his hand.

"Something is going on inside," he whispered to Katie.

"A ball? Dancing? Drinking?" She giggled.

"No, something more." He stood. "Maybe we should move back inside."

"No. I can't. Not yet. There is someone I don't want to see."

Before Cody could ask questions two men rushed out of the front door and headed straight toward them. Another two came from the side of the hotel where Cody had seen Katie dancing. Halfway across the muddy road one of the men raised his rifle.

There was no time for Cody to leave. He'd have to stay and see what was going on. He wasn't a man to back down from trouble. "I'll handle this, Katie. They probably just want to ask if we saw something. With all the money and jewelry in the hotel I wouldn't be surprised if there was a robbery."

He waited as the men closed in. Now two rifles were pointed at him. They were all hard men. He knew the type well; Cody was part of the tribe. The short leader stepped between two of his men. He wore a badge and his intelligent gaze took in everything around him.

"What's the trouble, gentlemen?" Cody asked when they were ten feet away.

"Raise your hands or you're a dead man," the man with the rifle shouted.

Cody slowly lifted his hands. "I'm former Captain Cody Lamar. I have a ranch half a day's ride from here." When the men didn't lower their guns, he lowered his voice. "I fought with Zachary Taylor in forty-six on the border. I was with Grant and Quitman's Fourth Division at the Battle for Mexico City. I watched the treaty signed when the war with Mexico ended. So if you boys think I'm going to back down, you've got another think coming."

Both men lowered their weapons. The man with the badge was the only one to take one step forward. "I'm Sheriff Wilson from Fort Worth. Me and a few of my boys came in to make sure all is calm tonight." He hesitated, then added, "Nice to meet you, Captain Lamar. I've heard a great deal about you."

Both men nodded once and Cody lowered his hands. "What's the problem? You men don't look like you just happened to drop by the party to dance."

The sheriff grinned. "A young woman is missing. Her father fears she's been kidnapped."

"What does she look like?"

"Don't rightly know, Captain Lamar. Her stepmother said she's wearing a pink dress with ribbons hanging off. I've heard said that she's on the plain side and so shy she hides away from folks, but Harry Hartman wants her found. Some marshal claims there is an outlaw loose tonight. Thinks he's the one who kidnapped the girl."

Cody looked down at Katie. She was wrapped up in his coat. Her big eyes looked up at him.

Cody never lied. "I haven't seen a soul for quite a while. Miss Katie and I have been enjoying a visit."

The sheriff tipped his hat. "Nice to meet you, Miss. I've seen you in church, I believe. You are a local."

Katie nodded once as she'd seen Cody do. "I saw Miss Jacqueline before the ball started. I helped her dress. She wore a blue velvet dress when she went down early to the ball, not pink." Katie grinned. "She said there would be hell to pay when her stepmother noticed she was not wearing the pink."

"Thank you. That will help us a great deal."

"I'll see that Katie gets home safe, Sheriff, then I'll join the search. The Hartmans are my neighbors. If Miss Jacqueline is being held against her will, we need to find her fast."

"Much obliged. Most of the men at the ball either didn't want to leave or were too drunk to be of any help." The sheriff motioned for the men to follow him and without a word the small band moved on down the street.

Cody turned to Katie. "I'd better see you home. I think it would be wise to keep my coat on until you're out of sight. If you are not Jacqueline Hartman, want to tell me why you're wearing her dress?"

"She hated it." Katie raised her chin. "She gave it to me. I'm no one, Mr. Lamar. I tried to tell you that. I'm not important. I'm one of those invisible people no one ever sees."

Cody looked down, not knowing how to answer. Part of him was glad she wasn't Hartman's daughter. He wanted to tell her that she was so much more to him, but he'd spent so many years being hard and cold to the world. The possibility that he could care, maybe even love, was too new for him to absorb. He stared down at the fire.

His coat suddenly slapped against his shoulder. When he looked up, the fairy was running across the street so fast she seemed to be flying.

When he turned to follow, she'd already vanished in the darkness between the lights of the hotel and the fire's glow beside him. He thought he heard the clank of the garden gate and knew she was out of his life, not just his sight. By the time he reached the back door of the hotel, there was no sign of her.

Katie. His Katie had vanished as quickly as she'd appeared, and he didn't even know how to find her.

Cody stepped into the back of the hotel where hallways led off in three directions. He picked the one lit and walked back into the kitchen. The chubby cook was still there.

"You see a woman rush by here in a pink dress with ribbons?"

The cook laughed. "I wish I had. Hartman offered a hundred-dollar reward for anyone who finds that daughter of his and another hundred to any man who kills the outlaw who took her."

"No." Cody stopped. How could he explain? The woman wearing the pink dress was not Hartman's daughter. She was his Katie.

Or was she? Maybe a moment in passing was all they'd shared. Nothing more. How could he explain that he didn't care who she was? He only cared that she might be willing someday to be his.

Chapter 9

Katie ran up the back stairs, leaving a trail of muddy footprints. When she reached the third floor, she stripped off her shoes. Her quarters were in the attic above, but she had to leave the pink dress where she'd picked it up.

No one was around. All the servants were downstairs working.

Without hesitation, she slipped into Jacqueline's room. She retrieved her uniform and rushed to the dressing room. There, finally alone and safe, she held the dress up to her one last time.

All she'd wanted to do was pretend for an hour. Mrs. Cockrell had told all the staff to stagger their times but take an hour break once all was set up because they'd been working before dawn and their shifts probably wouldn't end until long after the party was over.

Katie had decided that no one would miss her if she took a little time off. No one would notice if she wore the fancy dress and pretended in the garden that she was dancing at a fine party. Only someone *had* noticed. Cody Lamar. If he told anyone, she could be fired. She had to erase all signs of what she'd done. The dress, the shoes, the memory.

In a few years she'd move into middle age, probably be in charge of a floor or even become the head housekeeper. She'd grow old in service. Taking care of strangers who often didn't bother to learn her name.

She looked at her reflection as she held the dress in front of her. It was ruined now. The run she'd made had splashed mud almost to her knees. Her evening had ended. The pretending was over.

Slowly she washed and dressed in her black-and-white uniform. She wrapped her hair in her cover. When she looked back at her reflection, she saw a maid, not a fairy, not a lady, not a woman a man like Cody Lamar would even notice.

Slowly she folded the pink dress and put it in one of the laundry bags along with the pink slippers covered in mud. It was time to get back to work. She put on her black socks and tied the laces of her worn black shoes. Then she strapped on the leather band that held a small sheath for an old six-inch kitchen knife. Her worries and fears returned.

The last time Marshal Calaber had stayed at the hotel, he'd gone too far. The first time he'd teased her, chased her, and forced a kiss. But the last time, he'd been angry when he walked into the hotel and decided to take it out on her. A kiss was not enough. He needed to prove he had the power. He'd hurt her and she swore she wouldn't let him do what he did ever again. Six inches of blade would reach his heart.

She lifted the knife and slid it into its hiding place. Why couldn't she have met a man like Cody before she'd been damaged by the marshal?

When she turned back to the mirror, Katie barely recognized herself. The tall man who'd thought she was a fairy wouldn't even know her now if she walked right by him.

She didn't want him to see her like this. Angry, broken. Even if she was simply a memory, at least to Cody she wanted to be a good memory.

Chapter 10

Jacqueline woke to the music drifting up from two floors below. She felt warm and content in her hideaway between the trunks. A heart beat next to hers. Without thinking about it, she closed the distance between them and brushed her lips across his.

When Nate didn't move, she pressed harder, tasting his lips with the tip of her tongue. Boldly her hand moved over his heart. "I have your heart in my hand," she whispered against his ear.

Nate opened one eye and grinned. "What are you doing, my littlebird?"

"I'm making love to you while you dream," she answered.

He reacted to her next kiss, deepening it ever so slightly. When she finally pulled away, he whispered, "There is more to making love than kissing."

"Teach me," she answered, and kissed him again.

"My shy lady grows bold." He shifted her shoulders so he could cradle her in his arms. His kiss lingered for a moment, then turned real. She felt passion run through her veins and when she moved to be closer, he pushed her gently away with his hand covering the velvet over her breast. "Easy, now. This isn't something we have to hurry."

"But, I think I love you." She couldn't hold in her feelings any longer.

"I feel the same, but there are secrets between us. Things you have to know about me." He laughed without humor. "I must be the biggest idiot in the world. Making love to you would be heaven and I'm hesitating. But, it wouldn't be fair. It wouldn't be right, if you didn't know me."

She pulled away, pushing against his heart as she straightened. "You're right. There are secrets but you have to hold me while I tell you mine first. Promise you won't let go. Promise you won't turn away."

"I promise." He gently circled her throat with his fingers and pulled her close so he could kiss her cheek. "I'll not let go."

Jacqueline began to tell him of her life. The death of her mother. His father's coldness. Her stepmother's cruelty. Her plan to run away. "I've saved enough money to be able to travel for a while and that is exactly what I plan to do."

Nate kept his word. He never pulled away. He never stopped touching her.

Finally she told him the most embarrassing thing of all. "I'm to be given away to anyone who'll take me. My father was so afraid no man would offer he's sweetening the deal with land and cattle. If a man will walk me down the aisle, he'll win the prize. Not me, but land and cattle."

She straightened again and closed her eyes, but his hand never pulled away. She couldn't look at him. "I'm worthless. No one wants just me."

After a long pause, Nate answered, "That's not true. I want you. The girl who makes up stories. My pretty lady of the shadows. I see you. Nothing but you, dear one." He brushed his fingers over her hair. "I want to thread my hand through your hair while you sleep. I want to kiss you at sunrise and sunset. I want to talk to you until we both fall asleep in mid-sentence." He moved his hands over her bare shoulders and shoved the velvet lower down her arms, baring more of her breasts. "I want to steal your breath with my touch." His hand pushed the velvet lower until his fingers cupped around her.

She leaned back, letting him do just what he said he would; he took her breath away.

"Don't move. Don't open your eyes. Just feel." His kiss drifted down her throat and she realized she couldn't form words. She couldn't think. All her world was his now.

"I'll always be with you if only as a memory one day. Promise me you'll remember my touch. No matter what happens, just close your eyes and think of me touching you." He kissed her then and pulled her down beside him.

She floated on emotions she'd never felt, drifting with his embrace, tasting his passion. Loving how he treasured her.

He must have heard the rattle of the doorknob turning a moment before she did. Nate straightened, leaving her with a sudden chill.

"Remember," he whispered. "I love you. I always will. No matter what."

A lantern's glow flashed light into her hideaway. Their time together was over. If she could run back in time she would. She'd hold Nate tight and never let go.

As she straightened her dress, she realized he hadn't told her his story. He hadn't seen her except in shadows. There was far too much left unsaid.

The lantern swung wildly as men rushed into the room toward them. She heard one cuss as he stumbled over a hatbox. Other than Nate, her only defenses were empty trunks and fancy round boxes.

Nate stepped in front of her as if trying to draw them away

from their private corner, but the first two men caught him and jerked him forward. A moment later light filled the corner where they'd felt safe.

She bit into her hand, trying to keep from screaming as men surrounded her.

"Are you Jacqueline Hartman?" a low voice said almost calmly as if he was talking to a child.

"I am."

"Are you hurt, Miss?"

"No. Of course not."

The short man's words came harder. "Did this man harm you?"

She couldn't answer. Panic was washing over her in a tidal wave. The two men who had grabbed Nate began to pull him toward the door.

Nate fought back like a wild man but both men held his arms tight while another slammed a fist in his gut and mumbled something about Nate better not be any trouble or they'd have to carry out a dead man.

Before Nate could say a word, the butt of a rifle slammed against his head. Blood splattered across his dark hair.

Jacqueline finally screamed as they dragged his limp body over the trunks.

"It's all right, Miss," the low voice came again. "You're safe now. He can't hurt you anymore."

Anger, like she'd never known, built inside her. "He wasn't hurting me. He would never hurt me."

The men were not listening. The small man, barely as tall as she was, put his arm around her shoulder and guided her out. "She's been assaulted," he announced calmly. "The young lady is hysterical."

One of the men who'd bowed politely at her turned around and kicked Nate's unconscious body.

"No," she cried. "Stop."

The little man patted her hand. "Don't think about him, Miss. You'll never see him again. He'll be dead by morning." The sheriff turned to his deputies. "Take him out the back way. We don't want to interrupt the party downstairs." He glanced at a bellboy standing in the hallway. "Go tell Hartman that we found his daughter and she's fine. A father shouldn't have to worry over anything else so say nothing about a man being with her."

The bellboy met her gaze for only a second but she saw the sadness in his eyes. The pity.

The deputy next to Sam shook his head and whispered, "She ain't fine. Look at her. The poor thing's eyes look wild and crazy. There's no telling the hell she's had to suffer."

Sam turned away and ran to do his errand.

Other men mumbled but Jacqueline was finished with listening. If they didn't hear her, she would no longer hear them.

She looked down at her wrinkled blue dress. The sleeve had ripped when she'd jerked it up moments ago. They wouldn't understand. This had been her mother's dress. "I need to go to my room."

"Of course." The sheriff's voice had remained the same low tone, as if he'd seen so much in his job that nothing affected him. "I'll have the maid help you."

He walked her down the hallway to her room. At the door, he said, "I'm sorry, Miss, but don't you worry, we'll make sure this outlaw pays for what he did to you. I'll leave a guard at your door, making sure no one gets in but your maid."

"Including my stepmother?"

"If you wish."

She wanted to scream that all Nate had done was make her love him, but she knew no one would hear her. As she stepped into her room she heard Katie pushing her way through the men.

As soon as Katie was in she closed and locked the door, then without a word she wrapped her arms around Jacqueline and hugged her.

Jacqueline cried so hard her chest ached. Not because she was hurt or embarrassed, but because she knew she'd never see Nate again.

Then she remembered a story he'd told about dying in her arms. She'd said she would save him, yet when he'd been attacked she'd done nothing but whimper.

The tears stopped. That was exactly what she had to do and fast. Stop being shy and invisible. She had to save Nate.

Pulling away from Katie, she asked, "Will you help me change?"

The maid looked surprised. "Of course. I'll get your nightgown and robe."

"No." Jacqueline shoved the last of her tears off her cheeks. "I'll need my travel clothes." Her plan was simple. She'd break into the jail, free Nate, and they'd ride away.

The maid had been well trained. Never question a guest. Katie moved to the small dressing room and went to work.

She lit the small stove to heat water for washing, then helped Jacqueline remove her beautiful dress.

"Katie, can I tell you something?"

"Of course, Miss."

"I wasn't kidnapped. Nothing bad happened to me except I had a wonderful evening with a loveable man. Father would say he wasn't of my station, but he was perfect for me."

"I believe you, Miss. In fact, I know how you feel. I wore your dress and met your neighbor Cody Lamar. He didn't look like much in his worn black suit and muddy boots but he's a fine man. When he learns I'm nobody, just a maid, he probably won't speak to me again."

"I think I talked to him at the ball for a minute. In his case clothes didn't make the man. I fear you judge him too harshly. I've never heard my father say a single bad word about the man."

As Jacqueline dressed, they talked, not as maid and guest, but as two women finding love for the first time.

"Braid my hair, would you, Katie? If my plan works I'll be an outlaw before dawn."

"I can't imagine you ever doing something so wild."

"Maybe it's time. I've spent my life dreaming about adventures."

Before she could slip into her riding clothes, someone pounded on the door.

"Jacqueline, you open this door or I'll break it down right now!"

"We might as well let her in. She'll have to step over the guard the sheriff left. I have no doubt my stepmother's already bitten his head off." Jacqueline shrugged at Katie. "I'm sure the people downstairs can hear her."

The maid moved to the door. "No one will hear her. The dancers were stomping and laughing to an Irish reel. I wouldn't be surprised if the men trying to sleep at Fort Worth are hearing them." Katie turned the lock.

Margaret stormed into the room and the maid quietly closed the door.

"What have you done? I'm horrified. How was it possible for you to go and ruin yourself on the very night we'll be announcing your engagement?" Margaret saw Jacqueline standing in the dressing room in her undergarments. "You don't even look like you fought him. This is so embarrassing."

"I didn't fight him and he didn't hurt me."

"No, don't try that lie. It would make it worse. What proper husband will want a woman he can't trust? And once he's bedded you, he'll know you lied." Margaret wrinkled her entire

face in disgust. "For all I know you're already carrying the outlaw's bastard. Harry will disown you when he finds out you're
now a hussy who sleeps with bank robbers."

"We didn't sleep," Jacqueline answered. "We didn't have
time."

Margaret clapped her hands over her ears. "I can't be hearing this. You little tramp. You're ruining my plans."

"What plans?" Jacqueline took a step toward her stepmother.

"Never mind. We have to fix this." Without any warning
Margaret swung her fist hard, catching Jacqueline on the left jaw.
"There, at least you'll have one bruise. Maybe one of them men
will feel sorry for you and take you on as a wife."

"I'm not marrying anyone."

"Yes, you are, little girl. Harry's had three offers to take you
off his hands, providing he deeds the land and cattle, of course.
One is a bit old, nearing sixty, but look on the bright side, he'll
die soon. Two are young and wild, but nothing settles a man
like owning land."

"I'm not marrying anyone."

"Yes, you are!" Margaret shouted as if volume could make it
true.

Her stepmother swung again, but Jacqueline ducked. The
blow hit her arm, leaving another bruise.

"Good. Another mark. I don't mind planting a few more.
I've always hated the rule your father had about never hitting
you. Well, now you're grown and I don't think that rule ap-
plies."

Katie quickly opened the door. All three women saw the
two deputies just outside. Katie nodded. Jacqueline darted into
the dressing room and Margaret dropped her hand. Her expression changed instantly. "Well, you try to relax, dear child. I'll
go tell your father that you survived the attack."

She was gone before Jacqueline could say a word.

Katie moved closer and whispered, "She'd rather see that outlaw hang than face the truth."

"I know. Will you help me, Katie?"

The maid smiled. "Of course, Miss. That's my job."

Chapter 11

Cody had spent an hour with the deputies searching for Hartman's daughter and some outlaw Marshal Calaber seemed to have lost. No luck finding Harry's daughter or the so-called bad guy. When the deputies went in to search the hotel, Cody varied off to talk to his neighbor Harry Hartman. For a hard man who never seemed to notice he had a daughter, Harry was beside himself.

He was raging. One minute swearing he'd kill whoever took her and the next crying that he hadn't been a good father.

Cody had no idea how to calm him so he just nodded at whatever the man said.

"I never tucked her in. I couldn't, don't you see? She looked so much like her mother. I had one of the hands teach her to ride. Housekeepers took care of her until I found another to marry. I believed my new wife when she told me Jacqueline wanted to eat alone in her room. Jacqueline was never happy and I finally realized she never would be in my house. Maybe she blamed me for her mother's death. I never had the nerve to ask her." Harry dug his big hands into his curly gray hair and tugged as if he could pull out his problems.

"But, tonight I thought I was doing something right. I was getting her married off. Margaret said she needs her own house. I'm offering the land and cattle to make sure she doesn't ever want for anything. Hell, I'll even build her a house if she wants it. My foreman says she rides over to that grove of cottonwoods on my side of the river that runs between your land and mine. Says she just sits out there reading until evening comes on."

Cody drank his one bourbon while Hartman had half a dozen. The rancher's words began to slur. "I let her buy all the books she wants. I always gave my girl her own money when she went into town with the cook. Didn't want her to ever have to ask anybody for anything. My wife doesn't know it, but I set up an account for her the day the bank opened. She'll be a lady with her own means when she marries."

Cody felt like he needed to say something. "Sounds like you've done some things right by her, Harry."

"Yeah, I have. If she'd get married, she'd have kids. If I'm lucky there will be a grandson who'll run my ranch when I'm gone. Then that quarter of my ranch I'm deeding over will link up with Hartman land again."

Cody thought of telling him that wasn't likely. Jacqueline's husband might sell the land, or she might insult her father and only give birth to girls. And, what about Hartman's present wife? He had no doubt Margaret had plans once old Harry was gone and they didn't include giving her stepdaughter anything.

About the time Hartman started to fall asleep with the last inch of his drink balanced on his stomach, one of the bellboys rushed in.

"The deputies found her, sir!"

Hartman stumbled to his feet. "She hurt?"

"No, sir. Not a bruise on her."

"Where was she?"

"In a storage place on the third floor. I heard her say she was just talking to the man the deputies found with her. She didn't know anyone was looking for her. But the men looking for her weren't listening." The messenger hesitated. "They roughed up the fellow. Said he fits the description of the outlaw Marshal Calaber claims broke his arm."

"I'll kill him if he touched my little girl," Hartman shouted just before he crumbled to the floor.

Cody looked at the kid. "Help me get him in the chair. We'll tell folks he's sick with worry."

The bellboy did his best to lift one side of Hartman and added, "That might work if they don't get near enough to smell him."

Cody walked out of Hartman's suite of rooms and headed downstairs. All he wanted to do was find Katie, but that probably wouldn't happen. His fairy had vanished and he had a feeling if she didn't want him to find her, he wouldn't have a chance.

Who knows, after everything settled down maybe she'd find him. She knew where he was. He'd told her he'd be sleeping with his horse. The barn was so crowded most of the buggies and wagons were stored in the hay barn at the other end of town. And fools like him who didn't book a room ahead had no choice but to sleep in the hay.

He overheard people talking as he settled into the card room downstairs. The dancers might be unaware of anything going on, and the old men drinking might be slim on facts, but they were fat on guessing. A few even suggested that the outlaw should be hanged tonight. Then his body could be removed before folks woke up to Christmas morning. No one argued his guilt, only his timing.

Marshal Calaber was also sitting in the poker room, telling how the outlaw tricked him and then broke his arm so he couldn't follow. Calaber also liked to give details of how Miss Hartman must have been abducted and then treated. "She'll go insane, a gentle, shy girl like her. I heard her dress was ripped to shreds." The marshal lowered his voice as if releasing official secrets. "I've seen it before, gentlemen. She'll go mad within a year if she doesn't kill herself first. Timid, mousy girls like her are weak. I'd be tempted to marry her to try to save her, but I'll be running for governor and I can't have a crazy wife to keep watch over while I'm managing the big state of Texas."

Several men nodded.

Cody fought down anger. The woman in blue velvet that he'd talked to wasn't weak or mousy. If he thought he could get to her tonight, he'd tell her that he was still her friend.

He crossed to the kitchen, leaving as he had before. The round little cook was still there cleaning up. Half-empty trays of food surrounded her.

"Thanks for the biscuits, ma'am. I shared them with a fairy I met."

The cook laughed. "I noticed you talking to our Katie. She looked like she was happy in her pretty pink dress."

"She did," he answered, thinking he'd remember that dress for the rest of his life. Katie would dance through his dreams until he was too old to remember his own name.

"I'm guessing you're sleeping in the barn, aren't you, cowboy?"

He nodded as he looked down at his black suit that had gone from passable to pitiful. "Didn't decide to come until today. I'm not a man usually interested in balls." He smiled. "But I had a nice time visiting with Katie."

The cook grinned. "You come in here for breakfast in the kitchen tomorrow. I'll see you get a meal before you head out."

"Much obliged. I might do that. I didn't get a chance to say good-bye to her. Will she be near in the morning?"

"I don't know. She's up with Miss Hartman now. I'm thinking she's about as close as the little miss has to a friend right now."

Cody looked up as if he could see two lives cross somewhere above him. The two women he'd met tonight were obviously close if Katie was with Jacqueline. One became his friend even before he knew who she was and the other stole his heart. With his bad luck he'd probably never see either one of them again, but he was glad they were together.

Now there was no question. He had to act. Breaking a rule he'd set when he'd left the army, Cody decided he'd get involved in someone else's business.

"Any chance I could have a few of those cookies?" He winked at the cook.

"Sure. I'll wrap you up a dozen just in case you run into your fairy again."

Waving to the cook he slipped out the back door once more. It was snowing now, big feather-light flakes. Tomorrow would be Christmas, but to him it'd probably just be a messy day to ride home.

He headed for the jail. He needed answers, real answers, not the garbage Calaber was handing out and not the fears of a drunken father.

The barred windows of the sheriff's office and jail burned bright on the dark street two blocks from the hotel. When Cody stepped inside, he was welcomed. Two of the younger deputies were sitting near the potbellied stove trying to stay awake while on guard.

Cody smiled and offered the cookies. "I came to confess that I stole these cookies. Want to help me get rid of the evidence?"

Both Travis and Andy nodded.

"Want a cup of coffee, Captain? Least we can do for you backing us up tonight."

"Glad I could help." These had to be the two youngest of the town's deputies because they drew the short straw tonight.

"Coffee sounds good. Sheriff still putting a dirty sock in it to keep the beans strong?"

"Just the thought of that keeps me awake," the one Cody had heard called Travis answered.

Cody took the cup. "I'm in no hurry to turn in tonight. I'll be sleeping in the barn with my horse."

As he settled in, the deputy who'd helped with the capture began to talk. "I was near the back as we charged in, but when I saw her, her cheeks were red, but she didn't look hurt. The guy with her looked angry. He tried to block us from seeing her so Brad and Charlie had to beat him up a bit. One gut punch from Charlie usually knocks a man off his feet."

"What was the lady doing?" Cody asked.

"She was just standing there screaming for us to stop." Andy looked puzzled. "I couldn't see much. I was the last one in, but one of the men said she caught the outlaw's hand and wouldn't let go. Strange thing for a prisoner to do to her abductor."

Cody watched the young deputy. He was figuring out what Cody already had. The deputies weren't rescuing her. The man with her had been trying to protect her when the deputies stormed in because he cared about Jacqueline Hartman.

Flipping the paperwork over, Cody read the report while Andy put the pieces together as he talked. "Everyone was yelling and shouting orders. Even the sheriff had to raise his voice to be heard." Andy added more to himself than Cody, "I don't think anybody was listening to anyone there for a while."

"That's the definition of chaos, son." Cody might be only a dozen years older than the deputy but he felt much older tonight.

Andy stared at Cody. "They're going to hang him tomorrow. What if he wasn't the kidnapper? He could have just been some guy she met and they thought they'd found a place to talk. We only have Calaber's word he robbed a bank in Austin."

Cody stood and set his coffee cup down. "Talk is some of the men at the party want to hang him tonight. Your job is to protect that man in there. That's your duty, boys, and you do it."

"We will." Andy set his jaw and looked as if he'd aged in a moment's time. "You staying around, Captain Lamar? One of the men said that during the war you faced down a dozen armed men with nothing but a knife for a weapon."

"The story's grown. It was three men." Cody grinned remembering. "And no, I'm not staying here. I've got to go over and wake up the operator and send a telegraph." Cody walked over to the cell door and took a look at the prisoner bleeding on the one blanket they'd given him. He looked more dead than alive. "This is none of my business but you might want to move the prisoner."

"Where?"

"I'd say the doctor's office. The two of you should be able to carry him there if you leave out the back. He doesn't seem to have much fight left in him and no one will think to check at the doc's this time of night.

"Can you find your way without taking a lantern with you?" Both boys nodded.

"Then go as quickly and as silently as you can."

Cody's words came out as an order and the two didn't argue with him. They pulled on their coats and were wrapping the unconscious outlaw in the bloody blanket by the time Cody downed the last of his coffee. "Bar the front door and bolt the windows after I leave. If someone shows up, that'll slow them down."

Wishing he could stay to help, Cody moved back into the night knowing what he had to do. He didn't know if his plan would help the man who'd been with Jacqueline or not, but it wouldn't hurt to try.

By the time he sent his telegram, the snow had begun to blow. He went back to the barn and found a place in the loft where he could watch the hotel. If a mob got brave, they'd wake him as they headed toward the sheriff's office.

The beauty of the night calmed him. The hotel sparkled in the snow and the music was soft now, drifting in the night. Behind him he could hear men snoring, each one wrapped up in his own bedroll that made the loft look like a prairie dog town after dark.

He stretched out with his rifle beside him, one arm folded for a pillow and thoughts of Katie filling his mind. If he found her, he'd ask her right away to marry him. Then he'd kiss her. No, maybe he should kiss her first, then ask her. Either way, if she said yes, he'd start finishing the house. He'd have it built by spring.

There had been times, during the war, when he'd been out alone with the cattle for weeks without seeing a soul that he'd thought of having someone waiting for him.

Drifting in thoughts of what the future might be, he dreamed that he was dancing with his fairy. Her sunshine hair would be flying like a cape behind her and her laughter would be all the music he needed.

Chapter 12

Nate felt someone poking on his chest but he didn't open his eyes. He wasn't sure both weren't swollen closed. Every part of his body hurt.

"You all right, Mister?" a voice peppered with age asked. "I'm Doc Hollis. These deputies brought you over for me to patch up 'cause you're leaking blood all over their jail. You've got . . ."

"I know," Nate answered. He'd been beat up enough to know what was wrong. "Blacked eyes." He tried to open the left enough to see the doc. "One broken rib, maybe two. Several bruises. Bleeding from the forehead, my lip, and just below my right eye."

The old man laughed. "And bruises pretty much everywhere I can see. One on your back looks like a boot print. The deputies pulled off your jacket and shirt. I noticed several spots that need sewing up. It appears you've been dripping long enough to start a pond on your chest."

"The deputies are the ones who did this, Doc. I wouldn't trust them to help with the patching up."

"I didn't hurt you," the nearest deputy answered. "But I'm

Andy Potter and the one in charge of watching you tonight, so don't even think of running. We're both armed and you don't look like you can see good enough to find the door."

"I thought I was in charge," the other deputy said, moving closer. "I was deputized two days before you. Name's Travis, Mister, and you can take my word that we'll watch over you."

Nate groaned as he turned his head toward a kid who didn't look old enough to be wearing a badge. "You were both there when they arrested me for doing nothing?"

"I was in the back of the crowd," Andy answered. "Travis was closer but he didn't hit you."

"Do you know what happened to the lady I was with? Is she all right? Did the deputies hurt her too? Oh, God, tell me she wasn't hurt."

Travis moved closer, examining Nate over the doc's shoulder. "He don't sound like a man who was hurting Miss Jacqueline when we broke into that room under the stairs. He sounds worried about her, Andy."

"I saw Captain Lamar's eyes," Andy tried to whisper in the tiny back room of the doctor's home. "I don't think he believed this guy was guilty. What if we've made a mistake? The sheriff was getting pressure from both Marshal Calaber and Hartman."

"What if?" Andy whispered.

"What if?" Travis answered as he stepped back a foot as the doctor worked.

"You've been injured recently, son," Doctor Hollis said to Nate as if he hadn't been listening to the deputies. "Some of these bruises look to be a few days old."

"I was in a stagecoach turnover," Nate answered, then looked at the deputies. "I didn't rob a bank like the marshal claims and I didn't hurt the lady I was with. But, I'm worried about her." He swore through clenched teeth as the doc pinched his skin together and began to sew with a shaking hand.

The two deputies watched the show as if they'd paid to see

it. They were little more than boys, but Nate swore they were aging as they watched.

When the doc began to wrap his ribs, the deputies moved close to the door and whispered. Nate didn't care what they were planning since neither had agreed to go tell Jacqueline he was alive. The only good news Nate saw was the fact that they were no longer guarding him closely. Maybe they figured he was too injured to run. They were wrong. As soon as he saw a break, he'd take off and they'd have to shoot him in the back to stop him.

Nate closed his one good eye and tried to relax. He tried to remember every moment since he'd first seen the pretty lady rush into his hiding place. Jacqueline was a nice name but he liked Littlebird better. She'd said her mother called her that. In the back of his mind he'd put together that she might be the woman whose father was trying to marry off, but a few things didn't fit. The man downstairs had said she was plain. That couldn't be her.

Also his littlebird was about to run away. She'd even laughed and said she'd run away with him and live an outlaw's life or be a pirate. A rich girl wouldn't say that.

The doc's voice drifted into Nate's thoughts.

"Looks like you're patched up good enough to hang tomorrow."

"Thanks," Nate managed to say.

The doc started putting away his tools without bothering to clean them. "You boys help him back into his shirt. I'll get a clean blanket since he ain't got a coat. Wouldn't want him catching a cold on his last night on earth."

Nate grinned at the old man's humor.

Just as the two deputies lifted him to stand, the back door of the doctor's office blew open.

"Evening, Miss Hartman," the doc said as casually as if they'd passed on the street.

All three young men turned and stared. Jacqueline wore a black dress with a cap that whirled around her in the wind.

"Evening, gentlemen," Jacqueline said in little more than a whisper as she raised what looked like a new Colt revolver. "I'll ask you two deputies to lift your hands and step away from my friend."

If they'd been seasoned deputies they might have rushed her or even shouted orders for her to lower the weapon. But the idea of someone pointing a gun at them was too new to allow Andy or Travis to form words.

"You look mighty pretty tonight, Miss," the doc said. "This your fellow?"

Jacqueline smiled. "He is. Sorry we can't stay to visit, Doctor, but we must leave."

Nate didn't hesitate. He clenched his teeth, lifted himself off the table, and moved toward her. Then he stood right in front of her and lifted his hand to her cheek. "Who hurt you, darling?" He lightly brushed his fingers along her jawline.

She lowered her weapon so he could move closer. "My stepmother hit me, trying to make it look like you hurt me."

"I'd never . . ."

"I know." She sighed. Her gloved hand cupped his bruised face. "They beat you up pretty bad. I can't find a single place to kiss you. Oh, Nate, you look terrible and it's all my fault."

As they kissed very lightly, Nate heard the old doc mumble to the deputies, "Sounds like you boys got a really bad outlaw here. The little lady appears to be fighting him off with kisses."

"Someone made a mistake." Andy looked at Travis. "When they found these two in the storage room no one listened to them. You think there is any chance they'll listen to us? Calaber and Hartman want him dead."

"Don't forget the drunk mob the captain said might be headed our way? If they come, they won't take the time to listen to us. The sheriff already thinks he's solved the case. He's not likely to listen either." Travis swore. "If a mob comes for him tonight, they'll take one look at the lady's bruised face and hang him before anyone has time to explain anything."

"How'd you find us here, Miss?" Travis asked.

Jacqueline carefully cuddled against Nate. He couldn't stop staring at her and much as he hated it, he needed her support to stand.

She'd saved him. Just like she said she would. No one had ever cared enough to help him when he was in trouble.

"I followed the trail of blood in the snow. When I saw what was going on here, I left my lantern outside." Panic suddenly flashed in her beautiful eyes. "If someone followed me . . ."

She raised her Colt once more.

"Wait," Andy said, taking a step. "I'll get the lantern. We can't help a prisoner to escape, but we can walk back toward the jail accidentally stepping on any blood we see."

Everyone moved at once. The doctor suggested Nate and Jacqueline go through his home toward the front entrance. Travis balled up the bloody blanket and clothes the doctor had used. He shoved them out of sight as Andy stepped outside and lifted the lantern.

Nate caught one last glimpse of them as he looked back. Both of the deputies had worry in their eyes, but they waved, silently wishing them luck.

When the doc reached the front door, he warned Jacqueline. "He won't make it far with all those wounds, Miss. You'd be best to find a place to hide for a day or two. Maybe leave him somewhere where no one would look."

"I'm not leaving him," she whispered. "I'm never leaving him. I don't care if my father disowns me. I don't care at all. I'm not leaving him."

"We'll be on the run, Littlebird." Nate fought a darkness that circled in his mind. "I can't ask that of you."

She looked up at him, her eyes drowning in tears. "You don't want me?"

He saw a lifetime of pain floating in her gaze. "Of course I want you with me. I have no doubt that if I left you, I'd be sorry every day I drew breath. But you'd be giving up everything. Everything."

"No, Nate, I'd be winning a life, a world with you. Every day with you would be an adventure. My father said I could pick the man I wanted to marry and I pick you."

"If you're sure. We'll make it somehow."

The doctor opened the front door. "You've got to go. You have to get somewhere safe and this will not be it. Once they hear you've escaped, the sheriff will search every house in Dallas."

Nate leaned on her as they moved outside. A woman with a long black cape like Jacqueline's stood waiting for them. She was dressed like one of the maids from the St. Nicholas Hotel. Without a word she stepped to his other side and they half carried him off the porch and onto the snowy road.

Nate made it maybe ten steps before the world started spinning around. He went from seeing white snow to darkness closing in. The last thought as he collapsed was that he was breaking his promise.

He was leaving the one woman he'd ever thought he could love.

Chapter 13

Cody slept lightly on the hay in the barn's loft. His feet were cold in wet boots but his thoughts of Katie warmed the rest of his body. She'd be the best memory he'd ever had even if he never saw her again. And if he did find her, he planned to collect a few more memories that would remain with him forever. But, for tonight, he'd relive every moment. What she said. How she smelled of roses. How she touched him lightly.

The dog she'd said was her friend crawled up beside him and Cody couldn't help wondering if the pup missed her as much as he did.

The music from the St. Nicholas whirled in the cold air, reminding him that he was far from home tonight. The town didn't sleep in peace like the prairie did. Too many people, he thought. Too many problems.

If the mob decided to move from the gaming room at the St. Nicholas to the jail, he'd wake, but for now he liked the idea of drifting and thinking of his beautiful fairy who'd danced in the moonlight.

He could almost feel her lips on his. Hesitant, soft, cold.

Cold! He opened his eyes.

She straightened above him and smiled. His Katie had found him.

"Were you just kissing me?"

"I was, Mr. Lamar."

"Do it again."

"Only if you close your eyes. Then you'll think you're dreaming."

He did, but when her lips touched his, the kiss turned far more real than his thoughts could have conjured up. He raised his hand and gently touched her hair. "I was just dreaming of this and I got to tell you, this reality is far better." He tugged her closer until they touched. "Let me warm those cold lips up for you."

"I'd like that." She opened her mouth slightly in invitation.

It had been so long since he'd been kissed or tried to be gentle. Thoughts stumbled through as his logical mind tried to take hold. She liked him, maybe even wanted him, but he couldn't just take her home and build her a house. She'd need so much more than a roof and food. His Katie would need loving and kindness. She'd need a garden to dance in the moonlight.

As she rubbed her cold cheek against his, Cody decided he'd have a great deal to learn about this woman, but damn if he wasn't willing to die trying.

When she pulled a few inches away, he whispered so low it was more a thought passing between them. "I promised myself when I saw you again I'd either kiss you or ask you to marry me."

"But, Mr. Lamar, we barely know each other. It crosses my mind that you might be crazy, but it seemed a kind of insanity I could grow to love."

"We'll take our time learning all about each other. We've got the rest of the night to talk and come morning we'll find a preacher if you're willing."

"No." She straightened. "I need your help right now, then

we'll continue the talk about us. Jacqueline said you're her friend and to tell you she needs you." Suddenly she was tugging at him. "What is between us will have to wait. We have to help them."

"Jacqueline Hartman needs my help?" Cody felt like he blinked and the world shifted. The image of the little girl crying over her mother's grave flashed in his thoughts. He'd wanted to help her. Maybe now was his chance?

"We have to hurry. She said to tell you that the lady in blue velvet is calling in your promise to be her friend."

Cody rose and reached for his rifle. "I'm right behind you. Take me to her. But, Katie, when this is over, we're going to talk. We will have our time."

She didn't answer as she rushed toward the barn's ladder.

When she hesitated, Cody handed her his rifle, circled her waist with one arm, and headed down from the loft.

Katie laughed. "I feel like the world's biggest doll being carried under your arm."

"I just didn't want you getting all tangled up in your skirts." He reached the ground and let go of her.

She stood on tiptoes and kissed him again right on the mouth as several sleeping men mumbled for them to be quiet.

As they headed out of the barn he asked, "You planning to do that often?"

"What?"

"Kiss me right out in public."

"I do. Any objection?"

"Not a one." He couldn't stop grinning. She might not have time to talk, but he knew that come morning she'd be riding home with him.

"This way," she whispered as she turned into an alleyway.

Cody sobered. This was no time for dreaming. His entire mind and body shifted into the soldier he'd been in his early twenties.

He heard a moan before he saw two people huddled between buildings. Snow had dusted them almost invisible, but he made out their outline even in the dark. Two feet farther and he smelled blood.

In the dim light, he saw the face of the lady he'd met earlier. "My lady in blue," he whispered.

"Mr. Nobody," she answered. "My friend."

He knelt and lifted the blanket covering her lap. A man's bloody head rested there, so still he seemed to be sleeping. "Is he alive?"

She nodded. "He's lost a lot of blood. We have to get him to safety. He can't die." Her tears blinked like tiny diamonds on her cheeks.

Cody didn't pretend not to know Nate Ward. He'd seen him in the jail cell and if possible he looked worse than he had there. He handed Katie his rifle once more. "You know how to use this?"

"No," Katie whispered.

"I do," Jacqueline answered as she held her Colt in one hand and reached for his rifle. "If you can carry him, I'll stand guard. We have to get him somewhere warm and safe. The only place I can think of is my room at the hotel."

Katie began wrapping the blanket tightly around Nate. "I'll run ahead. Bring him in the back door and I'll make sure the path is clear."

As Cody lifted the man, Jacqueline stood and Katie disappeared.

"We'll have to move slowly because of the snow," Cody ordered. "Hold on to my arm. There's no hiding the fact I'm carrying a body, but visibility is so bad maybe we'll make it."

They stayed to the shadows of buildings. He could feel Jacqueline's hand tucked into the folds of his coat at the elbow. She was shivering from the cold, or fear, he couldn't tell which.

"I was at your mother's funeral," he whispered. "It was cold like this but the snow had turned to rain."

"I remember."

"I was young then. Just bought a piece of land and was headed to serve in the war with Mexico. Every time I came home, I'd look for you. Wanted to tell you I was sorry about your mother."

Her shaking stopped. "I remember seeing you a few times. I used to love to ride out to the river between our two ranches and watch as you moved the cattle down on your side for a drink." She tucked the blanket around Nate's face. "Thanks for helping me now. I love this man and if he's found, they'll hang him."

"I know. He didn't hurt you, did he?"

"No."

"Then we've got to help him. Maybe if he lives long enough to marry you, we'll be neighbors."

"Maybe." She stepped ahead of Cody, shoved the Colt deep into her cape pocket, and opened the garden gate.

As Cody stepped inside the garden, he heard boots stomping along the walk maybe ten feet behind them. He lowered Nate in the dead weeds near the three-foot stone wall and leaned close to Jacqueline.

"Who's there?" a man yelled as he materialized from the falling snow.

"Captain Lamar," Cody snapped back when he recognized one of the older deputies. "Go away. I'm talking to a lady." Cody leaned over the fence, blocking any view of Nate hidden below.

Jacqueline covered her face with her scarf and turned into Cody's shoulder as if hiding from prying eyes.

"Sorry, sir. Miss. We're covering the town. That outlaw escaped, but we'll catch him."

Cody nodded and pulled Jacqueline close. "Good night, then," he said as if in a hurry to be left alone.

The deputies marched on and Cody silently lifted Nate as Katie opened the back door.

Without a word Cody followed Katie through the hallway,

past the kitchen, and up the stairs. Jacqueline shadowed with the rifle at the ready. At each landing, a bellboy or maid stood guard. "They won't tell," Katie whispered. "We're taught to never tell what happens at the St. Nicholas."

Cody followed her into Jacqueline's suite. A parlor, a bedroom, and what looked like a small dressing room. Katie spread a blanket over the bed and he lowered Nate.

"Step aside," the round cook announced as she rushed in with two baskets of bandages and supplies. "You all have to leave. I know that old doctor and I'd bet he didn't clean a single one of them wounds. My mother always believed a clean man heals faster and if he doesn't, he's in proper shape to meet his maker." She looked at the three. "Out you go. I can handle this."

Cody might have argued with a general a few times in his life, but he didn't argue now. He held the door for the ladies and stepped into the parlor room. "We'll keep the lamps low and the door locked. If anyone gets in here they'll have to pass me to get to Nate."

He sat down in what looked like the sturdiest chair in the room while Jacqueline and Katie took the settee. They held hands like women tend to do.

Five minutes later a bellboy whom Jacqueline called Sam brought in hot water. Cody let him pass through to the bedroom. On his second trip, he brought in sandwiches and hot tea.

"Thank you, Sam," Jacqueline said, sounding tired and worried. "And thanks for keeping my hiding place secret for as long as you could."

"I didn't tell." Sam glanced at Cody and straightened slightly as if he were a soldier reporting in. "They were just searching every floor. I was surprised when they even noticed the door beneath the stairway. If I could have got past them, I would have warned you."

When Cody nodded once at him, Sam seemed to relax and

he turned back to Jacqueline. "The cook asked if I could find your outlaw more clothes. Everything we pulled off him is too bloody to put back on."

Jacqueline let a tiny smile raise the corner of her mouth. "You said he was about the size of the marshal?"

"Yes, Mr. Calaber claimed the outlaw stole his clothes tonight. The marshal complained it was downright embarrassing to have to wear his traveling clothes to a ball."

Jacqueline locked her hands behind her and passed back and forth across the small parlor. "Then I see only one solution. It couldn't hurt to take a few more of Calaber's things. I saw a trunk branded with double *CC* under the stairs. It's no wonder the marshal travels by stage, his wardrobe wouldn't fit in his saddlebags."

"Yes, Miss. I'll go fetch something the outlaw can wear." Sam vanished and five minutes later he was back with warm wool trousers and a shirt and leather jacket. Without waiting he rushed to Nate.

She turned to Cody. "He's not an outlaw."

"I've already figured that out. Never did judge a man by his duds."

"Which reminds me," Katie said, leaning toward Jacqueline, not Cody. "We need to work on the captain here. He wore what he has on to the ball."

Jacqueline nodded. "We'll have our work cut out for us if this is his dress clothes."

"What?" Cody had the feeling they were about to gang up on him.

"Nothing," they both said at once.

He leaned back, fighting down a laugh. He'd put up a fight against any idea they had, but he had a feeling he'd be losing the battle.

The cook stepped out of the bedroom before Cody could

finish the horrible cup of tea Katie poured him. "Miss Jacqueline, he's asking for you."

Jacqueline rushed to Nate. Katie followed, then Cody.

He stood at the door just behind Katie watching Nate and Jacqueline. She curled up beside him, her hand locked in his. Nate looked terrible, bruised and cut up, but in his stolen Western clothes, he now seemed to belong in this wild country.

"No one has ever cared enough about me to do what you did," he said to Jacqueline. "You risked your life."

"I told you I'd save you." She glanced back at Cody and Katie. "I did have help."

Cody pulled Katie back and closed the door. "We'll give them some time."

The cook picked up her rags and potions. "Don't be giving them too much time or I'll be delivering a baby next fall."

Cody laughed and kissed Katie right in front of the cook.

"Or two," the cook added as she left with Sam right behind her.

Drawing Katie close, he kissed her the way he wanted to from the first moment he'd seen her.

When she pulled away, he fought the urge to hold on tighter.

"I have to tell you things before we go any further, Mr. Lamar."

"I'm listening. Tell me what you have to say and then I'll ask you to marry me."

"Maybe," she said, staring at him with determination in her eyes. "I'm not afraid of you, Captain Lamar. I'll have my say. I'm twenty-eight. I don't have a penny to my name. I'm a maid here at the St. Nicholas. I'm not a virgin."

He smiled. "I'm thirty-four. I've got a ranch. Some years I'm rich and some I'm broke. I'm a soldier, been a loner most of my life. Folks say I'm a hard man, but I'll always be good to you. I'm not a virgin either and I think I'm more afraid of you than anyone I've ever come across, but I'm not backing down."

He saw a flash of panic in her eyes and added, "How about we forget about our lives before tonight? We're two newborns learning to love for the first time. Our lives are from this moment on and it's going to be what we make it."

She rested her head against his heart. "I have a feeling we'll rack up all the memories we can carry."

"That's my plan. Maybe I'll even learn to dance."

He brushed his hand over her hair, loving the feel of her so near. "Only we got to get one thing straight. You got to stop calling me Mr. Lamar."

"Yes, sir." She giggled.

Chapter 14

Jacqueline stood at the bedroom door. Nate was sleeping. For a while she watched Cody Lamar and Katie holding each other as if they never planned to let go.

"Cody," she finally said. "May I speak to you alone for a moment?"

The couple separated but neither one looked guilty. "Of course," Cody managed.

"I'll sit with your Nate," Katie said, crossing the room and closing the door behind her.

Jacqueline grinned. "We need to talk."

"I agree."

Chapter 15

The first light of dawn was fighting its way through the frosty windows of the hotel's ballroom when Jacqueline's father stood before her with the preacher at his side.

"Don't you think your stepmother should be here?" Harry Hartman bellowed, then groaned in pain. If his eyes were any more red he'd match the still-hanging decorations.

"No," Jacqueline said, staring straight at her father. "My stepmother does not need to be here."

"Fine. Let's get this over with." Harry looked at Cody, then back at his daughter. "So you agree to marry? Cody is a bit older than you, but he's a good man. Good neighbor too."

"I do plan to marry this very morning, if you keep your promise, Father."

Harry Hartman scratched his head. "I'll never hear the end of it if I don't get you settled. Margaret thinks it's the only way you'll be happy."

"For once I agree with her. First, we sign the papers, then the preacher will marry me off."

Harry scrubbed his face and seemed to be trying his best to

look sober. "I know Cody; he's been my neighbor for years. You picked a fine husband. But, who are these two people?" He glared at Katie and Nate. "Wait a minute. She's a maid and this man is the outlaw who kidnapped you and beat you up. I'll see him hang." Anger fired in the old rancher, but his hangover washed away any actions.

Before Harry could move toward Nate, Cody did what a friend would do. He locked his arm under Jacqueline's father, halfway stopping him and halfway holding him up. "He's no outlaw, Hartman. I've got a telegram from Austin to prove it. They caught the real bank robber." Cody gave him time to absorb the news, then he added, "Nate Ward never hurt your daughter. Margaret did."

Harry opened his mouth to argue, but somewhere in his whiskey-flooded brain he must have known the truth.

He backed up until his legs bumped a chair, then Harry Hartman crumbled. "I just wanted you to be happy. I wanted to see you married. Margaret said it was the only way."

"I am marrying. I found just the right man." Jacqueline knelt and looked up at her father. "And I will be happy."

The old man nodded. "Then I'll sign over what I promised. I said you could pick the man you marry. Tell me what part of the ranch you want?"

Jacqueline smiled. "Sign over the fourth of the ranch that borders Cody's land. It's not the best for grazing, but it's the part I've always loved. I'd like you to build a house in the cottonwoods near the river. And I'd like the entire second floor with big windows facing east and west to be for my books."

"Done." He touched her bruised jaw. "She really did hit you even after I said she never could?"

Jacqueline nodded. "It doesn't matter now, Father. It will fade along with the memory of her."

"What else can I do?" he asked.

"I'm giving Cody the cattle in exchange for half the profit

when he sells them. He'll also have grazing rights free until we return. Nate and I plan to spend at least a year traveling." She smiled at her father. "Thanks to you I have plenty of money in the bank in Dallas."

Harry sobered suddenly as if he'd been slapped. "Wait. You're marrying the outlaw? I thought it was Lamar?"

Nate straightened but didn't say a word. He was standing tall, but it was costing him dearly. Cody stood ready to catch him if the actor tumbled.

"You said I could pick the man I wanted. He's a good man."

"No. Not him." Harry started to stand.

She put her hand on her father's shoulder. "I'm marrying him, Father."

Harry huffed like a bull getting ready to fight. "He probably knows nothing of our life."

Nate laid his hand over Jacqueline's hold on Harry's shoulder. "Don't argue with your father. He's not a man who listens. We'll be fine without him, Littlebird."

Harry looked up at his only child. To her shock, huge tears rolled down his wrinkled, weathered face. All the anger had left him. "Her mother called her that," he said, really looking at Nate for the first time. "Her mother loved her."

"So do I," Nate answered. "We don't need anything from you. Tear up the papers. We don't need your cattle or land." He gently pulled Jacqueline's hand away and turned her into his waiting arms. "Come along with me."

She nodded.

Before they reached the door, Harry roared, "You can't tell me what to do. I'm doing what my daughter wants me to do. I'm a man who keeps his promises. It's her inheritance. She has a right to handle her own money and her own life." He glared at Nate. "Heaven help me, you seem to be what she wants. And you'd better be good to her."

"Nate, wait," Cody shouted out the command.

When Nate paused, Cody ordered again, "Turn around and shake hands with your new father-in-law."

Nate hesitated. A lifetime of rejection had left him strong.

Cody tried again. "This is probably as nice as he gets, but this is his way of telling you he loves his daughter and if she wants to marry you, that's all that matters."

Nate looked confused. "I've never had any family. Now I see what I didn't miss. But, if you are all the family she has, she'll probably want you around." He offered his hand to the old man. "I love your daughter. I'll put up with you for her sake."

Harry grabbed on tight and didn't let go as he pulled Nate toward him. "I'll do the same, but don't you ever call my daughter Littlebird again."

"Not a chance of agreeing to that," Nate answered. "And I'm thinking of teaching my sons to be actors or outlaws."

"Over my dead body."

"Can I have that in writing?"

Cody watched, swearing all the air left the room. The two men just stared at each other as if waiting for all hell to break out. With the old man still half drunk and Nate barely on his feet, it wouldn't be a fight he'd want to see.

Then, Katie, the one everyone had forgotten was there, began to laugh.

For a moment no one moved. Jacqueline smiled.

Cody decided both women had gone mad. Maybe the whole world had. It had been one hell of a night.

In a voice painted slightly with Ireland magic, Katie said, "Mr. Hartman, you sound just like my father did when my older sister married. He threatened to murder Shane in his sleep. Three years later he told my sister if she didn't start being nicer to Shane she'd have to move out. Of course, Shane could stay."

"What happened?" Jacqueline asked as if nothing of importance was going on in the room.

"My sister took my father's advice and stopped picking on her father's son-in-law. Three years later they had four boys and no longer had time to fight. I got a letter a few years ago saying they were up to eight sons now and living in Dublin. Shane became a banker."

Cody realized her story had worked. The yelling was over.

Harry offered his hand. "Maybe you'll grow on me, outlaw."

"Maybe you'll grow on me, old man. I love your daughter. I'll meet you halfway for her sake."

"Fair enough, but I'll teach my grandsons to ride. I won't have my kin being city boys."

The preacher, who'd been standing in the wings watching all the action as if it was a grand play, moved closer. "Can we get on with the wedding? I've got a Christmas service this morning."

Cody offered his hand to Katie. "Marry me, Katie."

She nodded and stepped to his side. She said all she needed to say when she kissed his cheek.

Jacqueline looped her arm through Nate's. "Please, marry me. You've already stolen my heart."

"We've only known each other one night, and we've both been beat up and almost killed. You think we can make it?"

"It'll be an adventure."

"Dearly beloved," the preacher started. "We'll keep this short . . ."

Margaret started pounding on the door, demanding they let her in.

". . . to join these men and these women . . ."

Marshal Calaber added his voice to Margaret's. He threatened to break in and arrest them all. He demanded in the name of the law. When that didn't work, he promised to shoot them all.

No one seemed nervous except the preacher. "I pronounce you two couples man and wife." The preacher was shaking so badly his Bible looked like it was dancing in his hands.

The door crashed in as he rushed through the service. "You may kiss the brides."

The marshal and Margaret were almost knocked down by the staff of the St. Nicholas rushing in to congratulate the two couples. Even Harry Hartman joined in all the hugging going on.

When Cody finally got a chance to hold Katie, he lifted her up and yelled above the crowd. "Let's go home."

"I'd like that, Mr. Lamar."

He frowned. "Don't you think you could call me Cody?"

Katie shook her head. "I will when I get to know you better."

He grinned. "Any objection to us going home and making that happen?"

"None at all, dear." She cupped his face with her small hands and kissed him. "Then, I'll teach you to dance."

As Cody turned toward home he whistled for the barn dog. "Come along, Friend," he said.

The dog didn't have to be asked twice.

Epilogue

Cody and his Katie eventually bought the land Harry deeded to his daughter and lived out their lives on the ranch. Through good times and bad they made memories. Some turned out to grow into six sons. Until Katie died in her eighties, Cody always saw her as his fairy.

Nate and Jacqueline traveled for two years before her first pregnancy brought them back to their house in the cottonwoods. There, she wrote stories of her adventures and Nate had a great time pestering his father-in-law. They had four daughters and the old man didn't seem to mind a bit.

Harry Hartman sent his wife, Margaret, back to New Orleans where he'd met her. He never saw her again.

Twenty Christmases later Nate and Jacqueline's second daughter married Cody and Katie's oldest son.

Marshal Calaber never became governor. Shortly after the ball of 1859 in Dallas, he moved to Oklahoma Territory. Those who saw him leave said he walked with a limp from an attack that Christmas season. They found him bloody and half frozen

in the garden of the St. Nicholas Hotel. Some say it was re-
venge, or payback for some terrible wrong he'd done. Others
noticed a few of the dents in his head looked more like pot
marks.

None of the staff of the hotel reported seeing a thing.

Birdie's Flight

CELIA BONADUCE

To Billy
Merry Christmas, my love

Chapter 1

December 1859
Dallas, Texas

Birdie Flanagan stood in front of the brand-new St. Nicholas Hotel. She willed her feet to take the final steps to the lobby of the gleaming three-story brick building. She tried to steady her hands. She'd traveled so far; she couldn't let her nerves fail her now. With exactly fourteen cents in her change purse, she was out of money.

Her luck had deserted her long ago.

She was a long way from County Clare, where two years ago, at age eighteen, she'd bought into the myth that all the streets in America were paved with gold. New York and New Orleans proved how wrong she'd been. There were no gold streets. Here in Dallas, half the streets weren't paved at all.

Birdie walked into the lobby, making sure her hair was tucked into the embroidered scarf under her hat. Her shoulders were squared and her head was held high. She patted the outside pocket of her valise, assuring herself her letter of recommendation was secure. She had to make a good impression on Sarah Cockrell, the woman who, against all odds, had built this hotel single-handedly after her husband's untimely death. Birdie told herself that any woman who could build a hotel in a man's world would understand the plight of another woman determined to prove herself.

But she'd been wrong before—and not just about the streets of America.

Birdie looked around the lobby. The first floor of the hotel was a flurry of holiday preparations. Fragrant evergreen was being strewn over balconies and the largest Christmas tree Birdie had ever seen was being settled in the middle of the lobby by four burly—and by the looks of the tipping treetop, optimistic—men.

Christmas was around the corner and the St. Nicholas Grand Ball, a gala that was the talk of Dallas, was a mere ten days away. There seemed to be more workers than guests in the lobby, which Birdie took as a good sign. It was obvious the hotel was sparing no expense. Surely they could use another employee. At least until the ball was over.

"Excuse me," Birdie said as she approached a woman in a black maid's outfit who was setting ornamental glass balls in a silver tureen.

"Yes?" the woman said as she looked up, a pleasant expression on her face. She eyed Birdie's travel-worn clothes and dusty suitcase. Her expression changed. Clearly, this was not someone she needed to indulge. "What is it, girl? I'm busy."

"I'd like to speak with Mrs. Cockrell," Birdie said, making sure her voice didn't quaver.

"You and every other floater," the woman snorted, and went back to arranging her centerpiece.

Birdie didn't flinch. *Floater* was not a word Birdie had ever heard in Bunratty, Ireland. In Bunratty, the woman would have been calling her a loafer. Although no one at home had ever called Birdie a loafer. She came from a good family who, while poor, always managed to make ends meet. Her family had been part of the fabric of the town. The first time *floater* had been hurled at her in New Orleans she didn't even know what it meant. The accusation stung, but like everything else in her life since stepping foot in America, she'd learned to brush it off.

"I have references," Birdie said.

The woman's hands fumbled with one of the glass balls. She lost her grip and she gasped as the ball slid out of her fingers. Birdie managed to rescue it before it hit the floor. The woman's hands flew to her heart.

"Thank you," the woman said, reaching for the ornament.

"I'd be so very grateful if you could point me to Mrs. Cockrell." Birdie smiled brightly but held the ball out of the woman's reach.

The woman watched Birdie's hand as she moved the ornament lightly through her fingers. It seemed impossible that Birdie wasn't dropping it, but the ball continued to balance perfectly. A hush descended on the lobby and the woman took her eyes off the ornament long enough to see what was going on, then turned back and looked Birdie in the eye.

"You're in luck," the woman said. "Mrs. Cockrell just walked into the lobby. Just follow the bowing and scraping."

"Thank you," Birdie said, tossing the ball back to the uniformed woman. "I appreciate your *kindness.*"

Birdie turned toward a small woman she could barely glimpse among the crush of people vying for her attention. How was she ever going to get Mrs. Cockrell to notice her in the middle of all these people? Birdie once more made sure every strand of hair was still tucked neatly in the embroidered scarf and tried to muscle through the crowd. She was not used to the aggression of Americans—even these Texans, who had only been Americans since the state was ratified fourteen years earlier. She put her suitcase in front of her, using it as a sort of battering ram. She needed a job. She could out-Texan these Texans if she had to.

She shouldered her way into the crowd, but suddenly stopped dead as she ran into . . . something. She looked up to see a wall of a man who stood between her and Mrs. Cockrell. He was handsome in his military uniform. He didn't need the stripes on his sleeve to announce he was an officer—his confidence and bearing attested to that.

"Can I help you with something?" the officer asked, steadying her.

He was staring into Birdie's eyes with a hint of a smile. If he thought he could dissuade her from getting to Mrs. Cockrell, he was mistaken.

"I need to speak with Mrs. Cockrell," Birdie said, staring back at him.

Poised for a fight, Birdie was surprised when the man stepped aside and she found herself face-to-face with the stranger who could give her a job and, even though it was a sprawling hotel, a place she could call home.

"Mrs. Cockrell," Birdie said in a strong, clear voice. She noticed the army officer was watching her with interest. "May I have a word, please?"

"Yes?" Mrs. Cockrell asked in a honeyed voice.

Birdie's mind froze. She hadn't actually expected Mrs. Cockrell to answer her. Birdie spent so much of her time trying to not be seen, she thought she'd made herself invisible. But Mrs. Cockrell had heard her and was waiting for her to speak.

Birdie knew she had only a moment to make an impression. She felt her head swim.

She fainted at the hotel owner's feet.

Birdie's sense of smell was the first of her senses to return. She breathed in the scent of warm tea. Then she felt a gentle touch on her cheek. In her dreamlike state, she thought for a moment she was home, asleep in her feather bed, and the delicate touch was that of her mother. A contented sigh escaped her before reality came rushing back. She remembered fainting in the lobby of the St. Nicholas Hotel! Her eyes sprang open and she bolted into a sitting position. Mrs. Cockrell had been leaning over her, but she took a tiny step backward as Birdie sat up, wild-eyed.

"You're all right? You scared us," Mrs. Cockrell said, putting a hand on Birdie's shoulder. "Take it easy. You might still feel dizzy if you spring up."

Birdie's head swam. Springing up was not in the cards. She wanted to lie back down, but she'd already made enough of a scene, so she just propped herself against some cushions and watched Mrs. Cockrell pour a cup of tea. While the hotel owner busied herself with the teapot, Birdie looked around the room. She was in a large office with beautiful furniture, opulent curtains, and fresh flowers. Birdie had never seen such elegance.

Mrs. Cockrell brought a tray with delicate blue-and-white-patterned china over to her. Birdie tried not to stare at the tiny sandwiches and steaming tea being offered.

"I had a feeling you might be hungry," Mrs. Cockrell said, sitting on the sofa beside her.

"A bit," Birdie managed.

She wanted to tip the entire plate of sandwiches into her mouth, but, with trembling fingers, picked up one perfectly cut triangle and forced herself to turn it into three ladylike bites. She was so hungry she couldn't tell what filling was between the two pieces of bread. She took another sandwich off the plate as Mrs. Cockrell poured some tea. Birdie suddenly noticed her bag propped against a side table. Then she noticed her hat was sitting on the table itself. She reached up frantically to make sure her headscarf was still in place.

It was.

"Captain Newcastle carried you up here," Mrs. Cockrell explained. "He removed your hat, but I suggested he leave your headscarf. I assume anyone who wears a scarf under a hat probably wants to keep it on."

Mrs. Cockrell passed her a cup of tea, apparently not requiring an explanation of the elaborately embroidered headscarf. Birdie sipped at the tea demurely.

"Thank you," Birdie said. "And I will have to thank Captain . . ."

"Captain Newcastle," Mrs. Cockrell said. "You're a very lucky woman. When word gets out that Captain Newcastle came to your aid, I guarantee there'll be a rush of fainting young women in the lobby every time he's here."

Birdie felt her cheeks flush. This was not the impression she'd hoped to make. She took another sip of tea. She decided it was time to change the subject.

"I was hoping . . ." Birdie said, realizing her voice sounded weak. She took a deep breath and tried again. "I know the ball is coming right up, and I was hoping you might need an extra girl."

She forced herself to look in Mrs. Cockrell's eyes. She knew the look she saw there. It was pity. There was a time when she would have shrunk from that look. Pride would have made her stand up, thank Mrs. Cockrell for her time—and sandwiches—and be on her way. But she didn't have that option now. She didn't care how or why Mrs. Cockrell gave her a job—as long as she gave her one.

"I have references," Birdie continued, putting the teacup down and reaching for her valise.

Mrs. Cockrell waited as Birdie rummaged through her bag with trembling fingers. Finally, she drew her tattered letter out of the bag and handed it to Mrs. Cockrell. Mrs. Cockrell took a pair of reading specs out of a pocket hidden deep in the folds of her dress.

"So you worked on a farm in Ireland, did you, Brigid Flanagan?" Mrs. Cockrell asked.

"Birdie," Birdie said.

She was about to say "My friends call me Birdie," but she was very much without friends—and frankly, Mrs. Cockrell probably had no interest what her friends called her. She started again.

"Most people call me Birdie," she said.

"All right, Birdie then. So you worked on a farm."

"Yes, ma'am," Birdie said, realizing it was hardly an obvious endorsement for a job in a hotel. "But I did more than farmwork. I did laundry, I cooked, I—"

"We've hired a full staff," Mrs. Cockrell said, handing the letter back to Birdie. "I'm sorry. I really am. But we've had so many applicants . . ."

Mrs. Cockrell's voice trailed off. Birdie could imagine Mrs. Cockrell had to give this bad news to girls several times a day. Why should Birdie's plight be any different?

Birdie took the letter back, trying not to cry.

"I understand," Birdie said, standing up and tucking the letter back into her bag. "And thank you so much for your . . ."

She hesitated. What should she say? Although she was crushed about the rejection, she really hadn't expected anything to go her way. Nothing had gone her way since she landed in America. But this woman had been so kind.

"Thank you for your kindness," Birdie said, feeling it was the perfect word.

"I wish I could be of more help."

Birdie managed a tight smile and a nod. She believed her. She picked up her bag and her hat and headed toward the door. Her feet were at least solid beneath her. No need to have Captain Newcastle carry her back to the lobby, she thought grimly.

At the door, she stopped for a moment to put on her hat, taking advantage of a mirror hung nearby. She tried not to be obvious, but she noticed Mrs. Cockrell studying her.

"Your scarf," Mrs. Cockrell said.

Birdie closed her eyes. Perhaps she was going to have to come up with some explanation after all for why she wore a scarf under her hat.

"Did you do that embroidery yourself?"

"I did," Birdie said, hoping to end the conversation.

"It's extraordinary," Mrs. Cockrell said. "And I noticed embroidery on your sleeve cuffs. Also your work?"

Birdie nodded. She turned around to see Mrs. Cockrell writing on a cream-colored piece of paper. Birdie had never seen a pen quite like the one in Mrs. Cockrell's hand. It appeared to have ink already in it! The pen made a scratching sound much like the chicken back at the farm. Mrs. Cockrell blotted the ink and handed the paper to Birdie.

"Take this letter to Miss Monica Quigley in the basement," Mrs. Cockrell said. "She is our head seamstress. I'd never hear the end of it if I let you get away."

"Oh! Mrs. Cockrell," Birdie gushed. "I can't—"

Mrs. Cockrell held up a hand.

"Just do your best," Mrs. Cockrell said. "Miss Quigley will not put up with anything less than perfection."

"Yes, ma'am," Birdie said. "You won't be sorry you hired me."

"You're hired if Miss Quigley says you're hired."

"Yes, ma'am. Well, if Miss Quigley hires me, you won't be sorry *she* hired me."

"Make sure of it," Mrs. Cockrell said. She looked stern, but her eyes were twinkling. "Everyone in the hotel is afraid of Miss Quigley."

"Even you?"

"Even me," Mrs. Cockrell said. "That woman could start a fight in an empty house."

Birdie was so overwhelmed with the idea that she actually had a job—if she passed muster with Miss Quigley—that she couldn't remember leaving Mrs. Cockrell's office. Back in the lobby, she realized she hadn't asked how to find the head seamstress. She remembered that Mrs. Cockrell said the sewing room was "in the basement," which certainly narrowed things down, but . . .

Birdie stopped in her tracks. Captain Newcastle, standing head and shoulders above a crowd of adoring women, met her eye. Birdie's thoughts momentarily shifted away from finding Miss Quigley as she had a fleeting memory of being swept up in his arms. She cursed her freckled skin, which she could feel growing warm as he smiled at her. She turned to find someone to ask about directions to the basement when she saw the captain breaking away from his admirers and heading her way. Frantically, she looked around for an escape route. She did not want to have a conversation with this man. Or any man, for that matter. She admitted he was incredibly handsome, but he looked like trouble.

And she'd had enough trouble with men to last her a lifetime.

"Miss," Captain Newcastle said. "I'm Douglas Newcastle, captain in the United States Army."

The captain took her hand and kissed the back of it. In Ireland, a gentleman never kissed a lady's hand unless it was offered. But here in America, it was not considered bad form for a man to lift the woman's hand and brush his lips against it. She found it hard to get used to, especially when a man was as enticing as Captain Newcastle.

"Yes, I know who you are," Birdie said, keeping her voice calm.

She noticed the envious glances from the cluster of women the captain had left behind.

She tried to put the vision of him carrying her limp body to Mrs. Cockrell's office and removing her hat out of her mind. The image seemed so intimate, her pink cheeks burned scarlet.

"Mrs. Cockrell tells me you—" she continued.

"No need to thank me," Captain Newcastle cut her off. He gave a little bow. "Just doing my duty."

If he was just doing his duty, there was no need for Birdie to feel embarrassed. A twinge of disappointment tugged at her, but she squashed it. "My mother wouldn't forgive me if I didn't thank you, so thank you very much."

"You may tell your mother I accept," he said.

Birdie could hear a few titters coming from the eavesdropping women.

"I'd better be on my way then," Birdie said, pushing past him.

"Do you think your mother would mind if you had dinner with me?"

Birdie was stunned. Had she heard him correctly?

"Dinner? With you?"

"Yes, dinner with me. Here at the hotel."

Birdie's mind reeled. Dinner? A real dinner? What would they eat? This was Texas. Texas was famous for beef, wasn't it? She could probably have a steak. And she would love a soup. She knew better than to have wine with a man, but perhaps dessert? She thought about the lovely puddings she'd had as a child.

Captain Newcastle's voice broke into her thoughts. "I'm hoping that silence is you deciding the answer is 'yes'?"

As hungry as she was, she could never agree to have dinner at the St. Nicholas with this man. The lobby was full of guests in their impeccable clothes. She would seem like a pauper.

She *was* a pauper.

"I'm sorry," she said, walking away from him. "That's very kind of you, but I really can't."

She realized she had no idea where she was going, but she moved purposefully through the lobby. She was a woman on a mission. Even a mission starting in a basement was progress. She had nowhere to go but up.

Chapter 2

Once belowstairs, there was another labyrinth of confusing hallways constituting the basement. But Birdie finally made her way to the head seamstress's office. The door was closed. Birdie stared down at her note from Mrs. Cockrell, to make sure it was real.

The letter read:

> *Dear Miss Quigley,*
>
> *May I introduce Miss Birdie Flanagan. I think you will find she has an extraordinary talent with a needle.*
>
> *Yours sincerely,*
> *Sarah Cockrell*

Compared to her tattered letter of recommendation from O'Connor's Farm, Birdie felt she held a magic ticket. If the woman who owned the hotel and was practically a legend throughout Texas recommended her, Miss Quigley couldn't very well refuse her.

Could she?

Birdie stood up straight and knocked on the door. She needed this job and she was going to get it.

"Come through," said a muffled voice.

Birdie detected a slight Irish brogue. Perhaps that might work in her favor. Feeling a little more confident, Birdie opened the door.

All confidence drained as she regarded Miss Quigley, a stern-looking woman who didn't glance up as Birdie entered. Miss Quigley was working on a traditional Irish tatted lace design, one which Birdie knew was extremely difficult.

"What is it you want?" Miss Quigley asked, still not looking up.

Birdie wasn't wrong about the voice. The woman spoke with a warm, rich brogue. Perhaps when Birdie spoke, her equally strong Irish accent might attract a glimmer of interest.

"I've been sent by Mrs. Cockrell," Birdie said, making sure she sounded as Irish as the day she landed in New York City.

"Have you now?"

If Miss Quigley felt a sister from across the waters had landed in her office, she kept it to herself.

"Yes, ma'am. I have a letter."

Miss Quigley put the needle down and finally looked up at Birdie. Birdie stared down at the head seamstress, who still hadn't risen from her chair.

"Well then?" Miss Quigley asked. "Hand it over."

Birdie tried to keep her hand from shaking as she handed the letter to the head seamstress. While Miss Quigley read the letter, Birdie studied her. Miss Quigley's graying hair was swept up in a bun. She was probably in her early forties, no-nonsense in her demeanor and clothes, the only ornamentation a key on a thin chain around her neck, which hung smoothly over a prim, full skirted dress. Birdie found the seamstress's lack of flair particularly interesting, since a quick glance around the room revealed that every inch was covered in opulence and glamour. Beautiful dresses, gowns, and men's frock coats on hangers and dress forms made the small room look like a rehearsal for a party. There were boxes of lace, feathers, buttons, and more embroidery thread than Birdie had ever seen. There was even a sewing machine!

Birdie was willing to take any possible job available at the hotel, but the thought of working in this room took her breath away. When she returned her gaze to Miss Quigley, the woman was looking sternly at her.

"So. Mrs. Cockrell thinks you can sew, does she?"

"Yes, ma'am."

"It's too bad Mrs. Cockrell doesn't know a thing about sewing."

Birdie's spirits plummeted. She had to convince this woman to take her on.

"She might not know anything about sewing, but she must know quality when she sees it."

"I suppose that's true." Miss Quigley sniffed.

"After all, she hired you." Birdie smiled.

Flattery was a sure way into almost anyone's heart.

"Don't go trying to flatter me, girl," Miss Quigley said, picking up her half specs off the table and pointing them at Birdie before perching them on her own nose. "I only care what you create with your needle, not your tongue."

"Yes, ma'am."

The two women stared at each other. Birdie wasn't sure what to do. The smell of stew wafting through the air distracted her. Finally, Miss Quigley broke the tension.

"You have some samples to show me?" she asked impatiently.

"Yes, ma'am," Birdie said, jumping up and retrieving her

bag. She pulled out two headscarves and a shawl. They were a little threadbare, but each showed a different skill—the shawl had a delicate lace edging and one of the headscarves was made from tatting, much like the technique Miss Quigley was using herself.

Birdie handed Miss Quigley her last sample, a headscarf covered in elaborate embroidery. The design was every Irish flower Birdie had ever seen—including her favorites, the lacy wild angelica, the trumpet-shaped bindweed, the delicate Little-Robin, and of course, the bright green shamrock.

Birdie held her breath while the woman looked over her handiwork.

"My mother taught me . . ." Birdie began, but stopped mid-sentence as Miss Quigley looked over her half-glasses at her. Clearly, Miss Quigley did not want her to speak.

"Can you use a sewing machine?" Miss Quigley finally inquired.

"No, ma'am."

"Pity."

Miss Quigley handed the headscarf back to Birdie. Birdie tried not to cry as she repacked her samples.

"I suppose we'll have to learn to use it together then," Miss Quigley said absently, as she refolded her glasses and put them back on the table.

Birdie's head spun. Did this mean she was hired? Dare she ask?

Miss Quigley smacked her hand on the table and Birdie jumped.

"Why Mrs. Cockrell insists that we share the same floor with Cook is beyond me," Miss Quigley said. "Can you smell that stew?"

"Yes, ma'am," Birdie said, dividing her attention between the heavenly sounding words *stew* and *we*.

"Night and day, that woman cooks," Miss Quigley said.

"But . . . isn't that her job?"

"Of course it's her job. She's called 'Cook' after all. But we've got a job too. And you know what that is?"

"To . . . sew?"

"Exactly! To sew and mend and fix and hem—and then return those clothes to our guests and have them not smelling of stew!"

"Yes, ma'am."

Birdie was still not certain she had the job.

"One of your jobs will be to walk the garments up and down the alley before returning them to guests. Air them out—it's the best we can do."

One of her jobs!

She wanted to embrace Miss Quigley but had a suspicion that would not go over well with the severe woman. Birdie wasn't sure she'd even appreciate a smile.

"I'll do my best," Birdie said with a simple nod.

Miss Quigley nodded back.

"From the looks of you, you just got off the boat."

Birdie didn't need to tell Miss Quigley the details of her journey from New Orleans to Galveston by a steamer ship so old and tired she was afraid it would sink, and then the flea-bitten coach to Dallas. The less said about that the better.

"Are you staying at Miss Hortense's Boarding House?" Miss Quigley asked.

"No, ma'am," said Birdie, who didn't have enough money to stay anywhere.

"I know you're not staying at Scarlett's"—Miss Quigley gave Birdie an appraising once-over—"or you wouldn't be looking for a job here."

"Yes, ma'am . . . I mean no, ma'am."

Birdie guessed that Scarlett's was the local house of ill repute. When Birdie left her sheltered life in Ireland, she had never even heard of a harlot. But in every city she'd visited since—the wharf towns on the Irish coast and all the stops she'd made in

America—she'd been propositioned not only by men but by women promising her an easy life if only she wanted it.

She didn't.

But Birdie made no judgments—she'd earned money sewing for the ladies of the night in more than one town. They always paid well. Though the women always had smiles plastered on their faces, they knew how hard it was to make a living in a man's world.

"I haven't . . . settled yet," Birdie continued.

"There's a storage closet you can clean out if you want it," Miss Quigley said, gesturing to a door behind two exquisite ball gowns. "It's large enough for a bed and a small dresser. It's not much but at least you'll be safe."

Safe. Could she even let herself think about being safe?

"Thank you," Birdie said, trying not to sound too eager. "I'm very grateful. I'm happy to clean it out . . . but I don't have a bed or a dresser."

"Don't be daft, girl," Miss Quigley said. "Haven't you noticed this is a hotel? We can get you a bed and a dresser."

"Yes, ma'am. Thank you, ma'am."

"In the meantime, get down to the kitchen and tell Cook to give you some of that stew. The sooner it's gone the better," Miss Quigley said, eyeing Birdie's thin frame. "From the looks of you, you could put away a good portion of it."

As Birdie headed down the hallway, she saw a now familiar figure propped against a wall. It was Captain Newcastle. Birdie surprised herself at the initial excitement she felt. She knew better than to make snap judgments about men. Especially positive snap judgments. She averted her eyes. She'd learned not to look at the floor. She just acted as if she didn't see him as she strode past.

"Are you following me?" she heard him ask.

"Excuse me?" She turned on him. "I was about to ask you the same question."

"Were you now?"

"Yes," she said, although she hadn't thought that until this very moment. "So . . . were you following me?"

"I hate to disappoint you, but no. I actually have business here."

"You have business?" Birdie was annoyed with his suggestion that she might be disappointed and forced herself not to sound it. She settled on a contemptuous tone. "You have business . . . in the basement."

"A soldier's lot takes him everywhere," he said with a wink. "You never know where you'll find danger, Miss Flanagan."

Birdie froze.

"How do you know my name?"

"I'm in the military," he said. "I have my ways."

"I suppose you're going to tell me it was through top-secret channels."

"No," he said. "I just asked Mrs. Cockrell. After all, it's not every day I carry a woman up two flights of stairs. I inquired as to your health and Mrs. Cockrell mentioned your name."

"You didn't mention you knew my name when you asked me to dinner."

"If I recall, you didn't give me the opportunity," he said. "Any chance you've changed your mind?"

Birdie tried to dislike this man, but she was finding it very hard to do.

"No, sir," she said, but could hear the regret in her own voice. "I can't. But thank you."

The captain saluted. Birdie tried not to smile.

"Would you know the way to the kitchen?" she asked.

She hoped it wasn't obvious she was just trying to prolong their conversation. Heaven knows, she could have just followed her nose to the kitchen.

"It's just down this hallway," Captain Newcastle said, walking in step with her. "I'll show you."

"In case there's danger in the kitchen?" Birdie couldn't help herself from playing his game.

"I can guarantee you there is no danger in the kitchen. I just came from there."

"Oh," Birdie said, envisioning a comely cook kneading bread.

"I was there on official business," he said. Birdie hoped he hadn't read her mind. "The kitchen staff cooks for the officers who are stationed here in Dallas. It's probably the only way we can keep the officers."

Birdie smiled. He really was incredibly charming. Perhaps she might lower her guard just a little.

The captain stopped abruptly.

"Here we are," he said as they turned a corner and faced a set of huge double doors.

He saluted again and turned on his heels. She watched as he disappeared around the corner. He did not look back.

All for the best.

Birdie opened the door and let herself into the kitchen. The heat of the ovens immediately washed over her. She remembered so many recent cold nights, she refused to be anything but grateful for the warmth. She could see a short, round woman standing on a stool, stirring an enormous pot of stew on a stove. Birdie's eyes widened. She was expecting to see a pot bubbling inside a huge fireplace, but clearly, the St. Nicholas had every modern convenience.

"Excuse me," Birdie said to the woman stirring the stew. Birdie wished she had asked Miss Quigley for Cook's name. "Are you . . . Cook?"

The woman turned around on her stool. She held a large ladle aloft and gave Birdie a smile.

"*Oui, cherie,*" she said, stepping off her stool and wiping her hands on her apron. "*Je suis Madam Durand. Est-ce que vous parlez français?*"

"Oh, I'm so sorry . . . I mean . . . *pardon,* but I don't speak French."

"Oh good," the woman said in a Texan twang. "Me neither. I just told you every word I know."

Birdie looked puzzled. Had the heat gone to this woman's head?

"Everybody likes a French chef and when people hear my name, they expect me to start jabbering in French," the woman said. "What can I do for you?"

"Well, Mrs. Durand—"

"Madam Durand," she corrected. "Gotta keep the romance alive."

"All right, Madam Durand . . . I . . ."

"Or 'Madam' is fine," she said.

"Yes, Madam."

"Or Cook," she said, sounding deflated.

"I think I'll call you 'Madam,' if you don't mind."

"That would be wonderful," Cook said, sounding surprised. "But you might as well call me 'Cook.' Everybody else does. Now, why are you here? Did you just tell me?"

"No, actually," Birdie said.

Now that she *was* here, Birdie wasn't sure how to demand a bowl of stew.

"I've just been hired by Miss Quigley to—" Birdie continued, but Cook silenced her.

"Are you the girl who fainted?" Cook cried, seizing Birdie's arm.

"How did you hear about that?" Birdie asked, embarrassed.

"Oh, you can't keep a secret in this hotel," Cook said.

Birdie stiffened. She prayed that wasn't true.

Chapter 3

"Excuse me, sir," the man said, pulling the badge out of his coat pocket. "I'm Detective Hilbrand. May I ask you a few questions?"

It was cold on the docks of New Orleans. All the detective wanted to do was call it a night. He'd been scouring the port for leads, but came up empty. He was on his way back to his hotel when he noticed a man sweeping up the day's debris. One more line of questioning couldn't hurt.

The man sweeping the dock stopped and rested on his broom. He gave a disinterested glance at the badge.

"You can put that away," the man said. "I can't read."

Detective Hilbrand snapped the rawhide case closed. He felt as if he'd been having the same conversation for weeks in every city to which his leads took him. Mostly dead ends, but always just enough information to keep going. He pulled out a worn black-and-white sketch from his pocket.

"Have you seen this girl?" he asked.

The sketch showed an unsmiling young woman in a white blouse and heavily embroidered shawl. Her hair was pulled up in a modest bun, but a few corkscrew curls escaped and curled around her neck as if they were already on the run.

The man with the broom squinted at the picture, tilting his head from side to side.

"We see a lot of people down here," he said.

Detective Hilbrand tried not to be impatient. It was as if the dockworkers had all memorized a script to use when talking to officials.

"Look," Detective Hilbrand said. "I'm with the Pinkerton Agency. I'm not a copper."

The man looked Detective Hilbrand right in the eye. It was as if he were deciding whether to proceed with the conversation or not. Detective Hilbrand forced himself to look as if he cared.

"I might have seen her," the man with the broom said with a shrug.

"How much?" Detective Hilbrand reached in his pocket. He knew the drill by heart.

Again, the man shrugged. Detective Hilbrand held out a few US dollars and the man took them.

"She was a pretty girl. You could tell she didn't want anybody to notice her. She had a scarf over her head, but . . ."

"But?"

"But, like I says, she was a pretty girl. And we don't get too many pretty girls down here."

"Can you tell me anything else?" The detective tried to keep the annoyance out of his voice.

What he wanted to say was "Can you tell me anything useful?"

By the time Birdie returned to the sewing room, Miss Quigley was gone for the evening. Birdie made her way to the storage closet, hoping she could just find a place to lie down for the night. She could clean everything up tomorrow. Tonight, she was too tired. She opened the door to the closet and gasped. Even in the dim light, she could see a bed with a beautiful comforter. There were two pillows with the letter "N"—for the St. Nicholas Hotel, no doubt—done in exquisite embroidery. A small dresser had also been added to the pristine space. Her travel bag was on the bed and a blue-and-white porcelain bowl and pitcher perched on the dresser. Birdie sank onto the bed, trying not to cry.

Over the last few weeks, she'd slept anywhere she felt she was away from prying eyes . . . fields, barns, in the shadow of stacks of luggage at train depots, and behind barrels at oceanfront ports. She'd never dreamed anything so beautiful would be waiting for her. She touched the embroidered "N," studying the design. She felt a boost of confidence. As lovely as the work was, she knew she was up to the task, should Miss Quigley ask her to replicate it. She wanted to write to her mother, thanking her for teaching her so many beautiful designs and techniques and insisting on perfection. Birdie had bristled at the time, but she shuddered to think where she would be now without them.

Perhaps she could make Dallas her home. She tried to put the thought out of her mind. She'd hoped for that very thing in every city she'd been in, but she only managed to stay one step ahead of the man who followed her relentlessly. Dallas seemed like the ends of the earth, so maybe he had finally lost the trail. But it was too soon to count on that.

But if, as a holiday miracle, she felt she was safe in Dallas, she might be able to write to her mother by Christmas. It was a lovely thought, writing a cheerful greeting filled with descriptions of her wonderful job, new friends, and possibly even an account of the St. Nicholas Grand Ball. She put her head down on the crisp pillowcase and went to sleep.

She awoke to a clatter. Springing out of bed, she saw Miss

Quigley filling the pitcher on the dresser. Birdie realized the closet had no window and she had no idea if it was day or night.

"I'm so sorry," Birdie stammered. "I must have overslept."

"You did," Miss Quigley said, keeping her eye on the pitcher, which she filled from a steaming pan. "It's five thirty. We start work at five fifteen."

"It won't happen again," Birdie said.

"I'd say that was a very good idea," Miss Quigley said, setting the bucket down and looking at Birdie. "Do you always sleep in your clothes?"

Birdie looked down at herself and gasped as she realized she hadn't changed into her nightdress. She'd gotten used to sleeping in her corset. She adjusted her scarf, which thankfully hadn't come off during the night.

"I . . . I was just exhausted," Birdie said.

"I've brought you a uniform," Miss Quigley said, motioning to a black pin-striped dress with a simple but elegant embroidered tulle mobcap.

The mention of a uniform nudged Captain Newcastle into Birdie's head. She quickly shut him out. She hadn't realized she'd been holding her breath until she saw that the cap would keep her hair neatly out of sight, without drawing attention to herself.

"Thank you, ma'am," Birdie said. "If the dress doesn't fit, I can take it in myself."

"The dress will fit. I picked it out myself. I didn't get to be head seamstress by haphazard guesswork, you know."

"Yes, ma'am."

"Now get cleaned up and let's get to work," Miss Quigley said. "I have biscuits and butter and coffee on the table, so be quick."

Birdie couldn't believe her ears. She'd just eaten last night! Miss Quigley swept out of the room and Birdie pulled off her worn traveling clothes and put them in the dresser. Even with all her sewing ability, she feared they would never be suitable to wear in the hotel lobby, but from what she'd seen of Dallas, she could certainly hold her head up on the town's sidewalks.

Miss Quigley was right: the dress fit perfectly, even to the length. Birdie tucked her hair into the cap, took a deep, calming breath, and opened the door to her new life.

Her new life smelled of coffee.

Birdie was not as hungry as she'd been the night before, so she managed ladylike sips of coffee—with cream and sugar! She took a large biscuit from a tray and started to slather butter on the warm bread but slowed her pace when she noticed Miss Quigley's arched eyebrow. Cook had been easy to talk to as Birdie downed her stew the night before and she gave Birdie a few tips on how to handle Miss Quigley.

"She scares everybody," Cook said. "But it's just an act. A very convincing act. But she has a heart of gold, that woman."

"That's good to hear."

"Well, it's true. I mean, she took you in off the street, didn't she? Pitiful little ragamuffin that you are."

Birdie looked up from her stew. Cook was looking at her with sympathetic eyes. Clearly, she wasn't being rude. Just stating the facts as she saw them. And what could Birdie say? She *was* a pitiful little ragamuffin.

"But she's a tough taskmaster," Cook continued. "So no sloughing off, you hear me?"

Birdie took another bite of biscuit as she reflected on Cook's words. Birdie was going to do everything she could to impress Miss Quigley.

A young man—almost a boy—arrived to take the tray back to the kitchen. While Miss Quigley talked to the kitchen boy, Birdie finished her breakfast, sorry to see anything on the tray being returned. But she told herself that there would always be something to eat as long as she was at the St. Nicholas. She smiled as the kitchen boy took the enormous tray and held it expertly aloft in one hand as he left the sewing room. It seemed everyone excelled at his or her particular duties.

"I'm going to send you up to see a very demanding guest," Miss Quigley said, sighing. "Miss Charlotte Rutherford. Spoiled beyond belief, this one."

Miss Quigley looked up to see the shocked look on Birdie's face.

"Just because we work for a living doesn't mean we're blind to the faults of our guests," Miss Quigley said. "You need to have a good head on your shoulders and see people for who they are, or else you're going to get in trouble."

Birdie knew exactly what she was talking about, and nodded her head.

"Charlotte is the daughter of a retired judge from Cincinnati. He's looking for investments in Dallas and the whole town is courting him. He's a lovely man, but he lets that girl get away with everything. You'll have your hands full."

"Should I get my sewing kit?" Birdie asked.

"That won't be necessary," Miss Quigley said. "We have everything you'll need."

"What *will* I need?" Birdie asked, eager to hear what Miss Charlotte would be requiring.

"Do you see those two dresses hanging by your room?"

"Yes, ma'am!" Birdie tried not to smile at the thought of her own room. She needed to keep her mind on the task at hand. "I noticed them when I first walked in yesterday. They're beautiful."

"Thank you. I made the green one and your . . . predecessor, Miss Paterson, made the yellow one with the jeweled décolleté," she said. "With my contributions, of course."

"Of course."

"Miss Rutherford hated them both. Pitched an almighty fit. She knew better than to confront me directly, but she called poor Miss Paterson every name in the book."

Birdie could feel herself starting to panic. Did this woman get her predecessor fired?

"Miss Paterson, a very talented seamstress, quit!"

"Oh! She *quit!*" Birdie tried not to sound pleased.

No matter how exhausting Miss Charlotte Rutherford turned out to be, she could never hold a candle to the last few months of Birdie's life. She would never quit. She took a quick glance at the dresses.

"I can't imagine owning either one of those dresses," she said, almost to herself.

"These girls are different," Miss Quigley said. "They're used to having everything. By the end of the ball, we'll have twenty or thirty discarded dresses—these girls will change their minds on what they're wearing until the last minute."

Birdie was surprised Miss Quigley had even heard her, let alone answered her.

She watched as Miss Quigley took the key from around her neck and opened a large wooden box near the fireplace. From Birdie's vantage point, she could not see inside, but Miss Quigley casually set a delicate pistol on the table as she continued rummaging in the box. Birdie stared at the weapon. Miss Quigley did not look like a woman who would own a gun. But this was the Wild West, where perhaps every woman had a pistol.

"Here it is," Miss Quigley said, holding up a pen much like the one Mrs. Cockrell had used the day before.

"How does that work?" Birdie asked. "If you don't mind me asking."

"It's a new idea," Miss Quigley said. "One of our guests, a Mr. Lyman, was working on a patent for something he was going to call a fountain pen. When he left the hotel, he made a gift of his prototypes for Mrs. Cockrell and me. He still has some work to do. The idea is to supply ink to the pen from a reservoir in the handle, instead of dipping the tip in ink every few words. I came into Mr. Lyman's good graces because I was forever getting spilled ink out of his shirts."

While Miss Quigley informed Birdie of the inner workings of the fountain pen, she returned the pistol to the wooden box and locked it. Miss Quigley took a sheet of the hotel's stationery and scratched a few words on it.

"Take this," Miss Quigley said, handing the note to Birdie. "It will introduce you to the Rutherfords. The judge is in room 207 and Miss Charlotte is in 208. Her father has a soldier, or a sheriff or some such man, stationed outside her door for protection, but this letter should get you in."

"What should I say to her?"

"You probably won't have to say anything. She's quite the talker, that one. I'm sure Miss Rutherford has another grand idea for a ball gown."

Birdie glanced at the finery behind her. She couldn't imagine rejecting either one of them. They were perfect.

"As tactfully as you can, please inform the little princess that we have other clients who also need dresses for the ball," Miss Quigley continued.

"I'll do my best," Birdie said, biting her lip. "Should I offer her some guidance or just listen to her ideas?"

"As my sainted mother used to say, never give cherries to a pig or advice to a fool. Just do what you can and we'll see if we make her happy this time."

"And if we don't?"

"God help you, child."

Birdie took the note and headed to the second floor. In the lobby, work for the ball continued. As rough as Dallas appeared beyond the doors of the hotel, once inside, the glamour of the St. Nicholas could rival that of any big city. But the glitter of the decorations only made Birdie wish for home. The holly and ivy, so lavishly festooned on tables and banisters, made her think of her family's own modest preparations. Her mother would hang a few berries tied with ribbon in the window. It was believed the berries on the holly would mean better luck in the new year—and her family could always use better luck. Everyone in the village also placed a large candle in the front window to symbolize guidance for Joseph and Mary on their journey.

Birdie found herself standing in front of room 208 and shook off her homesickness. The sentry, who was sitting on a stool, stood as Birdie approached. Without saying a word, he put out his hand and she placed the note in it. The man glanced at it, then nodded. Birdie knocked.

"Come in," a woman commanded.

Birdie looked at the sentry, who rolled his eyes.

"Good luck," he said under his breath.

Birdie took a deep breath, turned the knob, and headed into the room.

A woman was standing at the lace curtain, her back to Birdie. The light coming through the window cast the woman in silhouette. Birdie could only make out her general shape, which struck her as having much the same slim build as Birdie herself.

"Miss Rutherford?" Birdie asked.

"Yes," the woman said, not turning around.

"My name is Birdie Flanagan, Miss Rutherford," Birdie said. "I'm here to . . ."

Birdie glanced at the chifforobe, its dark mahogany doors ajar as dresses fought to escape the crush within. How could this woman possibly need another gown?

"I'm here to . . ." Birdie started again. "I understand you'd like a new gown for the ball?"

She did not answer Birdie's question. "Come over here," the woman said instead, still not turning around.

Birdie approached the window. She could now make out the delicate features of Miss Charlotte Rutherford. She had shiny, raven-black hair swept up in a chignon and flashing eyes, which were almost as dark. She pointed into the street.

"See that man down there?" Charlotte asked.

Birdie took a step toward the window, but Charlotte pulled her back.

"Don't let him see you!" Charlotte commanded.

Birdie looked from behind the curtain. The man Charlotte was pointing to was Captain Newcastle.

"Do you see him?" Charlotte asked breathlessly.

"I do," Birdie replied. She felt her heart beat a little faster. "It's Captain Newcastle, I think."

"How did you know that?" Charlotte asked. "Oh. Never mind, every girl in Dallas knows him, I suppose."

"Do they?" Birdie asked, trying not to sound alarmed.

He was talking to a group of fellow soldiers, but clearly was the center of attention. A woman who walked by the group pretended not to notice him, but once she'd passed by, she promenaded right back the way she came, hoping to catch his eye. Clearly, this man had his pick of any unmarried woman in Texas.

"They seem to. Anyway, I have to look perfect at the ball," Charlotte said, pointing to the man in uniform. "Captain Newcastle will be there, and my father is bound and determined that I make an impression. Father wants me to marry the captain, and Father does not take 'no' for an answer."

Birdie tried to hide her surprise—and disappointment. She tried to shake some sense into her own head. What did it matter if Charlotte had her sights set on Captain Newcastle? She took another look out the window. These women seemed shameless, although their tactics seemed to work. The soldiers had dispersed and the captain was now surrounded by hoop skirts and lace.

"I have an idea for a new dress," Charlotte said, pulling up a chair to a small table littered with papers. She motioned for

Birdie to take a seat as well. Birdie was hesitant. Should she really sit down? Charlotte motioned impatiently again to the chair and Birdie sat.

Charlotte started digging through the papers, which were all sketches of ball gowns. Birdie took a quick glance again at the chifforobe. There were at least a half dozen gowns in there—not to mention the two works of art down in the sewing room!

"Here it is!" Charlotte said triumphantly, pulling a sheet of paper and waving it in the air. "I want you to make this!"

The dress, well executed on paper, was stunning and complex. It had a tiered full skirt in two fabrics, one a crisp underskirt and one a frothy transparent fabric overlaid onto it. The skirt cascaded from a tight, low-cut bodice. The gown featured off-the-shoulder sleeves, which were little more than tiny rows of embellishments made from crystals. There were more strands of crystal embellishments sewn in a V-shape under the bust, mirrored by the long, pointed waist.

"What's wrong?" Charlotte asked, the first note of doubt creeping into her voice. "Don't you like it?"

"I do like it," Birdie said. "I like it very much."

"But . . ."

"But I can't imagine we could possibly get the gown ready in time for the ball," Birdie said. "I'm not even sure there is enough organza and silk in Dallas in the first place."

"There's only one way to find out," Charlotte said. "Let's go see."

"Let's go see what?" Birdie asked as Charlotte pulled a heavy wool shawl and hat out of the chifforobe.

"Let's go see what fabrics they have," Charlotte said. She glanced out the window. "Captain Newcastle is still outside. We can say hello. That will make Father so happy."

"I'll have to get permission to—"

"No, you don't. Your mistress is used to me. She knows you'll be busy all day."

"I have to get my shawl . . ."

"Here, take this," Charlotte said, pulling another beautiful shawl from the chifforobe. Was there no end to this woman's wardrobe? "We have no time to lose."

"That's very true," Birdie said, wondering how she would ever create the ball gown in less than two weeks, even if they could find the fabrics and embellishments.

Chapter 4

Detective Hilbrand considered tendering his resignation. Acting on the lead from the dockworker in New Orleans, the detective now found himself on a rickety steamship headed to Galveston. The dockworker was certain he'd seen the girl book the same passage, although he couldn't have been certain when. Maybe a week ago? Maybe a month? Even a few more dollars didn't help restore the man's memory. Now, as the detective gulped in the salt air, trying to ward off a roiling stomach as the ship surged through rough water, he wondered if the dockworker just wanted to get rid of him. He focused on the sight of Galveston as the town came into view. He might or might not be one step closer to finding Brigid Flanagan, but at least he'd be back on dry land.

"Ladies," Captain Newcastle said, tipping his kepi hat to Charlotte and Birdie as he looked over the tops of the bonnets milling around him.

"Pretend you're ignoring him," Charlotte whispered to Birdie as they marched toward Captain Newcastle.

"I *am* ignoring him," Birdie whispered back.

But Charlotte was right—Birdie was just pretending. The man was impossible to ignore.

"There are two general stores we can check for fabric," Charlotte said.

Birdie just nodded. She couldn't imagine any city outside of Paris or New York having fabric to meet Charlotte's standards.

A little bell over the front door announced Charlotte's and Birdie's arrival at the first general store. Birdie noticed the bolts of fabric lining a shelf behind a glass case full of sewing supplies. Birdie loved seeing the new scissors, some utilitarian and some with mother-of-pearl handles, needles in varying sizes, and several embroidery hoops. Birdie had gotten used to general stores as she traveled across the country. This store was modest compared to others she'd seen, but it was well stocked for a town without a railroad stop. There were foodstuffs: sacks of coffee beans and dried beans, jars of spices, baking powder, oatmeal, flour, sugar, honey, and molasses. There were also local items like eggs and cheese for sale.

Birdie spotted a corner of the store decorated for Christmas. A small evergreen, perched in a tin basin, and adorned with ribbons, reminded her of the "tree in a tub" her mother decorated every year in Bunratty. She expected to feel a pinch of homesickness, but instead, she felt closer to home than she had in years.

Birdie noticed the proprietress busy herself as she saw who was walking in. Birdie suspected Charlotte had already perused every fabric the store had to offer and found it wanting.

"Excuse me, Mrs. Snow," Charlotte said to the proprietress. "I've brought my new seamstress and we'd like to see any new fabrics you might have gotten in . . ."

"Since you were here last week?" Mrs. Snow asked, turning around.

"I thought perhaps you might have anticipated some need, since every woman in town will be going to the ball."

"Not *every* woman." Mrs. Snow sniffed. "Those of us who didn't receive the satin-bound invitation to the Grand Ball will be attending a dance on the other side of town."

Birdie's interest was piqued. She hadn't been to a dance since leaving Ireland. Could she possibly take a chance and go to it? Surely she wouldn't see anyone who knew her. She felt as if she'd run to the ends of the earth here in Dallas.

"It's called the Jingle Bobs and Belles Ball," Mrs. Snow said, sensing Birdie's curiosity. "You should come."

"Thank you, but I'm not sure," Birdie hedged. "I'm a newcomer and I wouldn't know anyone."

"You'll know lots of people!" Mrs. Snow said, smiling. "I'll be there. Have you met Cook? She'll be there."

"What about Miss Quigley?" Birdie asked.

"Not likely." Mrs. Snow snorted. "Miss Quigley doesn't approve of too much socializing."

"What about the stagecoach coming in from Jefferson?" Charlotte asked, turning the conversation back to her quest. "I've heard a rumor that there is a supply of dresses coming in."

"All of those dresses are spoken for," Mrs. Snow said. "Besides, I'm sure they would never meet with your exacting standards."

"That's probably true," Charlotte said.

"Our fabrics are good enough for some people," Mrs. Snow said pointedly to Birdie.

Birdie felt her cheeks redden. She was hoping Charlotte wouldn't pick up on the obvious slight. But Charlotte was eyeing the shelf of fabric intently.

"Is this your entire stock?" Charlotte asked. "I've already seen these."

"And if you come back tomorrow, you'll see them again."

Birdie turned her attention to a beautiful pair of scissors in the glass case holding the sewing supplies, leaving Charlotte and Mrs. Snow to their sparring. Her back was turned toward the front door and she didn't notice the tall, thin man enter the store. He wore a dusty brown wide-brimmed hat pulled low over his forehead. He strode over to the corner of the building used as the United States Post Office, soundlessly pulled down a WANTED poster for "Dangerous Jack Simon," and walked out again, quiet as a whisper.

"I guess we'll just have to go see what Mrs. Peak has on *her* shelves," Charlotte said.

"Please do," Mrs. Snow said. "*Please* do!"

Charlotte took Birdie's arm and they left the store.

"We might as well go back to the hotel," Charlotte said, straightening her hat.

"I thought you said we were headed to the other general store."

"Oh, Mrs. Peak's selection is even worse! I just said that to get Mrs. Snow's goat."

Birdie nodded, fairly certain Mrs. Snow remained unscathed.

Dallas was a hive of activity. Men in uniform or work clothes went about their business while the women who weren't busy in the shops tried to get their attention. It wasn't hard to tell which ladies were looking for love and which were looking for profit.

"Now, there's a handsome fellow," Charlotte said, indicating a lanky man wearing a vest and a battered badge who was helping a farmer unload a wagon of winter vegetables in front of Mrs. Snow's store.

"He must be the sheriff," Birdie said.

"Brave as well as handsome." Charlotte winked.

The two women watched as the sheriff tipped his hat to the farmer. Charlotte suddenly stepped into the street. A horse-drawn carriage was inches from her. Birdie couldn't find her own voice to shout a warning, but reached out. She was almost knocked over by the sheriff, who swooped Charlotte off her feet and carried her back to the safety of the boardwalk.

"Miss Charlotte," Birdie gasped, as the driver of the horse-drawn carriage swore and continued on his way. "Are you all right?"

Charlotte was not listening to Birdie. She was staring into the eyes of the man who had saved her—and who had not, as yet, put her down.

"You need to be more careful, ma'am," the sheriff said, putting her on the ground.

"Thank you," Charlotte said, shaking.

"Miss Charlotte," Birdie tried again. "Are you sure you're—"

Charlotte cut her off, stepping lightly in front of Birdie so only Charlotte was facing the sheriff.

"I don't believe I know your name, but I can see by the badge you're a lawman."

Is Charlotte flirting with this man? wondered Birdie. *What about her plans to marry Captain Newcastle? Did she step in front of the carriage on purpose?* Birdie had some questions, but she wasn't about to get any answers until Charlotte had finished her conversation with the sheriff.

"Sheriff Holden, ma'am," he said.

Birdie noticed he tipped his hat to Charlotte, in a slow salute. It was an innocent enough gesture, but somehow it had a lot more heat than the nod he gave the farmer. Whatever was going on here appeared to be mutual.

"Very nice to meet you, Sheriff Holden," Charlotte fluttered.

Sheriff Holden leaned lazily against a porch post and gave Charlotte a lopsided grin.

"And who have I had the pleasure of saving?" he asked.

"I'm Charlotte Rutherford," she said. "And I'm very grateful for your services just now."

Sheriff Holden stood up straight, any hint of impropriety

gone. The entire atmosphere changed from tropical heat to frosty.

"Miss Rutherford," he said. "I've had a few meetings with your father. I hope his continued interest in the town is not marred in any way by this unfortunate accident."

"Near-accident," Charlotte corrected, looking to Birdie for confirmation.

Birdie opened her mouth, but Charlotte returned her attention to Sheriff Holden.

"I'm sure Father will be very happy to hear you saved me just now."

"Oh, no need to mention it to your father. Really. I wouldn't want him to think Dallas was an unsafe place for a beautiful woman like yourself."

Birdie stifled a smile. The game was back on, apparently.

"Everything all right here?" came a familiar baritone. It was Captain Newcastle.

"Yes, Captain," Charlotte said, never taking her eyes off the sheriff. "Everything is just fine."

Birdie knew it was unreasonable to hope Charlotte would stay focused on Sheriff Holden. Captain Newcastle shifted his gaze to Birdie. She couldn't meet his eye but she knew he was looking at her. Was it possible he felt an attraction to her?

"I see you got the job," he said with a grin, indicating her dress. "Welcome to the world of uniforms."

Birdie felt the color rise in her cheeks. He only wanted to tease her.

"May I see you ladies back to the hotel?" Captain Newcastle asked.

"I was just about to offer my services," Sheriff Holden said.

Suddenly a man came flying through the double wooden half doors of the saloon two stores down. He landed facedown in the dust. Another man came running out and pulled the first man up by his shirtfront.

"Fight! Fight! Fight!" came the shouted encouragement from inside the saloon.

Birdie's stomach knotted. She'd seen enough drunken fights to last her a lifetime.

"Looks like your business calls, Sheriff," Captain Newcastle said to Sheriff Holden. "I'll see these ladies home."

Sheriff Holden, clearly having lost some silent game, quickly tipped his hat a final time and raced to break up the bar fight.

Captain Newcastle took Charlotte's arm and guided her across the street. Birdie knew this was protocol and tried not to wish it were she on his arm as they crossed the street. By the time they were safely on the hotel steps, the three of them looked back. Sheriff Holden had dispatched the fighters and sent them in different directions.

"What a brave man," Charlotte said.

"Are you trying to make me jealous?" Captain Newcastle asked with mock scorn.

"Not really," Charlotte said absently, and drifted into the hotel.

Birdie smiled sheepishly at the captain and followed Charlotte into the lobby.

If Charlotte was planning on marrying the man, she certainly had an interesting approach, Birdie thought.

Dangerous Jack Simon, the WANTED poster tucked safely in his back pocket, cleaned his fingernails with a pocketknife as he watched Birdie enter the hotel.

She was one beautiful woman, he thought. If he could stay ahead of the law, maybe he'd get a chance to speak to her.

He'd almost gone into the bar looking for a card game. No one noticed him as the fight started in the street. He smiled to himself. That man who landed in the dust could have been him. He'd been thrown out of better bars than this one. But luck had kept him outside—and out of the arms of the law. The fact that he had spotted Birdie and had identified both the sheriff and a captain of the military made him feel his luck was about to change. He knew who to follow and who to avoid. Once the sheriff was safely back in his office, maybe Jack would try his hand at starting a friendly game of poker after all. The men in the bar were definitely drunk enough to be easy marks. A few winning hands and there'd be enough money to buy several shots of Dallas's finest Irish whiskey.

He glanced up at the grand three-story St. Nicholas Hotel. He might not have enough money to get a room at the fanciest place in Dallas, but he could probably cheat his way into enough money to visit a hotel in the seedier part of town. Having just arrived, he didn't exactly know where that was, but he was sure a barmaid would be happy to steer him there.

Charlotte and Birdie made their way back to Charlotte's room. A middle-aged man was standing outside the door. Miss Quigley was with him.

"Father!" Charlotte exclaimed.

"Charlotte!" Judge Rutherford, a large man with an equally large walrus mustache, frowned at his daughter. "I've been looking for you for an hour!"

"Oh, I'm so sorry, Father," Charlotte said.

Birdie was surprised by Charlotte's tone. Every ounce of feistiness was gone. Although they had only known each other a few hours, Birdie was surprised to see Charlotte act so contrite. She suspected *act* was the operative word. Charlotte appeared to do whatever she liked.

"If it weren't for this lovely woman who assured me you were in good hands," Judge Rutherford said, nodding toward Miss Quigley, "I would have called the sheriff."

"If he's going to call the sheriff, maybe I should disappear more often," Charlotte whispered to Birdie before turning a brilliantly remorseful expression toward her father.

"Where have you been?" he asked.

"I was shopping," Charlotte said, opening her eyes wide to look as innocent as possible. "I still don't have a dress for the ball."

"I thought I'd paid for at least two dresses for the ball," he said.

"Three," Miss Quigley said under her breath.

"If you've no further need of my seamstress," Miss Quigley said to the judge, "I have other work that needs tending to."

"Of course, Miss Quigley," Judge Rutherford said. "And thank you."

"You're most welcome, Judge," Miss Quigley said. "Our Birdie is a very reliable young woman."

Birdie loved the sound of "our Birdie." Even though she'd been at the St. Nicholas less than twenty-four hours, it was the first time she'd belonged anywhere in two years. If her past was anything to go by, "reliable" might be stretching things, but she longed for an opportunity to rectify that. It was too soon to let her guard down, but images of a safe and warm Christmas and a new beginning in the new year were already popping up in her head.

"Now that I know you're all right," Judge Rutherford said, looking at his watch, "I have a meeting to attend."

"All right, Father," Charlotte said.

"You may have dinner in the dining room or have something sent to the room," the judge said.

"Yes, Father," Charlotte replied.

Birdie, who had only known Charlotte for one day, knew better than to believe she was going to stay put. How could her father not see that? But, of course, her own parents never had a hint that Birdie would up and leave in the middle of the night.

Birdie sighed. *If only we were the angels our parents thought we were.*

"We'll be off then," Miss Quigley said. "Good evening."

"Oh! I forgot, I have your shawl," Birdie said, pulling the

shawl from around her shoulders and holding it out to Charlotte.

"Oh no, you keep it," Charlotte said. "I have others and that one looks so nice on you."

Birdie looked to Miss Quigley, who gave her a curt nod.

"Thank you," Birdie said. Even if she had to move on, it would be lovely to have a warm shawl.

"And you'll be back tomorrow?" Charlotte asked. "We need to start working on my dress."

Birdie was about to point out that they still had no fabric or embellishments for Charlotte's great design but held her tongue. She looked at Miss Quigley once again for confirmation. The decision, after all, wasn't Birdie's. She knew Charlotte was a handful and certainly overindulged, but Birdie liked her. Charlotte seemed so sure of herself, never second-guessing her moves. Birdie was once like that—and it was comforting to see a woman who could still have confidence in herself.

One day, I'll have that confidence again. Until then, I'm happy to support a woman who still has hers, Birdie thought.

"Birdie will see you at ten in the morning," Miss Quigley said.

"Ten o'clock?" Charlotte started to protest, but the look in Miss Quigley's eyes silenced her. "Ten o'clock will be fine."

Confidence would only get you so far with Miss Quigley.

Chapter 5

Galveston was as far west as Detective Hilbrand had traveled in his life. He'd expected the island to be a small, sleepy hamlet but found himself in a bustling seaport full of busy people. People not particularly interested in helping a stranger locate a young woman from a black-and-white sketch.

No one on the docks had seen her. Was Galveston the end of the road? Had he lost her?

He patted the pockets of his jacket, locating the butt of a cigar he'd managed to make last the entire voyage from New Orleans. Lighting it, he headed into one of the wharf-side bars, hoping the whiskey would put the men—or women—in a talkative mood.

The bar was incredibly noisy. At first, the din was the only way the detective could gauge how crowded the place was. It was so dark it took a full minute for his eyes to register the various shapes slumped over tables as sailors, river rats, and long-shoremen looking for their next job. He threaded his way to the bar and ordered a shot. No need to specify a brand or a particular alcohol. You drank what was on hand.

Galveston was not New York.

Detective Hilbrand downed the shot and gritted his teeth against the rawness of the alcohol. As truly ghastly as the drink was, it did manage to warm him up. The boat ride had chilled him to the bone.

Experience had taught him that, in a place like this, it was better to wait for someone to engage him in conversation rather than start asking questions. If most people had something to hide, men and women holed up in a bar in a port town *all* had something to hide. Hoping someone would feel like talking, he ordered another drink.

"Buy a girl a drink?" came a smoky voice from behind him.

He turned to see a woman of indeterminate age. The cleavage spilling from her stained satin dress certainly left nothing to the imagination. But between the dim light and the pound of makeup the woman wore, it was hard to tell much more about her other than she knew how to pack a corset.

"Sure," he said, moving over to make a space for her at the bar.

"Brandy," she said.

"They have brandy?" he asked, impressed.

"No," she replied, a hard smile on her lips. "My name is Brandy. They do have champagne," she said as she signaled the bartender.

So we're going to play this game. Saloon girls always ordered glasses of "champagne" for top dollar.

He could tell by the look in her eyes that she was as tired of the game as he was—but neither of their professions left them much choice other than to proceed.

She took a sip of her drink as the detective pulled the sketch out of his jacket.

"Have you ever seen this woman?" he asked.

Brandy took the sketch from him and studied it. She took another sip, then met his gaze.

"She doesn't look like the type of girl who'd come to a place like this," she said sadly. "And if she did, she wouldn't look like that anymore."

She handed the picture back to him. "Sorry I can't be of more help."

"Look again," Detective Hilbrand said, refusing to take back the sketch.

He knew she'd keep the conversation going in order to get him to buy another round. If she had something to offer, she certainly wasn't going to tell him this early in the game. So he waited.

"She your wife?" Brandy asked. "Not that I care if you have a wife, you understand. But you're a handsome one, I'll say that. She must have been crazy to leave a man like you."

She moved closer to him. She must be new to her profession, he thought. She was moving much too quickly to make this encounter as profitable as possible.

"No, I'm just trying to find her," he said, pulling out his badge. Might as well make this as painless—and economical—as possible. The badge had its desired effect. Brandy pulled back.

"If you're a copper, why are you chasing some poor girl all over hell?" Brandy demanded. "Don't you have better things to do with your time?"

"As a matter of fact," he said, "I do. But let me ask you one other question. If you were a girl with a skill . . ."

Brandy's eyebrow shot up.

"If you were a seamstress and you landed in Galveston, where would you go?"

"Anywhere but Galveston," she said. "There are no jobs here for ladies with *skills*."

By midmorning, Birdie had hemmed a petticoat for a widow staying in one of the suites, sewn buttons onto several officers' uniforms, and added new boning to a corset for a guest whose seventeen-inch waist had grown a bit since her last gala.

Birdie eyed the two dresses Charlotte Rutherford had spurned. The sight of them made her extremely nervous. Even if Birdie managed to make a gown in time, what if Charlotte rejected it as she had the others?

"I wouldn't worry," Miss Quigley said, as if reading her mind. "Miss Rutherford seems to have taken to you. I'm sure you'll do fine."

The clock on the mantel chimed. Ten o'clock.

"Am I free to go to Miss Rutherford's?" Birdie asked.

Miss Quigley gave a nod. Birdie quickly retrieved her sewing supplies and headed out the door.

"If Miss Rutherford wishes to retain you for the day, make sure she remembers to order lunch for you. You need to keep up your strength."

"Yes, ma'am," Birdie said, smiling to herself. She wasn't sure whether she was smiling because she knew there would be lunch or because someone cared that she ate.

"And bring your shawl," Miss Quigley said. "Miss Rutherford always seems to have errands to run. She can't seem to stay still."

"Yes, ma'am," Birdie said, grabbing her new shawl.

Racing up the stairs, Birdie almost collided with a woman heading down.

"Oh, excuse me," Birdie said, suddenly realizing she was speaking to the mean-spirited woman who had been arranging the delicate glass balls in the lobby when she'd arrived.

The woman seemed to recognize her too.

"That was a pretty little trick, fainting to get Mrs. Cockrell's attention," the woman sneered. "Or was it to get Captain Newcastle's attention? Either way, I see it worked."

The woman looked Birdie up and down, studying the uniform.

"Won't help you any," she continued. "Seamstresses don't last long here. You may be the latest, but you won't be the last."

"I'm sorry, Mrs. . . . ." Birdie began, but realized she didn't have a name at hand for this woman.

"Mrs. Firestone," the woman said. "And I know you're Birdie. Everyone's heard of you after your shenanigans."

Birdie had never heard the word *shenanigans*, but she could tell by the woman's tone that it wasn't a compliment. Birdie took a deep breath. She could not afford to make enemies.

"I'm sorry, Mrs. Firestone," Birdie said, offering a smile. "I hope now that we're both working in this establishment, we can be friends."

"Not likely," Mrs. Firestone said, continuing down the stairs. "You'll be gone before I even learn your name."

But you've already learned my name, Birdie thought.

Charlotte's door opened before Birdie could knock.

"You're late," Charlotte said, although she seemed more excited than angry.

"I'm so sorry," Birdie stammered. "I ran into one of the other servants on the stairs and had a rather unpleasant exchange."

Birdie wondered why she was telling Charlotte this. Surely this was too much information to share with a hotel guest. But she thought Charlotte seemed as if she might be interested in hotel intrigue.

"Don't tell me it was that loathsome Mrs. Firestone," Charlotte asked, as she let Birdie into the room.

"You know her?" Birdie asked, surprised.

"Oh, I know everyone by this time," Charlotte said. "Don't take it personally. She absolutely despises every pretty young woman who comes into the hotel."

Birdie had had such a rough time of it these past two years, she couldn't imagine that anyone could still think of her as pretty. But it was still nice to hear.

"Why is that?" Birdie asked.

"She is sure Captain Newcastle is going to take one look at Olive . . ."

"Olive?"

"Her horse-faced daughter. Mrs. Firestone is sure he'll be her son-in-law by the end of the ball." Charlotte laughed. "Good luck, I say."

"She's no competition for you, then?"

"If my father has decided the captain is the man for me," Charlotte said with a shrug, "nobody is competition. Father can be very persuasive."

"Is it what you want?"

"I don't think that enters into it."

Birdie tried to be sympathetic. It wasn't Charlotte's fault her father had picked out a man for her to marry. Birdie herself had run from such an arrangement. But it was hard not to be the tiniest bit jealous that Charlotte was probably going to win over Captain Newcastle. Birdie couldn't help but imagine herself at the ball, in a beautiful gown, dancing with the captain, his strong arms around her even when she wasn't in a faint.

But that was just a dream. There was a time when Birdie followed her dreams, but they had all ended in heartache and hardship. Now, as soon as a fantasy formed, Birdie shut it out. Charlotte moved over to the window and looked down. Her face lit up.

"Oh! By the way, I've just confirmed he's not married!" Charlotte announced breathlessly.

"Captain Newcastle?" Birdie asked.

"No!" Charlotte replied, summoning Birdie to the window and pointing into the street at a knot of men that included both the captain and the sheriff. "Sheriff Holden."

Birdie peered at the man with the star on his chest.

"But what about Captain Newcastle?"

"What about him?"

"Didn't you just tell me your father has decided you were going to marry him?"

"Of course," Charlotte said. "And I know I'm going to have to dazzle him at the ball. That's why I have to have the perfect dress. But until then, I can do what I like."

Charlotte had such a sheltered view of the world, Birdie thought. She stared down at the men and realized that Captain Newcastle was staring up at the window. Her heart raced as he gave a tiny salute. Birdie backed away from the window—but with regret.

"We should start working on your dress," Birdie said, all business. "We don't have much time."

"All right," Charlotte said, taking one last look at Sheriff Holden. "I have a dress that is horrible, but I like the color. Shall we start with that?"

Charlotte moved to the chifforobe and pulled out a satin gown. The dress crackled as the folds of fabric were released from their bonds.

"What is this color?" Birdie asked, touching the dark purple fabric lightly. "I've never seen anything like it."

"It's called mauve, I think," Charlotte said. "It's the latest in Paris, I've heard. I agree that it's a beautiful color, but I hate the dress."

"The dress is amazing," Birdie said. "Not just the color, which is exquisite—and no other lady will be wearing it, I can assure you—but the gown itself."

"It's just so boring," Charlotte said. "Look at this neckline. It's something an old matron would wear. Not anything that would catch the eye of an officer. Since there doesn't seem to be any decent fabric in this town, maybe we could . . . I don't know . . . tear this dress apart and start over?"

Birdie's heart squeezed at the thought of dismantling such a lovely gown. "I don't know . . ."

Charlotte put the sketch of the dress she had in mind on the table next to Birdie and pointed to it.

"You could do this, couldn't you?" Charlotte asked. "For a friend?"

Birdie was momentarily confused. She didn't have any friends—especially not in Dallas. But then she realized Charlotte meant *she* was Birdie's friend. The idea of having someone in her corner was certainly enticing. But she knew it would not be fair to anyone, let alone someone as sheltered as Charlotte, to start down a road of shared confidences. There was too much danger involved.

But it was a lovely thought.

Birdie knew she was capable of transforming the gown into exactly what Charlotte wanted. But she wondered what the judge would say to the daring décolleté in the sketch.

"There is plenty of material in this gown to remake the bodice," Birdie said, her professional pride winning her over. "But we might have to adjust your design."

Birdie ran her finger over Charlotte's drawing.

"We don't have any glass beading for the bodice and sleeves," Birdie said. "Even if we could find the materials, there isn't enough time to create enough strands."

"But the beading is what makes the dress so elegant," Charlotte said. "Isn't there anything you can do?"

Birdie sighed. She thought of the beautiful gowns Charlotte had rejected. She hated to disappoint her, but she really had no recourse but to try to find another idea that would appeal to her. A knock on the door startled her out of her meditation. Charlotte moved swiftly to the door and answered it as Birdie hung the dress back in the chifforobe. Birdie turned quickly when she heard Miss Quigley's voice coming from the open doorway.

"I'm sorry to disturb you, Miss Rutherford." Miss Quigley's rich brogue floated through the room. "But I have an errand I must have Birdie run immediately. If it's not too much of an imposition."

"Come in, Miss Quigley," Charlotte said.

"Birdie, I bought this trim for the lampshades and I'm afraid the color doesn't work with the glass," Miss Quigley said, holding a small parcel in her hands.

Birdie reached out to take the package, but Miss Quigley lost her grip on it and the parcel dropped to the floor before Birdie could catch it. Birdie knelt to pick it up. The brown paper had torn and exposed the contents.

Birdie looked up at Miss Quigley as she retrieved the strands of perfect beads from the floor. They were every shade of purple Birdie had ever seen—and until today, some she'd never seen. They would be perfect for the dress.

"Such a waste." Miss Quigley sighed. "But they are just so wrong for what I had in mind. If you can't think of anything to do with these, could you take them over to Mrs. Snow and see if she could sell them? I hate for things to go to waste."

"They won't go to waste, ma'am," Birdie said, standing up and cradling the beading.

Birdie was silent, but her mind was racing with questions as Miss Quigley swept from the room.

Chapter 6

Birdie balanced a tray full of dishes as she stood outside the kitchen door, grateful to see it was ajar. Balancing the tray took both hands. She heard Captain Newcastle's voice booming from within. Peeking through the crack in the door, she could see Captain Newcastle sitting at the large center table. While she knew she shouldn't eavesdrop, her feet seemed frozen.

"I can't eat another bite," Captain Newcastle protested. "What if war broke out? I'd have to waddle my way into battle. Not a pretty picture."

"There'll be a war here at the hotel if I don't get these recipes perfected," Cook replied. "Let me know if there's too much cinnamon."

"I can only tell you if I like it or not."

"That's a start," Cook said, crossing her arms over her ample apron.

He took a bite.

"I'm waiting," Cook said.

"I think I need some cider," he said.

"Why?" Cook asked, sounding worried as she poured some cider into a mug. "Is it too dry?"

She held the cup of cider to her chest and stared at him with a worried expression.

"If I have to say it's too dry to get some cider, then yes, it's too dry."

Cook handed him the cup. She batted his shoulder playfully as he downed the glass.

"I'll cut you a slice of the 'wealthy cake,'" Cook said. "I need a man's opinion."

"I can't eat another bite," he said, standing up and kissing the top of her head.

"But I need to know if I've put in too much bourbon," said Cook.

"I think I can safely say—speaking for all men, or at least all the men I know—you can never put in too much bourbon."

"Go on, then," Cook said, pointing at the door.

"I'll be back later and maybe I could try a few more samples for you," he said.

Birdie realized she'd have to make a hasty retreat or go into the kitchen immediately if she didn't want to run into the captain in the hallway. The tray she was carrying was getting heavier and heavier, so she opted for the kitchen. She pretended to be so focused on balancing the dishes that she didn't notice the captain as she swung the door open with her foot.

"Cook, Miss Charlotte asked me if—" Birdie started to speak, but was cut off.

"That looks like a big load," Captain Newcastle said as he grabbed for the tray. "Let me help you."

"That's not necessary," Birdie said, keeping a grip on the tray.

The last thing she wanted was a reputation that she couldn't handle the chores assigned her—even if the tray *was* impossibly heavy.

"I insist," he said, pulling the tray toward himself.

"I am perfectly capable of delivering this to Cook, thank you very much," Birdie said, pulling the tray back.

"Consider them delivered!" Cook said as she suddenly appeared between them, lifting the tray right out of both their hands.

"Thank you," Birdie said.

She could feel her skin coloring from the neck of her dress all the way up to her cap.

"Let me send some cake up to Miss Charlotte," Cook said. "I know she loves a nice sweet in the afternoon."

"And it doesn't hurt to keep Rutherford happy," Captain Newcastle said, crossing his arms and leaning in the doorway. "It seems the whole town is doing what it can to butter him up."

"Don't you have someplace to be?" Cook challenged.

"My men can live without me for a few more minutes," he replied.

"Anything I can do to help?" Birdie asked Cook, pretending the captain wasn't there.

"No, dear," Cook said. "You just have a seat. I'll only be a minute."

Birdie sat. She took a handkerchief from her pocket. She pulled a needle from one corner and shook the linen square out. Whenever she had a moment, she worked on adding a row of vines around the edges for one of the hotel guests. She was grateful she'd remembered to bring it with her this morning. She wanted to at least look occupied as she waited for Cook to fill the tray.

"Weren't you leaving?" Cook asked Captain Newcastle.

"Maybe I should try that wealthy cake after all," the captain said, taking a seat. "I know how important this is to you."

"I thought you . . ." Cook started, but one look at the blushing Birdie and she stopped. She gave the captain a conspiratorial smile. "I'll cut you a nice big piece, now that you've obviously had a moment to digest."

Birdie couldn't help but steal glances at Captain Newcastle. Part of her wished he would just leave, but a larger part of her wanted him to stay right where he was.

She knew all of Dallas was trying to impress Judge Rutherford. She could only surmise that he would bring a level of respectability to the town, especially if his daughter were to marry the captain. Birdie felt a twinge of regret. Somebody had to win the captain's fancy, and since it could never be her, she might as well be rooting for her . . . friend? Even if it appeared her friend had very little interest in the captain.

A man in uniform strode into the kitchen and saluted Captain Newcastle, who was busy chewing the bourbon-soaked fruitcake.

"Sir," the soldier said, "the sheriff has requested you come to the jail immediately."

"Problems?" the captain asked.

Birdie noticed Captain Newcastle did not sound alarmed. Dallas was still a small town, so perhaps it was not yet a hotbed of crime. Birdie smiled to herself. She sounded so knowing. Not like the girl who had left Ireland two years ago. That girl was as naïve as Charlotte.

"No, sir," the soldier replied. "Sheriff Holden wants to coordinate security details for the dances."

"The dances?" Cook asked the soldier, putting a full tray in front of Birdie.

The soldier looked to the captain for permission to answer. The captain lazily waved his fork. Permission granted.

"The Grand Ball and the Jingle Bobs and Belles Ball, ma'am," the soldier said.

"Oh, so we'll have some soldiers at the Jingle Bobs and Belles, then?" Cook asked.

"Will you be there?" Birdie asked Cook.

"Oh, no," Cook said, shaking her head. "I have to be here, making sure everything goes as planned. But I'd be happy to know there were some upstanding soldiers going. The local boys can get a bit rowdy."

Birdie caught Captain Newcastle's eye. Clearly, Cook had a romanticized idea of soldiers. Birdie was sure they could give the locals a run for their money when not on duty. The soldier saluted the captain, turned smartly on his heels, and left.

"I'll make sure my men are on their best behavior," the captain said as he stood up. He bowed to Cook and Birdie. "Ladies . . ."

Birdie watched him leave. The kitchen seemed immediately less interesting.

The newly overloaded tray shook in Birdie's hands as she maneuvered herself upstairs to Charlotte's room. Cook had outdone herself, loading the tray with three different cakes, several sandwiches, and a large pot of tea. Birdie was wondering how she was going to knock on the door with her hands so full. Kicking at the door seemed positively rude. Perhaps she'd meet another hotel worker in the hallway who could knock for her.

Birdie could see the back of a black dress. Even from the distance of the entire hallway, Birdie knew it was the uniform of a St. Nicholas employee.

"Excuse me," Birdie called as softly as she could. "Could you knock on Miss Rutherford's door for me, please?"

She didn't have to mention the room number. Everyone knew which rooms the Rutherfords occupied.

The employee turned around. It was Mrs. Firestone. Birdie tried to smile.

"Hello, Mrs. Firestone," Birdie said. "Could you knock on Miss Rutherford's door for me, please?"

"I could," Mrs. Firestone said. "But I've heard such amazing things about you. I'm surprised you need help with anything."

Mrs. Firestone stood in front of the door. Birdie's arms were shaking from the weight of the tray.

"I'd so appreciate it," Birdie said through gritted teeth.

"I'm sure you would," Mrs. Firestone said. "I see Cook has sent the hotel's best china. It would be a shame if that tray should slip."

Mrs. Firestone suddenly put her hand on one end of the tray, tilting it precariously. Birdie let out a gasp. What if she lost her grip?

The door to Charlotte's room sprang open. Mrs. Firestone's hand flew to her side.

"Miss Charlotte!" Mrs. Firestone said breathlessly. "I was just giving your servant girl a hand with her tray. Cook appears to have outdone herself."

"Did you carry that all the way from the kitchen? It looks awfully heavy," Charlotte said, taking the tray from Birdie. "Thank you, Mrs. Firestone. My *servant girl* and I can take care of ourselves from here."

Mrs. Firestone gave a little bow as Charlotte closed the door.

"What a ghastly woman," Charlotte said, putting the tray on the table. "Referring to you as a servant."

"I am a servant," Birdie said, rubbing her upper arms.

"No, you are not," Charlotte replied. "You are a talented and skilled professional and don't you forget it, Birdie Flanagan."

"Yes, ma'am." Birdie smiled.

"This food looks delicious, but I think it will have to wait," Charlotte said. "I've been looking out the window and I think Mrs. Snow just got a few new dresses in."

"I thought the stagecoach wasn't supposed to come through for another few days," Birdie said. "And I thought all the dresses were spoken for."

"Not the stagecoach from Jefferson. This is the stagecoach from Galveston . . . it just came in. Isn't that the one that brought you here?"

Birdie nodded. Considering the horrid shape the Galveston stagecoach was in, she couldn't imagine it might be carrying dresses that would meet Charlotte's standards. Birdie shot a glance at the mauve dress, midway through its reformation.

"We really should be working on your gown," Birdie said.

"Oh, come on," Charlotte said. "It won't hurt to just go take a look."

Charlotte tossed Birdie's shawl to her. Charlotte seemed to find a reason to go out every day and Birdie decided to leave the shawl in Charlotte's room so it was always at the ready. Charlotte took her own shawl from the chifforobe, put the room key in her purse, and guided Birdie out the door.

Detective Hilbrand watched the stagecoach driver unload the contents brought up from Galveston. He felt shaken to his very core. The stagecoach had seen better days—and at this point, so had Detective Hilbrand.

He'd boarded the stagecoach on a whim. He'd gotten no leads in Galveston but a conversation with one of the working girls on the docks resonated with him.

"You say this girl has a skill? She can sew?" the woman had asked.

He knew she was trying to keep him talking, hoping her charms would suddenly become irresistible. He knew better than to let her know hell would have to freeze over before he took a chance on a sporting woman in a port town.

They were both playing games, but she got him thinking.

"She's probably not in Galveston," the woman said. "I know every seamstress in the city."

"Houston then?"

The woman shook her head.

"I know the girls up there too," she said.

"Where would she go then?"

A stagecoach rumbled past. It appeared to be so old, the detective wondered how the wheels stayed on. The woman eyed it.

"That coach goes all the way to Dallas," the woman said.

"Dallas?"

"Yeah. It's small, but there's a fancy hotel. There's going to be a big dance up there on Christmas Eve. If she was looking for work that might be a likely place."

It wasn't much, but it seemed a likely path, so he took it.

He looked around Dallas now, disheartened. The wind whipped through town, the makeshift buildings bending under its force. He noticed the large brick building across from the stagecoach stop. That must be the hotel the woman was talking about.

The wind kicked up so much dust, he couldn't make out the figures bent against it. The gusts made it impossible to speak, unless you were looking for a mouthful of gravel, so he didn't hear the accent of the Irish girl in the colorful shawl as she walked right by him.

As he headed across the street, he eyed a badge, visible even in the dust storm. A private detective had to be wary around lawmen. They didn't always welcome his kind on a new frontier.

He'd need to tread carefully.

Chapter 7

Birdie and Charlotte gathered their skirts against the wind and headed across the street. Birdie couldn't believe Charlotte would brave this awful weather to look at dresses that were sure to fail her standards. She heard footsteps bounding up beside her.

Sheriff Holden was suddenly walking alongside them.

"I hear we might be getting some snow for Christmas," Sheriff Holden yelled over the wind.

"How do you know?" Charlotte asked, falling right in step with him.

Birdie was surprised that Charlotte seemed so familiar with the sheriff. It was as if they were old friends.

"Old Man Langdon said his elbow was starting to ache," Sheriff Holden said. "His elbow is never wrong."

They had arrived at the general store. Sheriff Holden opened the door and smiled.

"Ladies," he said.

Birdie waited for Charlotte to go first, which she did. Birdie noticed that the sheriff guided her gently through the door, lightly touching the small of her back. Birdie noticed that Charlotte seemed pleased with the attention. Birdie followed Charlotte and noted that Sheriff Holden didn't extend the same intimate gesture to her.

What's going on here? Birdie wondered.

The sheriff didn't follow them into the store. Mrs. Snow was just signing some paperwork handed to her by the stagecoach driver. Two puppies, one solid black and the other black-and-white, lay on an old blanket next to the stove.

"These pups were born in the barn over at the St. Nicholas," Mrs. Snow was telling the stagecoach driver. "I told Mrs. Cockrell I'd help find a home for a few of them. Any need of a ferocious dog on the coach, Wilbur?"

"Sure," Wilbur said. "And when these little guys grow up, if one of them turns out to be ferocious, you let me know."

Wilbur tipped his hat to Birdie and Charlotte as he left the store. Birdie realized that she had been so exhausted on her own stagecoach ride from Galveston, she couldn't remember if he had been her stagecoach driver or not.

She'd come to view Dallas as a haven more quickly than she ever could have imagined.

Charlotte was right—several new dresses lay on the countertop. Birdie noticed that Mrs. Snow's smile disappeared as soon as she saw Charlotte.

"You might as well turn right around, Miss Charlotte," Mrs. Snow said. "These dresses won't be of any interest to you."

"That's an interesting sales technique," Charlotte said, pulling a dress from the counter. "What if you're wrong?"

Mrs. Snow sighed and started to stock the shelves with the canned goods from Galveston. Charlotte picked up a two-piece dove-gray dress with black embroidery around the tightly fitted sleeves and full skirt.

"What do you think of this?" Charlotte asked Birdie.

Birdie studied the dress. It had a high collar and jet buttons. Lovely, but certainly not anything Charlotte would wear.

"It's very nice," Birdie said cautiously.

"I know the embroidery isn't up to your standards, but do you think it would do in a pinch?"

Birdie felt her heart race. Did Charlotte think Birdie might not get her dress done in time?

"It's a lovely dress," Birdie tried again, "but I think you'll be happier if we finish the dress we're working on. When I get the beading on, it's going to—"

"Oh, it's not for me," Charlotte trilled. "It's for you."

"For me?"

"Yes. For the . . . what's that other dance called?"

"The Jingle Bobs and Belles Ball," Birdie said. "But I can't accept this, Miss Charlotte, it wouldn't be right."

"Why wouldn't it?"

"Because I . . ." Birdie hadn't accepted charity to this point in her life and she didn't want to start now. But she didn't want to sound ungrateful for the gesture. She was very touched by Charlotte's generosity.

"I'll tell you what," Mrs. Snow interjected, surprising both Birdie and Charlotte. "It really is a lovely dress. What if Miss Charlotte buys the dress for herself and lends it to you for the dance? How is that?"

"I still don't think . . ." Birdie murmured.

"What a good idea! You and I are about the same size, I think," Charlotte said, holding the dress up to Birdie.

Birdie couldn't resist. She touched the beautiful fabric. She would love to wear the dress.

"Thank you, Mrs. Snow," Charlotte said. "Wrap it up. Please."

Mrs. Snow carefully wrapped the dress and handed it to Birdie. It was surprisingly heavy.

"Send the bill to my father," Charlotte said as she opened the door.

"I will do that right away, Miss Charlotte." Mrs. Snow beamed. She turned to Birdie and added, in a whisper, "Not a bad sales technique after all."

Dangerous Jack stood in the shadows and studied the man who got off the stagecoach. Was he someone to worry about? He watched the man pull his hat down over his ears and his jacket closed against the wind as he headed over to the hotel.

Probably just another rich guest coming into town for that ball, Jack thought.

Jack memorized the man's clothes, since he couldn't see his features. The man might be an easy mark if he showed up at the saloon. Jack hadn't started any big-stakes games, worried about drawing too much attention to himself, but he'd done all right for himself with pickpocketing.

Enough money to keep himself warm, fed, and full of whiskey.

Which was enough for now.

Birdie and the very chatty woman with whom Birdie was keeping company headed back into the St. Nicholas. Jack stayed where he was. He would have to play his cards very close to the vest. Dallas was too small a town to get lost in, but it did have a lawman.

Jack waited until the stagecoach pulled away. He would have to go back into the store to make sure there was no new WANTED poster on the wall. He doubted the fleabag coach from Galveston would be delivering one, but you couldn't be too careful. He'd stayed one step ahead of the law all these years, it wouldn't do to let down his guard now. Many of the Texans he'd met seemed to be as suspicious of the law as he was, but the sheriff in this town seemed pretty humorless when it came to people breaking the law. He'd have to watch that one.

And that captain in the army.

He seemed like he could be trouble.

Jack plastered on his most charming smile and headed to the back door of the hotel. He wished it were summer and he could pick some wildflowers for the woman he was romancing. That old cow Mrs. Firestone would definitely fall for a fistful of flowers. But his charm never failed—even when he was empty-handed.

Birdie's cheeks still burned from the cold as she and Charlotte settled down to try Cook's offerings. Charlotte had unwrapped the dress from Mrs. Snow's and hung it outside the chifforobe. Birdie could hardly take her eyes off it.

"I guess the tea is probably cold," Charlotte said, frowning into the teapot.

"I'll run down and ask Cook for some hot water," Birdie said.

"We can live without it," Charlotte said.

"It's no trouble," Birdie said.

A crisp knock on the door startled them both. Birdie opened it to find Miss Quigley standing in the hallway with a teapot.

"I suspect you might need a hot pot of tea," Miss Quigley said, sweeping into the room. "After a day of shopping."

Birdie's cheeked burned. Was this an admonishment? She could never tell with Miss Quigley. The only thing she knew for sure was that the woman always seemed to show up at the perfect time.

Miss Quigley put the teapot on the tray.

"Is this new?" Miss Quigley asked, going over to the dove-gray dress on the hanger.

Birdie was shocked—and impressed—that Miss Quigley never stayed "in her place." She treated everyone as an equal and expected to be treated as such.

"Yes," Charlotte said. "We . . . I just bought it. Do you like it?"

Miss Quigley looked the dress up and down.

"May I?" Miss Quigley asked, but was already flipping the dress inside out to see the seams.

"What do you think?" Charlotte asked.

Birdie smiled. She could tell Charlotte wanted Miss Quigley's approval.

"Birdie's handiwork is far superior," Miss Quigley said. "But it will do in a pinch."

"That's exactly what I said," Charlotte marveled, as Miss Quigley left the room.

"Thank you for the tea," Birdie called after her.

The whole building seemed to relax as the wind suddenly died down. Charlotte went to the window.

"There's our sheriff patrolling the streets," Charlotte said with undisguised admiration.

Birdie picked up the mauve gown and studied it. The Grand Ball was only a couple of days away and there was still a lot of work to be done. If Charlotte wanted the dress finished, Birdie would have to be firm with her. There would be no finding excuses to go out every time the sheriff walked down the street.

Chapter 8

"Good morning and happy Christmas Eve," Cook trilled as she wheeled a tray into the sewing room. "Here's the breakfast you ordered, Miss Quigley."

Birdie and Miss Quigley looked up from their tasks. Miss Quigley was changing the buttons on a guest's formal tailcoat, while Birdie was finishing the trim on Charlotte's gown.

"Oh, isn't this a treat!" Miss Quigley said as Cook presented a full Irish breakfast. Birdie watched Miss Quigley lift the silver lids off plates piled high with bacon, sausage, baked beans, eggs, and some potato hash. There was also Irish soda bread, butter, marmalade, and a pot of steaming tea on the cart. "Cook, you've outdone yourself."

"We're lucky to have so much food in the place," Cook said. "The kitchen is bursting with preparations for the Grand Ball . . . and I've made a dish for Birdie to take across town to the Jingle Bobs and Belles Ball."

Birdie felt a lump of homesickness well up in her throat. Her mother always made an opulent Irish breakfast every Christmas Eve. The smell of so many familiar dishes was bittersweet.

But, as Miss Quigley said herself, what a treat! Birdie would never have dreamed that she would be eating all her favorite foods on Christmas Eve morning. There was no way for Miss Quigley to know about her mother's tradition. This had to be a coincidence!

Coincidence or not, Birdie was ready to sample everything on the tray. She put the gown well out of reach of the delicacies and gave Cook an impromptu hug.

"Happy Christmas Eve to you too, Cook," Birdie said. "This is a wonderful way to start the holiday."

"Eat up," Cook said. "I suspect you've both been hard at work since dawn, so you must be hungry."

Birdie had been concentrating on the trim and realized suddenly that she was very hungry. She waited for Miss Quigley to sample everything on the tray—in very delicate proportions, Birdie noticed—before heaping her own plate high.

"Careful, Missy," Cook said. "Don't forget you have a dance tonight. You don't want to be busting your corset."

Birdie blushed, but Cook laughed.

"I'm only teasing you," Cook said. "It's good to see you've put some meat on your bones since you got here."

Birdie smiled. How could she resist an Irish breakfast? She buttered a slice of the Irish soda bread and took a big bite. While it certainly wasn't nearly as good as her mother made at home, sinking her teeth into Christmas memories warmed her to her soul.

"Have you had a chance to look outside?" Cook asked.

Both women shook their heads, too involved in food and memories of home to answer.

"It snowed last night," Cook said. "Looks like we're going to have a white Christmas."

"Do you think they'll still have the dances?" Birdie asked.

"Oh, you haven't been in Texas very long," Cook said. "A little snow isn't going to stop them."

* * *

Detective Hilbrand warmed his hands over the stove in the saloon. It had taken him a while to get used to the fact that, in the West, saloons functioned as hotels as well as bars and were open all day and all night. The sporting women who worked at the bar finally decided he meant it when he said he wasn't interested in having a drink or sharing a bed with them. He rented a small, private room, which he knew was a ridiculous luxury, but if he didn't want to share a bed with one of the women working there, he certainly couldn't bring himself to share it with two or more drunken cowboys. But the room had no heat, so he found himself in the saloon trying to thaw.

He was running out of money fast and if this hunch didn't play out, he'd have to pack it in.

After he finally felt warm enough to go back to his room and go over the facts he'd gathered since arriving, he locked the door and sat at a small table by the window. Dawn's first light flickered into the room. While it illuminated the room, the sun brought no real warmth from the snowstorm that had blown through during the night.

Everyone in town seemed distracted by the two dances that would be happening this evening. Surmising that Birdie would have to be working at the fancy hotel across the street, he'd tried to strike up a conversation with a few of the workers. But nobody had a minute for him.

Until he found Mrs. Firestone.

She was standing outside one of the servants' entrances at the back of the hotel. At first, she'd tried to give him the brush, but he persisted, thrusting the sketch of Brigid Flanagan into her hands. She took a cursory glance.

"No, never seen her," Mrs. Firestone said.

"Look again," he found himself pleading.

Mrs. Firestone's mouth formed into a rigid, straight line and she looked again. He could see a glint come into her eyes.

"Yes," Mrs. Firestone said, covering up the top of the sketch so the woman's hair was hidden. "She works here. I knew she was a bad egg!"

Once he'd shown her a picture of Birdie, she'd given him all the time in the world. Now he knew Birdie was working at the hotel. He asked if Mrs. Firestone could manage to get him into the hotel, but she said that was impossible.

"You can't go disrupting the guests," she said firmly. "Not before the ball. If it ever got back to Mrs. Cockrell that I—"

"She'd never know," Detective Hilbrand said, having already discovered that Mrs. Cockrell was the woman who owned the hotel. He really had no justification of making this promise, but he was ready to say anything.

Mrs. Firestone stood in the doorway of the hotel, blocking his way.

"I've gone out on a limb for another very nice man," she'd said. "And I can't push my luck."

The detective tried not to show his frustration. Birdie had given him the slip more times than he could count. He had to get into the hotel.

"But I will tell you this," Mrs. Firestone said. "I know for a fact that your girl will be attending the Jingle Bobs and Belles Ball tonight across town. And she'll be wearing a gray dress that she could ill afford and a beautiful hand-me-down shawl. Just go to the dance. You don't need an invitation for that one."

Mrs. Firestone swore she would keep his presence in town a secret and from her apparent glee in telling him everything he wanted to know about Birdie, he believed her. As she started to close the door, he debated showing her another sketch he had with him but, to use her own words, he did not want to push his luck.

He would just have to wait until tonight to make his move.

* * *

Birdie put the last stitch in Miss Charlotte's dress and held it up in front of the mirror. It was the most stunning gown Birdie had ever seen, if she did say so herself. Working late every night, Birdie had even managed to stitch some delicate embroidery around the bottom of the dress.

She'd been working on the final touches of the gown two evenings ago when she looked up to see Miss Quigley studying the dress.

"That gown could use some interest around the hem," Miss Quigley had said. "Some dark purple embroidery. And something to catch the light, I think. A few gold strands."

"That would be lovely," Birdie said, imagining the design she would use. "But I haven't seen any embroidery floss like that in our supplies."

"So true," Miss Quigley said, pulling out the large box Birdie had seen her open with the key around her neck.

She opened the box once more, laying the pistol on the table and rummaging inside. She smiled as she pulled out the perfect shade of embroidery floss. The gold strands caught the candlelight as she handed it over to Birdie.

"It will be a lot of work," Miss Quigley said, returning the pistol and locking the box. "But I think it will be worth it."

Birdie worked until her fingers cramped, but she finished. She envisioned the embroidery floss catching the candlelight as Miss Charlotte swirled around the dance floor.

Birdie sighed. Miss Charlotte was going to be the most beautiful woman at the ball. Every man was going to fall in love with her.

And that included Captain Newcastle.

Birdie tried to ignore the ache in her heart.

Miss Quigley had said she'd be gone most of the morning catering to guests who all seemed to need last-minute adjustments to gowns, trousers, and shirts. Birdie had offered to help, but the guests were all demanding the head seamstress attend to their needs.

Miss Quigley's approval had become more important to Birdie by the day. Especially on Christmas Eve, when Birdie was missing her family so fiercely, it was lovely to have someone who appeared to be watching over her. Birdie wanted to show her the finished dress. But she knew Charlotte would be waiting anxiously for the gown to be delivered and she couldn't put it off any longer.

A knock on the door of the sewing room startled Birdie. She almost dropped the gown, but caught it as Mrs. Firestone, carrying four new servants' dresses, strode in.

"These need to be hemmed by six o'clock. Absolutely not a minute later. I've marked each one for length," Mrs. Firestone said, as if they were in the middle of a conversation. She laid the dresses across the sewing table.

"These need to be done for the ball *tonight?*" Birdie gasped.

"Yes, tonight," Mrs. Firestone said, picking up the first one. "Start with this one. It's for my Olive. Even though she'll be working at the dance, I want her to look perfect. She's such a pretty girl, I'm sure she'll catch someone's eye."

"I'm not sure I can get these finished by then."

"It's your job to have them finished," Mrs. Firestone snapped. She eyed the gown in Birdie's hands. "You clearly can do amazing work when you put your mind to it."

"Mrs. Firestone," Miss Quigley's voice broke into the conversation. "What a pleasant surprise. To what could we possibly owe the honor?"

"Mrs. Firestone needs these four uniforms hemmed by six o'clock," Birdie answered the question.

"Six o'clock, you say?"

"Yes," Mrs. Firestone said.

Miss Quigley frowned and studied the crisp dresses laid before her.

"Is this on Mrs. Cockrell's orders?" Miss Quigley asked.

"It is," Mrs. Firestone said, sounding vaguely triumphant as she shot Birdie a fierce glance. "And if that means some of us are going to be late to the Jingle Bobs and Belles Ball, well, so be it."

Birdie bit her lip. She didn't mind being late to the dance. But she did mind failing at an impossible task.

"My work comes first. I might not get to the ball at all," Birdie said defensively.

A shadow passed over Mrs. Firestone's face.

"Oh, you have to go to the ball," Mrs. Firestone said, her tiny teeth showing through a mean smile. "Just get the dresses done first."

Why would Mrs. Firestone suddenly want to make sure I get to the dance? Birdie asked herself.

"If Mrs. Cockrell needs the dresses done for the ball, we'll get them done," Miss Quigley said. "Thank you for bringing these down to us. You may pick them up at six. But not a minute sooner."

Miss Quigley held up a butler's uniform from the pile Mrs. Firestone laid on the sewing table.

"What about this?" Miss Quigley asked.

"Don't you worry about that," Miss Quigley said, snatching it back.

"But the cuff is frayed," Miss Quigley said. "That will need to be fixed."

"Just concentrate on the dresses," Mrs. Firestone said.

Folding the butler's uniform over her arm, Mrs. Firestone swept past Birdie and closed the door behind her.

"That woman!" Miss Quigley said.

"The nerve!" Birdie agreed.

"I don't know how she runs a hotel."

Birdie was about to say something, but closed her mouth. Did Mrs. Firestone run the hotel?

"Sending Mrs. Firestone down here and expecting us to hem four full skirts by six o'clock," Miss Quigley said. "I swear she doesn't know the first thing about sewing."

Oh, we're talking about Mrs. Cockrell, Birdie thought. *Good think I didn't run my mouth any further.*

"I'll take this gown up to Miss Charlotte and come right back," Birdie said. "It looks like we're going to have a long day."

Birdie rushed up the stairs, carefully cradling the gown. Charlotte's door was ajar. Birdie was about to take a step into the room when she heard a sneeze so violent it shook the floor.

"Father, I told you that you should have worn your scarf last night!" Charlotte said. "You sound terrible."

"I'm fine," the judge said. "Just a cold. It's just been damned impossible to get anyone in the town to focus on business with this damn Grand Ball breathing down our necks. I have to talk business when I can, even if it's at a poker game."

"Life can be very hard, Father," Charlotte said.

Birdie recognized Charlotte's sarcasm and tried to stifle a giggle. She coughed to cover it.

Judge Rutherford turned toward the sound and swung the door open.

"Birdie," he said, sounding more stuffed up by the minute. "I was just leaving. Come in."

Birdie smiled. With all the hardships she'd endured since coming to America, one thing she had to give these friendly people was their lack of pretention. A man of the judge's stature back home would never have bothered to learn her name.

"Take care of yourself, Judge," Birdie said as he walked back to his room, sneezing the whole way.

"It's finished," Birdie said, trying not to sound too proud.

Her mother had taught her that being prideful was not an admirable quality. She found that Americans had less of a problem admitting to one's own talents . . . many didn't even have a problem boasting about them.

"Let me see," Charlotte said.

Charlotte took the gown over to the window and ran her hands over the beading and down to the embroidery on the hem. Then she stared out the window.

"You should try it on," Birdie said, perplexed by Charlotte's apparent lack of enthusiasm.

"Yes, of course," Charlotte said. "Come give me a hand."

Getting Miss Charlotte out of one set of corsets and petticoats and into another took almost twenty minutes. Finally, Birdie slipped the new gown over Charlotte's head, careful not to muss her hair, and laced her into it.

The dress was all the more beautiful with Charlotte in it.

Birdie tried to look humble, staring at her shoes and peeking up and then waiting for Miss Charlotte's reaction. She didn't have to wait long.

Charlotte suddenly sank to her knees, crying violently into the skirt of the dress. Birdie rushed to her.

"What's the matter?" Birdie asked.

Fearing the gown would get stained, Birdie gently guided Miss Charlotte to her feet, handing her an ornately embroidered handkerchief to stem the flood of Miss Charlotte's tears. "Don't you like it?"

"It's perfect," Charlotte said. "But I don't want to go to the ball."

"What do you mean, you don't want to go to the ball?" Birdie asked. "Everybody who is anybody is going to be there."

"I don't care," Charlotte sobbed. "I don't want to go."

"But what about Captain Newcastle?" Birdie said, her loyalty to Charlotte outweighing her complicated feelings about the captain.

"What about him?"

"How can you marry a man you haven't danced with?" Birdie tried to sound teasing.

"I don't want to marry Captain Newcastle," Charlotte sobbed. "I want to marry Joey."

"Joey?"

Who was Joey?

"Sheriff Holden," Charlotte moaned. "I want to marry Sheriff Holden."

Chapter 9

As his mother used to say, Dangerous Jack was a gambler in his heart and soul, "if he had either one."

He had a big gamble ahead of him: stay focused on the business at hand or temporarily put it aside for a potential bonanza.

He decided to gamble on the bonanza.

Thanks to Mrs. Firestone, he would be working at the Grand Ball, moving quietly, like a good servant, clearing away plates and glasses. The entire hotel would be crowded. He would practically have his pick of jewels and rawhide wallets. When he had enough loot to get him through the winter—he'd learned the hard way not to be *too* greedy—he'd head over to the Jingle Bobs and Belles Ball and finish up the business that brought him to Dallas in the first place. Impatient by nature, Jack had forced himself to be a good listener. And listening to Mrs. Firestone would test a saint. But Mrs. Firestone knew just about everything about everybody who lived or worked at the hotel. It didn't take long for Mrs. Firestone to mention that Birdie would be among the girls going to the Jingle Bobs and

Belles Ball. Jack relied on his poker face not to show how pleased he was to get this news.

"Here's your suit." Mrs. Firestone's voice broke his concentration. "The girls in the sewing room were going to be busy, busy, busy, so I took it up myself."

"Aren't you just a darlin'?" Jack said with his most engaging smile.

He slipped into the jacket and turned to show it off to Mrs. Firestone.

"Fits like a glove," Mrs. Firestone said, standing behind him and smoothing the shoulders. "I hear the snow is going to keep on until tomorrow."

Jack turned to face her.

"With your beautiful, warm smile, I'm sure nobody at the ball will notice the cold."

Mrs. Firestone blushed coquettishly.

Sometimes, life was just too easy, Jack thought.

Charlotte lay on the fainting couch, sobbing into Birdie's handkerchief. Birdie knew she had to get back to the sewing room as quickly as possible to hem the servants' uniforms, but she could hardly leave Charlotte in such a state. Birdie wasn't sure how to proceed. Should she ask about Sheriff . . . Joey? Or would it be best to leave it alone? The choice was made for her when Charlotte suddenly sat up and dried her eyes.

"I've been meeting Joey secretly for the past few weeks," Miss Charlotte announced.

"When? How?"

"At night, when my father leaves to . . . to do whatever it is he does."

"So he doesn't know any of this?"

"Of course not! It's a secret," Charlotte said. "A deep, deep secret."

"I understand."

"Do you? I can't imagine that you have any deep secrets."
You have no idea.

"What are you going to do?" Birdie asked.

"What can I do?" Charlotte asked. "My father has his plans for me, and that's that."

Birdie knew this was probably true.

Charlotte stood up and looked at herself in the looking glass.

"It really is the most beautiful dress ever, Birdie," Charlotte sniffed. "I can't imagine Captain Newcastle will be able to resist me, frankly."

"I was thinking that too," Birdie said.

Birdie felt like she might burst into tears herself.

"The ball is still hours away," Birdie continued. "Do you want me to help you out of it, so it stays fresh?"

"No, that's all right," Charlotte said. "I want to wear it. Maybe I can slip away and show Joey."

"It's snowing," Birdie said. "You'll have to be very careful out there."

"I will be."

"But seeing Joey before going to . . . to the Grand Ball," Birdie said carefully. "Won't that make matters worse?"

"Nothing can make matters worse," Charlotte said, her lower lip trembling. "He knows the situation is as impossible as I do."

"I need to go back to work," Birdie said. "But I'll try to come back before the ball, if I can."

"Oh, don't worry about me. I'll be fine," Charlotte said. "But promise me one thing."

"Anything."

"When you get to the Jingle Bobs and Belles Ball, make sure Joey doesn't have *too* good a time."

Birdie smiled, unsure if Charlotte was kidding or not. She promised and quietly closed Miss Charlotte's door.

Birdie could hear the judge coughing and sneezing as she passed his room. She wondered if he was really as inflexible as Charlotte thought he was.

We misjudge people all the time.

She adjusted her mobcap before heading down the stairs. She knew it was imperative that all staff look their smartest, especially today, with so many high-powered guests milling around, and she was glad she'd taken the time to embroider the edges of her cap. She saw Miss Quigley coming out of the sewing room carrying three enormous hatboxes. Birdie rushed to her.

"I'm sorry I took so long," Birdie said. "Can I help you with those?"

"No, thank you," Miss Quigley said. "They're not heavy. I'm just taking them to the trunk room."

"The trunk room?"

"It's a room we use to store trunks that don't fit in the guests' rooms. Miss Adelaide in room 12 just rejected the three headpieces I made for her and there's no space left in her room for these boxes."

"There's no room for *hat* boxes?" Birdie asked, then blushed.

She should not be judgmental.

"She didn't even look at these," Miss Quigley said, shaking her head. "God only knows what she's going to wear to the ball now."

Birdie knew Miss Quigley had spent hours on the various caps, sewing cloth leaves and berries into one elaborately designed cap and attaching several streamers of ribbon to another. Birdie couldn't imagine how Miss Quigley stayed so calm in the face of these pampered women. Birdie realized she was being unkind. Since getting to know Miss Charlotte, she could see that the privileged had just as many problems as the rest of the world.

"I'm so sorry," Birdie said. She suddenly remembered the uniforms that needed to be hemmed. "I know we only have a couple of hours left, but I'll start on those uniforms right away."

"I've finished three of them," Miss Quigley said as she headed down the hall. "There's one left. I'm sure Mrs. Firestone will find everything satisfactory when she comes to collect them."

Birdie's jaw dropped. How could Miss Quigley have finished three gowns and have a consultation with Miss Adelaide all in the space of time it took Birdie to get Miss Charlotte into her gown?

There was no time to worry about that now, she had to hem a dress—and it had to be perfect.

Birdie concentrated on the rhythm of the needle and thread moving across the hemline. Sewing had always been her solace as well as a way to make a living. She could block out all thoughts of the problems around her. She heard the door open and called out.

"I don't know how you got three dresses done, but I've just put the final stitch in this one."

"That's good to hear, but I don't think I'll be needing one tonight," Captain Newcastle said teasingly. "It's mandatory dress uniform for officers, I'm afraid."

Birdie stood up and faced him, mortified.

"I thought you were Miss Quigley."

"Clearly."

"Is there something I can do for you, Captain?"

"No. I just got lost on my way to the kitchen."

"That seems highly unlikely," Birdie said. She could feel herself blushing furiously.

"You caught me," Captain Newcastle said, taking a seat on a large trunk full of ribbons, trims, and furbelows. "Actually, I just wanted a minute alone."

"Sorry to disappoint you," Birdie said.

"What do you mean?"

"Well, I'm here, aren't I?" Birdie said, bristling. "So you can't be here alone, can you?"

"You caught me again," he said. "What I really meant was, I wanted a minute alone with you."

Birdie felt frozen to the spot. She hugged the dress tightly to her chest, but loosened her grip when she realized she'd get it wrinkled. Captain Newcastle looked perfectly at ease as he looked at her.

"I'm very busy," Birdie said, trying to sound efficient and businesslike. "There is a Miss Carpenter from England who needs me to look at a dress immediately."

"I'd better let you go, then," the captain said, looking disappointed. Birdie felt a prickle of annoyance. What kind of officer gave up so easily? And she had to admit, she didn't really want him to leave.

"Why did you want to be alone with me?" Birdie asked softly.

She hoped she hadn't given any indication of the attraction she felt. It would be unseemly for a girl of her station to have feelings for an officer. And even if Miss Charlotte didn't have any romantic inclination toward the captain, Birdie felt she would be being disloyal to her friend to be entertaining such notions.

"Ah, Birdie," Captain Newcastle said. "Do you know what it's going to be like tonight?"

"At the Grand Ball?"

"Yes."

"No, Captain," Birdie said. "I don't know. And I won't know because I'll be going to the dance across town."

Why did she feel the need to say that? Did she want him to know she had plans? Her own life? He probably didn't even care. This conversation was about *him*.

"I'm on all the eligible ladies' dance cards," the captain said. "With others waiting in line."

Could he be more conceited?

"I'm sure that must be preferable to war," Birdie said dryly.

"The thing is," Captain Newcastle said, standing up and walking toward her. "It's all about the uniform. These girls don't want to dance with me, they want to dance with the captain in the United States Army."

"I'm sure that's not true," Birdie said, although she knew that it was true for Charlotte, or if not exactly for Charlotte herself, for her father.

"It is true. Trust me. When I was just Douglas Newcastle from St. Louis, Missouri, I wasn't on anyone's dance card."

"I'm sure you'll be brave in the face of battle," Birdie said, squeezing the dress again as the captain stood over her.

"Maybe I'm wrong, but I had the feeling you'd seen beyond the uniform," the captain said, brushing aside her sarcasm. "I just thought it would be nice to have a few moments of real conversation before that infernal dance envelops me."

He leaned in. Birdie wanted him to kiss her, but she felt she was being disloyal to Charlotte, even if Charlotte no longer had any interest in the man. He lifted her chin and looked into her eyes. She looked back at him. Birdie had been duped in the past by a man who said all the right things. She now knew how to spot the truth in a man's eyes.

Captain Newcastle's eyes spoke the truth.

The door banged open and he pulled away. It was Mrs. Firestone.

"I've come for the uniforms," Mrs. Firestone said, eyebrow arching. "Am I interrupting something?"

"No, ma'am," Captain Newcastle said, and bowed to Mrs. Firestone.

Birdie noticed the captain didn't offer Mrs. Firestone any explanation.

He did keep his cool in heated situations.

"I hope you have a wonderful time at the dance tonight," Captain Newcastle said to Birdie, taking her hand and kissing it. The captain seemed anxious to have some further words with Birdie, but the moment had passed.

"Let me help you with these uniforms," the captain said to Mrs. Firestone as he gathered the four dresses in one sweep. He gestured to Mrs. Firestone to lead the way. "After you."

Birdie stood in the middle of the room, slowly letting out the breath she seemed to have been holding forever. She shook her head and told herself very sternly that romantic dreams were not for her. She gathered her sewing kit and headed out to fix the dresses for those girls to whom the dreams were offered.

Chapter 10

Detective Hilbrand stomped his feet in the snow, trying to get some warmth back into his toes. He had stationed himself behind the closed feed store, where he could get a view of the entire main street that ran between the St. Nicholas Hotel and the entrance to the Jingle Bobs and Belles Ball. This way, he would be able to spot Birdie when she left the hotel. While he was usually very careful to avoid the lawmen in any given town, Detective Hilbrand decided to take Sheriff Holden into his confidence. After all, none of the detective's strategies had panned out so far. Perhaps a new approach in a new frontier was the way to go. His very enlightening conversation with Sheriff Holden had given him every confidence that his plan would go smoothly.

From time to time his sight line was obscured by the snow wafting through town. Carriages had been letting off men and women dressed in their finery at the entrance to the St. Nicholas for over an hour. He looked at his watch. It was almost nine o'clock. The servants at the hotel would be finishing up their last-minute duties and would soon be heading over to the other end of town.

He would be ready.

"We haven't had any requests in over an hour. I think we've finished for the night," Miss Quigley said to Birdie. "You should get ready for the dance."

"Are you sure?" Birdie asked. "I'm happy to stay."

"No, you go ahead. I'm sure we won't get any more emergencies at this hour."

A loud banging on the door made both women jump.

"Just a minute," Miss Quigley said, striding to the door and opening it.

A young woman with flushed cheeks stood on the other side of the door. Birdie didn't recognize her.

"Yes, Miss Adelaide?" Miss Quigley asked.

Birdie remembered this was the young woman who didn't have space in her room for three hatboxes.

"I've changed my mind," Miss Adelaide said. "Everyone has beautiful headpieces at the ball!"

Miss Adelaide strode into the room. She started looking frantically around. She didn't look at Birdie; it was as if she wasn't even there.

At first, Birdie was annoyed, but then she smiled. She had spent the last two years trying to be invisible. She certainly shouldn't hold it against someone if she'd accomplished her goal.

"The headpieces aren't here," Miss Quigley said. "I took them to the trunk room."

"That is certainly not helpful," Miss Adelaide said.

"Why don't you go up to your room?" Miss Quigley said as she steered Miss Adelaide out the door. "I'll retrieve the headpieces and meet you there. It will only take me a minute."

Miss Adelaide and Miss Quigley headed out the door, but Miss Quigley turned back to Birdie.

"Go ahead and get dressed now," Miss Quigley said. "I'm sure I'll be back before you're ready and I'll see you off."

"But what if—" Birdie started, wanting to offer her assistance, but Miss Quigley put up a finger.

"You get ready now," Miss Quigley said. "You deserve a good time."

As Miss Quigley closed the door, Birdie could hear the orchestra strike up a waltz she knew. It was a slower version of waltzes she'd heard and danced to at home. Americans called it the "Boston Waltz." She loved the unhurried tempo. So full of romance. Birdie pretended Captain Newcastle put his arm around her waist, ready to lead her in a dance. She quickly put all thoughts of Captain Newcastle out of her mind and danced over to her beautiful dove-gray dress. She was determined to have a good time tonight, captain or no captain.

The door to the sewing room flew open. An eruption of mauve satin, lace, and trim exploded into the room.

It was a breathless Charlotte.

"Thank goodness you're still here!" Charlotte said.

Birdie still had the dove-gray dress on the hanger. With everything it would entail getting out of her uniform and into the dove-gray dress, it wasn't as if Charlotte almost missed her.

"Is everything all right?" Birdie asked.

"Everything is perfect," Charlotte said. "Father is too under the weather to go to the ball!"

Clearly, this news made Charlotte very happy, but to say "I'm so happy to hear this!" sounded downright rude. She knew if she just kept silent, Charlotte would fill the empty space. She didn't have to wait long.

"Don't you see?" Charlotte continued. "If Father isn't at the ball, it means I don't have to be either!"

Birdie was now at a complete loss for words. Nothing Miss Charlotte was saying made sense.

"What do you mean you don't have to go to the ball?"

"I can go to the Jingle Bobs and Belles Ball! I can be with Joey."

"I'm not sure your father would think much of that idea."

"Of course not! That's why it's the perfect plan! He'll never know."

"But what about Captain Newcastle?"

"Oh, I don't give a hoot about Captain Newcastle. And he doesn't give a hoot about me. Why should he? We've only said a few words to each other since I've been here."

Birdie tried not to be excited about this news.

"Besides," Charlotte continued, "Captain Newcastle has his pick of any girl at the ball. He'll be just fine."

Birdie's hopes plummeted. Of course, Charlotte was right.

"I should get dressed," Birdie said, trying to regain some semblance of composure. "I'm not sure it's a good idea for you to go to the ball with me, but . . ."

"You're right about that. Going with you to the ball is a very bad idea," Charlotte said, reaching out and taking the dove-gray dress from Birdie and appraising it. "But going to the ball in your place is a fantastic idea."

"That is insanity, Miss Charlotte. Just insanity."

"I've thought the whole thing through. We're the same size! I'll wear your dress and go to the Jingle Bobs and Belles Ball, and you wear my gown and go upstairs to the Grand Ball. It will be perfect."

"I think your father might not be the only one with a fever."

"Think of it, Birdie. I can go be with my Joey and you can try your luck with Captain Newcastle."

"What do you mean?"

"Don't think I haven't noticed *your* feelings for the captain," Charlotte said.

"My feelings?" Birdie gasped.

"You turn red as a beet whenever he's around. You're like an open book."

Birdie could feel herself turning red as a beet just discussing him.

Dangerous Jack knew he should limit his drinking if he was planning on lifting wallets and jewels from the crowd at the ball. But Mrs. Firestone would drive even the most devout man to the bottle. Every time he turned around, she was at his heels.

He just had to be patient. He would only be at the Grand Ball for another hour or so, then over to the dance across town to conclude his business in this backwater town. Dallas would be nothing but a memory in a few short hours. Then it would be off to Houston to unload the spoils of the evening. He already had a diamond necklace and a ruby bracelet in his pocket. If the evening continued to go as planned, he'd be a very rich man by the end of the night.

He let his mind wander to the possibility of life after Dallas—back to the East Coast? Maybe head west to California?

Whether he would be alone or have a companion remained to be seen. He reflexively patted his pocket to make sure his gun was there.

He caught Olive Firestone's eye. She gave him a bold look. He looked right back at her, knowing he'd have to tread carefully. One whiff of an interest in her daughter, no matter how passing, would have Mrs. Firestone tossing him out on his ear. Mrs. Firestone appeared from the kitchen. She gave him a wide smile and headed toward him. Olive looked away quickly. She was as good at playing the game as he was.

Maybe if things played out differently, he could have explored the possibilities of Olive a little further. Although having to deal with Mrs. Firestone would slow any man down. No wonder the poor girl was single.

Mrs. Firestone threaded through the crowd, headed right at him. Jack picked up a glass of half-drunk whiskey from his crowded tray of discarded drinks and downed it.

Birdie, dressed in the marvelous mauve gown and mobcap, and Charlotte, wearing the demure but lovely dove-gray dress, stared at themselves in the looking glass.

"This is never going to work," Birdie said.

"What could go wrong?"

"What could go wrong?" Birdie squeaked. "Your father could decide to check on you and come to the ball after all. Joey might not arrest you, but he could arrest me as an imposter. I might be needed to sew up a ripped petticoat and I would be nowhere to be found. Or worse, found dancing at the ball. You might—"

"Oh, all right, something could go wrong. But think how fun this will be. Not doing what we're supposed to be doing. Taking life into our own hands for once. We just need to be a tiny bit brave."

Birdie, in her own beautiful mauve creation, looked at Charlotte. Maybe she had a point. Birdie had mustered all her bravery over the past two years, but it had been because she was living in fear and had no choice. What would it feel like to take a chance just for fun?

She decided to find out. Not quite trusting her voice, she nodded to Charlotte.

Charlotte stood behind Birdie and regarded her in the mirror.

"You can't wear that awful cap to the ball, you know," Charlotte said.

Birdie started to protest, but Charlotte was too quick for her. She pulled the cap off Birdie's head. Her fingers flew to her lips. Birdie stood frozen as carrot-red hair tumbled past her shoulders.

The door banged open and Miss Quigley strode in, looking at a squashed hatbox in her hands.

"Miss Adelaide decided on a headpiece and has returned, triumphant, to the ball," Miss Quigley said.

She looked up and saw the two young women. Two children caught with their hands in the cookie jar could not have looked guiltier. Miss Quigley didn't appear the least ruffled that she was staring at Birdie, magnificent in mauve, with her red hair cascading down her back, and the flamboyant Charlotte in subtle gray.

"I never even showed her this one," Miss Quigley said, addressing the two well-dressed little elephants in the room. "Which is a good thing, Birdie, since it will go perfectly with your gown."

"Well, isn't that nice," Charlotte said with far too much enthusiasm. "Well, I'd better be going."

She gave Birdie a quick hug, grabbed the mobcap and Birdie's shawl, and flew out of the room.

Birdie closed her eyes as Miss Charlotte escaped the room.

"I'm not sure how to explain . . ." Birdie began.

"No need," Miss Quigley said, prying the lid off the crushed hatbox.

Miss Quigley pulled some bobby pins from her own hair and began to work the delicate headpiece into Birdie's curls.

"I can only assume Miss Charlotte wants to go to the Jingle Bobs and Belles Ball to be with Sheriff Holden and you are going to try your luck with Captain Newcastle—or something like that," Miss Quigley continued.

"Exactly like that."

It appeared the discussion was over. Birdie stood still, watching in the looking glass while Miss Quigley worked her magic, weaving Birdie's hair into beautiful soft waves framed by the headpiece. She looked at Miss Quigley, realizing that "magic" was exactly what Miss Quigley seemed to be. She shook her head. She sounded like a child, believing in a fairy godmother.

But Miss Quigley always seemed to know exactly what was going on, what exactly needed to be fixed and exactly how to fix it.

Was it just a coincidence?

Birdie shook her head. If she'd learned anything in these two years, it was that fairy tales did not exist.

"Oh no!" Birdie exclaimed. "Don't I need an invitation to go to the ball?"

"Yes," Miss Quigley said absently, focusing on the head-piece. "Stand still!"

"But I have to get Miss Charlotte's invitation or I won't be able to go!"

Birdie had been of two minds as to whether or not attending the ball was a good idea. But now that it appeared out of reach, she'd decided she had to go.

Miss Quigley stood back and examined Birdie.

"You look more than presentable," Miss Quigley said.

From the head seamstress, this was high praise. Birdie nodded her thanks.

"I really have to chase after Miss Charlotte," Birdie said.

"That would be a very bad idea," Miss Quigley said. "Miss Charlotte is probably halfway across town by now. You can't afford drawing attention to either one of you."

Birdie knew Miss Quigley was right. She sank down on a chair and buried her head in her hands. She should have known better than to get her hopes up for a crazy scheme. Would she never learn?

She heard Miss Quigley moving around the room and heard the familiar sound of the head seamstress unlocking her mysterious box of treasures. Birdie looked up to see Miss Quigley lift the satin-bound invitation out of the box, then close the lid.

"I think we can solve that little problem," Miss Quigley said, handing Birdie the invitation.

Birdie stared at the parchment in her hand. She looked up at Miss Quigley, who stared back at her impassively.

"How did you—" Birdie began, but Miss Quigley cut her off.

"It's almost ten o'clock," Miss Quigley said. "The dance will be in full swing by now. You'd better go."

"You've been so kind. I don't know how to thank you, Miss Quigley, for everything," Birdie said.

"Have a good time," Miss Quigley said, brushing aside the compliment. "Tonight belongs to you, Birdie. Make the most of it."

Miss Quigley guided Birdie to the door and gently pushed her into the hallway, closing the door between them. Birdie stared at the door, not believing what was happening.

Birdie took a deep breath, picked up her skirts, and stood tentatively at the doorway.

Maybe the magic of Christmas was real, she wondered.

The night seemed so full of possibilities.

Birdie turned back. She wanted to hug Miss Quigley, but the head seamstress was already sewing by the fire. Birdie headed down the hall to the staircase, toward the music. At the other end of the hall, she glimpsed a woman in a beautiful pink gown, ribbons floating down the back. Birdie ducked into a doorway. She knew that dress! She'd reinforced the ribbons for the local lady they called the "Texas Princess."

What was she doing in the servants' quarters?

Birdie's instincts as a helpful servant got the better of her and she stepped back into the hallway, ready to be of assistance to the obviously lost lady. But the lady must have found her way. The hallway was empty.

Birdie headed toward the music, coming from the ballroom above.

* * *

Detective Hilbrand was still standing in the snow. The carriages going to the Grand Ball had slowed to a trickle. People bundled against the snow coming around the corner from the servants' entrance and headed in the opposite direction had also subsided. He wondered if somehow he had missed Birdie.

It wouldn't be the first time.

He looked up and saw a woman appear on the front steps of the St. Nicholas, dressed exactly as Mrs. Firestone had described.

This girl is brazen, the detective thought. *Doesn't even use the servants' entrance.* He moved closer as the woman, dressed in dove gray with a mobcap and a shawl, made her way down the stairs. The detective noticed her body language. Even at a distance, he could tell she was nervous and didn't make eye contact with anyone.

This had to be her.

Could I really be at the end of this journey? he wondered as he followed at a safe distance.

The night seemed so full of possibilities, he thought grimly. The problem with his job was—a successful mission never really made anybody happy.

Something to think about on Christmas Eve.

Chapter 11

Kerosene-fueled chandeliers cast a warm golden glow over the ballroom. Beautifully dressed men and women glided around the dance floor as Birdie stepped lightly into the room. She expected the man at the entrance to question her about her invitation. She recognized him as one of the hotel's servants—they had passed each other dozens of times over the last few weeks. But he did not seem to know her.

She froze as she caught a woman's eye. It was Mrs. Fitzgerald from room 200. Birdie had sewn new stays into her corset two days ago. But Mrs. Fitzgerald didn't seem to recognize her either.

Birdie knew she'd been wise never to show her hair.

Everyone remembered her hair.

She stepped timidly into the room.

"Where have you been all evening?" came a voice from behind her.

She recognized it as Captain Newcastle's. Although he was the reason she was here, now that the dream had become a reality, she wasn't sure what to do. Her feet seemed to want to run out of the room. But she realized if she bolted, she might be discovered in her deception. Not to mention Miss Charlotte's and even Miss Quigley's subterfuge. She'd hurt the people she loved—something she vowed never to do again.

And of course, there were myriad reasons she couldn't be discovered in the first place.

Birdie turned around. She was so nervous. She took a deep breath, remembering her mother's advice to always smile, no matter how nervous or frightened you were.

She smiled.

"I saw you come in," the captain said, casting an eye around the room. "*Everyone* saw you come in. You've caused quite a stir."

Was this a warning of some sort? She was about to ask when the captain continued.

"I'm Captain Newcastle," he said.

Birdie's breath caught.

Was it possible that *he* did not recognize her? Her hopes for the evening plummeted.

"I'm Brigid Flanagan," Birdie said coldly, holding out her hand.

The captain kissed her hand. The thrill of his touch was just as electric as it was the day she'd arrived.

"Brigid Flanagan," the captain said, seeming to savor her name. "Well, Brigid Flanagan, the orchestra just announced an Irish reel. May I have this dance?"

"I would think your dance card is full," Birdie countered. She didn't trust herself to be in his arms.

"I seem to have forgotten all about dance cards," the captain said, leading her to the dance floor. "I blame an old war injury."

"How convenient," Birdie said.

Birdie and Captain Newcastle lined up with the other dancers and joined in the Irish reel. Birdie couldn't help but be swept away by the music. Happy memories of home combined with the good fellowship of the dancers at the ball made her forget her problems. The Irish reel was a formation dance—she danced with other men as well as the captain. There was none of the passion and romance of a waltz. Maybe the evening would turn out all right after all.

I'm fairly skilled at lowering my expectations at this point, she thought.

The dancers burst into spontaneous applause at the end of the reel. Birdie loved the energy of Texans. They weren't afraid to show they were having a good time, no matter what their social standing. The captain escorted her off the dance floor.

"Thank you, Captain Newcastle," she said, flushed from the dance and his close proximity. She offered her hand.

He took it, but instead of a farewell kiss to the back of her hand, he gently held her wrist and smiled.

"Listen," he said.

Birdie cocked her head to one side.

"What am I listening for?" she asked.

"You're not listening *for* anything," he said. "You're listening *to* my favorite Viennese waltz. Please do me the honor?"

She knew she should politely reject this request. If Captain Newcastle couldn't see past her red hair to recognize the woman he'd carried up the steps while she was in a dead faint and whom he'd tried to kiss in an unguarded moment, he was certainly not worthy of her. She told herself it might be better to keep those thoughts—rather than his broad shoulders—in mind.

Birdie chided herself. This was only a dance. It had been such a long time since she'd allowed herself to have a good time. If Captain Newcastle wanted to dance with her, why shouldn't she? What harm could there be in it?

She gave a small curtsey and allowed him to lead her back to the dance floor. She reminded herself to keep her emotions in check. She could feel the eyes of the other young women on her—presumably the girls whose dance cards bore his name. She decided not to worry about them and enjoy herself.

As he put his arm around her waist and the opening measures of the waltz began, all thoughts of what she should feel drifted away. As she looked into his eyes, their fellow dancers ceased to exist. When the song ended, she realized she'd even stopped hearing the music. Somehow, he had escorted her off the dance floor again. Captain Newcastle was looking into her eyes. He pressed his lips to her ear.

"Birdie, I—"

A hand clasped the captain on the shoulder, bringing Birdie back to reality. From Captain Newcastle's sudden change of posture, Birdie knew this was a senior officer.

"You need to stop monopolizing this young lady," the officer said to the captain. "I'm sure she has other gentlemen just waiting to dance with her. And I know you have your own . . . obligations."

"Yes, sir," Captain Newcastle said.

He'd called her by name. Birdie took a seat, just in time to not lose her balance.

He knew it was me.

Birdie watched as Captain Newcastle was led away. The officer guided the captain over to the bar, where he introduced him to a young lady in a bright green dress. Would the captain be able to come back to her before the evening was out?

Another dance, this time a lively polka, began. Dozens of dancers were now between her and the captain. She could only catch a glimpse of him now and then as couples whirled between them. She did manage to catch his eye—and the apology in it. Captain Newcastle wanted to make his way back to her, she knew.

A piece of ice in her heart that she had carried for so long it felt a part of her suddenly seemed to melt away. She closed her eyes. Perhaps she could stop running after all.

She opened her eyes and looked for the captain, but he was nowhere to be seen. Might he be dancing with the girl in green? She scanned the dance floor, but didn't see him.

What she did see brought the ice back to her heart and soul. Standing at the bar, staring right at her, staring through her, in a hotel uniform, was the man she'd been running from for two years.

Birdie ran out of the ballroom. She heard someone call "Birdie" but in her panic, she couldn't tell if it was Captain Newcastle or Dangerous Jack.

She did not turn around to find out.

She took flight.

Chapter 12

Birdie tried to force herself to think as she ran down the steps toward the sewing room. She wanted to convince herself that she must have been mistaken. How could it be him? How could he be working at the hotel?

She knew better than to turn around and see if he was after her. In her heart, she knew that he'd been on her heels these two long years. She had not a second to lose. She needed to get her few belongings and get away from this town as quickly as possible. She hoped the labyrinth of hallways in the basement would slow him down.

As she fumbled with the doorknob to the sewing room, she prayed Miss Quigley would be out. She did not want to involve her in this mess. The door opened and a hand grabbed her and pulled her inside. Dangerous Jack had somehow beaten her to her destination. He seemed to know the hotel as well as she did.

"Stop fighting me," he said as Birdie slapped at his arms. "It's over, Birdie, my pet."

Ice water ran through her veins hearing him call her his pet. She tried to find something she could use as a weapon, but she stopped struggling immediately as she saw he'd tied Miss Quigley to a chair.

"Miss Quigley, please forgive me," Birdie sobbed. "I never meant—"

"Shut up," Jack said, pushing Birdie to the floor.

There was a time when Birdie would have stayed on the floor and hoped Jack would have mercy. But she had not spent two years crossing America without learning a few things, one of which was not to show weakness.

She mustered all her courage and stood up.

"Let my friend go," Birdie said to Jack. "She has nothing to do with you."

"Well, look at you, all powerful and mighty," Jack said in his sneering, mocking tone. "Get your things. We're leaving. Your friend will be discovered soon enough."

Birdie started to untie Miss Quigley from the chair.

"I said no," Jack hissed.

Birdie's heart was pounding but she tried to give the impression that she was not frightened. She gambled on the notion that he would not make a scene. The kitchen was right next door and any commotion would send Cook to investigate.

"You might be more trouble than you're worth," Jack said as Birdie helped Miss Quigley to her feet. Her hands were still bound.

"Miss Quigley, I'm so sorry," Birdie said.

"I'm all right," Miss Quigley replied calmly.

Birdie had entertained such fanciful thoughts that Miss Quigley knew how to solve any problem. Birdie realized that was just being carried away with the magic of the season. She wanted to cry as she started to untie Miss Quigley's hands.

Jack suddenly pulled a gun from his waistcoat.

"Leave her hands tied," he commanded. "I'm not taking any chances."

Birdie looked him in the eye. She saw no pity there. In her

heart, she knew he would never leave her in peace. She might as well go with him quietly and save Miss Quigley from the possibility of harm.

"I'll get my things," Birdie said dejectedly.

"And change out of that dress!" Jack commanded. "We won't get far with you parading yourself like that!"

Birdie noticed the frayed cuff on his shirt.

Mrs. Firestone had that shirt with her when she came to leave off the dresses to be hemmed. She must have given Jack the job. She was outraged by this betrayal, but realized Jack had probably talked his way into many a woman's heart. She couldn't blame her.

She knew that from experience.

"You should take the money in the strongbox," Miss Quigley said. "You'll need it."

Birdie looked at her. What did she mean? Miss Quigley's eyes went to the large box near the fireplace.

The box where she keeps her gun!

Birdie looked at the box and realized it wasn't locked. She thought back to when Miss Quigley had unlocked the box to get out the invitation to the ball. She hadn't relocked it.

Which was strange, because Miss Quigley always relocked that box.

Miss Quigley arched an eyebrow at Birdie.

Birdie opened the box and, with a shaking hand, laid her fingertips on the gun. She prayed that Miss Quigley's uncanny ability to be one step ahead of any situation would hold true and that the gun was loaded. She pulled the gun out and pointed it as she heard a shot ring out. Then another.

She panicked. What was happening? She knew she had not been hit. In the smoke that filled the room, she tried to find Miss Quigley.

As the smoke cleared, she saw Miss Quigley was also fine, sitting calmly with Dangerous Jack Simon at her feet, blood pooling around his shoulders. Captain Newcastle stood in the doorway, tendrils of smoke curling in the air around his gun.

"Birdie," he said.

"I'm all right," she said. "Help me untie Miss Quigley!"

By the time Miss Quigley was free, a crowd had gathered. Cook, Mrs. Firestone, Judge Rutherford in a dressing robe, Miss Charlotte, Detective Hilbrand, and Sheriff Holden were all there.

"What's going on?" Sheriff Holden demanded. "Who shot this man?"

"I did," Captain Newcastle said. "I was either saving these two ladies, or I shot him in self-defense. Both are true. Your choice."

Birdie noticed that the sheriff seemed satisfied with the explanation. He turned to Detective Hilbrand as he pointed to the man on the floor. "Is that the man you're looking for?"

The detective nodded.

"That's him, all right," the detective said.

"He's wanted in five states, for gambling, theft, and murder," the detective said.

"I don't understand," Birdie said.

Detective Hilbrand showed her his badge.

"I'm with the Pinkerton Detective Agency. I've been following your trail since you left New York."

"I had no idea," Birdie said.

"That's why I've still got a job," the detective said, and smiled. "Anyway, we knew Dangerous Jack was hell-bent on finding you. I knew if I found you first, I'd eventually get him."

"Thank you for not giving up," Birdie said.

"I did give up! When I got to town, I explained to the sheriff that I was making one last attempt to locate Dangerous Jack through Brigid 'Birdie' Flanagan," the detective said, turning to Birdie. "I knew you'd be going to the dance across town, so I waited for you to leave the St. Nicholas. I followed you but when I got to the dance, it turned out I was following the wrong woman."

He looked pointedly at Charlotte, who was busy avoiding her father's eyes.

"I thought I'd played my last card," the detective continued. "I decided to enjoy the party and head back east on the first stagecoach."

The sheriff bent over the body and felt for a heartbeat.

While he found no pulse, he did find a pocketful of jewels.

"Is he dead?" Birdie asked, never taking her eyes off the body.

"Yes," Sheriff Holden said. "He's dead."

"You know this man?" Captain Newcastle asked Birdie.

"Her husband," Detective Hilbrand said.

"My late husband," Birdie said, lifting her eyes to Captain Newcastle, the man who'd saved her life.

"We can deal with the body later," Sheriff Holden said. "We don't want to bring any more attention to this unfortunate event than we have to. Bad for the town's morale. Luckily those lawmen Mrs. Cockrell brought in from out of town have had their hands full upstairs. We can deal with this ourselves."

Miss Quigley threw a sheet she'd been embroidering over Dangerous Jack's body as the little group in the sewing room retired to the kitchen.

Cook poured shots of brandy as everyone tried to make sense of what had happened that night.

"I got a message that a few of the ladies had missing jewelry," the sheriff said. "I left the dance down the street and was on my way into the ballroom with Charlotte when I heard the shot. I came down here and Charlotte followed."

Sheriff Holden turned to Judge Rutherford.

"I told her to stay upstairs, but you know how headstrong she is," the sheriff said.

"I knocked on your door to see if you'd returned from the

ball when I heard the shot and came down," Judge Rutherford said.

"I'm sorry you had to get involved, sir," the sheriff said miserably.

"Why was Charlotte with you?" Judge Rutherford asked the sheriff. He turned toward his daughter. "And why is Birdie wearing your dress?"

Miss Charlotte gave an impassioned version of her scheme. She professed her love for Sheriff Holden, which quieted the room.

"And are those feelings reciprocated?" the judge growled, downing his brandy and looking at Sheriff Holden.

"Yes, sir," Sheriff Holden said. "Very much so."

"What I want to know is," Detective Hilbrand said, "how did Jack get into the hotel? He had a uniform! Someone was working with him."

Birdie looked at Mrs. Firestone, who visibly paled. Birdie instantly took pity on her. Dangerous Jack had convinced Birdie to leave her family in Ireland to follow him to New York, where he made her life a living hell. How could Birdie blame Mrs. Firestone for falling for his smooth talk when she herself was a victim of the same thing? She stole a glance at Miss Quigley, who was also looking at Mrs. Firestone.

"Perhaps we'll never know," Miss Quigley said, letting Mrs. Firestone off the hook.

"I think I'll take Birdie out for some air," Captain Newcastle said, reaching for her hand and pulling her to her feet.

"It's still snowing out there," Charlotte said, pulling off her shawl and handing it to Birdie. "You'd better take this."

Captain Newcastle wrapped Birdie in the shawl and led her up the grand staircase to the glittering lobby and onto the front porch. The ball was winding down and couples drifted into carriages pulled by horses whose jingling sleigh bells cheered the night air with their music.

"I can't believe I almost lost you," Captain Newcastle said.

Birdie could hear his voice constrict with emotion.

"Why did you pretend you didn't know who I was?" Birdie asked.

"Why did you pretend to be someone you weren't?" he asked, then grinned. "Well, it's obvious now, isn't it? But at the time, I thought, she must have her reasons. Out here in the West, a lady is entitled to her secrets."

"I never want to have any secrets from you. I want to be totally honest from here to . . ."

Birdie stopped herself. Was she being too forward?

Church bells rang out through the silent night.

"Midnight," Captain Newcastle said. He took Birdie's face in his hands and looked deep into her eyes. "This is our very first Christmas together."

He kissed her. The years of weariness in her heart drifted up to join the song created by the church bells on the wind, replaced by the promise of all good things to come.

"Merry Christmas, my love," Birdie said.

Epilogue

December 24, 1860

Dear Mam,

   *Christmas will be gone by the time you get this
letter, but I wanted to let you know that after a
year's courtship, Captain Douglas Newcastle and I
will be getting married on New Year's Day. My
friend Charlotte will also be marrying her beau who
is the sheriff in our town. Her father is a judge who
is going to help make Dallas a great city. He is going
to marry us in a double ceremony.*

   *I am still working at the hotel. My lovely head
seamstress, Miss Quigley, whom I've told you so
much about, has made me her successor. She is moving to Houston to work in a beautiful new hotel. I
would never say this to her, but I think she needs a
new challenge now that she's straightened out my
life!*

*In your last letter, you asked about Mrs. Firestone.
Please do not worry. While we will never be the best
of friends, we keep each other's secrets, so all is well.
Besides, she is very busy trying to procure a husband
for her daughter. She really doesn't have time to
focus on me.*

*Give Da my love. I dream of Ireland and plan on
making your Irish soda bread a Christmas tradition.
I've even given our cook at the hotel a few lessons on
how you make it at home.*

But my heart is here and so here I will stay.
Merry Christmas, Mam.

Your loving daughter,
Birdie

Spirit of Texas

Rachael Miles

Acknowledgments

Thanks to the following for their assistance: Lynn Rushton, the Public Art Collection and Conservation Manager at the City of Dallas's Office of Cultural Affairs, for telling me stories about Sarah Cockrell and her influence on Dallas; Joan Gosnell, University Archivist, at Southern Methodist University's DeGolyer Library for providing access to their Cockrell family papers and artifacts; John Slate, Senior Archivist, City of Dallas Municipal Archives, for helpful direction; and Sam Childers, historian and author of *Historic Dallas Hotels,* who solved the puzzle of whether the St. Nicholas sat on the northwest or the northeast corner of Commerce and Broadway. It's northeast.

Chapter 1

Some say that the Hudson Valley with its verdant greens and moody skies is the most picturesque landscape in these great states. They have never seen a field of bluebonnets and scarlet paintbrush under the blaze of a Texas sunset.

—Garrand Kent, *Texas: Her Land, Her Peoples*

"*Miss* CARP-*in-ter.*"

Lost in her book, Eugenie Charpentier didn't hear the hotel manager's voice until he stood before her. When Eugenie lifted her gaze from the page, Jones—the manager—stiffened a little. She sighed inwardly. Ever since her maid had "confided" in the hotel staff that Eugenie's grandfather was an English duke, Jones had treated her alternately like a sleeping dragon or an ignorant child.

Eugenie had wanted nothing more than to be treated like any other guest, knowing that her family's status in England had no claim in this wild land. But her great-aunt Judith had taught her how to respond in any situation—"Darling Genie, always signal your mettle by standing tall and looking anyone you meet straight in the eye."—so Eugenie placed her finger in the book to hold her place, then rose, straightening her back.

"Miss CARP-in-ter." Jones looked around the drawing room. Seeing it empty, he lowered his voice anyway. "Your guide has arrived in town."

"Excellent. Please send him to me and bring us tea." She waited, letting the silence emphasize her directions.

Jones fingered the chain of his pocket watch nervously. Then he turned away from her to look out the window.

If I remain in Jefferson much longer, he will have worn the chain completely through. Eugenie tapped her foot, and Jones returned his attention to her.

"Do you object to me using this room to meet my guide?" Eugenie raised one eyebrow, a trick she'd learned as a child from her great-aunt. Years later, she'd realized that Judith's strength of presence, not her eyebrow, caused dilatory servants and tradesmen to jump to attention. For Eugenie, the eyebrow worked only about half the time.

"Oh no, miss, no objection at all. The next steamboat isn't expected for hours. But he's not here, miss. Your guide, I mean. He's at the dry goods, loading supplies." Jones, if possible, looked more nervous. He crumpled an envelope stuck partway into his waistcoat pocket. "Asher says a storm's coming, and he wants to be halfway to Marshall before it hits."

"Asher? My guide is a Mr. Graham."

"That's him, miss. Asher Graham. He's a bit distant, and, like the other Rangers, you wouldn't want to cross him in a fight, but no one knows this land better." For the first time since her arrival, Jones spoke easily.

"Ranger?" Eugenie said more to herself than to Jones, wondering what else her mother had neglected to mention.

"Yes, ma'am. He fought with Rip Ford eight or nine years back, and I've heard he intends to join Ford's new troop at Fort Brown by Christmas." Jones returned to shifting his feet, all eloquence gone. "He's called for your bags to be sent down. He will meet you here—ready to travel—on the hour."

"No." She sat down, holding her book in her lap.

"No, miss?" The man sounded stunned. No one, apparently, refused the order of a former Ranger.

"My mother may say Mr. Graham is trustworthy. But I will use my own judgment. Please call for my maid and send tea."

Jones, looking forlorn, worried the crumpled envelope. "My wife can pack some vittles for the road," he cajoled. "It's no trouble, you being paid up through the end of the week and all."

"No. If there's a storm coming, we can wait it out here." Eugenie sat silently until Jones nodded uncomfortably and hurried off.

She turned Garrand Kent's *Texas* over in her hand. Once she'd decided to make the long journey from England to Texas, Eugenie had gathered all the information she could, scouring the newspapers for any mention of the state and interviewing anyone who had ever made the trip. But in Kent's book, she'd glimpsed the heart and soul of the state, one that made her spinster heart long for adventure. She opened *Texas* and picked up where she had left off.

> Unlike the appearance of the sky in other parts of
> the country, a Texas sky is limitless, high and blue.
> In the East, it's easy to imagine that if one merely
> climbed a high mountain one could touch the sky.
> But that isn't the case in Texas. No. A Texas sky is
> ferociously distant.

A bellman delivered the tea tray, and Eugenie looked out the window. Ferociously blue skies as far as the eye could see. Hrumph. "Trust your own judgment, Genie, and you'll do well," Judith had always told her.

A pang of grief and loneliness caught her off-guard, and she waited, breathing slowly, until the threat of tears passed. It wouldn't do to meet her Ranger with tears in her eyes.

To soothe herself, she traced the indentations of Kent's name embossed in gold lettering in the center of the book's deep green morocco leather cover. Her mother, Lilly, had sent the manuscript to England for publication, and she'd requested that Eugenie bring fifty copies from London. But Eugenie knew her mother too well to agree too quickly. Lilly had a penchant for mischief and had once brought a collection of erotic prints to Eugenie's engagement tea. Eugenie could still see her mother's look of gleeful pleasure when Eugenie had opened the portfolio and the rector's wife had fainted. So Eugenie had read *Texas* first.

But Kent's *Texas* mixed philosophy, history, and reflection, and Eugenie had adored it from the start. Kent's pages resonated with the heartbeat of an honest man, and sometimes, in the darkness of a lonely night, Eugenie even allowed herself to imagine what might happen if she could only meet him. Kent would be a man so unlike her suitors in England that she could imagine herself trusting again. He would be a man who would care more for her and her character than he did for her connections or her money. Though she'd never admit it to anyone but herself, she'd agreed to fetch her mother from Texas partially out of a hope that she might encounter the man whose sensibility so mirrored her own.

She turned away from her reverie and back to Kent's pages.

> Living under a limitless sky, Texans are a new breed, seeing possibilities where others have only seen obstacles. In lands where the sky sits heavy on its people, the old clothes of habit and custom bind men up. But Texas calls her people to cut new clothes out of new cloth, eschewing tradition and rules in exchange for honest lives and true hearts.

Eugenie sensed rather than heard her guide enter the room. His movements were so silent that she imagined him as a raccoon-hatted Daniel Boone. But she didn't look up.

Her mother may have sent Mr. Graham to be her guide, but he needed to understand Eugenie was not some simpering young miss who needed to be delivered to her mother. No, she was a fully capable woman who knew her own mind and made her own decisions, one who had traveled halfway across the world to escort her mother back to England.

Without raising her head, she glanced over the edge of her book at his shoes. Her uncle Ian swore that the cut of a man's shoe indicated his character better than the cut of his jacket. She'd hoped he might be wearing Boone's well-known moccasins, but her guide—disappointingly—wore boots.

They were neither Hessians as was currently fashionable in Europe nor Wellingtons as most colonists still wore. Nor did they look anything like the finely polished shoes of the tradesmen and gamblers in Jefferson. Instead, her guide tucked the legs of his trousers into tall stovepipe boots.

The boots, decorated on the top and sides with stitched swirls, stopped an appropriate distance from her.

"Eugenie Charpentier." Her guide's voice was deep, and the sound of it rumbled pleasantly in her belly. Even better, he pronounced her name correctly. A relief.

She lowered her book and examined him, boots to hat. His long legs were clothed in heavy dark trousers, utilitarian mostly, but with a narrow light-colored pinstriping that gave them a hint of fashion. His waistcoat was unbuttoned, revealing a starched white (and surprisingly clean) linen shirt and leather braces. His stomach was lean and his shoulders broad. A short, narrow neckerchief, more like a bandanna than a cravat, was tied near his neck.

She'd expected her guide to be one of the wiry, weather-hardened men that she'd watched from the parlor window as they made their way to the local saloon. But even dusty from the trail, Eugenie's guide was handsome: tall and lean as a birch, with raven hair and deep green eyes.

She should have known not to trust her mother's tepid description: "A man of the frontier, straightforward and honest, but largely unable to carry on a conversation on any topic but cattle or the weather." Liliana, Countess of an extinct Habsburg duchy, would always prefer a man with polish and a veneer of court life to this strong, vital specimen of American life.

Asher's presence seemed to fill the room, and she imagined him as one of the heroes in the novels she'd read, picking her up in his strong arms and carrying her away to a romantic hideaway for a passionate affair. She pushed the fantasy away. She wasn't like her mother: a dreamer, running from one great love to the next. No, all her life she'd been practical where her mother was whimsical; dependable where her mother was headstrong; plain where her mother was beautiful. Even so, she could still regret that she wasn't the sort of woman a dashing Ranger would choose for a grand romance.

Tamping down her unexpected attraction, Eugenie gave her guide the smile she reserved for visits from the rector's wife. Welcoming but distant, her smile indicated that no matter the other appearances of civility, he was her hired guide and she was in charge.

"Ah, you must be Mr. Graham." She rose. Doing so closed some of the distance between them, but somehow her rising made him appear even taller. If they were to embrace, her head would nestle comfortably below his chin. Something about this man made her wish she were young again with a face almost pretty rather than a spinster firmly on the shelf. Resisting the unexpected impulse to touch his chest with her hand, she gestured to the chair across from the small tea table.

"Graham is my father's name; folks call me Asher." He remained standing, his expression remote. "Your mother sent word to expect me."

"I have been *expecting* you every day for the last week." She studied his face. His cheekbones and jaw were strong. His dark eyes flashed with a hint of irritation. Somehow that pleased her.

He held out a crumpled envelope. "Jones sent this: your maid intends to stay in Jefferson with a young man she's met."

His fingers brushed hers as she took the note, and Eugenie imagined a frisson of electricity passing between them. It surprised and unsettled her. Not even during her engagement had she felt such chemistry. She focused on unfolding the envelope. Her maid's note began and ended with apologies, reserving the middle for her lover's merits. "His name is Beauregard; I hope he lives up to it," Eugenie reported, shaking her head. "Love at first sight. Foolish girl. "

She looked up to see Asher raise one eyebrow.

"We arrived only two weeks ago." She felt compelled to explain. "Not nearly enough time to know the heart and soul of a person." Her finger rubbed the spine of Kent's book.

"Depends on the person, I reckon." He stared at her intently, and the moment stretched out between them. She was about to speak, when he looked out the window to the waiting stagecoach. Several trunks were already loaded on the top and back.

When she looked back at him, he was studying her face once more.

"Mrs. Jones sent down those fancy trunks of yours. Should I load them with the rest?"

"How many passengers are traveling to Dallas?" She counted the number of trunks, trying to estimate how many others he might be taking.

"Just you. I would have brought a wagon, but your mother insisted on a carriage. Said you'd be more comfortable."

She felt her jaw tighten, wondering whose funds—hers or her mother's—would pay for the hire of a guide and an entire coach.

"I'm uncertain I wish to travel *alone* with a man I have only just met," she objected. "I'll need some time to find another maid."

"Time's something we haven't got." He pulled a second note from a pocket inside his waistcoat and held it out. Her mother's florid handwriting decorated the cover. This time, as his fingers brushed hers, she felt the spark of electricity run down her spine. "There's a storm brewing out west that's going to level trees here to Shreveport."

She pulled her hand back and looked out the window. The sky remained a limitless clear blue.

Asher studied the clock over Eugenie's shoulder. "If you want to be in Dallas by Christmas, you best come with me. Of course, you can wait until your mother finds another guide she trusts, but I won't be back this way for some time."

The clock chimed the quarter hour.

"I can give you until the hour to make up your mind, but if you aren't outside then, I'll leave that fancy luggage of yours on the porch." He settled his wide-brimmed hat on his head. "Pleasure meeting you, Miss Charpentier." His voice caressed the syllables of her name.

With long purposeful strides, he walked away.

A minute or two later, Eugenie saw him walk past the drawing-room window to the carriage. She moved to the window, watching Asher test each piece of the horse's rigging.

Growing up under Judith's care, she'd learned to judge a man on how well he treated his livestock. "A just man respects the life of his animal, but a wicked man's mercy is cruel," her aunt would paraphrase her prayer book whenever they observed a man jerk too tight on his horse's bit or use a whip to punish, not direct. Despite his hurry, Asher moved carefully, methodically, talking to each horse as he pulled, tightened, and adjusted the various leathers. Eugenie was relieved to see that the horses responded to his voice and touch with no hint of fear.

She opened her mother's note. It was brief. "You will find the bearer of this note, Mr. Asher Graham, a faithful guide. If luck is with us, you will arrive in Dallas in time for the Christmas ball at the St. Nicholas hotel—it will be, as you would say in England, the event of the season. The thought that I might spend Christmas with my daughter fills me with joy."

Eugenie rolled her eyes. Joy?

It was much like the note her mother had left seven years before when she'd run off to America without saying good-bye: "If you were only older, we could travel together to that new land of limitless possibilities. As it is, fate leads us to live on different continents. But as your doting mother, I must enjoin you: do not marry that Sherman boy, he will give you only grief." Eugenie had been twenty-one, more than old enough to travel with her mother. But she'd known, even then, that by leaving, she'd merely trade one sort of heartache for another.

Pushing away the memory before it could do much harm, Eugenie tucked her mother's note inside her book's back cover and returned to her reading.

> But as limitless as a Texas sky is, it is also a difficult mistress. I've seen hail the size of a silver dollar fall from a clear blue sky—all because the weather shifted somewhere in the Oregon Territory. Texans learn fast that if the breeze turns cool and dark clouds roll in, you should run—not walk—for cover. Texas storms wait for no man—or woman.

Stepping to the window, she studied the sky—still blue and clear—and Asher. He lifted her heaviest trunk without seeming to notice its weight, then strapped it onto the back of the carriage. Each of his movements were strong and fluid, even graceful.

Asher saw her at the window and stared back with a strange intensity. The feeling of electricity, of attraction, shimmered between them, once more catching Eugenie off guard. She should look away, refusing the intimacy of his gaze, or frown disapprovingly as she would with an impertinent servant. But she didn't.

Somehow her mother's note—and the memory of Jeremy—had made her feel defiant. London with its strictures and obligations was a world away. No one here was cataloging her every move. Indeed, other than the skittish Mr. Jones, no one showed any particular interest in her at all. It was liberating to be unknown, to set aside the rules that had governed every moment of her life, and to drink deep in the spirit of this wild, reckless land.

And why shouldn't she? No one would know—or care. And what was the purpose of traveling through a new country if one never let go of the old country's rules?

Recklessly, then, she held his long gaze. Asher was the sort of man she had always found attractive: strong, confident, a good horseman. But hard experience had taught her to be wary. Still waters might run deep if one were considering a river, but too often, she'd learned, a man of few words displayed little intellectual depth. No, if a spinster could find romance in this wild land, it would be with a thoughtful man like Garrand Kent, one who could see and feel deeply into the heart of things.

As if he read her thoughts, Asher gave her a slow wink and touched the brim of his hat. Eugenie felt his acknowledgment flip in her belly.

At that moment, the hotel manager Jones engaged Asher in conversation, and the two men walked to the far side of the carriage, out of her sight. The loss of Asher's gaze left her feeling oddly bereft. She'd left England for Texas, hoping somehow that she might meet with a grand adventure. But thus far her trip had offered not even a good squall at sea. Even so, a fortnight's travel with a handsome stranger—a Texas Ranger, no less—might give her a taste of the people and landscapes Kent described. Then, when the nights in her small English cottage drew out cold and lonely, she could reread Kent's book, accompanied by her own memories.

But was she brave enough to leap? The clock ticked away the minutes. She needed to decide.

No one would fault her for remaining in Jefferson until she could find a new maid. Other than her mother, Dallas offered little of interest, having neither the culture of Jefferson nor the size of San Antonio, Galveston, or Houston. And once she arrived at the dusty township, she would find herself somewhat cut off, without a regular stagecoach or mail service. But though staying in Jefferson offered many amenities, she wasn't certain she could endure another month of tedious conversation with strangers or Jones's barely contained anxiety.

As she weighed her choices, Jones appeared outside the open window. "Excuse me, miss." He unhooked the shutters. "If you'd latch these shut, then close the window, it'd be much appreciated." Behind Jones, merchants up and down the street were doing the same.

As Jones closed the shutters, Eugenie caught one last glimpse of Asher, climbing effortlessly up the side of the carriage to settle behind his team.

Eugenie followed Jones's instructions, then, refusing to think, she gathered her things. Wrapping several tea cakes in a large piece of writing paper, she tucked them and her book into her reticule and hurried through the hotel lobby into the street.

She arrived at the carriage as the clock struck the hour.

The corners of Asher's mouth twitched when he saw her, as if he was a man who had forgotten how to smile. He extended his hand. "Step on the axle, and I'll help you up."

Jones, frowning, held open the carriage door instead, gesturing for her to ride inside the coach.

One of the hotel shutters banged open, picked up by a change in the wind, and Eugenie looked down the street at Jefferson's fine storefronts and elegant hotels, then at the two men. Here was her choice laid bare: Jones held out the path of propriety, while Asher tempted her with adventure.

Asher waited for her decision, his face impassive, but his dark eyes invited her to trust him.

Gathering up her skirts, she took Asher's hand. His touch—even through their gloves—warmed her spine and pooled in her belly. She pulled herself up to sit beside him.

Asher waited for Jones, clearly disapproving, to shut the carriage door. Then he pulled the coach deftly away from the boardwalk. "I see your mother was right."

"In what way?" Eugenie wasn't certain she wished to know.

"She said you might be stubborn as a mule, but you were no fool." Asher led the team skillfully out of town, the streets now almost deserted.

Chapter 2

Stubborn as a mule. Was she surprised that Lilly would describe her in such unflattering terms? And to a stranger? Or was Asher another of Lilly's devotees? Perhaps he was neither, and Lilly was *as usual* merely being indiscreet. It would be important to know which was the case. "We'll have to see if my mother was right about you as well."

"Should I guess what she told you?" Asher seemed unconcerned.

"That you can talk only of cattle and the weather."

"Well, I suppose that's about right."

The corner of his mouth wanted to grin: she was certain of it.

Eugenie alternated between watching Asher and the landscape. The weather had been unseasonably warm, the shopkeepers in Jefferson had told her. Though it was early December, the deciduous trees still held their fall colors against a backdrop of live oaks and evergreens. The road was cut wide enough for two wagons to pass side by side, yet still the woods felt ancient, with veils of gray moss hanging down, thick and eerie. She shuddered, wondering if the giant alligators she'd seen sunning themselves on the banks of the Red River or walking through the streets of Jefferson were also in the woods.

"Only cattle and weather? Nothing more?" she asked.

"That's mostly what we got."

"And you find no other topics interesting?"

He gave a slight shrug. "I suppose every thing has a little interest, if you look at it right."

"What about alligators? I heard it takes only minutes for one to drown a man."

"It's a good thing, then, that we're in a carriage." His eyes never left the road. "You needn't worry too much about gators: we'll be out of their territory tomorrow, though we'll keep an eye out until then. It would be a right shame to travel all the way from London only to settle in the inside of a gator's belly."

He might have been teasing her, but Eugenie couldn't quite tell.

"If not alligators, what about snakes?" In England, one never pressed another person to converse with them. But if she were to spend a fortnight traveling with Asher, she wanted to know about his character and interests. If he was tempting her to smile, she wanted to know how to tempt him as well. "How are snakes interesting, if you look at them right, of course?"

"Well, let's see." He thought for a moment. "Some say alligators have the power to control the rain, while others say a rattler staked belly-up breaks a drought."

"So, alligators and snakes are interesting because of their connection to the weather."

"Suppose so." Asher signaled the team to move faster. "And if you see birds flying low to the ground or cattle lying down as they are over yonder, you know a storm is coming."

Cattle or weather. He had to be teasing her, but she refused to laugh. Instead, she watched his hands on the reins, long slender fingers in heavy leather gloves, guiding his horses with the slightest of motions. From his hands, her gaze traveled up strong arms to broad shoulders. What would he do if she put her hand on his? She pushed her thoughts away: men only found her attractive for her inheritance or her family's influence. But both her inheritance and her family were far away.

"How long will it take us, this trip to Dallas?" Eugenie tried to keep her voice light and easy. Jefferson had disappeared into the trees, and even its sounds were far behind them.

"Depends on how far we get before that storm hits," Asher said, nodding toward the horizon. "If all goes well, a fortnight, give or take a day or two."

"Is there something in that clear blue sky that's supposed to give me pause?" Eugenie still saw nothing.

"At the top of the next hill, you should have a good view of the horizon." Asher kept the team at a steady pace, not so fast to wear them out quickly, but fast enough to show he wished to make good time.

They lapsed into silence, and Eugenie studied the narrow road. The dirt was packed down and dry. But a rainstorm could easily make the road unpassable, whether it leveled trees or not. As far as she could see, before them and behind, no one else was on the road. In England, even the most remote roads had some traffic. She had never felt so isolated.

"For cold or rain, you'll find a blanket and a heavy canvas under the seat." Asher's voice interrupted Eugenie's thoughts. "Though, if we don't outrun the storm, we'll both be waiting it out in the coach."

Eugenie looked to the sky, still a remote blue. Rather than question his expertise, she deferred. "Our perch here gives a lovely view of the land as it passes. I've grown tired of sea and water."

"Land's something we have plenty of." He paused. "In fact, some Texas ranches cover so much territory that it takes days to ride from one end to the other."

"Perhaps you need a faster horse," Eugenie quipped without thinking.

Asher gave her a look that she couldn't interpret, then turned his attention back to his team. His hands held the reins with a gentle ease, and Eugenie couldn't help wondering how her hand might feel in his. To avoid such thoughts, she pulled her book out of her reticule, turning the pages somewhat aimlessly.

Periodically his leg brushed up against hers, making him a hard man to ignore. The silence between them felt comfortable like the silence between old friends.

Several miles out of town, they reached the rocky bed of a shallow stream. Asher surveyed the area, then whistled two tones in sharp, quick succession. Eugenie waited for a fat alligator to emerge from the shadows near the bank, but nothing happened.

With a slight grimace, he whistled again. Before she could ask if they were meeting someone, Asher, half shaking his head, drove the carriage forward. They crossed the creek easily. Asher, silent, studied the area once more before moving on.

As they made their way out of the valley, the breeze turned from warm to cool. She breathed it in gratefully, until she noticed the line of gray-blue clouds low on the horizon. Asher flicked the reins, increasing the horses' pace.

The temperature dropped from refreshing to brisk in just a few minutes, leaving Eugenie's fingers cold even through her gloves. She rubbed her arms, then pulled the blanket from beneath her seat.

Tucking her hands under the blanket, she skipped to the part of Kent's book that described the many ways Texans predicted the weather. Most centered on the behavior of animals or insects. Singing locusts foretold drought. She listened, but heard nothing. Large squirrel nests predicted cold. She studied the trees, but couldn't determine if the nests were unusually sized for the region. Dancing coyotes signaled rain.

"What does a coyote look like?"

"Bigger than a fox, meaner than a dog."

The wind, bitterly cold, blew down from the north, pushing a thick mass of dark blue clouds closer.

Asher pulled the wagon to a stop, positioning it as close as he could against the side of a steep hill.

"Storm's here." He jumped down from the carriage seat and began to unhitch the horses. As if on cue, hail as small as the head of a pin fell like hard rain, though the sky was still clear blue above them.

Asher reassured the horses with calm low tones. But when lightning struck in the distance, the team grew restive. The dark clouds drew closer, a heavy mass that seemed to turn as it approached.

The hail, grown into tiny pebbles, thudded on the carriage. A long bolt divided the sky, and the horses tugged against their traces, making it hard for Asher to free them.

"Get under the carriage," Asher called out.

Tucking her book under the seat, Eugenie flung herself to the ground. But instead of seeking cover, she made her way to the leader on her side.

The horse, finding her unfamiliar, shied away, and she struggled against the laces. The hail grew larger, sometimes as big as cherries. Her hat kept the strikes from hitting her head or face. But with each hail strike, the horse struggled to be free.

She forced herself to focus, to keep her fingers steady. Though the hail beat heavier on her head, back, and shoulders, she eventually loosened all the ties. The leader ran free. She moved to unhitch the wheeler from the shafts, hail falling heavy around them. She struggled against the traces, then pulled them loose.

Her horse and Asher's ran free at almost the same instant. Lightning struck so close that she could smell its smoke. It illuminated the horses, escaping into the trees.

Suddenly Asher was at her side. He grabbed her arm. "Under the coach—now."

The hail had grown to the size of walnuts. She put her arms over her head to protect her face. It beat against her forearms, each hit hard and painful.

This time she followed Asher's direction. Throwing herself to the ground, she crawled under the carriage, Asher following.

The hail thundered down on the coach. One piece, the size of a silver dollar, rolled beside her, and she weighed it in her hand. Under the protection of the carriage, she felt a rush of excitement and wonder—at last, an adventure! "I've never seen hail fall from a clear sky. Or hail this big."

Asher's attention never left the dark clouds now looming near them. "If you stay in Texas, this won't be the last time."

Stay in Texas. That wasn't in her plan, though she kept the words to herself. No, this trip was a rescue: collect her mother, return her to England, nothing more.

She tossed the hail out onto the road before them. There dozens punctuated the dirt and grass like pale wildflowers. Asher's body, lying next to hers, was warm, and she wanted to move closer until the chill left her limbs, but she resisted. She watched him watch the storm, studying his face so focused on the approaching weather. His expression was grim, sober, his jaw tight. If Michelangelo or da Vinci had painted a Texas Ranger, Asher would have been the model. He seemed the very embodiment of the Texas people as she'd read in Kent's *Texas:* rough, brave, decisive.

How, she wondered, would his face transform if she reached out and touched his cheek, or if she let her fingers trace the line of his strong jaw? She turned the thought away. It was a fantasy born of excitement and the sense of freedom she'd felt since she'd landed on US soil.

Not for the first time she wondered who she might be in this rough land. Could she allow herself to forget that in England she was the ward of a duke, the granddaughter of an earl, and the daughter of a count? At times, all those hundreds of years of obligation threatened to stifle the very life from her, but here, she imagined she could breathe free.

The hail stopped, but the clouds loomed more threateningly. The land had grown silent, as if all the wildlife had disappeared. No sounds, not of insects, nor of birds. It was eerie and unnatural.

"If you are a praying woman, you might wish to make your peace." Asher's voice sounded tight, constrained, even in some way apologetic. "If that cloud doesn't turn, we'll be meeting St. Peter for supper."

"Which one?" She studied the clouds: blue, black, and purple, with portions a sickly green. She hadn't considered that her adventure might prove fatal.

"The twister." He pointed at the dark heart of the storm. There, the black, blue, and gray formed a swirling mass, with the cloud reaching toward the earth in a cylindrical mass.

He put his arm around her, pulling her farther under the carriage. She knew he was merely protecting her from the weather, but she let herself melt into his touch. If they were to die, why not allow Asher's comforting closeness?

"We need to move. We aren't safe here. The twister could crush the coach and us in the bargain."

She looked around, forest behind them, a vast plain before them.

"Where?" She waited for his direction. She didn't have time to feel anxious. Every cell of her body felt tensed, ready to run. Her heart beat fast, but time seemed to move slowly.

"There." He pointed to a narrow ditch running along the cleft of the hill.

"There?" she repeated, but he was already crawling out from under the coach. She tried to follow, but her boots tangled in her skirts. She kicked against the fabric, but couldn't get free.

Her panic rose as the light of day faded into the dark of the on-coming storm.

"I . . ." She barely spoke the word before Asher pulled her from under the coach, setting her on her feet with strong, gentle hands. He took a heavy quilt from inside the carriage, before hurrying her away from the coach. His arm remained around her shoulders to ensure she had her balance.

"We need to get below the level of the road."

She expected him to lay out the quilt for them to lie on. But instead, he sat down in the ditch, pulling her down to sit beside him. The storm's pulsing pressure hurt her ears.

Moving quickly, he tucked one quilt end under their lower legs. "It's not much, but it might give us a little buffer." Then he lay down, drawing her down with him, her back nestled against his chest, his arms enfolding her.

She'd read about Texas storms in Kent's book. But his prose had been so lyrical, his descriptions so thrilling, that she'd imagined the storms more like an exciting painting than a murderous explosion. Her rush of excitement faded as the noise of the storm drew nearer, leaving cold dread in its place.

Asher pulled the quilt over their heads, tucking it under their shoulders and pressing the material into the ground beneath them. If the situation hadn't been so terrifying, she might have found it pleasant, her body cradled into his.

Then the storm was upon them, a rush of pulsing, screaming, sucking wind. Tree roots cracked as they were torn from the earth. The wind tugged at the quilt, pulling it from under their legs, and then it was gone. Asher flung his body over hers to take the brunt of the storm.

In a single instant, she relived all her joys and sorrows, her regrets and her desires, and found her life lacking. Sadly, one didn't measure the quality of a life by the cups of tea poured for visitors and guests. Though she'd wanted to be daring, she had resisted, not wishing to follow in her mother's footsteps. And nothing in her life had ever called upon her to be brave. If she were to die . . . she would never know if she'd had those characteristics within her.

What else of life would she have missed?

But it was too late for anything but prayer, and that one the most simple of all. *Our Father. . . .*

Then the storm was gone.

They lay unmoving, waiting.

She tensed the muscles of her body in succession, feet to arms, to see if she was in one piece. He was so close she could feel his breath warm on her neck.

She opened her eyes, and Asher was studying her face. His eyes were a dark green, deep as a cavern, rich as a fine ore . . . and as inscrutable. If he were a smiling man, his would be the sort of face that made giddy debutantes swoon and giggle.

His hand rested on her shoulder, as if he would press her farther into the dirt if the danger had not passed.

"Are we alive?" she whispered, feeling relief rush through each cell of her body. Alive. Both of them. Together.

She noticed for the first time the long scar that ran along his cheek in front of his ear. Without thinking, she touched it, gently tracing the line of it down to his jaw. He mirrored her action, cradling her jaw in his palm. They searched each other's eyes, both knowing that the moment was precious, that life was precious. In that gaze, she met him as an equal, not hesitant or afraid, but daring as she had never been.

Unwilling to let the moment pass, she leaned toward him, stopping only when she could feel the warmth of his lips close, but not touching. She searched his eyes, but he only watched her, letting her choose. Refusing to wait or wonder, she closed the distance, pressing her lips against his.

It was pure reaction—they both knew it—to the fear and the excitement, joined with a joy of still being alive and, on her part, a spinster-wish to be more than she was. The kiss was perfect, sweet, and tender, then growing in intensity each time their lips pressed together.

When the kiss ended, her hand found his, neither of them willing to let the moment go. He sat up, surveying the area next to them, then rose, helping her out of the ditch and onto the road. The tornado had brought hail and wind, but little rain.

"It's cold," she said without thinking, as her breath misted white.

He placed his arm around her shoulders and pulled her body into his side.

They stood together, surveying the damage. Tree branches lay all around them, along with other debris, papers from a lawyer's office from a town some forty miles away, and a man's hat. But, other than a thick stick thrust through the carriage wall, the carriage itself, tucked against the hill, appeared relatively unscathed. None of the boxes or trunks appeared to be missing, a testament to Asher's extra care at tying them down.

"We were lucky," he said, nodding her attention to the distance where the damage was far more severe. There, trees lay toppled from their roots. Those still standing were entirely stripped of their remaining leaves. In the gaps where the trees used to be, the sky appeared a cold gray-blue.

"A twister's unpredictable. If you're right in its path, you'll be singing in St. Peter's choir unless you can get underground. But if you're out of its path—even by a hundred yards—it's as good as living in the next county." He paused, removing a leaf from her hair. The storm seemed to have made him garrulous.

Her hand still gripped his tight. She relaxed it, thinking Asher would release hers as well. But he didn't. Instead he turned to face her, his gaze meeting hers.

"That was a mighty fine kiss."

"I . . ." Suddenly shy, she forced herself not to look away. She struggled for words. "I don't typically kiss—I mean I've never kissed—I mean, not a man I've just met. I understand we're stranded, but . . ."

"I wouldn't call us stranded." He continued to study her face, his eyes smiling, even though his mouth hadn't yet figured out how.

His mouth, his lips, continued to invite her, and she felt herself rise on her toes. He pulled her into another kiss. This one spurred not by fear, or relief, but by pure desire. She kissed him in return, allowing herself another taste of him, his lips so sweet, and his embrace so thrilling. Her insides warmed to his touch, and she let herself ignore all the reasons why she shouldn't kiss him again.

But soon her internal monitor won over her fledgling desire. When she pulled back, he let her go.

"You could have hobbled the horses," she said, still somewhat dazed by their kisses.

"They deserved a fair chance of surviving. If we're lucky, they won't have gone far." He whistled once, twice, three times.

Eugenie half expected the horses to come galloping back over the rise, responding to his call as easily as she had to his kisses. But nothing happened.

She followed him to the coach. There, Asher pulled a box from under the seat, dislodging her book, which had been tucked safely on top of it. The book fell to the ground, narrowly missing a puddle. Grateful it hadn't been swept away with their quilt, she picked it up, cleaning its cover with her skirt, then clasping it to her chest.

Asher, watching, shook his head as if she were a strange creature. Then, opening his box, he loaded a revolver and shot into the air three times in quick succession.

"Why did you do that?" The cold bit through her clothes, and she tightened her jaw to keep her teeth from chattering.

"Well, we have to decide whether to walk or to wait." He opened the carriage door, his hand inviting her to enter. "But we should eat first, and there's no need to shiver out here when we have more blankets inside."

"Wait for what?" She stepped to the open carriage door, but she was too short to pull herself in neatly. Before she could ask for the stairs, Asher's strong hands encircled her waist, lifting her up. She slid across the seat, as he climbed in behind her.

"Horses." He pulled the door shut, then rolled up the carriage windows near him. She followed his lead with those on her side.

"I've never known a man to train his horses to *return* to gunshots. Isn't that dangerous?" She wanted to nestle close to him, to feel his warmth, but she kept her distance. Before she could consider kissing him again, she needed to know more of his character and opinions.

"I suppose we'll find out." He held out a heavy blanket. "This should warm you up. Surviving a storm usually leaves me plumb tuckered out."

"Tuckered?" She wrapped the blanket around her shoulders.

"Tired, exhausted, depleted." Asher stretched a second blanket out over their legs, his hand brushing her knee. "Fatigued, wearied, worn."

The excitement over, she felt exhaustion envelop her with each word.

"You sound like *Roget's Thesaurus.*" Shaking off the spell of his voice, she unlaced her boots, then curled her feet up under her.

"We had a copy when I was young. My brothers and I made a game of it, picking a word, then seeing who could remember the most synonyms." Asher's face shuttered. Silently he removed his gloves, then held his hand out for hers. She caught a glimpse of shiny, puckered skin on the backs of his hands. Old burns, and bad ones.

As he laid out their gloves carefully on the seat before them, she searched for some topic that could bring him back from his memories. "A thesaurus," she repeated. "And to think my mother wrote that you were a man of few words."

His barked laugh surprised and delighted her.

"Depends." He gave her a sly wink, warming the inside of her chest. "I have plenty to say to the right person."

Eugenie felt suddenly happy in his presence. Her mother—indiscreet on many topics—was tight-lipped where money was concerned, so Asher likely knew nothing about her inheritance.

"Besides, your mother's got enough words of her own." Asher lifted a basket from beneath the forward seat. "She doesn't need anyone else's, much less mine."

Eugenie laughed out loud. "Most people find conversation with my mother delightful."

"It can be. But it's rarely a conversation. Mostly your mother likes to have an audience." His fingers brushing hers, Asher handed Eugenie a packet of cotton tea towels all folded together.

"My uncle Ian says Lilly is happiest when she's holding court. All she needs is a few adoring admirers and someone to torment."

"Torment." He laughed, a full, deep laugh, and she liked the sound of it. "That's the perfect way to put it."

"Does she torment you?" Eugenie leaned forward, breathing in the enticing smells of Mrs. Jones's cookery.

"No, Lilly leaves me be. But she likes to *torment* my business partner." From the basket, Asher lifted out fat heavy-paper packets filled with various foodstuffs.

"Did he not pay her adequate court in the beginning?" Eugenie unfolded the cotton tea towels, keeping one and handing the other to Asher. "She does expect a certain amount of deference."

"Rafe finds your mother a curiosity." Opening the packets, Asher revealed slices of salt pork and venison roast, biscuits, butter, jam, and several thick slices of yellow pound cake.

"Lilly would hate that."

"Oh, she does, but Rafe makes the most of it." From the bottom of the basket, he removed several glass jars, their lids sealed with wax, and a single apple.

"What's a plum got to do with exhaustion?" Eugenie picked up the apple, wondering what Asher would think if she made a joke about Eve tempting Adam in the Garden of Eden.

"A plum?" Asher looked at the apple, confused.

"You said *plum* tuckered out." Eugenie set the apple on the seat. What was it about this man that made her wish to be daring? Perhaps she'd make the joke another time.

"Ah," he said, almost grinning. "*Plumb* is an adverb, not a fruit." He buttered a biscuit, then stuffed it with pork. "*Plumb* answers the question 'How?' as in 'How tuckered out are you?'" Eugenie watched his hands, their movements surprisingly elegant.

"An adverb?" She inspected one of the jars filled with liquid. Seeing tea leaves resting at the bottom, she broke the seal and drank deeply. "A thesaurus and a grammar book. Were those odd books for a boy on the frontier?"

"My father only allowed useful books in the house: the Bible, the *Farmer's Almanac,* and a set of Carey and Lea's *Encyclopedia Americana* he won in a poker game." With his toe, he tapped a box sitting underneath the seat in front of them. "Perhaps that's why I collect books for Mrs. Cockrell's circulating library when I travel."

"Mrs. Cockrell?" Eugenie, suddenly wary, studied his face for signs of affection but saw nothing in particular.

"She owns the St. Nicholas Hotel where your mother lodges." He placed the sandwich on one of the large linen tea towels and held both out to her. "She's our most famous citizen, owning the saw mill, the grist mill, and both the ferry and the bridge across the Trinity River."

"Would she mind if I read her books while we travel?" Eugenie accepted the sandwich, letting her fingers brush the back of his hand. The spark of energy was still there.

"I can't see why anybody'd mind." He leaned forward, filling another biscuit for them both.

The sound of thunder rolled across the sky, and Eugenie flinched.

"There's often a storm after a twister." Asher wiped the frost from the window to look out, then nodded to the magazines. "Why don't you find us some game to play while we wait? It'll take your mind off the storm."

"Not another tornado?" Eugenie wrapped her arms around her belly, as the rain pounded on the carriage roof.

"Not likely at this point, but I'll watch." Asher held out another biscuit, but Eugenie, suddenly no longer hungry, refused.

The thunder rolled closer, lightning flashing just a few seconds behind.

Eugenie's stomach twisted. She was uneasy but unwilling to show it, so she affected a light tone. "Tell me one book that has shaped how you view the world."

Asher studied her face, as if he'd never seen a creature like her. She added quickly, "We can discuss the weather and hide in ditches only so often before it fades as a form of entertainment."

"You are an odd woman." Asher shook his head.

Eugenie's heart deflated a bit. Jeremy had said as much oh-so-publicly at the Moreton ball when he'd broken their engagement. But, as Judith had taught her, she raised her chin and met Asher's criticism. "You are not the first to say it."

"Ah, but I might be the first to mean it as a compliment." His eyes never left her. "Few women—even those born here—would have weathered a tornado with as much sangfroid as you."

"I'm not sure which word in that sentence amuses me most," Eugenie quipped. "*Weathered* for an experience with weather or *sangfroid* from a Texas Ranger."

"We aren't all rogues and rustlers. Some of us have even read a book, once or twice, if the print's not too small and there are enough pictures to justify the time." He was teasing her. She could tell now, and it pleased her. Teasing suggested he had a regard for her "odd" mind.

"Then tell me what book you have found most significant?" Her heart felt lighter. "One with big enough print and plenty of illustrations to justify the reading, of course."

"If I agree, you must do the same in return. And neither of us may make fun of the other for their choice."

Eugenie nodded, wondering who had "made fun of" him in the past for his reading.

"Then I'll be honest with you. Until about five years ago, I would have said John Milton's *Paradise Lost*. But then a friend gave me a copy of Harriet Beecher Stowe's *Uncle Tom's Cabin*, and it has proved a book I can't forget."

"That's an odd pairing. Why *Paradise Lost*?" She leaned forward, intrigued. Perhaps he would prove more like Garrand Kent, after all. Someone she could trust with her ideas and hopes and dreams.

"It's all about ambition and authority, free will and human love. Satan wants to rule, even if the only place he can rule is hell. God gives Adam and Eve free will, even if it's the free will to make the wrong choice. But, in the end, Adam chooses the love and companionship of Eve over living in paradise. The two leave Eden hand in hand—'the world all before them'—to make their way in the wilderness together."

A flash of lightning drew her attention to the window.

"'*To lose thee were to lose myself . . . Thou to me are all things under heaven, all places thou,*'" Asher recited in almost a whisper, but with such great feeling that Eugenie felt the sentiment resonate deep in the center of her chest. Sadly, when she looked to him, he was looking out the window, not at her.

"And Stowe?" She shifted the conversation, hoping to hide that she'd thought he was speaking to her, not quoting Adam's speech to Eve.

"Though Stowe examines slavery, at the heart of her book, she addresses the same issues as Milton. Some settlers believe themselves to be new Adams in a new Eden, with authority to rule the land and the peoples already in it, and the ambition to match." He looked away from the window directly at her. "They build their prosperity on the backs of the many. And our only hope of redemption is in loving our neighbors."

"Stowe says that?" She studied his face, so honest, so open.

"In a way."

When she'd asked what book mattered to him, she'd meant it to be a game, a diversion from the weather. But his answers revealed the soul of a just man. And if that were the case, she owed him a glimpse into her own.

She'd intended to choose an unobjectionable book, something a bit witty, a bit wise, the sort of book one could have as a favorite, without revealing too much of herself or her heart. As a spinster, she'd gained the privilege of telling the truth. But too often the price of her honesty was loneliness. She hadn't had a friend outside of family or servants in a long time.

What could be the disadvantage of being honest to Asher? He seemed to have the makings of a friend, but if she were mistaken in his character, it would be only the loss of a brief acquaintance, not long lamented. If he disliked her choice of book or her reasons, their journey might be uncomfortable, despite their promises. But the journey would end, and they would part, and soon after she'd leave Texas forever. That allowed her a certain freedom. She decided for truth, perhaps even for a little challenge.

"Since you altered the game to choose *two* books, I'd like to choose an *author* rather than a single work."

"It's our game." He winked. "We make the rules. We change them."

"Then I choose the poet Elizabeth Barrett Browning. Her works praise women who choose their own paths, even when those paths lead outside of the roles society has established for them. Yet she doesn't exclude the possibility of love, believing it to result not from choice or habit, but from a mystical connection of souls."

He said nothing, merely studying her face, his own unreadable. Suddenly uncomfortable, she hurried on, "By that I mean—*Browning* means—that our souls are winged, and two humans fall in love when the tips of their souls' wings touch. "

"Ah, yes: '*How do I love thee, let me count the ways.*' "

He quoted the first line of Browning's Sonnet 43. But instead of being pleased, she felt disappointed. It was the one line everyone knew and quoted, even those who had never read a line of Browning. If Asher thought—like them—that the line was a bit of poetic fluff and romantic gibberish, how could she explain what Browning meant to her? She looked away, watching the rain. When she looked back at him, he was still watching her with those deep green eyes that caught her breath.

After a moment's pause, he spoke, " '*I love you to the depth and breadth and height that my soul can reach when feeling out of sight . . . for the ends of being and ideal grace.*' " It was the next sentence of the poem.

Her surprise mingled with a sort of joy. She hesitantly, cautiously, quoted the next line: " '*I love thee to the level of every day's Most quiet need, by sun and candlelight.*' " She studied his face for a reaction.

" '*I love thee freely, as men strive for Right.*' " His eyes never left hers.

" '*I love thee purely, as they turn from Praise.*' " She paused, and the coach grew quiet.

Neither finished the poem. The intensity of his gaze caught her breath. In that silent moment, feeling the beat of her heart quicken, and the arc of attraction pulse between them, she could believe that the wing-tips of their souls touched.

He reached out and brushed a fallen curl behind her ear.

After a few moments, she found her voice again.

"I first read Barrett Browning for her love poems. But her political works changed the way I saw the world: her opposition to child labor in 'Cry of the Children,' to the repression in the corn laws in 'Cry of the Human,' and to slavery in the 'Runaway Slave at Pilgrim's Point.' She encouraged me to act against injustice, though I must admit my first efforts weren't quite successful."

He waited, encouraging her with a nod.

"I placed my pin money in the parish poor box." She paused, uncertain if she could confess it all. But his smile—his first real smile—encouraged her. "And, at twelve, I rejected the comfort of my bedroom to sleep in the barn . . . until one of the grooms discovered me there, and my guardian called me to his study."

"He told you that nice young women of good family do not sleep in barns."

"No. He told me that I changed nothing for those in need by sleeping in a barn, and if I wanted to help others, I should do something useful. I'd never been useful, so I asked my great-aunt Judith to help me." She smiled at the memory. "Judith led me to the library. 'If you wish to do good, Genie, you must first understand the problem, what has caused it and what solutions others have tried. Only then can you find a path that effects real change.' And she created a shelf of books for me to read."

"She called you Jeannie." Her nickname in his voice sounded like a caress.

"She did." Eugenie smiled. "And over Lilly's quite strong objection." She wiped away unexpected tears. "Forgive me: I'm sometimes still caught off guard by her loss."

"Grief does that: lets you go months enjoying happy memories, then stabs you in the heart and belly when you least expect it." His hand found hers, squeezed it, then withdrew.

"I learned everything from her . . . everything important at least."

"And she gave you books." He led the conversation to a less tender subject.

"And I read." She caught her breath. "And I asked questions, and eventually I found ways to be useful."

"Why did your family wait so long to teach you about the political conditions of England?"

"Politics, in the home of a duke, was in the very air. But Lilly didn't send me to live in England until I was eight or so." Suddenly she felt shy, on display, as if she had said far too much. "You must excuse me: I've made an intellectual game something entirely too personal."

"Being *stranded*"—he winked again—"in the rain on a deserted road encourages confidences. It feels too easily like you're in another world, and that's fine, as long as you don't forget to keep watch."

At that moment, thunder and lightning boomed and flashed together.

"Ah, it's upon us now." Asher brushed the fog from the window. Suddenly the rain changed to a torrent, falling in sheets down the glass and beating heavy against the roof of the carriage. The carriage swayed under the wind and rain.

To regain some emotional distance, Eugenie picked up the newspaper from Dallas, dated the previous week. The headline read INDIAN DEPREDATIONS! Disturbed, she read the first notice—"*Patrick Murphy of Young County is offering a $1000 reward for the recovery and restoration of his Sister, recently carried* *into captivity by the Indians"*—then the second, *"In Cameron County, the Cortinas band swear to hang every American, man, woman, or child."*

"It's only rain; it should pass us soon." Asher stared out the window, then reached for the packet of pound cake.

"Buchanan and Cameron Counties. How far are they from Dallas?" Eugenie asked.

"Buchanan is four, maybe five, days by coach; Cameron, though, is past San Antone, at the tip-end of Texas. Getting there would take the better part of two months. Why?" He spread butter then jam on the cake.

She held out the paper, pointing at the stories with her finger. "Are these cause for concern?"

He read carefully, shaking his head. "Most newsmen just want to sell a paper. They entertain a little, frighten a little. But in everyday life, newspapers are little good against a prairie fire, or a snakebite, or a herd of cattle spooked and stompeding."

"Unless they also *inform* you how to stop a prairie fire, how to treat a snakebite, and how to survive a *stampede*." She was disappointed. After their earlier conversation about books, she'd expected a more appreciative response. Even so, his slow half smile caught her breath.

"I suppose that English cattle stampede in pretty English accents." He tossed a bit of cake into the air and caught it in his mouth. "But spook a couple hundred head of Texas cattle, and them critters will stomp all the way to Kansas City." Something about his manner—his drop into a chummy Texas slang—rankled. *Pretty English accent, my foot.*

"Mr. Graham." She infused her voice with Judith-taught steel. "While spook, critters, and stompedes offer me a delightful glimpse into a Texas vernacular, I am not some sweet young thing unable to bear hard truths. As far as I can tell, we *are* stranded miles from any city, without ready help against Indian depredations or Cortinas. Do I have cause for concern?"

He sighed. "Depends on which group captures you. This land first belonged to the Native peoples, then the Spanish came, then the French, and now the English. So, it's a constant tug-of-war. Drawn by the promise of rich land, settlers encroach into Indian territory, and the Native peoples push back with various levels of hostility."

"Show me." She held Kent's book open. Its frontispiece was a lithographed map of Texas. As she'd read, she'd penciled in the names of more than twenty Native peoples over the places associated with them. "Which should I be wary of?"

Asher, putting down his cake, took the book from her hands, turning the cover over so he could read the spine. " '*Texas: Her Land, Her Peoples,*'" he read aloud. "Another greenhorn visitor, telling all sorts of questionable stories, I bet."

"No, the author is one of your native sons, a Texian, he calls himself. I find his work enthralling."

"A Texian? Not likely." Asher examined the book more closely. "Only those of us who lived under both Mexico and the Republic can call themselves that. My family came soon after the Old Three Hundred, the original settlers under Stephen F. Austen. And I've never heard of any Garrand Kent, though there was a Garrand and a Kent at the Alamo."

"We can debate later whether Mr. Kent is or isn't a Texian. For now, I wish to know what sort of danger we might be in."

"If I say you are in no more danger than you would be walking the streets of London at night, you won't be satisfied, will you?" His voice mirrored the firmness of her own.

"Already you understand me quite well." She tried to ignore the way his fingers caressed the leather binding of Kent's book. "I had trusted that Mr. Kent's assessment of the state of Texas was a good one. But if he isn't a reputable guide, I have only you . . . or the newspapers."

He sighed and pointed to a spot on the map. "Buchanan County is here, west and north of Dallas. Until six months ago, four peaceable tribes—the Caddo, Anadarko, Waco, and Tonkawa—farmed there on the Brazos reservation."

"What happened six months ago?" She was grateful that he had agreed to answer. It signaled that in a way he respected her and her concerns.

"Settlers farther west were being attacked by the Comanche and Kiowa." His finger traced a circle around the western territories of those groups. "But to the Anglo settlers, one Indian is pretty much the same as another. They demanded that the Brazos reservation be closed, and its inhabitants moved to the Oklahoma Indian Territory here. But the Comanche refuse to move from their hereditary lands, and they are fierce warriors, feared even by the other Native peoples. You wouldn't want to be captured by them."

"What about the Cortinas?"

He laughed, though his voice quickly turned serious again. "Cortinas isn't a people, it's a man. Juan Cortina. But whatever that newspaper says, many in Brownsville call him a hero for fighting to protect those who have been falsely accused." He pointed to the tip-end of Texas by the Gulf of Mexico. "And he has the loyalty of a small army, all men who believe the Treaty of Hidalgo gave the land south of the Nueces to Mexico. Rip Ford's men are heading there now to keep the peace." His face grew pensive.

"Rip Ford. Mr. Jones said you were joining his Rangers later this month." She wanted him to say it wasn't true. Already she hated the thought of him dead or wounded.

"I haven't decided." He started to hand Kent's book back to her, then stopped. "Books like this one underestimate the dangers, while the newspapers overblow them. The truth is this: men may be dangerous, but so is this land. We have wild spaces with so few people, that if you needed help to survive, you'd likely die before you found it. Predators of all kinds, both animal and man. Weather that changes four times between sunrise and sunset." Asher studied her face. "It's a land for the brave and the reckless, not for the faint of heart."

She felt her cheeks warm. "I have never been accused of being reckless or faint of heart, though I've never been called brave either."

"A fearful woman doesn't leap from a coach to free unfamiliar horses. She doesn't leave her home to travel alone to a new land."

"You needed the help, and I didn't travel alone." Eugenie folded her hands in her lap. "The maid who accompanied me from England to Boston took one look at your new land and demanded to be sent back to London. In Boston I hired the one who refused to leave Jefferson today."

"Yet *you* didn't turn back. Why?" he quizzed her. But he'd answered her questions. It was only fair to answer his.

"Since my mother isn't well enough to travel on her own, I have come to retrieve her from her latest scrape and return her to her family." Eugenie kept her voice matter-of-fact, refusing to let him hear any hint of resentment or annoyance.

"Your mother isn't well?" Asher sounded surprised. "What scrape?"

"My mother believes herself a revolutionary, but in truth she's an enthusiast, chasing cause after cause. This time, she fell in with a colony of Swiss, Belgian, and French socialists. They wished to enact the ideals of the French Revolution, starting with full equality of the sexes in every realm, political, social, and even sexual." The moment she said the word *sexual,* she wished she hadn't, not with Asher sitting so close by. She hurried on, hoping he wouldn't notice the word. "But their colony has failed, and now that she's hurt, she wants a companion to carry her back to our family."

"Hurt," Asher repeated, searching Eugenie's eyes. He turned his attention somewhat abruptly to repacking the food basket.

"The La Réunion colony's ideals were less at fault than the weather."

"The weather?" Eugenie paused, trying to determine if he was teasing her again. But he seemed perfectly serious.

"The last year that the La Réunion colony tried to grow crops, a long winter delayed planting until late spring, then a devastatingly hot summer burned everything to the ground." He shrugged. "They came here as craftsmen, but they needed to be ranchers and farmers. Perhaps, given better weather, they could have learned to be both."

"I can't imagine Lilly as a farmer," Eugenie said, almost to herself.

"She makes delicious jams." Asher offered her another jar of tea, seeming to wish to change the subject. But Eugenie waved it away.

"Makes? Jams?" Eugenie closed her eyes. She had agreed to travel with this man—this handsome Ranger—largely on her mother's recommendation—and he clearly didn't know her mother at all. Her fingers moved to her lips—and she'd kissed him.

"I like her prickly pear jam best."

Eugenie opened one eye, stared at him, then closed it. A prickly pear. Of course Asher-of-the-almost-smile would like *prickly* pears. She opened both eyes and stared into his. "What exactly is a prickly pear?"

"The fruit of a cactus. In the spring, I'll bring you one." Asher finished packing the basket. "Lilly's just one of the colonists who moved across the river to Dallas, bringing their professions with them. Scientists and architects, coach- and watch-makers, jewelers, milliners, lithographers, and even dancing in-structors, Dallas needs them all if it ever hopes to rival Galveston or San Antonio."

"And my mother's profession is jam-making," she said flatly, still not quite believing it.

"Jams, and she teaches art. Her studio is quite popular, and one afternoon a week, she teaches those who can't afford lessons."

"I'm lost in a world gone utterly mad." Eugenie couldn't decide whether laughter was an appropriate response. "Lilly has become a jam-making, art-teaching doyenne."

"You always call your mother Lilly," Asher observed.

"She prefers it. 'No society of true equals can allow titles,' she says. Of course, the family suspects she merely wishes to conceal that she has a daughter as old as I am."

"She did lead me to believe you were . . . somewhat younger."

Eugenie felt her stomach drop. She knew she wasn't the sweet young thing that most men looked for in a wife. Certainly, Jeremy's new heiress-bride was barely out of the schoolroom. And she'd long ago given up the idea that a man might find her attractive for anything other than her fortune. But something in her interactions with Asher—their kisses, his glances that warmed her skin, their shared appreciation of Sonnet 43—had allowed her for a moment to forget her age.

"You said we would decide to wait or walk after we ate. Should we decide now?" She knew her voice sounded cold, but she couldn't help it.

Asher rubbed the fog from the window glass and looked out. "I'd hoped by now someone would have come by. But at this point, we should walk to the next town, hire some horses, and come back for the coach."

"And my trunks?"

"You *could* drag them behind you. But I'd leave them here until we return."

Eugenie imagined herself, hunched over, pulling one of her trunks down the road by a rope over her shoulder. "I'll need to collect some things before we go. But what of your supplies and your other cargo, will you drag or leave them?"

"It's cold now, but in a couple of hours, when the sun sets, it'll fall well below freezing." He loaded two revolvers. "We'll simply have to hope we return before someone happens on the carriage."

"How far is it to the next town?"

"It's a piece." Asher tucked the guns in his belt.

"Is a *piece* a measure of distance?" She'd enjoyed their earlier teasing over words, but somehow she'd lost her heart for it. Now she merely wanted to get to Dallas, whatever it took.

"I think of a *piece* as a distance somewhat more than a mile, but less than five."

"What do you call a distance five miles or more?"

"Well, that's a *fer* piece. But those are just my own estimates. I can't say they hold true for anyone else."

"If it's just a piece to the next town, we could walk there in an hour or two, rent a team, then be back here before sunset." She gathered her reticule, her book, and the apple he'd left out of the basket.

"Let's hope they have enough horses to rent us a team. Knowing Trudy, she's already run halfway to the Oklahoma territories."

"You named a horse Trudy?" She almost laughed. "Not something strong and masculine?"

"It seemed apt. When I was young, Mrs. Trudy ran the closest school; she was quiet and easygoing, until you crossed her, then terrifying. Rain's stopped." Asher opened the carriage door and climbed out. A gust of frigid air blew through the cabin. "Do you want anything from your trunks? A heavy cloak, perhaps?"

She nodded yes, following him out of the carriage and pointing out which trunk to untie.

He climbed up on the coach, but somehow the joy had gone out of watching him. They were clearly close to the same age, but as single men aged, they preferred to court girls younger and younger still. Even with her fortune, she'd garnered less and less attention as she'd matured . . . until Jeremy. She shook off the memory.

She walked down the road, hoping someone—some wagon or coach—would come by and offer to carry them to the next town, but the world was silent.

A hint of movement in a stand of trees some fifty feet away caught her attention. She could barely make out the figure of a tall man wearing a turban, then the light shifted, and he disappeared.

Pretending she hadn't seen anything—had she?—she returned to the carriage, walking slowly and stopping to look at things along the way. If a man was in the woods, she didn't want him to know he'd been seen.

"Asher?" she asked softly when she'd reached the side of the carriage.

"Yes." His head was down as he worked the rope loose. "There!" He dropped Eugenie's small valise to the ground.

"What sorts of clothes would a Comanche warrior wear?"

"This time of year, a hide coat, hide boots, and hair in two long braids with a single feather." Asher looked up, surveying the woods and the fields around them.

She looked with him, but saw nothing.

Had all their talk of Native peoples simply caused her to create one out of light and shadow? She looked around again, this time more anxiously. If someone intended them no harm, why wouldn't he come forward?

"What of colorful beaded cloth?"

"Get back in the carriage, Miss Charpentier . . . slowly."

Chapter 3

Her full name, more than his instruction, formed a cold, hard lump in the pit of her stomach. She moved to the door of the carriage, her heart suddenly beating hard.

If she were taken captive, would her mother offer a ransom? Would anyone ever know what had happened to her? First a tornado, and now Indian depredations. She'd come so far not to reach the dusty village of Dallas.

At the door of the carriage, she pulled the stairs out to climb in.

Asher leaned down, appearing to struggle with part of the rigging. When she looked up, she realized his revolver sat next to his hand. Pitching his voice low, he asked, "What did you see?"

"I'm not certain. It could have merely been an illusion. He seemed to be wearing a turban."

"Turban? You're sure?" Asher's whole body relaxed.

"I'm not certain of anything."

He climbed down from the coach to stand beside her. "John? I know it's you. Come out!"

A young boy, around nine or ten, ebony-skinned and dressed

as a ranch hand, ran out from behind the trees. The boy called out to Asher, "John says my grandfather may be from Africa, but I'm getting almost as good at hiding as any Cherokee." The boy disappeared back into the shadows.

In his place, a tall man, dressed almost like the Westerners she'd grown used to seeing in Jefferson, stepped into the light. His turban was decorated with feathers and stickpins. A wide colorful swath of beaded cloth was wound around his midriff. In one hand, he carried a rifle; the other hand was hidden behind his back. He stopped at the edge of the trees, waiting.

Asher took her hand. He had not yet put back on his gloves, and his flesh against hers felt thrilling, even though she knew it shouldn't.

"You're frightening my passenger, Ware," Asher called out, and the young boy reemerged from the darkness, grinning.

The turbaned man handed Ware something, and the boy ran forward, holding the reins for Asher's team. The horses followed behind obediently.

John and Ware joined Asher, embracing warmly.

"Eugenie, meet my eldest brother, John."

John bowed from the waist and brushed the back of her hand with his lips. An oddly European action for a man sporting feathers.

"John?" Eugenie felt confused by the ordinary Englishness of the name. She studied the two men's faces for a family resemblance.

"Our father had an odd sense of humor," Asher said flatly.

"Our father was originally from Belgium," John explained. "The name my mother gave me—Yanasa—sounded to him like his native Jan, so . . . John."

She studied Asher with renewed interest. "Are you also a Native?"

"I'm native to Texas—as are all my brothers."

"Asher pretends not to understand you," John intervened.

"We are all half brothers. Like Sam Houston, our father lived among the Cherokee people in Tennessee as an adopted son. When Houston became President of the Republic, many Cherokee moved to Texas, our father and his first wife, my mother, among them."

"I see," she said, not seeing very clearly at all.

"Our father had three wives and a son from each marriage," Asher broke in.

John picked up the story. "My mother divorced our father and took me to live with her people outside Dallas. Asher's mother—a widow from New Orleans—died when he was two. My mother reared us both."

"What of your other brother? Is he in Texas as well?"

John raised his eyebrow at Asher, asking a silent question, and Asher nodded.

"I've spoken of Rafe already; you'll meet him in Dallas," Asher explained.

"The business partner Lilly torments is your brother?"

"Our father married his third wife while his second was still living. With one family in Dallas and the other in San Antonio, he never intended his sons to meet. But by luck or chance or fate, Rafe, John, and I all served in the same Ranger troop, along with our other business partner, Ware's father, Ben Payne."

"So you are brothers *and* brothers-at-arms? Does Rafe's mother know?"

"Even if she did, Dona Julia is a very devout woman. She would never admit it, and we keep the secret for her sake."

"I will not break your trust." Eugenie was surprised and touched that Asher trusted her. She wanted to ask more questions but couldn't imagine how to frame them.

Ware, having tied the horses to the coach, demanded to be noticed.

"Eugenie, please meet our youngest cattle drover, Ware."

"I'm not just a drover; we are all partners," Ware announced, proudly.

"Partners?" Eugenie said with only a little surprise.

"Yep," Ware said with a smug grin. "Asher, my parents and me, Rafe, and John. When we get near to Dallas, I can show you our place."

"Your place? Is that the same as a ranch?" She found the young man delightful, a mix of childhood bravado and seriousness.

Ware thought before answering, "It's like a ranch but somewhat bigger."

"Like a coyote is bigger than a fox?" Eugenie recognized Asher's influence already.

"Never thought of it that way, but I suppose so." Ware tilted his head in concentration. "The dog that lives behind the farrier's shed growled at me so much, I was sure she was a coyote. But she was simply protecting her pups. Asher's promised me a black pup when we return to Dallas. Perhaps he'll get you one too."

As Eugenie talked with Ware about his anticipated pet, Asher and John stepped to the side of the wagon. She could hear their voices pitched low, but not their words. A few moments later they rejoined her and Ware.

"Fallen trees block this road two miles down. John says we can move the trees enough to pass by, but we'll lose time and tire the horses. Or we can take a second route he's scouted: the rain passed it by, so the roads are dry. But it will require us to sleep on the trail."

"You are the guide. How could I have an opinion as to which road to take?"

"I don't know," he said, giving one of the half grins that flipped her stomach, but she forced herself to ignore it. "You are a formidable woman, and I thought it would be best to ask your preference."

* * *

Within minutes, Asher, John, and Ware had hitched the horses, who seemed happy to be back in their traces. While the men strapped Eugenie's luggage back to the carriage, Eugenie spoke to each of the horses, especially Trudy, scratching the horse's neck until she found that spot where Trudy's lip drooped in pleasure.

Within minutes, they were back on the road. Asher and John shared the driving, while Ware sat like a prince on the luggage on top of the coach.

Eugenie traveled in the coach alone, left to her own thoughts. She relived each moment of her trip with Asher, from their first meeting to the tornado to their kisses. Before her lips had found his, she'd never believed that two souls could touch.

But whatever attraction she felt for him, she couldn't trust it. Asher had admitted she was older than he'd expected. To him, it likely was a turn of phrase, or even an observation about how Lilly manipulated words as well as people. But for Eugenie it was a necessary reminder of Jeremy's cold assessment of her shortcomings: "I can describe my fiancée in six words, boys: plain, bookish, dull, opinionated, old, and . . . rich, boys, rich as Croesus." She'd misjudged Jeremy—or rather she'd judged him on the face he'd chosen to show her—and she would not make that mistake again. She would be suspicious, where before she'd been trusting.

Asher Graham might be handsome and clever, but he was still rough and tumble, with ways more suited to life on the frontier than the drawing room. She would reserve her affections for someone like Garrand Kent, a man who could navigate both the land and the niceties of social interaction and whose writings showed to be wise, witty, and kind.

A tap at the window interrupted her reverie.

Startled, she jumped to see Ware, hanging down from the top of the coach, pressing his face to the cold glass. A wide smile spread across his face; clearly, half the fun was shocking her.

Her sad thoughts interrupted, she picked up Kent's *Texas,* intending to read. Yet somehow every page reminded her of Asher. She set the book aside, but the scenery through the window had lost its appeal.

Remembering the box of books for the circulating library, she pulled it out. When in London, she'd spent her happiest childhood hours at a bookstore called the African's Daughter. The owner, Constance Equiano, had been her grandmother Sophia's dear friend and Eugenie's favorite tutor. The daughter of bestselling author and former slave Olaudah Equiano, Constance had taken her father's abolitionist legacy seriously. Her shop had for almost forty years been a center for radical liberal thought, most recently encouraging women to begin the fight for suffrage. Eugenie had learned to think broadly under Constance's tutelage, and she hoped that the books Asher had collected would give her a glimpse into his mind.

Sadly, the contents of the box were a hodgepodge, telling her nothing at all of Asher's interests.

On top were a pile of magazines, and she amused herself by imagining who would read each one. Godey's *Lady's Book* would be for the young miss about to enter her first season—did Dallas have such a thing? *Harper's New Monthly Magazine* for the new resident wishing to remain connected to the world outside Texas. The *Atlantic Monthly* for the elderly lawyer, lonely for intelligent conversation. The suffragette magazine the *Lily* for a middle-aged widow no longer concerned with public opinion, *Scientific American* for the local school headmaster—Dallas was big enough for a school, wasn't it?

But her interest in the game quickly faded, and she set the magazines aside to see what else might be in the box.

Underneath the magazines were a collection of books for young children. She studied each book carefully, trying to imagine how the local schoolmaster or mistress would use it to teach. The fattest of the books, Jacob Abbott's *Rollo Learning to Read*, surprisingly wasn't about learning to read at all. Instead the book offered a series of stories on a variety of topics intended to encourage practice in reading. She read one or two but found the pictures more interesting than the text. She was about to close the book when she noticed the opening lines to the story of 'Contrary Charles':

"Do you know what a contrary boy is? He is one who is never satisfied with what he has, but always wants something different."

Before Jeremy, she would have thought that an accurate description of Lilly. But after, she'd wondered if she were the contrary one.

She leaned her head back against the carriage wall and shut her eyes.

She hadn't loved Jeremy, not in any way that mattered. But as a woman longing for a family of her own and with few prospects who weren't fortune-hunters, Eugenie had thought they would suit. He'd appeared to be steady and responsible, if a bit tedious and proud. And Judith—ever-perceptive Judith— had liked him. Eugenie needed no other recommendation.

Only Lilly had seen through him. She'd disliked Jeremy immediately, and he her. As Eugenie's courtship progressed, Lilly's interactions with Jeremy increasingly bordered on the uncivil. Jeremy had explained away the problem in flattering terms: Lilly needed to be admired, and he admired only Eugenie. For once shy Eugenie found herself the center of a handsome man's attention, while her vibrant mother sat in the shadows.

Lilly's note on leaving for Texas had ruined it all. Had Lilly enumerated all of Jeremy's faults, Eugenie would have shaken her head over the list and ignored it. Instead Lilly said only, "He will bring you grief." No explanations, no justifications.

The sentence slipped into Eugenie's heart like the slender blade of a penknife.

Her uncles had already investigated Jeremy, so Eugenie made her own inquiries. Using the resources available to a woman—the testimony of maids, servants, and shopkeepers—she discovered everything she didn't want to know. After that, it was easy to make him want to break their engagement, though she hadn't expected him to choose the season's best-attended ball for his announcement.

No, she hadn't loved him, and except for the public nature of the scandal, she had barely missed him. But he'd cost her Judith.

Judith, more her mother than Lilly ever was.

She should have seen the signs: the hesitant look, the forgotten reticule, the repeated question. But for more than a year, she had been too caught up in Jeremy's attentions. Not until Judith, confused, started calling her Lilly, did Eugenie realize how much she'd already lost. And then Judith was gone.

After Jeremy's deception and Judith's loss, all Eugenie's expectations of what her life would be like disappeared. She was left with only a bone-deep sadness. She'd learned to live with the sorrow, never confronting it directly, fearing that if she did—if she let herself feel it, even for a moment—she might never find her way out of the darkness again. But in the quiet safety of the carriage, she let herself touch the edge of that pain, and five thousand miles from home, she finally let herself cry.

A long time later, when she brushed away her tears, she considered the question from a different angle: if she couldn't be satisfied in England, could she expect to feel any differently in Texas?

She closed Rollo's book, wondering if Asher had brought the book for Ware, and if the young boy knew how to read well enough to enjoy it.

Under the children's books, she found the sorts of books she'd expected for a lending library—recent British novels by the Brontë sisters, Charles Dickens, and Anthony Trollope alongside American works by Herman Melville, Nathaniel Hawthorne, and Lydia Maria Child. A thin volume of Lydia Sigourney's pious, devotional poems fit her expectations of a Western town's taste. But who in Dallas wanted to read Margaret Fuller's *Woman in the Nineteenth Century*? If the books were those Asher had chosen himself, he had a wide, eclectic, and even odd taste. No, Mrs. Cockrell and the other subscribers must have given him a list.

Once the box became merely a collection of books rather than an insight into Asher's mind, she lost interest. She was about to choose a book to read, when, underneath all the other books, she found a package wrapped in brown paper and tied separately with twine. She ran her finger along the package's edge. More books. But why separate them from the others?

Curious, she carefully unwrapped the books. She knew them all from Constance's bookshop, and she greeted each one as an old friend. *Narrative of the Life of Frederick Douglass, An American Slave*, written by Douglass himself, published over a decade before to great acclaim both in the US and abroad; William Wells Brown's *Clotel, or the President's Daughter*, a novel imagining the tragic lives of Thomas Jefferson's fictional slave daughters; and a book of poetry by Frances Ellen Watkins Harper.

Eugenie touched the spine of each book reverently. She knew that relations between the races were tense in the States. She knew that many thought that a war was coming, one that would pit the Southern states against the Northern. But somehow the sequestering of books by African-Americans into their own packet disturbed her. Had Asher done it? And why?

Carefully she wrapped the books back up and returned them to the bottom of the box.

Picking up Margaret Fuller's radical call for equality, she began to read.

The new road led them through land less populated, and John stayed with them, offering another set of eyes and hands. On the new road, the travelers quickly fell into a routine. Each day they would rise to hard bread and tack, then start their travels, riding two or three hours, followed by an hour to water, feed, and rest the team. In the middle of the day, they would rest for several hours—Asher called it their *siesta*—then return to the road, traveling another two or three, before stopping again.

They would travel this way from dawn until dusk, able to cover in ten hours around fifteen to twenty miles a day. With each stop, Ware and John prepared food over the fire, and Asher saved the coals for the foot warmers in the carriage. At night, she would sleep in the carriage, curled under heavy blankets, with Ware—her self-appointed protector—stretched out in the gutter between the seats. Asher and John remained outside near the fire, alternating between sleep and keeping watch.

On the third day, she surprised the men by asking if she could ride sometimes on the driver's seat, and they began to take turns. Sometimes she and Asher would ride together, other times she and John. Ware almost always rode on the roof behind them, adding his own quaint commentary to their conversation. When after several more days Eugenie asked if she could drive the carriage, the men devoted themselves to teaching her how to read the road and the horses on it. It wasn't exactly like driving her uncle's curricle, but she quickly adapted to the new challenge.

She soon discovered that John was a natural storyteller. He entertained her for hours with stories of training as a lawyer and a diplomat under the charismatic Sam Houston. He alternated his stories of strange Dallas court cases with fantastic

tales of Texas Kent's book hadn't included. The headless horseman of the mustangs, believed to be the restless ghost of a mur-
dered cattle rustler; the wild woman of Navidad who could slip
in and out of houses, stealing food and supplies, without the
families or their dogs ever waking; and the secret gold of the
Guadalupe Mountains. John made her laugh as often as he made
her cry.

Asher filled in her education with more useful knowledge,
telling her about the distinct geographical regions of Texas: the
steamy swamps and timber forests in the east; the sand hills and
dunes of the southern coast; the tall grass plains of the north;
the arid deserts of the far west; and the majestic mountain region of the southwest. His stories were more humble than
John's, focused on the land and the people and animals in it.
But somehow his quiet stories and his rich sonorous voice kept
her riveted.

Every time they rode together, he made her feel like the
world contained only the two of them. And yet, at the same
time, he was never inattentive to his team or his surroundings.
He was a rare man, kind, interesting, gentle, and passionate,
and she looked forward to sitting beside him as she had looked
forward to little else for years.

But when they asked her to reciprocate with stories of England, she chose carefully. To hide her wealth, she told stories of
living with her widowed uncle as his housekeeper or of helping
the ladies of the Muses' Salon—her grandmother's club—with
their various schemes and projects.

All her stories were true, but what they suggested of her circumstances was utterly a lie. She was no poor relation, but an
heiress with money and land of her own. She regretted her deception, but justified it, by reminding herself that soon she
would return to England and never see him again. The thought
hurt her heart and her conscience more than she cared to admit.

Though she warmed under each man's tutelage, she felt

Asher's praise and attention most deeply. Each night at the fire-side, when he brought her a dish of whatever he and John had cooked and his hand brushed hers, she wished that the trip could last more than just a fortnight.

Some nights they would sit wrapped in blankets by the dying fire, and she and Asher would trace the constellations, making up new ones to go with the old and giving them all stories. She'd wanted her trip to be an adventure, giving her memories to treasure during the solitary winter nights in her future English village. And somehow, without her saying it, Asher seemed to understand.

By the end of the first week, the Texas landscape had changed dramatically. No longer the pine forests and swamps in the easternmost part of the state, the land in front of them was mostly flat, having been largely converted to farm and ranch land by the settlers. Too late to see the crops in the fields, she imagined what the fields would look like covered with the many wildflowers that Kent's book and Asher had described. In other places, the grasses still stood so tall that they reached almost to the top of the carriage.

During their journey, Ware was John's constant companion, making it impossible to ask the boy if he wished her to help him read. Four days out of Dallas, however, John rode on ahead, saying he would meet up with them near Ware's home. Even though they had only a few days left on the road, Eugenie believed a boy as clever and intelligent as Ware could learn to read quickly.

After their siesta, she removed the box of books from the carriage and placed it on the ground, calling Ware to her side. Seeing the box, the boy's face grew eager. Pleased with herself for broaching the subject, she removed *Rollo Learning to Read* from the box and held it out.

Ware backed away. "Have you read that?" the boy asked, looking horrified.

"I was hoping we might read it together." She smiled encouragingly.

"Isn't there anything more interesting in the box?"

She picked up the other children's books and held them out. Ware leaned forward to examine the spines, then pulled back, shaking his head. "I'd rather not."

She felt stymied. "There's some lovely pictures." She opened the book, hoping to engage the boy in the pictures, then encourage him to read the text. But Ware kept his distance.

Asher came up behind her and took the books from her hands. Returning them to the box, he removed the small packet tied with twine and held it out to Ware. "I was hoping to keep these for your Christmas gift, but there's no harm in you having them now. You would have discovered them soon enough anyway."

Ware, pleased, clasped the packet to his chest.

"You'll like the poetry," Asher said, squeezing the boy's shoulder affectionately. "While we're on the road, make sure to read in the carriage. Better to avoid trouble than to chase it."

Asher turned to her, his face amused. "Ware's our prodigy: he learned to read at three, how to brand at five, and this year how to drive cattle at nine."

"Asher says when I'm older, I can go to Harvard College." Ware had already unwrapped the books and was looking through them.

"I thought you wanted to be a cowhand when you were older." She was a little bewildered. She hadn't imagined Ware as one of the possible recipients for the books.

Ware shook his head as if she were dim. "I'm a cowhand *now*. When I'm older, I want to be a judge."

"A judge?"

The boy's face turned serious. "My people, like John's, need someone to argue for them."

Looking through the pile of books, Ware smiled broadly

when he saw Frederick Douglass's book. "I want to meet Douglass someday. Asher's promised to take me to hear him if he's ever close by."

"I heard him speak in England when he was a fugitive slave, and I have never forgotten the power of his oratory. You would do well to hear him—if he is ever close by."

"Do you know any of the others?" Ware held them out, and Asher leaned in to listen.

"I wept when I first read Brown's imagination of what the lives of Jefferson's slave daughters might have been like after his death." She looked at Asher to see his response, but he only nodded encouragingly. "As for the Harper poetry, I find her stoic faith in the face of injustice more than admirable. Asher chose a fine selection for you."

Asher put his hand on her shoulder, and she felt the warmth of it down her spine.

"When you finish those, perhaps I might suggest some others."

Ware nodded. The boy picked up his books and started to climb into the carriage, but he stopped, looking directly at Eugenie. "There's a Christmas ball at the St. Nicholas. Asher should take you." The boy pulled himself up into the carriage and nestled in with his books.

"Did you teach him to read?" she asked with a sort of awe.

"His parents did, but John and I supply the books. That's why I wrap them up differently: to keep them separate from those for the circulating library. But he does let us circulate his books through the community when he finishes with them."

Asher wrapped his arms around her shoulders, turning her body against his chest. Eugenie let herself melt a little into his embrace. Somehow he surprised her at every turn, and she was quickly growing too fond of him for her heart's good.

"As for the St. Nicholas ball . . ." He paused, clearly searching for words.

"There's no need," she said, hurrying to stop him, embarrassed that Ware had shamed him into offering to escort her. "I haven't an invitation, and besides, I'm sure my time will be full managing Lilly's return to England." As she said the words, though, she felt the lie in them. Now that she knew there was to be a ball, she wanted to go with Asher.

Asher nuzzled her head. "You may not have an invitation, but I do. And if you'd be willin', I'd be pleased to escort you to the St. Nicholas ball. As your mother told you, it's the event of the season."

"Do you even know how to dance?"

"Of course. You do this." He lifted her feet from the ground and swirled her in a circle over and over, until they were both laughing. Then he kissed her, a head-spinning kiss that led to another and another, until Ware called out from the carriage, "That's not a dance." And they stepped apart.

"Well"—she caught her breath—"I suppose with dancing skills like those, I couldn't refuse, but I haven't anything appropriate to wear."

"Neither do I. We'll make a perfect couple."

And he kissed her again.

Chapter 4

On the tenth day, Eugenie woke to the sounds of Asher hitching the horses. Ware was still asleep in the well of the carriage. She slipped out past him, picking up Kent's *Texas* as she climbed out of the carriage.

The early dawn was filled with animals, rabbits hopping from the side of the road back to the safety of the tall grass. She could name the birds now, easily recognizing the difference between them and their British cousins, just as she could look on the horizon and see that the day was going to be beautiful.

Asher had already climbed up to the seat, and, seeing her, he held out his hand. They sat together in a companionable silence, watching the Texas sunrise light the sky with oranges, purples, and pinks. Then when the sky had turned a perfect cornflower blue, Eugenie opened Kent's book.

Asher interrupted her. "Tell me about this fella's book you admire so much."

She paused, choosing her words to do Kent justice. "He's a masterful writer. He's obviously well educated, but he writes so clearly that he doesn't appear pedantic or heavy-handed. He is careful to provide accurate scientific descriptions of Texas flora and fauna, but he accompanies those descriptions with a palpable sense of wonder at the yet-unspoiled land. He describes both the tragedies and triumphs of life on the plains, but he balances that dark and that light in a vision both honest and hopeful."

"Is that all?"

She shook her head, smiling. "Somehow he speaks directly to my heart with the voice of an old friend. And I know that if he were my friend, his subtle wit and kind heart would make it easier to bear the bad times and to rejoice in the good. But more than that: he imagines a *future* Texas, where all its peoples have learned to live together peacefully and respectfully. And every time I read it, my heart soars."

"That's a tall order for any one book." He thought for a moment. "But the real question is this: does he talk about the weather?" He smiled at her, the broad teasing smile she'd grown to love.

"Of course he does; he's a Texian." She turned the pages of the book until she found something Asher might like. "Let me see.

"'*Most say Texas has four seasons: drought, flood, blizzard, and twister. Sometimes a man can experience all four in a single day. Near Fort Chadbourne on what is called the Llano Estacado, or the Staked Plains, those in the west add a fifth season: dust. Carried on a blistering hot wind, the dust rains pink and brown out of a cloud so dense that it can suffocate both man and animal. As one newspaper put it, the dust "comes in at the window, at the door, over the furniture, over the floor; rolling and curling and whirling it flies, stopping your guzzle and closing your eyes.'*"

"Read me that again."

Eugenie was thrilled; it was the first interest Asher had shown in Kent's book. For some reason, she wanted him to like it as much as she did. She read the section again, letting the syllables roll pleasantly against one another.

"Well, that damn . . ." He bit the sentence back, glancing at Eugenie.

"That damn what?"

He rubbed the back of his neck, thinking before he spoke. But his face showed signs of irritation. "It's nothing that can be helped now." He stared into the distance for a long time.

Eugenie waited.

"Tell me about the author, this Garrand Kent." His voice was cold. "How do you know him?"

"I know very little. My mother sent me the manuscript with directions to convey it to a particular publisher and to hire a lithographer to create a map of Texas for the front. I had my grandfather's solicitor review the publisher's contract to ensure that Kent's interests were secure." She paused, waiting for a response.

"So you approved the publication."

"On behalf of the author, yes." She felt bewildered. "It's been a huge success; by the time I left England, it had sold through eight editions in as many months. The *Monthly Review* even praised the book as 'the honest musings of a native son.' "

"Well, at least they got that right." He muttered under his breath, "The fool."

"Who is the fool? The *Monthly Review* or Garrand Kent?" She studied his face and watched the way his hands tensed on the reins. "Wait! You know him." She leaned forward, eager. "Who is he? Where does he live? Would you introduce me to him? He can't possibly be a fool. His book: it's so, so exhilarating. His descriptions of the land—even when at its most challenging—make living here seem possible."

"He's a no-good, no-account rancher with more land than sense, and little enough of that." He brushed his hair back, his hand trembling with anger. "If his book encourages people to settle here, then he's a fraud as well. I've told you: this isn't an easy land. Take the La Réunion colonists: they struggled for years, but the land gave them only heartache."

He paused, pulling his frustration under control, and she waited.

"When people read that damn book of yours, they won't see that half the people who settle here starve to death. No, they'll respond to that man's underlying optimism. They will travel here, stake a claim, and then the land will fail them. Or they will run afoul of Natives or Cortinas, and they will die. No, you won't like him at all."

"Whether I like him in person or not, the publisher wants another volume of his observations. I have the letter to deliver myself. And despite what you say, I'm looking forward to meeting him."

Asher was about to say something more, when Ware called out for them to stop. John had emerged from the tall grass as the carriage passed.

"Well, this is as good a time for a rest as any." Asher pulled the carriage to a stop and leapt down from the seat. "But you would have been better off reading Frederick Law Olmstead's *A Journey Through Texas*. At least it's clear what he hates."

He turned back to give Eugenie a helping hand down.

"I did," she answered, wanting to explain she'd found Olmstead's descriptions mean-spirited and unkind.

But Asher had already walked away. Instead of checking the horses immediately, he stalked off down the road. It was unlike him.

She reread the section of Kent's book silently. What could Asher have found offensive in such lovely prose? She shook her head, hoping to have a chance to ask him later.

After John had arrived, Eugenie returned to the carriage, letting the two brothers share the driving. John offered no explanation of where he had been, or why he'd gone. He had merely returned, and Ware once more became his constant companion.

Late in the afternoon, they turned off the broad road onto one little better than a trail, and some two hours later Eugenie sighted a cabin in the distance.

Ware, hanging on the side of the carriage, stuck his arm through the window and undid the latch on the door. Opening it, in a feat of real agility, he swung himself inside.

"I've been wanting to try that. And this was my last chance." The boy began to wrap up the stack of books he'd left on the backward-facing seat.

"Why is it your last chance?" Eugenie asked.

"Because I'm home. Look!" He pointed at the cabin now close enough for Eugenie to notice its construction. The cabin had four rooms, two on each side, separated by a covered breezeway, and the whole shared a single roof. Across the front, the roof extended out to shade a long porch. Asher pulled the carriage to a stop a polite distance from the cabin, and the men and Eugenie disembarked.

A tall woman with ebony skin and wearing a linen head scarf watched from the porch, a rifle on her hip. When she recognized Asher and John, she set the rifle aside and stepped out to greet them.

"Well, that's somethin' fancy." She gestured at the carriage.

"Fancy but comfortable." Asher quickly introduced the two women, Eugenie as Lilly's daughter, and Eva as Ware's mother. Eva looked Eugenie over head to toe.

Eugenie bore Eva's inspection with good grace. "You have a fine son, Mrs. Payne."

Eva's face softened. "He is a good boy, in spite of the influence of that one there." She pointed to Asher.

"If anyone is the bad influence," Asher objected, "it's Rafe, filling Ware's head with stories of the glories of the buffalo hunt."

"Rafe!" Eva called out, laughing, and a tall man sharing a family resemblance with his half brothers came out of the cabin. "You ain't never hunted a buffalo, and don't tell my son you have."

Rafe joined the group. He raised a single eyebrow when Asher introduced him as their brother. Carefully examining Eugenie, he extended his hand in greeting.

Ware ran to his mother's side, wrapping his arms around her waist. In that moment, he seemed wholly a child, rather than the small adult Eugenie had come to expect.

"Ah, there's my boy." Ware's mother leaned down, hugging her child to her side. "Did you have your adventure?"

The boy nodded, strangely tongue-tied.

"We are in Ware's debt," Eugenie said, holding out her hand.

Eva, after the slightest hesitation, grasped Eugenie's hand in hers.

"Had he and John not found our horses, we would still be walking."

"He's a good boy, if mischievous." Eva gestured toward the doorway. "But come in; I've beans and cornbread to fill your stomach. And Ware can rest the horses."

The dining room, which also served as a pantry, held a bench and table with a covered pot in the middle. Eva spooned a healthy portion of beans onto their bowls, then passed around a plate of cornbread.

Asher took a seat beside Eugenie, grinning as he ate. "Eva, you are the best cook this side of the Mississippi."

Eugenie bit into the bread, not knowing what to expect, but she found it chewy and a little sweet, crisp on the bottom where the oil had fried the bread.

"What do you know of the Mississippi, Asher?" Eva teased. "You barely get outside the Texas border on a cattle drive before you run your way back inside the state again."

"In my younger days, I visited all the states and most of the territories. I simply prefer Texas," Asher explained, breaking a piece of cornbread into his beans. "Ware, tell your mother about the stompede." He gave Eugenie a sly wink.

Eugenie raised an eyebrow in return. For all the stories they'd told her on the road, this was one she hadn't heard yet.

"Ah, Lawd, perhaps you shouldn't." Eva straightened her gingham dress.

"We only had one stompede, Mama, and I knew to find a safe place to hide. So I climbed a tree, and I watched the horns of the cattle run below me."

"Good boy, Ware." Eva smiled with relief.

"But after a few minutes I heard a sound above me, and sitting there, watching me, was a panther."

His mother breathed in sharply in alarm. She began to study Ware as if she were counting his limbs.

Eugenie was fascinated. "Ware, what did you do?"

"If I'd stay'd in the tree, I could have been mauled or eaten. But if I jumped, I could have been gored by the horns of the cattle running beneath. So, I hung down, real careful-like, until my heels grazed the backs of the cattle as they passed."

The boy demonstrated, holding his arms up above his head. "Then I let myself drop, praying that I would hit a back and not a horn. And that's how I landed. Then I just rode the running cattle, until I could slip off, safe and sound with nary a scratch."

Eva hugged her child into her side. "You didn't."

Ware's smile broadened wide.

"He did," Asher confirmed.

Eva twisted her towel and swatted Asher, not entirely without heat. "You take my blessed child on a drive, and you can't manage to keep him away from stomps and panthers."

"I kept him from getting snake bit." Asher shrugged, not completely apologetically.

"Well, thank the Lord for small favors." She nuzzled Ware's

head, kissing his forehead. The boy blushed but allowed his mother's affection. "I'm expecting your daddy any minute, and I'm not sure how happy he's gonna be when he hears your adventures."

"But I had to have an adventure, else I couldn't partner with Asher and John like you and Daddy do," Ware explained seriously.

"I worked for some years helping my uncle manage his estate. How does your partnership work?" Eugenie asked.

"Depending on our labor, we divide our produce and profits," Asher explained. "But this year, I barely worked hard enough to justify any part of Eva's vegetables. Most, I think, she gave me just out of pity."

"We can't have you starve, Asher." Eva shook her head, smiling, then gestured at the room around them. "Besides, every day when I enjoy this cabin, I think you deserve another plate of okra."

"What is the relationship between the cabin and okra?" Eugenie asked.

"This used to be Asher's cabin," Eva explained.

"Until he built that fancy one for Miss Sadie," Ware added.

An expression Eugenie couldn't decipher crossed Asher's face, and Eva gave her son a stern look.

Sadie.

He wore no ring. But how could a man like Asher not be spoken for? The thought deflated her. Surely, he'd had a dozen opportunities to tell her about Sadie over the last fortnight. It would have stung, but she would have preferred it to finding out from the offhanded remark of a child. From Ware, it felt like a hard slap. And if Asher had left out something so significant, what other important parts of his life had he neglected to mention? And to think she'd believed she'd learned his character.

Ware looked pained at his mother's silent rebuke, but Asher gently patted the young boy's shoulder.

"Fancy?" Eugenie kept her voice light, even teasing, but she watched Asher's face to see how it changed.

He shrugged, not meeting her eyes. "All I did was make a shed for the horses and put two seats in the privy."

"I believe you put in a glass window or two," Eva interjected, trying to lighten the mood.

"Might've done." Asher rubbed the scarred flesh on the back of his hand.

Eva touched his shoulder. "There's not a day goes by that I don't miss her."

Relief flooded Eugenie's belly, and she felt immediately guilty. He had lost someone, a woman who was important to him, and she'd responded with jealousy and suspicion.

Asher merely nodded.

A moment or two later, he rose, his face inscrutable. "That was a good meal, Eva, and a good break for the horses, but if we're to make Dallas by nightfall, I should tend the team." He slipped from the room, and Rafe and John followed. Ware kissed his mother on the cheek, then scrambled after them.

Eugenie watched the men go, her shoulders and chest growing tight in response to Asher's obvious pain.

Solemn and quiet, Eva cleared the table, covering the food with linen. Eugenie watched for something she could do, then followed Eva's lead, wiping out the plates and placing them in the dry sink. After a few minutes of activity, Eva gestured to the cabin door.

"Would you like to sit outside and watch the men? If we pull the chairs into the sun, we'll be warm enough."

"Shouldn't I do something to help?"

"No, leave them be. Besides, they'd just refuse your offer anyway."

Agreeing, Eugenie followed Eva to the porch, pulling her chair into the sunlight as Eva did hers.

As the two women watched, the men together checked each joint, each rigging, each strap, and each wheel.

"He's a careful man," Eugenie said, more to herself than Eva.

"You have to be in these parts."

Asher, seeing the women, paused to study Eugenie for a moment, then nodded and smiled. Eugenie felt the tension in her back release.

"Well, well. Asher Graham smiling," Eva exclaimed. "That's something I didn't expect to see."

"Is that unusual?" Eugenie thought of all the smiles he'd given her over the last fortnight.

"Has been for some time now. Since Miss Sadie died. Before that, he was a smiling man."

"What was she like?"

"Sadie? Oh, she was a little thing and sunny. The whole world smiled on Miss Sadie, until the day it didn't. He was visiting his mother's people in New Orleans when they met. He was traveling with the Rangers then, and he wrote her letters from all over Texas for more than a year before she agreed to come to Dallas and marry him."

Eugenie wondered what a letter from Asher would be like. Would his wry wit transfer to the page? Or would he spend all his time describing the weather? No, much as she enjoyed the quiet, thorough way Asher's mind worked during their conversations, she couldn't imagine he would be very interesting as a letter writer. Even so, she wanted one, and she was jealous of Sadie for having gotten them for a year.

"What happened to them? The letters, I mean."

"I saw them once; she'd collected them all in a big book. But I fear he burned them."

"Is that where he got the scar—on the back of his hand?"

"Oh, no, that's from a prairie fire. In the summer, it gets so hot and dry that almost anything can start a fire. And once it's started, it can burn half the county . . . or more."

"Like what?" Eugenie wondered how in all their conversations prairie fire had never come up.

"Ashes from a camp left smoldering, or even those new-fangled matches Mr. Peak sells at his general store in Dallas. I had a box of them catch fire all by themselves last year."

Eva paused, clearly considering her next words. "He stayed here after she died, you know. Up there." She pointed to an opening in the porch ceiling. "That leads to a bit of attic we use for sleeping or storing goods. He refused to stay at their cabin, and though I offered him a room here, he refused that too. Said he couldn't escape her ghost in the rooms they'd lived in together."

Eva turned silent, and Eugenie waited, wanting to hear everything Eva might tell her.

"He turned his back to the wall, and we thought he'd die of grief. Ware would crawl up and stay with him, but by summer my Ben had to roust him out of there, or he would have died of the heat."

"I didn't know." Clearly, Eugenie didn't know a great deal, and it called into question everything she thought she knew. "May I ask you a question?"

"You may ask, but I may not answer."

"How did she die?"

"No one knows for certain." Eva shrugged. "Asher had left her in town while he went to answer another Ranger's call for help. But she wouldn't stay; she had too much to do at their cabin. Asher hadn't been gone a week, when Mrs. Cockrell went out to visit. She found Sadie, sitting in a chair, all peaceful-like, as if she'd just sat down to rest."

"How did you let Asher know?"

"There was no way to tell him. Dallas didn't have a telegraph, and besides, we didn't know where our men had gone. But I was in town the day they returned—Asher, Rafe, John, and my Ben, all together."

"Your husband was a Ranger as well."

"A Ranger never quite stops being a Ranger, but the four of them served together and became best of friends."

"I didn't mean to interrupt," Eugenie apologized.

"Sad stories tell themselves at their own pace." Eva watched the men, almost finished with their inspection. "Asher knew the moment he rode back into town. When the Rangers return home, it always draws a crowd. But this time, no one went out but me and Sheriff Holden. When Asher's eyes met mine, I couldn't do nothing but shake my head."

"What did he do?"

"He turned his horse and rode straight to his family cemetery. I've not seen him smile since . . . until today." Eva patted Eugenie's arm as Asher approached. "I'm grateful to you for that."

Within minutes, Asher and Eugenie were back on the road, this time alone. John had decided to stay with the Paynes for a few days, and Ware, exhausted from their travels, had already fallen sound asleep on the porch bench. His mother had covered him with a patchwork quilt.

Eugenie felt unexpectedly sad on leaving. The thought that she wouldn't see Ware or John, or even Eva again, weighed heavy on her heart.

But that was what she'd expected, wasn't it? To come to Texas, retrieve her mother, and return home to England. Not to make friends, and certainly not friends she already missed. Her time for adventure was drawing to a close.

Though Asher had been all smiles when they said good-bye to the Paynes, once they were back on the road, he grew distant. Eugenie let him have his silence, needing to prepare herself for her meeting with Lilly. The two sat in peaceable silence for most of the way to Dallas.

After an hour or so, Eugenie saw the beginnings of a more

concentrated population: the occasional rustic building grew to two or three, and after that, into streets and intersections.

Soon she would be caring for her invalid mother and trying to determine the best route back to London. But she turned her mind away from that problem.

For a little while longer, she had Asher at her side. In two short weeks, she'd learned so much, about the land and its peoples, about law and rebellion, animals and, not unexpectedly, weather. But most importantly she'd learned to value Asher, not for his good looks, but for his kindness and honesty. Traits she'd thought she'd not easily find in a man outside her family.

"Is it far to the St. Nicholas?"

"Less than a mile." Asher kept his eyes on his team.

"When we arrive there . . ." She struggled to find words to explain her relationship with her mother. "I haven't seen Lilly in almost a decade. Would you accompany me to meet her?"

Asher's mouth formed a hard line. "Wouldn't miss it for the world."

"We've never been . . . close, she and I. Once I went to live with my grandparents, I rarely saw her. She's always had too little care for her social obligations, and I've perhaps had too much. Once every couple of years she would arrive, bearing gifts and toys. And for a few days, a week, sometimes even two, she'd be this delightful, spontaneous presence. And then one day she would simply be gone, often without even a good-bye. It took me a long time to learn not to have expectations."

Asher didn't respond, navigating the increased traffic on the road. The street was well developed with businesses and homes on either side for several blocks before the town square. But she could see it—the St. Nicholas—in the distance, towering over the other shops.

"So, I'm not quite sure what to expect when I see her again, particularly now that she's an invalid. It's all—I must admit—a little overwhelming."

Two young boys ran alongside the carriage, then, as Asher stopped to let another carriage pass, ran on ahead down the street, waving. All down the street, people stepped to their doorways and watched them drive past, women waving, men tipping hats. It must have been like this when he had returned to find Sadie dead, she thought, him riding into town with his brothers-at-arms, except then the townspeople, seeing his approach, had disappeared into their houses and shops.

As they approached the town square, the St. Nicholas, a three-story brick building at the intersection of Commerce and Broadway, came more fully into view. A grand hotel for the plains, the St. Nicholas stood a full story over the rest of the shops and businesses in the center of town. Beyond it, Eugenie could see the Trinity River and the wooden bridge that connected Dallas to the remains of the La Réunion colony.

Asher pulled the carriage in front of the hotel.

He turned to her, his face grim, "About your mother . . ."

At that moment, several young women, their mothers in tow, arrived chattering excitedly. "Do you have them?" the girls asked in almost the same voice.

Asher turned pleasant. "Yes, ladies, I collected everything you requested."

A crowd gathered, men joining their wives and daughters.

He turned back to her, speaking low. "Do you want to wait or go in now?"

"I want to wait," she whispered.

He began to unrope the luggage, calling out names and handing down trunks and boxes. The crowd—the girls particularly—responded with squeals of laughter and delight.

She could feel the excitement in the crowd. What could Asher be delivering that mattered so much to so many? She didn't have long to wonder.

"Mine next, Mr. Graham. Mine next!" a girl barely old enough to be out of the schoolroom called out.

Asher opened a large wooden-slatted trunk. Inside, Eugenie could see long paper-wrapped packages.

"Let's see. Minnalee Rice. One bolt of . . ."

"Don't say the color, Mr. Graham. It's a surprise." The girl stepped to the side of the carriage and held out her arms.

"Then a surprise it will be." Asher handed down the bolt, and the girl clasped it to her chest and ran away.

One by one the women and girls stepped forward, excited, as Asher called out their names.

"I've never been so glad to see a coach arrive, except perhaps the one that takes my mother-in-law back to San Antone." A portly man with twin daughters stepped forward, pulling a hand wagon. "My girls have been staring out the parlor window for more than a week, praying you'd bring their dresses in time."

"Happy to be of service, Anselmo." Asher handed down five boxes as long as his arm. "But why do you have more boxes than daughters?"

"When the twins couldn't decide which dresses they wanted, I let them order extra as long as they were all in the same color."

"Why the same color?"

"To keep track of my girls at the ball," Anselmo said, proud of his strategy.

The twins looked at each other with mischievous glances, and Eugenie wondered if they had already made plans to trade their dresses for ones in a different color.

Asher met Eugenie's eyes. "Anselmo, what are your plans for the extra dresses?"

"I've already got buyers lined up three deep," Anselmo answered.

Asher looked an apology to Eugenie, and Anselmo led his girls away, the five packages piled up high in the wagon. Asher continued handing down packages, until only Eugenie's luggage was left.

As quickly as it had formed, the crowd dispersed, the towns-people carrying away their deliveries, all still chattering excitedly.

Asher stood beside Eugenie's perch, and she descended holding his hand. After two weeks of travel, she still felt a thrill whenever his hand—even gloved—touched hers.

As Asher lifted her down, Eugenie heard her mother's voice calling her name. As her feet touched the ground, she was wrapped in her mother's embrace.

"Oh, my girl, my darling, darling, girl." Lilly kissed both Eugenie's cheeks.

Eugenie looked over her shoulder, mouthing "help" to Asher. He set her luggage on the hotel porch, then instructed the bellmen where to take it.

Lilly entwined her arm through Eugenie's and led her daughter to the hotel entrance. Asher followed the women in.

Eugenie tried to take everything in: the names of the bellmen, the manager at the registration desk, and the craftsmen still employed by the hotel. As they passed the giant central staircase, Lilly waved directions toward the room already set aside for her daughter.

Eugenie wanted nothing more than to wash her face and hands and change into a dress less travel weary, but Lilly barely paused before leading Eugenie into a private drawing room near the back of the hotel lobby. Asher slipped in before the door closed.

"Mrs. Cockrell, you must meet my Eugenie." Her mother's voice slid gracefully over the syllables. "Mr. Graham has ful-filled his promise. And here she is, safe and sound."

A slight woman with sad gray eyes and dressed in mourning was seated before the fireplace. Asher went to her side and spoke something privately in her ear.

Mrs. Cockrell nodded, then rose to meet Eugenie and Lilly. She clasped Eugenie's hands. "The winter has been so unpredictable and cold that we were worried you might be delayed. I hope the weather didn't give you much trouble."

In an instant, Eugenie remembered the storm and the tornado, lying against Asher's chest, the warmth of his embrace, and the passion of his kisses. "No, no trouble at all."

"As we'd hoped, you have arrived in time to attend the St. Nicholas Grand Ball," Mrs. Cockrell continued. "It's at the end of the week. Our ladies have been fretting that Asher might not return in time. You must attend, of course. It will give you a chance to see our society at its finest."

"Oh yes, dear, you must!" Lilly exclaimed. "I'm certain we can find *someone* to escort you." Lilly threw the *someone* openly at Asher, but he stood immobile, looking out the window.

Eugenie recoiled inwardly from her mother's presumption. She had no question that the Dallas ladies would fret if a handsome man like Asher weren't present at the ball. Yet the thought of it—of him with another woman, even Sadie—roused feelings she found unsettling. Certainly, she'd never cared much if Jeremy or any of her other suitors danced with the other women in attendance; that was expected of all the men. But somehow with Asher, the situation felt different. It wasn't jealousy, rather a sort of longing tinged with sadness.

More than anything, she felt a deep sense of loss; their friendship, their affection, their passion (if she could call it that) had clearly been a feature of the road. It had been an interlude away from responsibilities and other relationships. But now that they were in town, other obligations required their attention. And the gossamer web of attraction and connection between them, so strong on the road, had little place in town.

Her mother would make too much of it, if she knew that Asher had already asked to escort her. And since he hadn't responded to Lilly's very obvious hint, Eugenie would not reveal it either. "I'm grateful for the invitation, Mrs. Cockrell, but I have brought nothing suitable to wear to such a grand occasion."

Asher glanced her way, but said nothing to suggest he intended to take her to the ball. Her heart sunk a little.

"As for the dress, my head seamstress, Miss Quigley, may be able to arrange something." Mrs. Cockrell crossed the room to the drawing room door. "She is our fairy godmother in these sorts of situations. I hope to see you at dinner, Miss Charpentier. Your mother dines at my table, and I will have a place set for you."

Asher opened the door for Mrs. Cockrell's exit, and Eugenie found herself alone with her mother and Asher.

Her mother had collapsed delicately into a chair, a powder puff of lace and ribbons. Eugenie took the opportunity to study her. On the way in from the carriage, Eugenie had noticed no limp, no slowed pace, no labored breathing. No, on the contrary, Lilly's color was good, quite good, and her face showed no sign of pain or discomfort. Instead her mother looked pleased, much like a cat who'd stolen a pot of cream.

"An invalid." Eugenie said the word. The lie of it filled her mouth like alum. "How could you?" She kept her voice cold and level, but anger flared in the pit of her stomach.

Lilly shrugged beautifully, as if she had practiced the motion in a mirror. "I never felt at ease in England nor in Italy. But here, no one is higher or lower. I make jam and draw, and from my window, I can gaze on a countryside that stretches out forever. I finally found a land to match my spirit . . . and to awaken yours."

"I've traveled for the better part of a year because you asked for my help, because you said you finally wanted to come home." Her anger swelled, fed by the long months of purposeless travel and decades of Lilly's neglect. But she bit it back.

"My darling, you must understand."

Eugenie shook her head, holding up her palms to stop her mother's words. "You don't intend to leave. You never intended to leave. Why did you ask for me to come for you?"

"How else would I have drawn you here?" Lilly's voice broke with emotion. "When Judith wrote about Jeremy's cruelty, I knew I had to act. I couldn't let you settle for a narrow life in some narrow village, knitting with the other spinsters."

Asher stood away from them, watching the floor, his body taut and tense.

"Haven't these months of travel made you wish for more?" Lilly extended her arms, but Eugenie backed away. "When you stood at the railing on the ship, didn't you feel something waiting for you? With each mile of ocean, couldn't you feel the constraints of being a duke's ward fall away? When you arrived in Boston, in New Orleans, in Jefferson, and now in Dallas, did you not see a civilization so new and fresh that it makes London for all its appeal look old and stale?"

"Those are your reactions, Lilly, not mine." Eugenie felt her mother's deception twist along the length of her spine.

"My dear child, you have more spirit in you than you've ever allowed yourself. Here you can stretch your limits, see yourself more clearly. Here you can live your own life, not some pale version of Judith's. She wouldn't have wanted that for you; she had too much spirit of her own."

"Don't speak of Judith."

But Lilly, in the rush of her own words, didn't seem to hear. "Dallas is only a hint of a city, but Galveston and San Antonio already rival those in the Eastern states. You could make your home in one of those, though I would lament your loss now that we are finally together."

"Whatever I choose, whatever I make or don't make of myself, it will result from something *I* did, not from something you manipulated." She would not show Lilly her anger. She would not show Lilly anything of how she felt.

"You had no right, Lilly," Asher finally spoke. But Eugenie wanted none of his help. *He* had betrayed her trust as well.

"No right." Her anger prodded by hurt swelled to include him. "You have the gall to speak of no right. What right did you have to keep this from me?" She waved her hand at her mother, still seated in her overstuffed chair. "Two weeks ago I told you I believed she was unable to travel alone."

"What right? What right have you to be angry with me? You had traveled halfway around the world to see your mother. It wasn't my place to stop you only one hundred and seventy miles away."

"If you'd told me, I could be halfway back to Boston by now." She pointed her finger sharply.

"What right did *you* have to help her publish *my* manuscript?" His accusation spilled out, hot and angry.

"Your manuscript?" She spoke a second before the realization hit. It made sense: he was Kent. And her anger turned cold and hard. "And you didn't think to tell me?"

"I had no obligation to tell you—all that fawning over a book."

"*Your* book."

"Not mine—Sadie's. I wrote it for her, not you, not nobody else, and certainly not for the whole damn island of England. You hadn't the right, neither of you, to publish it without asking." He stared hard at Lilly. "What makes you think you can manipulate other people's lives in that way?"

"Because she always has," Eugenie answered.

He turned on his heel and stormed from the room.

Lilly looked half penitent and half pleased. "You should follow him."

Eugenie didn't know whether to rail at her mother or follow Asher.

After a moment, she rushed out after him, but she was too

late. The carriage was gone, and he and Rafe were already riding their horses out of town.

There would be another time. Perhaps at the ball, if he intended still to escort her. But neither of them had revealed their earlier arrangement to Mrs. Cockrell or Lilly. Would he believe she wasn't interested in going to the ball with him after all?

She shook her head in frustration.

It was a fine mess.

She had no way to contact him, so no way of knowing his plans. If she asked her mother or Mrs. Cockrell or even one of the servants where he lived or how to contact him, she risked raising questions she couldn't answer. And if somehow she managed to contact him, she risked another public rejection if he wished to have nothing to do with her.

His horse out of sight, she returned to the hotel lobby.

She had no option but to wait. Besides, she had much to discuss with Lilly, and knowing her mother, Eugenie would need every minute of that time to be able to leave her mother in Texas without further regrets.

Chapter 5

Since her falling-out with Asher, Eugenie had spent days listening—and pining. The women who crowded Mrs. Cockrell's drawing room could talk of nothing but the upcoming ball. Some had doubted that Sarah Cockrell would finish the hotel after her husband's murder, but she did, and the ball was her celebration of the accomplishment.

Some ladies who could not afford to buy a fancy dress had—with surprising ingenuity—salvaged silk from hatboxes or reused the satin, taffeta, and lace from gowns long stored away to make new ones. Others of more means had ordered bolts of material from St. Louis, Boston, or Philadelphia, then waited months for them to arrive by the irregular mail coach or by way of trips—like the one Asher had made—to Jefferson. Still others ordered new dresses from the most fashionable modistes in New Orleans or Houston. For many, their dresses—ordered months in advance—still hadn't arrived.

Those with dresses to spare had loaned or sold them to those without. Even Lilly, usually so careful with her clothing, had promised all her spare dresses to women in her drawing classes long before Eugenie arrived.

Eugenie admired their patience and even, in some odd way, their fatalism. It was a land in which one could make one's own way, through hard work and ingenuity and luck. So much luck. But it wasn't a land that promised success. And the settlers embraced that challenge.

Giving the conversation only half her attention, she considered whether she should attend the ball at all. Asher had made no attempt to contact her since he'd stormed out of the drawing room, and her heart ached to speak to him again. Even so, even in the face of his lack of communication, she still hoped . . . and longed.

Perhaps that hope and longing explained why—with less than an hour before the start of the ball—she was standing on a stool in the middle of her mother's sitting room, having a stranger's dress fitted to her figure. Miss Quigley had approached another resident of the hotel—a Miss Rutherford—to see if she would allow Eugenie to have one of the half dozen dresses she'd commissioned, but rejected. And Miss Rutherford had agreed. Apparently at the St. Nicholas Ball, most of the women would be wearing someone else's clothes.

The room was filled with maids and seamstresses and several of Lilly's friends. All the women seemed to be talking simultaneously.

The seamstress, Birdie, was examining the dress's embroidery. "Ah, this was done in the old country," she said in her Irish brogue. "I've not seen this whipped running stitch used much here—shame that: it's so elegant."

Lilly's maid couldn't stop talking about Mrs. Cockrell's scheme for lighting the affair. "The small chandeliers in the dining room and the large one in the main entry came all the way from New Orleans. They take kerosene for fuel, which is, you know, much safer than candles. And Mrs. Cockrell has hired her own fireman to light, watch over, and put out the flames."

While the seamstress brought in the dress's waist, Lilly attempted to settle a cluster of greenhouse flowers on Eugenie's head.

"Ouch," Eugenie said, putting her hand to her forehead.

"Stop fidgeting, Eugenie." Lilly batted away Eugenie's hand.

"Stop stabbing me with pins. I have no need of hothouse flowers in my hair."

"But with them you will be the belle of the ball."

"I'm too old to be the belle. Besides, I'd prefer not to bleed on another woman's dress."

"It's a red dress—bleed all you want." Lilly was not to be dissuaded from the flowers.

In the days since her argument with Asher, Eugenie had made a curious peace with her mother. She had never known her mother, not as an adult at least. So, she had set aside a child's hurt at feeling abandoned to ask why Lilly had left her with Judith. Lilly's answer had surprised and troubled her.

Lilly had pulled a locket on a chain from under her blouse and held it open. On one side was a miniature of a man Eugenie recognized as her father; on the other were three dark curls of hair, each tied with a silk string.

"I was so young when I married your father, and so in love, and then he was gone. But I had you, my precious girl, just two, with those ringlets of dark hair around your face, and I had your brother." Lilly pointed at the curls of hair, one for each of her children and one for their father.

Though Eugenie had often seen her mother wearing the locket, she had never known what was inside. She'd never imagined it might be a remembrance of her.

"On your father's death, you and your brother became the new count's ward. I had no legal right to my children; no mother does. He sent your brother to school, but he allowed me to keep you. Then he changed his mind."

"Why?"

"Because he did. It is the way of such men. They decide. You comply. The count never expected me to refuse. But I'd already met my dear Charles, and he agreed to help me take you to my own guardians in England. His only requirement was that we marry. So, we spirited you away."

"To my grandparents and to Judith." Eugenie kept the conversation going.

Lilly nodded. "Your uncle was a petty count of an insignificant territory. Your grandfather was a duke of the English realm. You were safe with him."

"Why didn't you tell me?"

"What child understands such power?" Lilly closed the locket and slipped it back under her blouse. "Besides, from the beginning, you and Lady Judith shared a bond. Everyone could see it."

The hints of tears formed in the corners of Lilly's eyes. "I was a willful, flighty girl, a butterfly, in love with the idea of love as much as with the men I married. You were your father's daughter, all serious and thoughtful, so I left you in the care of someone who could nurture those qualities, not destroy them."

"You wouldn't have destroyed . . ."

Lilly held up her hand, stopping Eugenie's words. "If I know anything, I know myself. And if you are honest with yourself, you know I was right."

Eugenie, though she found her mother's reasoning odd, had to admit its truth. "Why did you always leave without telling me?"

"Because I never knew myself. Whenever I woke up crying at the thought of leaving you again, I packed my bags. I told myself it was for the best. I never wanted you to remember me crying."

Eugenie had almost objected, but she let it go. In some way, Lilly's odd incomplete explanations had been enough.

"Ouch." Eugenie came out of her reverie with a start. "Now you've stuck a pin in my ear."

"Don't worry—it's just a tiny bit of blood. Next to this red rose, no one will see it. There. All done."

"Ah, look! The guests have begun to arrive! Look at that carriage: all decked with ribbons." The maid pointed at the street.

Lilly and Eugenie joined the maid to watch the guests arrive. It was shortly before dusk, and the streets were suffused with a golden glow. Guests arrived both on foot and in carriages. The women wore their finest jewelry, rivaling that worn at the best Brahmin party in Boston. The men in their gleaming white shirts and black suits sported jeweled studs and cuff links. All of them—men and women both—wore white gloves, the women's extending all the way to their elbows.

Eugenie studied the crowd, looking for the tall, lean Ranger who had somehow in just two weeks captured her heart. She hadn't realized that she loved him when they'd parted, but since then, she'd felt as if a portion of her soul had been torn away.

If he didn't come to the ball, she would know there was nothing between them. She would proceed with her plan to travel back to New Orleans and from there to Boston and home. She didn't want to be Eve in the New World, without Asher as her Adam.

Lilly whispered, "He'll come, my darling girl; Asher's no fool. He'll come."

To avoid Lilly seeing her cry, Eugenie squeezed her mother's hand and slipped from the room.

In the main ballroom, converted from the dining hall, kerosene lamps flickered from sconces on the walls between each window. Each table was lit by its own oil lamp, though the wicks were kept low to create the appearance of a mellow glow throughout the room. The ballroom walls were hung with fine tapestries, many borrowed from Dallas's leading citizens, and around each window hung garlands of cedar and other evergreens. From the half-circle balustrade before the balcony, flags of Texas and the United States hung down. There the honored guests sat with an unparalleled view of the proceedings.

The preliminary music was unexpectedly fine, with the local music teacher Mrs. Reinhardt directing her students on the piano and guitar. Then, the orchestra master played several melodies solo on the violin. Once he was done, a bugle signaled the grand march.

Eugenie found herself in a space against the wall. From there, she watched the couples enter the ballroom in a long, elegant line.

Near her, a woman in blue velvet stood half-hidden both by the drapes and a giant bear of a man in a respectable but worn black suit. Eugenie couldn't hear their whispered conversation, but both were clearly at ease with the other. Eugenie had begun to spin a story about them, when the man left to join a garish woman dressed in red. Eugenie felt disappointed that the romance she'd imagined just starting had ended so quickly. Like hers.

The ball began with a waltz. As the couples moved so gracefully across the floor, Eugenie imagined herself twirling around the room in Asher's arms. But the memory hurt more than soothed her. How had she imagined she was storing up memories for the future? Every one made her heart break.

The waltz transitioned to a minuet, then the minuet to a polka, followed by dance after dance she didn't know. A helpful young servant told her the names: schottische, mazurka, lancers, Virginia reel, and a dozen others.

She waited. Still Asher did not come.

Around nine, she noticed a group of rough men with badges had arrived. She assumed they had been hired to ensure that none of the ladies or gentlemen lost their jewels. But they circled the dance floor, staring at all the women and the men, like animals in search of prey. One, crossing in front of her, stopped to give her a hard look.

She drew herself up tall. "What are you looking at, my good sir?"

The man grinned, revealing broken-out teeth. Probably from a brawl, she thought.

"I'm looking for a missing heiress. Her daddy thinks she's kidnapped, as if any man would want a girl as homely as she is."

She thought of the woman in blue velvet hiding behind the curtains and the man talking to her. Perhaps their whispers had been a plan to escape. Had it been Asher asking, she would have offered the information gladly, but she wouldn't tell this half-drunken bully anything.

The man's eyes ranked over her body. "Pink dress, she's wearing, with ribbons."

"I'm not wearing pink," she said flatly, letting her voice carry all the steel she'd learned from years of avoiding rakes and other predators.

"No, ma'am. You're not." He leered at her, his breath stinking of liquor. "But that red is mighty fine. Let's take a twirl around the dance floor."

He reached for her hand, but she pulled it back decisively.

"I could never enjoy a dance knowing a young girl is in danger." Inwardly rolling her eyes, she played to the drunk lawman's sense of importance. "You must go . . . and find her."

"Of course, Miss . . . ?" He waited for her to fill in her name. She didn't.

"Well, I better go. That girl's pappy won't be able to sleep until he knows she's safe. But if you need anything, you just holler for Chase. Chase Johnson."

"I'll keep that in mind."

She watched Chase saunter away, happy she'd been able to

get rid of him so easily. But men like him were like bad pennies, and it was inevitable he would show back up before the evening was done.

Chase rejoined the other lawmen and military officers at the door to the poker room. They were hard men, cleaned up for the ball, but still rough in a way Asher had never been. Asher would never leer at any woman. No, everything with Asher had been an invitation, an outstretched hand inviting her to a life bigger than she'd ever imagined. She blinked back the tears.

If only he'd come . . .

Suddenly she didn't want him to find her standing against a wall, waiting. If there were the slightest chance that he might come for her, he needed to know—and she did as well—that she could make a life here.

For the next several hours, she met those who had come to the ball. Shopkeepers and craftsmen, headmasters and school-mistresses, ministers and lawmen, ranchers and cattlemen, lawyers, judges, and a legislator or two. As the end of the dance drew near, she felt like she'd made polite conversation with most of Dallas and some of Texas. And still he did not come.

Worst yet, in one of the conversations, she learned that a group of Dallas Rangers had left that morning for Fort Worth, about three hours away. There they would meet with other Rangers and travel south to join Rip Ford. She prayed Asher wasn't with them.

Near midnight, she was standing on the porch along the back of the hotel, planning to effect an escape from the ball as soon as she could. She gazed up into the sky, the cold air making the stars especially bright.

He hadn't come.

She had her ticket for the stagecoach at least. She could leave on any of the days it came to Dallas. Her heart still ached to think that Asher would let her go. But that was the way of things, and she knew her place. Though she'd seen glimpses of what her life could be like in Texas—what she could be in that vast wild land—it was only a dream, fading with daylight.

Her home, she understood it now, was in England. Safe. Without rattlesnakes or scorpions or alligators or stampedes. England was a civilized land. The problem was she felt . . . no longer civilized.

Perhaps she would go to Galveston instead. She could start a school and wait to see if she wanted to take that ship back to London. Perhaps her mother was right, and she should give Texas a chance. There would always be England . . . if she needed it.

But now she needed something she couldn't have. A man who was too rough and tumble to understand how a book might speak so deeply to her soul, even when he was the one who had written it. A man who had shown glimpses of a soul like hers. A remarkable man. A man who didn't want her.

The porch creaked behind her, and she turned hoping it would be Asher.

But a man and a woman giggled in each other's arms. She decided to leave the porch to them.

As she walked back into the ballroom, Asher was there. Not as she had seen him last, dusty from the road, but sleek and polished in a pressed suit. He carried himself as if he wore such clothes every day. She stared. His face was clean-shaven, his dark green eyes flecked with gold. Without his beard, his jaw looked even firmer.

He'd dressed and shaved for her. She knew it. He'd dressed as she'd described Garrand Kent: urbane, cultured, polished. Nothing else would make him wear such clothes.

He caught her eyes and smiled, and she felt the warmth of it down to her belly.

He had come . . . for her.

But the fact that he'd waited almost to the end of the dance made her wary.

He made his way to her, the crowd parting to allow him through.

"Miss Eugenie Charpentier." As before, his pronunciation was perfect, as if he had studied for years in France, not read a thesaurus on the plains of Texas. "Might I have the pleasure of this dance?" He held out his hand, inviting her—as he had in Jefferson—to trust him.

"It's Jeannie to you," she whispered, wondering if every eye were not already watching them.

She stretched out her hand, the long white of her glove fitting neatly into his. He led her onto the dance floor, and again the crowd seemed to part at their approach. Their first real dance was a waltz, slow and elegant.

He placed one hand on her waist, and she placed one of hers on his shoulder.

She felt the now-familiar thrill of his presence. The sense of electricity that came from their souls' wings touching. But she refused to acknowledge it: he'd made her wait a week without any contact. Even so, he led her gracefully, expertly across the dance floor.

"I thought all you could do was twirl a girl in the air. How did you learn to dance?"

"I would have told you, but you never asked."

"Is that all it takes? A simple question and you answer?"

"I suppose it depends on whether the question is appropriate to the moment."

"What sort of question would be 'appropriate' to this moment?"

"It's another game: I get to decide once you ask."

Annoyed, she began to pull out of his arms, but he held her close, breathing in the hot-house roses in her hair.

"Ask," his voice pled.

"How did you learn to dance . . . out here?"

"I didn't always live out here. For some years, I went to school in New Orleans living with my mother's family."

"Your mother is French?"

"Was. French Huguenots."

"Did you meet Sadie there?"

"Yes. But why don't you ask something more appropriate?"

"What should I ask?

"Like why I'm here, in this suit, dancing with you."

"Why?"

"Because after Sadie died, I refused to consider that I might love another woman. I refused to live in the places I'd lived with her. I refused to live without her."

She started to pull out of his arms.

"But I find that you have crept into the very corners of my soul, and I can't imagine a life without you in it," he whispered.

She blinked back the tears. "I don't know what to say."

"Say that you love me. Say that we have a chance for happiness together. Say that you can love the ornery rancher who stands before you more than you love the polished ideal of a man you found in that damn book. Say that you'll come to my cabin tomorrow for Christmas dinner. Say something, anything."

"Have you forgiven me for having it published?"

He looked surprised, but still he answered. "I've thought about that—and you—every moment since we parted. Can a man be both angry and grateful?"

"I don't know."

"If Lilly hadn't sent the book to you, if you hadn't read it, you might not have come here prepared to love this land as much as I do. You might even have refused to come—I hear you have a brother she could have sent for instead."

"She wanted me to come, not him."

"And if you hadn't fallen half in love with that damn book, you wouldn't have been able to fall half in love with me. Even if I'd met you on the street, you wouldn't have known me, not the way you knew me after reading the book."

"You thought about me every moment?" The idea felt heady, but she couldn't believe it.

"I'm here, Jeannie, to try and make things right, though I find this outfit scratchy and uncomfortable."

"I wish you'd saved your money: I would have danced with you no matter what you wore."

"Is there something wrong with it—other than being scratchy and uncomfortable?" He looked down at his suit.

"No, no." She touched his face. "It's handsome—you—are handsome in it." Somehow the idea that he had spent money he didn't have to come to the ball . . . for her . . . made her feel guilty.

"Handsome until I go scratch my back against that column like a bear in the forest on a hot summer day." He sounded relieved, even pleased.

"Have you ever seen such a bear?"

"If *you* see such a bear, make sure you are downwind, so that he doesn't see *you*." He gave her a twirl. "My suit may be handsome, but your dress—lovely as it is—isn't half as becoming as the one you wore on our first day on the road."

"The one that ended up covered in mud and me along with it."

"Yes, but it showed your grit."

"Grit. As in sand?"

"Here we use 'grit' to signal character, mettle, or even gumption, as the Scots would say."

"More words from your thesaurus?"

"It's a big book. It has lots of words."

"It's important that you know: I don't require fancy clothes or other frivolous purchases, not when you find yourself in such reduced circumstances." It was an awkward moment to raise the issue of finances, but she should have told him earlier who she was and what her resources were. If there was any hope for them to be together, she had to broach the subject.

"Who told you my circumstances are . . . reduced?" His face grew distant.

"You did, when you criticized Garrand Kent, as a no-good, no-account rancher with little sense and less land. And when you admitted that without Eva's help, you would have starved this year."

"I have enough means to be here with you." He spoke firmly, before his voice turned questioning. "Does it matter so much to you whether I have money?"

"Yes, I mean, no. *I* have money. You don't need to have it, if I do."

He said nothing.

"You don't know what it is like to have more money than others do," she quickly added. "It changes things, relationships, people."

"I think I know." He drew the words out slowly.

She thought of Eva Payne's log cabin where he had slept in the attic. "I never had a conversation with a man in England— an eligible man that is—who wasn't somehow calculating my worth at the same time. And I wasn't always wise enough to know that the desire they professed wasn't for me, but was for my money."

"What matters in Texas is who you *are* and what you *do*. If you lost your money tomorrow, could you still be happy living with me in a cabin on the plains?"

She paused, having never considered the question from that angle.

He waited. "What are you going to say?"

"I don't think . . ." She searched for words to convey that as long as he was near her, she needed nothing more than him. But she hesitated too long.

"You don't think so." Asher looked wounded. "I came here to tell you I love you. And you don't think . . ."

She opened her mouth to clarify, but before she could, Chase Johnson tapped her on the shoulder

"This lady promised me a dance." Chase pressed his way between them.

"Of course." Asher dropped her hand and stepped back. "We're finished here."

And he was gone.

The next moment Lilly was at her side, guiding her out of the ballroom.

She dressed for the Christmas service as if by rote, choosing a perfectly respectable dress of the sort she'd worn as Ian's housekeeper. As soon as she'd arrived in Dallas, her mother had commissioned three pretty dresses for her, and Eugenie had agreed, imagining she would wear them for Asher. When she left Dallas, she would give them to one of the maids, unworn.

Following Mrs. Cockrell and her mother, she walked to the church—a fine Methodist edifice for which Mrs. Cockrell had donated the land. Dallas already had five churches, and all were full to celebrate Christmas morning. The minister was apparently engaging, but Eugenie couldn't focus on his words. At the appropriate moments, she repeated the Apostles' Creed and sang the hymns.

As she sat beside her mother and the widowed Mrs. Cockrell, she could see her future returning to the one she'd imagined before she'd met Asher, before her weeks in the wildness of Texas had held out other possibilities.

She would return to her cottage in England. She would be once more a pleasant churchwoman of no close family devoted to good works and the care of others. She had been satisfied with it before, if a little lonely, and she could be satisfied again. It would be enough again. It had to be.

But even as she thought the words, she felt her heart, already shattered, break some more.

After the service, Lilly was, as usual, sociable, talking to each and every member of the congregation. For the first time, Eugenie was grateful for her mother's social good will. It saved her from having to make more than pleasantries.

Luckily, everyone wanted to return home for their own celebrations. In the crowd of well-wishers, Eugenie easily slipped back to the hotel and to her room.

She took up a place at her window. Hours later, she was still there, watching the road, knowing he wouldn't be riding it to her.

As the sun made its way across the afternoon sky, she knew she should dress for the St. Nicholas Christmas dinner. But she didn't have the energy.

Sometime later, she heard her mother's voice at the door. "Eugenie. Eugenie. Let me in." But she ignored her, and after a while her mother left her alone with her thoughts and losses.

Eventually, her mother returned. "Eugenie, let us in."

When she didn't respond, her mother added, "We're opening the door."

She wasn't surprised to hear the key turn the lock and the door open: Lilly could be very persuasive.

But she couldn't object, not when grief made breathing hard.

Her mother entered, followed by Mrs. Cockrell, who closed the door behind them.

"We were surprised not to see you at Christmas dinner after services. We thought to see if you were feeling ill." Sarah's voice was kind.

"I . . ." Eugenie started to say she was well, but the gaping hole in her heart made her unable to speak the words. Instead she tried to change the subject. "The street has grown quieter as the day has progressed. I don't think I've ever seen it this still."

"You should go to him." The firmness in Sarah's voice startled her.

Eugenie shook her head. "He doesn't want me."

Lilly put her hand on Eugenie's arm. "Darling, he's merely afraid, afraid of losing another woman he loves in this inhospitable land."

Eugenie said nothing, letting her mother believe that was the conflict between them. When Lilly folded her in her arms, she let herself accept her mother's comfort.

"I know that you've thought I was wrong to send his book to London without telling him. But now I hope you can see why: that book was his heart."

Eugenie pulled back to study her mother's face. "When he said he wrote that book for Sadie, he meant you published his love letters, didn't he? All the chapters were his letters to her about the places he'd visited and seen." Eugenie brushed tears back. "Eva told me Sadie had bound them into a book, but she thought he'd burned it. How did you even get the manuscript?"

Lilly and Sarah looked at each other, as if deciding what to say.

"Sadie copied out the letters, retaining only the parts about Texas and leaving out all of the more personal sections," Lilly spoke first. "She was surprised to find he had written so much. She asked us to read it to see if it was worth printing."

"She was considering offering sections to Mr. Pryor at the *Dallas Herald*. She'd even chosen a pseudonym, using the last names of men who died at the Alamo," Sarah added.

"When we told her that it should be a book instead, she was so pleased." Lilly brushed a tear from her eyes. "She was thrilled to have it published. Knowing how little Asher likes being on display, she wanted to present it to him, all printed and bound, as a surprise."

Sarah touched Eugenie's arm. "In all the time they were together, he never dressed up for a dance the way he did for you."

"He loves her still." Eugenie shook her head sadly.

"Do you love Judith still?" Lilly countered.

"That's different."

"Eugenie, we do not stop loving those we've lost." Sarah's face turned sad and wise. "Love isn't a commodity that one must ration out like grain in a famine or water in a drought. No, the more we love, the more we are capable of loving."

"He'll always love Sadie, yes." Lilly set her hand comfortingly on Eugenie's shoulder. "But that doesn't mean he can't, doesn't, also love you. And in that book, his loves exist simultaneously. For Sadie, the book recorded their courtship. For you, it offered a glimpse into his soul."

"That book is also a love letter to this land, to his home, with all its beauties and dangers," Sarah added. "Asher has always been a bighearted man. As a Ranger, he was never interested in the glory or the fight. No, he wanted to care for the people of this land and protect them."

"When he lost Sadie, he lost the ability to see the beauty. The whole land became a dangerous place, not to be trusted or enjoyed." Lilly paused. "But with you, he found that joy again."

"Do you love him?" Sarah asked the question quietly.

"How can you ask such a question? I've only known him for a few weeks." Eugenie shrugged.

"But you know his heart; you've seen it in how he treats people, his friendships, his regard in the community . . ." Sarah's voice trailed off.

"And in his words. You loved his book, the feeling intellect you found there, before you knew Asher wrote it." Lilly knelt down before her daughter. "Can you honestly tell us that you do not love him?"

"No, I can't." Eugenie let the tears fall on her cheeks without wiping them away. "But I hurt him, and he said we were finished. He won't come back. If I were Sadie, he would have come back."

"That's true." Sarah said the sentence with an absolute conviction that would have crushed Eugenie's heart, if she had any heart left. "Every love is different. Every love brings out different strengths and weaknesses in us." She placed her hand on Eugenie's shoulder. "Asher treats you as his equal. No different from how he treats Rafe or John or Eva. He treats you as someone he admires and respects. So you are right: if your words sent him away, he will not return."

"But you can go to him." Lilly squeezed Eugenie's hand. "I've never been one to apologize, or even to forgive. If you follow my example, you'll let him go, despite how much you love him. You'll wait for the next mail coach to Matagorda Bay, then you'll be gone, traveling back to your safe life in England. Or you can follow Judith's example and act."

Eugenie started to rise, then sat back down again. "But I don't know where he is or how to reach him."

Sarah smiled. "Rafe rode in this morning to see if we had any pie left over from last night's ball."

For the first time since the ball, Eugenie felt a moment of hope.

"He agreed to wait until we got your decision."

Eugenie looked into their two faces, both sympathetic and encouraging.

Eugenie rose. "He may send me back."

Sarah laughed. "I doubt it, but you are welcome here if he does. Now let's get you changed." Sarah loaned Eugenie a Western riding habit, while Lilly packed a small valise, with a dress, rolled tight, undergarments, and some toiletries. She tucked Kent's *Texas* on the very top.

* * *

"It's a good forty minutes," Rafe warned, "but the only horse I have is Asher's. If you're willin', we can pick her up at the farrier's."

"Asher left town without Trudy?"

"She needed her hooves trimmed. But, what with the ball bringing in so many travelers, the farrier was too busy to take care of her right away." Rafe looked sheepish. "It's a bit of luck, actually. Other than Trudy, there's not a horse to be rented at any price within fifty miles."

It was a test of her grit and her desire.

Using her hand, she measured the distance between the sun and the horizon. Only an hour of daylight remained before a moonless night. He might send her away. That would be his right. And she would face it, if he did.

But she refused to think about how awkward his rejection would be: her with no horse to return to town, and him with only a small cabin for her to stay in overnight. Better to think only of her apology and to plan her words. If nothing else, she needed him to hear how very sorry she was and how much she loved him.

She'd been wrong to think she could settle for a useful life in a rural English village. Perhaps before she'd met him, but not now. Now she'd seen the challenge of a life on the prairies. Now she'd always be missing him. Him. Not Garrand Kent.

"I can manage. Trudy and I are old friends." Once decided, she refused to be afraid.

Rafe smiled, then pointed their way to the farrier.

A natural storyteller like his brothers, Rafe entertained her as they traveled. First he told her stories of the ciboleros who hunted buffalo on the Llano Estacado, far into Comanche territory, then of his adventures with Asher, John, and Ben in the Rangers. His stories made the time pass quickly.

"Here we are." Rafe gestured toward the narrow path of beaten-down snow in front of them.

"Here?" She looked around, hoping to see evidence of Asher's cabin. But all that she could see was a grove of leafless trees. As Asher and John had taught her, she identified the trees from their bark: peaches and pecans. But from her own experience as an estate manager, she could tell that the trees, though dormant, were healthy.

"Those should provide good yields in the spring." It comforted her to think that she might have something useful to offer, if Asher would let her stay.

"We hope so. Eva's promised us peach-pecan pies, if we harvest enough fruit. Last year, we only had enough for cookies."

Rafe had the same understated sense of humor as his brother. But she'd learned how to respond.

"Well, pies are just like cookies, only bigger."

Rafe laughed out loud. "When Asher came home last night angry as a bear, I was pretty sure you were the right woman for him. Now I'm certain. Come along: the cabin's this way."

They turned in among the barren trees and rode until she could see the beginnings of a structure, set back into a low-rising hill.

"Whoa, Trudy." She pulled back on the reins, stunned.

"When Asher built the cabin, he nestled it into that hill. He didn't want anyone to see it from a distance," Rafe explained. "But after he finished the building, the hill wasn't tall enough, so he carted load after load of rocks and dirt up to the top. We ridiculed him something awful."

Asher's cabin wasn't a cabin at all. It was a house. A two-story rock house with small windows on the upper floor and larger ones on the bottom. It wasn't anything like the dog-trot house he'd originally built that Eva and her family now occupied. This was the home of a wealthy landowner.

Fancy was the word Ware had used. She should have listened.

For a moment she was angry. He'd lied to her. He wasn't some no-account small rancher.

Then she began to laugh. Rafe looked at her with concern.

But she waved it away.

She would have done the same thing. *Had* done the same thing.

He hadn't wanted her to know he was a man of means, that he didn't need the proceeds of the book, because he'd wanted her to love him for himself, not his money.

She'd had the same problem; she could understand.

And how could he have told her, once she believed him poor, that he wasn't? When she'd tried to explain her own circumstances, she'd failed miserably.

But how could she convince him to give her—to give them—another chance?

"Rafe!" Ware raced out the door, then stopped. His eyes widened when he saw Eugenie.

Rafe motioned "don't tell" with his hand.

Ware yelled back into the house, "Rafe's back with Trudy. I'll help him with the horses."

Eugenie dismounted, and Ware flung his arms around her, saying "Barn's this way."

She followed, grateful for a little more time to compose herself.

Just as Asher's house wasn't a cabin, the barn wasn't a shed.

Though her grandfather had employed plenty of grooms, Eugenie had always found caring for her mount peaceful. She let the old motions—combing, brushing, and drying—soothe her. Then, following Rafe's lead, she covered Trudy's back with straw then a blanket. They led the horses to their stalls. Past the horse stalls, she could see the outlines of a carriage, the side still punched through from the tornado.

"Ready to meet the bear in his cave?" Rafe teased.

She nodded, reminding herself that she had less to lose by trying and everything to gain. "I'll follow you. But I want to enter on my own."

Rafe nodded understandingly and directed the boy to the house. Eugenie followed close behind, wanting her approach to be covered by Rafe's and Ware's. It wouldn't do for Asher or one of his hands to think she was an intruder.

She stepped onto the porch, breathing in deeply. Rafe left the door slightly ajar for her.

Then, gathering all her courage, she pulled the door open and stepped into the room. It was already a boisterous party.

The table looked like Texas—or at least the Texas she'd learned to see with Asher.

Asher was seated at the head of the table. At his right and left hands were his brothers, Rafe and John. Next to them was Ben Payne, his brother-at-arms, and Payne's family, Eva and Ware. At Ware's feet was the black puppy Asher had promised him for finishing the cattle drive. At the other end were a half dozen men, Asher's hands on the ranch.

The table itself was covered with food: meats and root vegetables, corn and spoon bread, a pot of a Creole dish Eugenie recognized from her time in Jefferson as red beans and rice. Several pies waited on the sideboard.

Eugenie looked from the pies to Rafe, and the Ranger gave her a wink. The pies had been a diversion to give her one last chance to reconcile with Asher. And she was grateful.

The ranch hands looked her over, "sizing her up," as she'd heard it called, and she lifted her chin to meet their gaze as an equal.

Asher rose slowly, but his eyes never left her. "You came."

"I was invited. And a lady never ignores an invitation."

"Is that the only reason?" He stepped away from the table toward her.

She looked around the room; all eyes were watching her. "No, no, it's not. I should have trusted you. I should have believed you." She paused; no one was moving. She wasn't certain anyone was even breathing. One of the cowhands held his fork suspended halfway to his mouth.

She stepped toward Asher. Letting the rest of the room melt away, she focused her gaze only on him. "I love you—all the parts of you. I opened your book, and I became infatuated with your mind, your witty observations, your understanding of this land and its people. I thought that all I had to do was come here, walk down the street, and somehow I would know you, and, stranger still, you would know me. Yet I didn't."

She breathed deeply and continued. "Instead I fell in love with a handsome Ranger, with a heart as big as this state and whose table welcomes everyone, even an odd Englishwoman. I'm sorry I never saw that Garrand Kent and Asher Graham were the same man, until you told me. Can you forgive me?"

He stepped forward, and then she was in his arms.

Seeing Asher's welcome, the men nodded and returned to their food, ignoring the couple, as Asher led Eugenie out onto the wide porch.

The sun was setting over the fruit trees, its colors a brilliant orange, purple, pink, and blue. They faced the sky together, looking out over Asher's land.

"They say that the stars on a Texas night light the sky from east to west," Asher whispered in her hair.

"You read your book." She looked into his face, searching for any sign of anger. She found nothing but peace.

"I needed to discover what I said." He shrugged. After a moment he continued, "But I say that nothing in Texas is brighter than the light in my love's eyes."

"That's not in the book."

"It should be. Next book I write, I'll put it in, and you can read it back to me every time we ride across Texas."

"Your love?"

"My love. I made the light in your eyes go out a bit at the dance. But I was wrong. Because I want nothing more than to see your face, to hear your voice, and to hold your hand for the rest of my days."

"You forgot kisses." She pressed her palm to his cheek.

"A man should never forget kisses." He placed a kiss on her forehead, then on the top of her nose, then firmly on her lips.

"I could stand here with you every night and never grow tired of this." She nestled into him.

"But will this be enough for *you*?" Asher wrapped his arms around her. "This land, this people. You've seen Dallas: it's growing, but it's not Jefferson or Galveston, and it will take more than our lifetimes for it to rival London."

"Will you be by my side?" she asked, still facing the sunset, not daring to look at his face. "If you will, it will be enough."

He turned her to face him, whispering into her hair, "As long as day follows night, as long as the wind blows on the Texas plains, as long as the sun shines bright in the heavens, I will love you."

"And I you," she promised.

Their kiss was long and gentle. And one turned to two, and two to three, until she couldn't count anymore.

At the end of that long kiss, side by side, hands clasped, they looked out over the plains. And as far as the eye could see, the world was before them.

Historical Notes: Dallas, Sarah Cockrell,
and the St. Nicholas Hotel

We hadn't heard of Sarah Horton Cockrell (1819–1892) or her St. Nicholas Hotel before we began this anthology. And that's a shame.

On the frontier, a town could thrive or fail depending on a single event or person. Take for example the city of Jefferson (where Rachael's story opens): navigation so far inland was made possible by a giant log jam, and when the Army Corps of Engineers destroyed that jam in 1870, it also destroyed Jefferson's trade. Similarly, the 1858 killing of Sarah's husband, Alexander (1820–1858) could have signaled disaster for Dallas, a town not yet fifteen years old, with roughly 400 residents.

John Neely Bryan had staked his 1841 claim for the city at the low-water crossing of the Trinity River and built a ferry. In 1850, in a hotly contested election, Dallas had been named the county seat, and Bryan sold his remaining interest in the town in 1852, to the Cockrells, who used the revenue from the ferry to establish other enterprises.

Dallas beckoned settlers with ample water (from the forks of the Trinity River and natural springs) and a rich black soil that supported cattle, horses, sheep, and mules. The city drew its populace from many cultures: African-American, Belgian, Canadian, English, French, German, Mexican, Swiss, Tejano and Texian, along with those Native peoples who had not been relocated. Those peoples who remained in Texas—if not specifically in Dallas—included the Cherokee, Anadarko, Tonkawa, and the widely feared Comanche. (For a more comprehensive listing of Texas's Native peoples, see the annotated 1846 map on Rachael Miles's website: rachaelmiles.com.) The region grew barley, corn, oats, rye, wheat, sweet potatoes, and peaches; and the woods were replete with ash, cottonwood, elm, spotted oak, and post oak.

But Dallas's prosperity rested heavily on the Cockrells' industries—a ferry, freighting business, brickyard, lumberyard, sawmill, grist mill, and downtown building rented out to other businesses. The Cockrells also built the first wooden bridge across the river, connecting Dallas to those communities on the west side of the river. So, in 1858, when Alexander was shot eight times by a man who owed him money, the many Dallas residents reliant on the Cockrells' enterprises, particularly those associated with Alexander's grand hotel project, held their breath.

Sarah had always been her husband's amanuensis and adviser, but with his death, the management of their holdings fell to her. Most expected her to sell and move back to Virginia. But she didn't. Instead, Sarah—a thirty-eight-year-old widow with five small children—became an entrepreneur in her own right. Her first act: finishing her husband's last project, the luxurious St. Nicholas Hotel.

A three-story brick building that commanded the town square, the St. Nicholas stood at the northeast corner of Dallas's main streets, Commerce and Broadway. Lavishly furnished, the St. Nicholas boasted a giant crystal chandelier, elaborate kerosene lighting, and a grand piano, along with other luxuries imported from Shreveport, Houston, and New Orleans. Both its July inaugural ball and the Christmas ball drew visitors from across the state. Engraved invitations were sent by special messenger, since the mail coach only came to Dallas somewhat irregularly. We drew our descriptions of the ball from the contemporary notices in the *Dallas Herald* newspaper (available at The Portal to Texas History, texashistory.unt.edu) and from Vivian Castleberry's 1994 *Daughters of Dallas* and 2004 *Sarah—the Bridge Builder*. We hope our stories give Sarah's hotel life once more.

By 1860, almost 2,000 settlers called Dallas home, including many former La Réunion colonists. Even so, Dallas was far from populous, coming in a distant ninth in the list of Texas's ten most populated cities. San Antonio (8,235) and Galveston (7,307) headed that list, followed by Houston (4,845), Marshall (4,000), New Braunfels (3,500), Austin (3,490), Brownsville (2,734), and Sulphur Springs (2,500). Sarah's St. Nicholas was home to forty-three residents, including Sarah and her children Aurelia, Frank, and Alex. Doctors, lawyers, merchants, craftsmen, they came from sixteen states, including Maine and New York, and six countries. The editor of the *Dallas Herald* and his printers made their homes there. In the 1860 census, Sarah valued her real estate as worth $78,500 and her personal property at $13,525.

But the St. Nicholas was fated to have a short life. In July 1860, in 105-degree heat, sulphur matches at the W. W. Peak & Brothers Drug store spontaneously caught fire, reducing most of Dallas to ashes. Even so, the city—and Sarah—refused to concede.

Sarah, having lost much of her fortune in the fire, went on to make her own history. She became, in 1860, the first woman to testify before the Texas legislature, winning the right to build an iron bridge across the Trinity; she opened it in 1872. She built the first steam-powered mill and donated land to the Methodist church and to the city for a park (later Dealey Plaza). Her second hotel, the St. Charles (later renamed the Dallas Hotel), was still standing in 1967 when it was razed for the J. F. K. cenotaph.

At her death, Sarah Horton Cockrell owned a quarter of Dallas.

Connect with Us